# Hattie's Home

MARY GIBSON was born and brought up in Bermondsey, where both her grandmother and mother were factory girls. She is the author of the bestselling *Custard Tarts and Broken Hearts*, which was selected for World Book Night in 2015, and three other novels, *Jam and Roses*, *Gunner Girls and Fighter Boys* and *Bourbon Creams and Tattered Dreams*. She lives in Kent.

# Mary Gibson

## Hattie's Home

First published in the UK in 2018 by Head of Zeus, Ltd

This paperback edition published in 2018 by Head of Zeus, Ltd

9 7 5 3 1 2 4 6 8

A catalogue record for this book is available from
the British Library.

ISBN (PB): 9781784973391
ISBN (E): 9781784973360

Typeset by Adrian McLaughlin

Printed and bound in Great Britain by CPI Group (UK) Ltd, Croydon, CR0 4YY

First Floor East
5–8 Hardwick Street
London EC1R 4RG

WWW.HEADOFZEUS.COM

*Dedicated to the memory of my aunt*
*Amelia Ellen Cooper, who spent all her working life*
*in the Alaska fur factory in Bermondsey*

Earth cares for her own ruins, naught for ours.
Nothing is certain, only the certain spring.

—LAURENCE BINYON, *The Burning of the Leaves*

# 1

## The Wasteland

*January 1947*

Life was moving on for Hattie Wright, but it seemed the number forty-seven bus to Bermondsey was not. Too much snow and too little skill on the part of the driver had brought the bus to a halt in Tooley Street. A resigned groan from her fellow passengers rippled along the bus. Hattie stood up. Hefting her well worn army kitbag down from the overhead rack, she hopped off the running board into the deep bank of snow piled against the kerb. Still wearing her stout army shoes and ATS greatcoat, at least she'd be warm. They were calling this the worst winter in living memory, but she'd been hardened up by three biting winters in Belgium.

The journey by rail from Southampton had been predictably slow. Everything in the country seemed broken. Trains, rails, ticket machines, buffet cars, signals and even the people, hustling along platforms, huddling in smoke-filled, freezing carriages, seemed worn out beyond repair. There was a national stoop she'd noticed – which surely hadn't been there last time she was home – a universal taut-faced, clenched-fist bowing to the bitter Arctic wind sweeping across the country. She marched along Tooley Street, glimpsing herself in an office window. Had she developed the stoop? Not yet. Her tall figure was slim and strong. Perhaps staying on in the army had saved her. Her shoulders were square beneath the kitbag's weight and, in spite of the hampering snow, her stride purposeful. At twenty-seven, her pale ivory skin was still good, her pointed chin taut and her red-gold hair still abundant. The war hadn't worn her out; it had honed her.

Hattie hadn't been back to Bermondsey since 1942; five long years and it hadn't been long enough. She certainly didn't want to be here now. But what choice did she have? Eight years as an ATS sergeant fighting the war hadn't prepared her at all for the peace. The sort of roles she felt ready for were being reserved for returning servicemen. Besides, her mother had made a rare plea for her to come home. She was, she'd said, finding it hard to cope these days and was nearly blind. Sometimes her mother was prone to exaggeration, but the spidery, blotted handwriting of her letter spoke more persuasively than her words.

The devastation along the riverside was plainly visible from Tooley Street. It wasn't so much what was still there, as what was now gone that struck her. Here, the Thames had always been obscured by slab-faced offices and docks, but now through jagged gaps she could see the river riding high, a dull afternoon sun raddling its ice-black surface. The destruction in this area was exactly what she'd expected. The docks had always been the target, of course.

Hattie cut down Bermondsey Street – a whole tract of which had disappeared in a tumbled wreckage. Burned, eyeless windows stared from shells of buildings and she passed one tall house, still inhabited by the looks of it, which stood exposed on three sides. Wallpaper and fireplaces patterned its outside walls as it stood in isolation amongst the piles of rubble. She wondered who would have wanted to stay living there, and yet where else would they go? She wasn't the only one facing a life of limited choices.

But as she came to the end of Bermondsey Street shock hit her like a bomb blast. She was about to cut across one of the many small side streets leading into Abbey Street, but she couldn't find one of them. Where was Larnaca Street? Stanworth Street? There was nothing left. Instead she was forced to cross a moraine of tumbled bricks, stone boulders and splintered timber. Where rows of terraced houses ought to have been, was instead a wide tract of wasteland, littered with rubble, heaped with pyramids of charred beams, punctuated by twisted metal. In one street, only the back wall of a row of houses was left standing – a patchwork mural of water- and fire-damaged wallpapers.

She pushed on, astonished that in the twenty months since the war's end so few areas had been cleared. But in those that had, no sign was left of their former occupants or usage, all trace of the life that had gone on in that place had been eradicated. The cleared sites looked somehow more forlorn than the jumble of walls and collapsed roofs. At least they remained a memorial to the life that had been lived before the war.

So many once familiar landmarks had vanished, it made her feel queasy and disorientated, as if set adrift on a featureless ocean and washed up on a barren island, where some giant's scythe had cut down houses like so many stalks of corn, leaving only an irregular stubble of truncated walls and crushed plaster behind. The air was thick with dust, picked up on the chill breeze, which swirled the beginnings of a new snowfall around her feet. Panic seized her and she had to fight for her breath as a great weight seemed to press on her chest. But she knew the stifling, choking feeling wasn't simply a result of the fields of debris. She was approaching the place where she feared her spirit might be crushed into as many particles as the dust at her feet. The Alaska.

During all the war years she'd feared nothing so much as the prospect of returning here, but now it seemed her only hope. Bermondsey smelled of death to Hattie, and right now it felt like her own. The Alaska fur factory, brimful with the pelts of dead animals, was somewhere she'd vowed never to return. She'd experienced another life, another country and another self; now she was determined to do more with her life than paint stripes onto beaver lamb furs. She'd be the one wearing the musquash and the mink, and she wouldn't put up with any fake beaver lamb either. She passed some hastily erected ten-year bungalows in The Grange – prefabs people were calling them. Uninspiring barrack-like cubes they might be, but at least they were evidence of life going on.

Her feeling of nausea increased as the Alaska's square white tower came into view. The high tower had proved its worth for spotting approaching Heinkels during the war, but she thought it resembled a watchtower in a German prison camp. Once in Grange Road she stood outside the Alaska's gates, staring up at the sad-eyed seal carved above its entrance arch, along with the date – 1869. The creature's mournful, drooping eyes mirrored her mood, and she lifted her gaze beyond the arch to the hotch-potch of Victorian and modern buildings that made up the factory. The white tower was one of the newer buildings, only fifteen years old but already looking worn out by the war. Though the factory had largely escaped the bombs, she'd heard one had dropped through several floors of K building without ever exploding. A guilty wish crossed her mind that the German bomb-maker had been more efficient. But she dismissed it, horrified at her callousness, for her friend Buster Golding and a few hundred workers had been sheltering in the factory basement at the time. She peered between the gates into the yard and thought of Buster. He was the foreman in charge of the Alaska girls and he'd been exempted military service so that he could continue doing war work at the Alaska. He'd stayed throughout the war, working day and night to produce sheepskin flying jackets for the RAF and fur mittens for Arctic manoeuvres. All that patriotic team spirit and sacrifice and what had they ended up with? A wasteland.

She turned away. Time enough for thinking about the Alaska when she was actually clocking on. She didn't even know if they'd take her back. Besides, there was still hope that one of her office job applications might be successful. For now, she was tired, hungry and looking forward to falling into a bed at her mother's house in the Square. Dusk was coming on as she hurried along Spa Road, stopping only to look at the half-ruined town hall. There was evidence of some shoring-up work, but little attempt had been made to repair it. She crossed the road, intending to take a short cut across an uncleared bombsite, but as she moved through its stone-strewn heart something made her stop. A fire was burning. Made from roof timbers stacked teepee-like and packed with assorted smaller debris, the fire's heart was white-hot and red flames flicked up into a yellowish evening sky. Figures were silhouetted against its glare. They were moving; dancing round the pyre, hopping first on to one foot, then another, stomping the ground and whooping.

*Kids.* She shifted the kitbag on to the other shoulder, considering whether to tell them to clear off. She didn't mind if the rest of Bermondsey burned down, but she supposed she ought to care that a child in one of the nearby prefabs might get fried to a crisp. She sighed and in her loudest parade-ground voice roared: 'Oi, you lot, clear off out of there!' But the whoopers continued to whoop, oblivious to her order. She began picking her way towards them across the rubble-strewn ground.

Thick oily smoke serpented from the fire. She smelled creosote and soon spotted the fuel source: a pile of tarred roadblocks, no doubt dug up by the little 'Red Indians' for their fire-lighting potential. Heat rolled towards her in billowing waves, searing her cheeks as she drew nearer. How the kids weren't getting their hair singed she didn't know. She tugged on the unravelling jumper sleeve of the nearest boy, who spun round, fists already raised to defend himself. Each cheek bore three charcoal stripes and he had a grey pigeon's feather stuck in his hair.

'Oi, get yer bleedin' hands off me!' His voice was hoarse, perhaps from the smoke or else from continual shouting to his mates. His bony, elfin face had the street-urchin's pallor, and wary eyes stared at her beneath pale lashes. His hair was brittle straw, spikey with dirt and sweat. Around his neck, in spite of the failing light, she saw a visible tidemark. *Just where the noose might go one day*, she prophesied.

'If you want to burn yourself to a cinder that's up to you, but if those flames catch the prefabs all the little children in bed where they *ought* to be will go up in smoke too. So, sling yer hook,

5

you, Sitting Bull, or whatever your name is, and take your tribe with you!'

The straw-headed boy thrust out his chin. 'This is our place, not your'n! Piss off, scrubber!' he said, using the pejorative term for ATS girls she hadn't heard in a while.

'That's enough of that, you cheeky 'apporth,' she said as he put two fingers in his mouth and emitted a shrill whistle, at which the rest of his tribe moved away from the fire and fanned out round her. Soon she was encircled by a crowd of street rakers, one as young as four or five. The straw-headed boy, obviously the leader and about eleven, squatted down and wrapped dirty fingers around a broken brick. Before she realized what was happening the brick was hurtling towards her. She ducked, but its jagged edge caught her cheek and she heard the crack of brick on bone even as she felt the sting. Rubbing at her face, she brought away blood-smeared fingers.

The gang of kids shuffled closer. Each now held a missile of some sort and she felt a growing unease as something like fear prickled up her spine. There were two girls amongst them, obviously twins, sporting identical bows in their hair, but the looks of glee on their pretty faces were even more unsettling than the stony-faced boys. The girls were the first to scream, 'Let's get her!'

The street was deserted. Too early for the night shift to be clocking on or the pubs to be turning out. The smallest kid darted behind her, harrying like a yapping terrier before giving her a sharp kick in the ankle.

'Oi! Stop that!' She made a grab for his shirt collar, but he eluded her, to hoots of laughter from the others.

One of the twins produced a sharpened wooden stave and now, like a spear-wielding Amazon, launched it at Hattie, who dodged aside just in time. The missile whizzed past her ear. But now the boys began to howl and leap with strange high-kicking steps round her. It reminded her of country-dancing lessons at school, where the boys had been taught to leap over the sticks, shaking their ankles to make the bells ring. But this cavorting was nothing so innocent. She didn't know what had happened to kids in her absence, but this lot were more vicious than any she'd ever seen. When straw-head picked up a piece of pipe so heavy it required two hands to lift, she judged it time to retreat. But it was too late – a wall of kids blocked her way.

She turned back to straw-head. 'I know your name,' she said, 'and I know who your mother is!' A complete lie, but it was a threat that had always worked on her as a child.

A lanky, black-haired boy sniggered. 'His mum! *Everyone* knows that slag!'

Suddenly the other children froze and straw-head's face flushed red. He seemed to catch fire, as the flames behind him licked higher and higher. His face twisted in fury and raising the rusted piping like a golf club, he slashed at the lanky boy, catching him behind the knees. The boy yelped in pain and fell forward on hands and knees. But straw-head hadn't finished. He swung the pipe above his head and charged at Hattie, roaring, 'Don't you talk about my mum!'

Hattie turned and ran, but the phalanx of dirty-faced kids was like a shield wall and she felt the pipe smash into her back with the force of a kidney punch. She fell on to her knees as straw-head followed up with another whack across her shoulders. She covered her head with her hands as he smashed the iron across knuckles and wrists. He was trying to break her skull! They would kill her if she didn't get up. The time for reasoning had gone. She curled up into a ball as small fists wielding bricks and wooden sticks battered the tender places of her body. She dug her toes into the frozen earth and sprang to her feet, but not before straw-head caught her another glancing blow to the head. Now she swung her kitbag like a shield around her, fending them off. Then she ran. Turning her ankle on bricks, tripping over beams, she daren't look back but she heard them whooping as they chased after her. She sprinted, as fast as her injuries allowed, along Spa Road, not stopping until she reached the corner of Pearce Duff's custard factory. The kitbag, heavy as lead, had bitten into her shoulder.

Hoarse breaths raked at her chest and she coughed up residue from the tarry fire, which seemed to have coated her throat. She could run no further; they would be on her in seconds. Venturing a look behind, expecting to see them closing in, she was surprised to see they had retreated to the bombsite perimeter. Stony-faced little sentinels, they stood to attention, each holding their weapon, staring hard in her direction, daring her to return.

She felt a rush of humiliation. So much for being honed by the war. So much for all those ju-jitsu lessons in PT. A crowd of kids had done what no German ever could. She'd been terrified. She slumped against Pearce Duff's wall, letting her forehead rest on the ice-cold green tiles.

'Should have let them burn. The little gits,' she muttered to herself, and pushed herself off the wall and headed for the Square.

Hattie's mother, Cissie, lived in the Square – its full name was never used. In the distant past it had been the 'posh' part of Bermondsey. But its three-storey Victorian houses had long since been deserted by the posh and taken over by the poor. Three or four families were crammed into each house, though the corner villas were still reserved for the vicar and doctor and other better-offs. Four streets led into the Square, so that it formed a sort of cross at the heart of Bermondsey and at its centre was a church. Cissie occupied the top floor of an end house adjoining one of the incoming streets. Hattie hoped her mother had received her telegram. She'd sent it two days ago before she'd caught the train to Ostend.

The last time Hattie had seen Cissie was in 1944, shortly after D-Day, when she'd taken her chance and volunteered to join a new battery going to Belgium. Cissie had made the trek down to Southampton to see her off. She'd been touched. Cissie had never been a typical mother and perhaps that's why Hattie rarely called her 'Mum'. But obviously the thought Hattie might never come back had penetrated her normal cavalier indifference to her daughter's life. When after VE day Hattie still hadn't come home, Cissie didn't complain. By then Hattie had switched from big guns to a pen – transferring to the army records office in Brussels. She was doing important work, helping to wind up the war in Europe, that was why she couldn't go home, or this was what she told her mother. But Hattie knew better. When she'd received her notice to leave Brussels, she'd actually cried.

Now she stood outside Cissie's house, the only one in the Square with bomb damage by the looks of it. Adrenaline had sustained her this far, but now her battered ribs and legs began to scream in pain. She hadn't stopped to wipe the blood trickling down her forehead and caking her hair. She put a hand to her ribcage and looked up. A snow-covered tarpaulin stretched across her mother's roof, and she noticed with alarm that the three top-floor windows were boarded up. *What if Cissie had been forced to move out?* She groaned. There was nowhere else for her to go. She staggered, propping herself up against the low wall in front of the basement area, breathing painfully. If Cissie was still living on the top floor it must be very dark and damp in there. The front door was reached by some stone stairs, which Hattie mounted slowly, wincing at each step. As she waited for someone to answer her knock, she peered down into the airey where the basement flat was also boarded up and deserted.

'Hattie? Is that you, Hattie?' Cissie stood at the door, squinting hard. Vanity usually prevented her from wearing the round, pebble glasses she needed to see any distance.

'It's me, Ciss, it's Hattie. Let me in for chrissake.' She slumped against the door jamb, feeling splintered wood under her palm. A band of pain tightened around her ribcage. Something was broken.

'Good gawd, Hattie? What are you doing here?' The look of surprise on her mother's face told her either the telegram hadn't been received or had been forgotten about, which wasn't impossible with Cissie, who had always had a jumbled-up, disorganized sort of existence, however much Hattie had tried to combat it with her own tidy, ordered mind.

'Didn't you get the telegram?' She stumbled into the passage and into an awkward embrace, which was absolutely necessary if Hattie were to keep upright. Cissie threw her arms round her.

'Don't stand on the doorstep, love, come in!' Cissie said, helping Hattie into the house. 'Whatever's happened, are you all right, love? I wasn't expecting you.'

They staggered together along the passage, Hattie leaning heavily on her mother, who barely had strength to support her. 'Why wouldn't you be expecting me? You asked me to come home!'

Streaks of water damage had lifted the passage wallpaper and a damp smell permeated the place. She waited for her mother to lead her upstairs to the top-floor rooms, but instead, Cissie stopped at the first door in the passage. It had once been the Weller family's front room.

'We're in here now, love. The Wellers moved out to Beckenham when we got bombed.'

'Why didn't you tell me about the bomb, Ciss?'

'Oh, there's worse off than us, it was just blast damage. But the Wellers and the family that was in the basement couldn't take it no more and moved out. I've just got the one room now. They say all the rest of the house is inunhabitable,' Cissie said, flashing a red-lipsticked smile in her direction as she fumbled for the door handle. Sometimes her mother's words were as jumbled as her life. Cissie lowered her voice. 'Just to warn you, I've got a new friend staying.' She dropped her voice to a whisper. ''Scuse the mess. Now don't start jawing me – we was just having a bit of fun.'

Net curtains were stretched taut round the front bay window and the room was lit by a single gas mantle. In the orange glow, Hattie saw that what appeared to be all the furniture from her mother's upstairs flat had now been crammed into this single room: table, chairs, a sofa, a metal kitchen cabinet and a gas ring. A heavy green satin curtain was strung across the room and from behind it she heard a rumbling cough.

'That's my new chap,' Cissie mouthed. 'Mario! Well, his name's Marian really – he's Polish! But I can't call a feller Marian, can I? Come out here and meet me daughter, darlin'!' Cissie tweaked aside the curtain, revealing a dark-complexioned, black-haired middle-aged man lying on the bed, dressed only in vest and underpants. When he saw Hattie, he sprang up.

'Cecilia, she is hurt!' he said in a heavy Polish accent, taking hold of Hattie's arm, as Cissie finally registered the blood and bruises.

'Oh, gawd above, you've been in the wars!'

Hattie gave a wry smile, which hurt, and said, 'Yes, Ciss. I have, for eight years...'

Mario helped her to the sofa, then turned away while he pulled on trousers and shirt. Hattie looked in vain for the bed she had hoped to fall into, while Cissie cleared space on the sofa.

'Who did this to you?' Mario asked. 'I will find them and beat them.' He seemed eager to go out into the night and avenge her, but she was too exhausted for any more battles.

'I was crossing a bombsite, bunch of street rakers set on me...' She put a hand to her ribs. 'Think I might have bruised a rib or two... nothing to worry about.' Mario looked unconvinced, but Hattie saw him register Cissie's bewildered expression.

'Is it bad, Mario?' she asked in her little-girl voice, which she often reverted to when a problem presented itself.

'I get bandages,' Mario said helpfully.

'I'm fine!' Hattie snapped, pain fraying her manners.

'I will make tea,' he said, looking hurt.

'Well, if you're boiling water, I'll have some in a bowl to clean up this mess... thanks, Mario.'

He smiled. A nice smile, that puffed his cheeks into two pouches.

'Did I say he's *Polish*?' Cissie puckered her red lips in appreci-ation, as if she had just eaten a juicy peach. 'Very polite. Ex-airman. I saw him one day down by John Bull Arch clearing a bomb-site, had his shirt off, the physique on him! Didn't even have me glasses on – but I saw enough.' She lowered her voice. 'I offered him the basement on the "share a house" scheme, but we ended sharing a bit more, if you know what I mean.' Cissie gave her a knowing look, which would have scandalized any other daughter, but Hattie had grown up being her mother's confidante. 'Well, that basement's not fit to live in now,' her mother continued. 'The drains is up, pipes froze, water everywhere, and the rats! 'Course you can stay here with us as long as you like, darlin',' she said.

'That's big of you, as you're the one asked me to come home and then forgot all about it!'

She'd raised her voice and Mario looked alarmed as he came back with a bowl of steaming water. He offered her a rag and a mirror.

'Take no notice, darl'. I'm used to it. Talks to me like shit, her own mother.'

Hattie ignored her and began wiping her grazed knuckles and knees, then dabbing the cuts on her face. She couldn't reach the gash on her neck, because her shoulder didn't seem to be functioning as it should.

'I will help?' Mario asked cautiously, and Hattie nodded.

He was remarkably light-handed for a large man, gently bathing her cuts, then applying Germolene and dressings made from an old sheet that had already been topped and tailed into a patchwork.

'Thanks, Mario, you're a better mother than Ciss ever was!'

He gave a warm, deep laugh, which she was relieved to see Cissie join in.

They fished out some blankets from a box under her mother's bed and made up the sofa. After pulling the dividing curtain closed and saying good night, she examined the wounds to her legs. They were covered in grazes and purple bruises but she didn't think anything was broken. Her main worry was her ribs, which hurt with each breath. She turned down the gas mantle and eased herself back into the sofa. For all its lumpiness and the suffocatingly overcrowded room, Hattie found herself drifting off gratefully within minutes. She'd been on the move for two days and her tiredness was almost as painful as her wounds. But her relief was short-lived for she was kept awake by the unmistakable sound of Cissie and Mario sharing more than just the house.

'For chrissake!' she muttered, throwing off the stifling blankets and getting up. She'd spent most of her childhood, ever since Dad left, accommodating Cissie's string of 'gentleman friends', but never at such close proximity. There were limits. She padded over to the front bay window. A thick freezing fog now enveloped the Square and a full moon hung over the church, washing it with an opaque, silvery light. It looked pretty, under the earlier snowfall, an undamaged incongruity in this war-ravaged place. She'd almost rather be out there than cooped up in here with the two lovebirds behind the curtain. For now, proceedings had come to a halt but she knew sleep wouldn't come again for her tonight. She was about to let the curtain fall when she thought she heard a noise coming from downstairs in the basement. She craned her neck, but couldn't see down into the airey; the angle was impossible and she daren't open the window. The sound came again. Just a cat, crying like a baby. She shuddered, remembering her mother's description of the rat-infested place below. The cats would have good hunting tonight.

\* \* \*

That night, as the embers from the bonfire opposite the town hall folded into grey ash, a woman picked her way across the moon-washed bombsite. Dressed only in a thin frock and a wraparound pinafore stretched taut across her swollen stomach, revealing her heavy pregnancy, she was wearing carpet slippers and, though she wore no coat, didn't seem to feel the bitter cold. She was a short, skinny woman of about thirty-five, though she looked older, with unkempt, pale, straw-coloured hair. Her stockings were falling down, wrinkled at the ankle, and as she walked her head moved from side to side, as if searching the rubble. She wove an aimless path through scattered masonry and mangled wooden window frames. And though there was no one to hear her, she continually asked invisible passers-by, 'Have you seen my Sue, my little Sue? I'm sure it was here I left her. She was with me mum and dad. Have you seen my Sue?' And then she raised her voice. 'Sue! It's time to come in for bed, darlin'. Sue?'

A slight figure rose up from behind the fire where he had been poking at it with a piece of rusty pipe. He rubbed at his elfin features, smearing the charcoal stripes on each of his cheeks, then ran dirty fingers through his straw-coloured hair. He walked over to the woman who seemed not to notice him. He tugged at her arm. 'Mum, it's me, Ronnie. Sue ain't here. I told you that before – she's gone! Come on, you're catchin' your death. Hurry up, it's time to go home!' But when the woman did not move, the boy took his mother's hand and, pulling her gently, led her out of the rubble-strewn wasteland.

# 2

# Clara's Baby

## January 1947

The baby's eyes were rich brown, speckled gold and amber, like a thrush's breast. She had a button version of her father's bridgeless nose and the black curls, coiled like tiny springs on her small round head, were a looser version of his. Her golden-brown skin seemed to glow with the light of those sun-blessed days the child had known in her early weeks. But today, Australia, the place of her baby's birth, seemed as far away to Clara Young as the sun itself. Clara hoped that under Bermondsey's leaden sky, her daughter Martha's skin would not pale. But perhaps life would be easier for her here if it did.

Martha had a sunny smile, which began in her eyes, crinkling at the edges then almost closing, as with a shy turn of her head the cupid's bow mouth broadened until her little face was lit with joy. Every time she saw it, Clara's heart hurt with love and she wanted nothing more than to preserve that smile, so that it would never be spurned, never be dimmed. But she knew that in this place, the chances of that were slim.

The baby nestled into Clara's breast, perhaps sensing her mother's foreboding as she approached her old home in the Square. Feeling a wave of nausea rise in her throat, she almost turned back, but Martha looked up at that moment, with eyes full of unquestioning trust and undisguised dependence. Clara would swallow any amount of pride or fear not to disappoint that trust, and so, though her knees were weak as water and her mouth dry as an Australian desert, she knocked on her parents' front door, refusing to quail when her mother took one look at the bundle in her arms and exclaimed, 'Well, that takes the cake, she's only come home with a brown baby!' And she slammed the door in Clara's face.

Clara knocked hard on the door, startling Martha, who tried, unsuccessfully, to raise her head from the folds of the blanket. Clara was grateful the child couldn't see the look on her grandmother's face as she reopened the door.

'We told you when you married him you wasn't welcome here no more. Just because he's sent you home with his bastard, don't make no difference. You broke your father's heart when he found out you was nothing but a common slut... and I'll never forgive you for it.' She was about to close the door when Clara shot out a foot to stop it. She held the baby up.

'Mum!' she pleaded. 'Just look at her, see how beautiful she is!'

But her plea ended with a sob. Martha's mouth turned down, her lower lip trembled as, sensing Clara's distress, she began to cry. Clara's mother's expression softened a little at the baby's cry.

'You can come in,' she said brusquely. 'He's not back from the parish meeting.'

Her father was a regular attender at the church in the middle of the Square and proud of his position on the parish council. It had been a particular hardship for him to put up with the earnest, well-meaning sympathy of his fellow parishioners when Clara had first taken up with Barry. She breathed a sigh of relief he was out and hoped the parish meeting would be a long one. She followed her mother inside, shushing the baby as she went.

'You can stay for a cup of tea, but I can't have you here when he comes home, Clara. He won't have you in the house.' She looked at her daughter with resigned disappointment, as Clara put her cheek against the baby's to soothe her crying. 'You've made a rod for your own back there.' Her mother nodded towards the child.

As her grandmother made tea, Martha's curiosity was piqued and she attempted to pull herself up, examining, with wide, questioning eyes, first Mrs Young then the teapot. Clara smiled with pride at her daughter's forwardness and looked to her mother for approval, 'See, Mum, she can already pull herself up.' But she was crushed by a look of disapproval.

'She looks like him. You'll have no life. No feller's going to look at you now, not with a bastard brown baby in tow,' she said.

Clara felt the words sting like a whip and pulled her child closer.

'Don't call her that. I'm married. My baby's not a …' She couldn't bring herself to say the word.

'That's exactly what she is!' Her father's voice made Clara jump and she twisted her head round to see him standing in the kitchen doorway. He looked through her and addressed his wife. 'What's she doing here?'

Mrs Young stood up, smoothing her pinafore as if she were soothing her husband's ire.

'I've told her you won't let her stay. But she's got the baby now, Arthur… our granddaughter.'

Not daring to say a word to her father, Clara glanced warily at her mother. Perhaps she was going to change her mind after all. Surely she would take her side, for the baby's sake.

Arthur Young walked into the room. He was a tall man, always neat and tidy, ramrod straight, and there was little else about him that would bend. Her mother was taking a chance, with that smallest of rebellions, calling the child their granddaughter. Her father silently took off his trilby and overcoat, hanging them in the passage. Then he came to sit on a kitchen chair and nodded to his wife. 'You sit there and tell her how we know it's a bastard and not any grandchild of ours.' His cool blue eyes seemed to pin Mrs Young to the spot and she sat obediently.

Clara's heart stopped. How could they know? She'd only been in the country a couple of days.

'Mrs Almond's daughter wrote and told us what happened.'

Betty Almond was a girl who'd sailed out with Clara last year on the bride ship to Australia. She herself had married an acceptable white Aussie airman.

'So, we know you ain't really married to him, not that you was any the wiser at the time…' her mother continued, dry-mouthed, shooting a quick look at her husband, who interrupted.

'She *should* have known! I warned her about him. And married or not, any woman who goes with a black man's a slut and I'm not having her here!' He slammed the flat of his hand on the tabletop. 'If she'd taken notice of me she might have asked a few more questions and found out her so-called husband already had a wife at home, before she run halfway round the world after him!' Now he looked Clara in the eyes, a withering look, so cold it seemed to quench the embers of any remaining hope that her parents might rally round and help her.

She looked to her mother for help. Her mouth had gone dry and her body trembled. It was bad enough she had to go back to the Alaska and have them talking about her behind her back, but she couldn't bear it if they started calling her daughter a black bastard. 'You haven't told anyone, have you?' Clara asked her mother. 'Martha's innocent. She doesn't deserve to suffer for her mother's mistakes.' Clara stroked her daughter's sleeping head.

'Don't you try and pull that one – you'll get no sympathy from your mother!' Mr Young interrupted. 'All that nonsense you give us, about "we love each other", and you was no more than his tart. That's how much he thought of you. It'll come out sooner or later and say what you like, that child's a bastard!' Her father's pale face was now marbled with fine thread veins. He wasn't a heavy drinker, just a regular one, and now he got up and pulled a half-bottle of whiskey from the sideboard. The large vein in his neck began to bulge.

'Don't upset yourself, Arthur,' her mother said, and Clara's heart sank. Of course, she would always side with him over her.

'I'll stop upsetting meself when you get her out of here,' he said, downing the whiskey. 'And make sure no one sees her.'

Her mother stood up and ushered her to the front door.

'How could you let him say that about your own granddaughter?' Clara looked to see if her mother's face held any sign of shame.

'It's your own fault, gel. You've made your bed.' Her lips were tight-pressed, her eyes hard.

'Get back in here and close that door,' her father bellowed down the passage. 'You're letting all the heat out.' Her mother slammed the door and, startled, Martha began to cry again. Tears rose in Clara's own eyes. It seemed she had already failed to protect her child's beautiful smile.

Clara banged on the door with her fist, rage for her child suddenly making her bold, and she called through the letterbox, 'You're the bastard! And you're a bitch!' In all her life she had never once sworn at her parents, but now she was a parent herself and she thought they deserved it. She sank down on to the front doorstep, trying at once to comfort her child and stem her own sobs. She wiped her eyes, unable to still the trembling that shook every inch of her body.

'It ain't *you* that's not good enough, it's *them*! They're not good enough to be your nan and grandad, my darling,' she whispered. 'You're better off without 'em and I won't let anyone hurt you, not ever!' she promised with a kiss. At that moment, she believed she could keep her promise and so, it seemed, did little Martha, for with two teardrops still trembling on her cheeks, the baby looked up and smiled.

It had grown dark. The night sky was sharp, icy, and the earlier snowfall had made the streets treacherous. Her parents hadn't asked if she had anywhere to stay. She didn't. Almost penniless and with little else than the clothes she and the baby were wearing, she had got herself home by stowing away on a ship from Sydney. Sometimes she was in awe of her own daring. She still didn't know how she'd managed such a thing. She'd been discovered, of course, and the crewmen had a whip-round for her, to pay her passage and give her a bit extra. That was all she had to live on and it was running out fast. But her sudden flight had meant she'd had no chance to prepare – hers and Martha's clothes were intended for sunnier climes. Now she shivered on her parents' doorstep, pierced by a freezing wind that blew round the Square. The cold weather had come as a shock to her and she was sure the thin blanket would barely keep the baby warm. She opened her coat and nestled Martha into its folds.

'There, nice and warm now, aren't you?' And Martha gurgled her agreement.

She was still in unbelieving shock that her parents' hearts hadn't melted at their first glimpse of Martha. She'd naively believed that the long voyage home was the hard part, and that once here she would be forgiven, not for her sake, but for the baby's. It seemed inconceivable that anyone could look at her child's innocent face and not love her. And yet her tiny presence had only seemed to intensify their disapproval, the baby merely evidence that she'd slept with a black man, which, according to the harsh judgements of her parents and their kind, made her a slut, married or not. But Mrs Almond's daughter was right, Barry was indeed a bigamist who'd broken her heart; she could understand it if her parents had blamed him for that, but not for the colour of his skin.

Where could she go now? She had no backup plan. And that was her all over, acting before she had thought things through. Letting her heart lead her halfway round the world, without asking any questions, thinking that love could overcome any amount of prejudice. She was a prize fool and Barry had seen her coming. If she'd only stopped to think before marrying him… but this was no time for 'if only's. She shivered. Either she'd forgotten how cold English winters could be or this one was particularly biting, and now she might have to face it out on the street.

Lights were spilling from kitchens and parlour windows into the Square and Clara found herself envying the occupants who took their shelter and warmth for granted. She thought of going to her brother Pete's, but he and his wife lived the other side of the Old Kent Road, too far to go tonight. Besides Pete was his father's darling and would always side with him. When she'd left for her new life in Australia with Barry, she believed she'd left her family and their condemnation behind forever. But they'd made it clear they didn't want her and she wouldn't give them the satisfaction of begging again.

She stood up and, carrying the baby and her small suitcase, walked towards St Anne's, the pretty church in the Square where she'd been christened and gone to Sunday School. She used to win prizes, coloured postcards of Bible stories. Her favourite had always been the Good Samaritan story, and the memory prompted her to walk up to the church door. It was locked, but she knew another way in. She walked round the Square to the parish room at the rear of the church. This was where her father spent those interminable parish meetings, this was where she'd earned her Girl Guide badges and where they'd put on amateur dramatics. She never thought she'd be so desperate to be let in. She rattled the hall doors, but with little hope. It was as she turned away that Martha began a tentative grizzling, which Clara knew would intensify to a banshee scream if she didn't stop soon and feed her.

'Shhh, shhh, Mummy knows you're hungry, babe. It's coming soon...' She looked around for some private space and her eye was caught by a light in an upstairs window of the house opposite. The ridiculous idea came to her that she should knock on the door. Surely kindness existed in Bermondsey, even for a woman with a brown baby? But as she was about to mount the stairs to the front door, the light went out and her courage failed her. She hurried down the basement steps. At least down here no one could see her from the pavement. She sat on the damp bottom step, shielded from view by the airey wall, and fed her ravenous child, grateful that she could at least provide her with food, if not shelter.

Martha's gold-flecked brown eyes took on a glazed calm that eased Clara's battered heart. 'I love you, sweet baby,' she crooned, not wanting to look away.

But when Martha was satisfied and her eyes closed, Clara began to look around her. She was sitting a few feet from the basement's boarded-up front bay window. The place had obviously suffered some bomb damage for her feet were resting on a jumble of broken bricks, from part of the collapsed airey wall. The basement door on her left was within touching distance and something made her reach out and give it a shove. She jumped when it swung open with a long, low creak. In spite of the cold, she felt herself break into a sweat. *Why not?* The place looked empty. The pitch-black passage was uninviting, but however damp and cold it was inside, it must surely better than spending the night on the street.

She stepped over the high wooden flood step and felt her way along the passage. Her fingers brushed walls of embossed Lincrusta and came away wet. There was a mouldy stench of damp and urine, which became overpowering as she ventured further into the basement. She froze at a scuffling sound. Perhaps someone else was using the place for a shelter? The scuffling came again and she squealed, jumping back as something ran over her foot. A mouse? No, bigger. She took shallow gasps of breath as she crept to the back kitchen. Pearly moonlight streamed through the backyard window, allowing her to investigate the abandoned remnants of someone else's life. Two broken-backed chairs, a table, an iron bedstead with no mattress, a nest of old army blankets near an unlit fire. She ventured into the scullery beyond. There was a sink, so at least she'd have water. She turned the tap and a stagnant trickle of water sputtered out, then stopped. Perhaps the pipes had frozen, it was certainly cold enough. It was then she realized her feet were splashing around in water. The scullery was an inch deep in it and the smell told her it was rising from a broken drain somewhere. Perhaps she'd be better off on the street after all. But a freezing draught penetrating a broken windowpane was enough to persuade her to stay; it was colder outside. She could sit with her feet up on the kitchen chairs all night, holding the baby so the rats didn't bite her.

She prepared herself to stay awake all night. But it was so dark and cold, she soon found herself longing for the warmth and blue skies of Australia. It wasn't the country she'd hated, only him, and even that hatred had taken a long while to grow in her. She'd so wanted to believe it had all been a terrible mistake, that he really had loved her.

She opened a cupboard and felt about inside, quickly pulling out her hand as a disturbed spider brushed her fingers. 'Oh dear God, help me,' she prayed. 'I need a light, a candle, a match, anything...' But there was no light apart from the snow-bright moon.

She left the scullery, feeling her way back into the kitchen. She poked the pile of blankets with her foot, but decided to suffer the cold rather than wrap those around her. Placing the two chairs together, she sat on one and raised her feet to the other. Eyes wide and ears pricked, she sat nestling Martha inside her coat, following the path of the moon through the window for what seemed like hours. Her eyes began to droop but a sound made her start – perhaps it was only the wind rattling the rotten window frame. She blinked and forced her eyes open, but as soon as she nodded off again another noise jolted her awake to a cold sweat. This time it sounded like the thump of a loose fence board outside. But she was grateful for the sounds, as they kept her vigilant.

It wasn't long after she had succumbed to sleep that a figure crept into the basement. He made no more noise than a rat and Clara did not wake as he approached her with a stooped, shuffling gate. He stopped and cocked his head to one side as, by the light of the moon, he studied the baby's face, peering up at him from the folds of Clara's coat. Martha's trusting, curious eyes were wide open and a joyful smile lit up her face. It was the smell rather than any noise that woke Clara. At the sight of a man standing over her, she let out a scream which she quickly stifled, plugging her mouth with a fist. The man was short and wide, with long muscular arms and a marked stoop. His face was bony and his large head was tilted to one side. It was too dark to make out his age, but the immediately obvious thing about him was that he stank. An eye-watering mixture of urine and body odour emanated from him. The baby stirred in her arms and made the loud, bright two-toned sound that Clara was convinced was the child's version of 'hello'. It seemed Martha had already seen the intruder and was greeting him.

Clara put up a hand, palm outward as if to fend him off. 'Please, don't hurt my baby! D-d-don't...' she pleaded, her teeth chattering so much she was unable to finish. The man lumbered forward and she leaped off the chair, backing away into the flooded scullery. 'I'll go... I'm sorry, if this is your place. I didn't mean to take it.' Now she found herself backed into ankle-deep smelly drainwater in the scullery. Her hand felt the backyard door. She yanked it, trying to twist the knob. It was stuck fast, though she rattled it with all her strength. Giving up, she turned and pressed her face to the wall. Curls of peeling wallpaper brushed her cheeks as she stood rigid with fear, shivering in the freezing scullery, shielding Martha from whatever was to come.

She stayed there, wrapped around her child, frozen to the wall, and it seemed as if the basement must become her tomb. But the blow she was expecting never came, and eventually Clara heard sounds other than her own half-choked breath and banging heart. Footsteps shuffling back along the passage, then the unmistakable click of the front door closing. Had he gone? She inched round, listening to the faint scurrying noises of a rodent's claws on lino and the wind whistling through the broken window. There was no other presence in the basement, she was sure of it. But when she finally plucked up courage to return to the pitch-dark kitchen she found the visitor had left them two gifts. A rare, if rather wrinkled, tangerine and a lingering aroma of unwashed body.

# 3

## *Lou's Baby*

### *January 1947*

Ronnie didn't know what to do. His mother had returned from Fairby Grange, the council's convalescent home out in Kent, even more doolally than when she'd left. He wished she'd stayed there. He'd been doing all right on his own. He was meant to have stayed with his uncle while his mum was away, but Ronnie hadn't fancied that. He'd bunked off school and shifted for himself on the bombsites. Now his mother was sitting on the kitchen floor, rubbing her great big stomach and groaning. Usually he could persuade her to get into bed, but tonight she wouldn't budge. She'd told him she had a tummy ache. She would sit up, she said, and wait for Dad and Sue to come home. But his dad was dead and so was his little sister, Sue. Neither would be coming home. Their two-room flat in Barnham Street Buildings had only the one bedroom, where his mum slept. His bed was in the other room – the kitchen. Eventually he decided to leave her where she was and crept into his little cot-bed, wedged between the range and the table.

He was woken in the middle of the night by her weeping. He sat up sharply, rocking the flimsy cot-bed. His mother sat on the kitchen floor exactly where he'd left her, surrounded by a puddle of water.

'Mum, no! You've gone and wet yourself!' he cried, getting out of bed to pull her up. 'What you do that for?' he asked crossly. The room they called the kitchen had a range, but no sink or tap, so he grabbed a cloth from the bucket they kept under the table and began mopping up the mess.

'Ronnie, love, leave that, get me Mrs Wren...' His mother's voice was faint, her body rigid. Pain rippled across her face, twisting her mouth, wrinkling her forehead. He was about to protest that Mrs Wren would tell him off for waking her up, when his mother let out a loud groan, and he jumped up. He charged out of their flat and downstairs to the second-floor landing where Mrs Wren lived with her husband and elderly in-laws. He banged on the door until a light appeared and it was opened.

'Ronnie, come in. Don't stand out there in the freezing cold, boy. What's happened?' Mr Wren was in his pyjamas and his unBrylcreemed hair was fluffy as a white candyfloss. 'Is it your mother?'

Ronnie nodded. 'She's wet herself.' He explained, and Mr Wren, seeming unsurprised, called into the bedroom to his wife, who acted as the unofficial midwife of Barnham Street Buildings. 'Mina, it's Lou's time!'

The commotion had woken up the elderly Wrens, who slept in a double bed that took up half the kitchen. Mrs Wren appeared in her curlers and told Ronnie not to worry. Not stopping to dress, she threw a coat over her nightie and led the way upstairs. Once in their flat she took Ronnie by the shoulders. 'I'll need you to get me plenty of water. How many buckets you got?'

'One.'

'Well, get filling and don't get in me way.'

The five flats on each landing were served by a single stone sink and cold tap outside. Now he trotted along the freezing landing and hoisted the zinc bucket into the sink, turning it full on so that water splashed up to soak him. He was trembling under the full weight of the bucket by the time he got it indoors.

'Mind out, you're slopping it everywhere!' Mrs Wren was red-faced and seemed flustered. 'Giss it here, gawd's sake, I'll heat it up in the saucepans, you fill it up again.'

His mum was now in her bedroom, but Ronnie could still

hear her groaning all the way down the landing, and he was tempted to leave the bucket and run. But Mrs Wren shouted at him to hurry up and someone in another flat ordered them to pipe down. He deposited the bucket in the kitchen and hunkered down behind the closed bedroom door, watching through the crack as Mrs Wren leaned over his mother.

They had forgotten him. He stuffed fingers in his ears to shut out his mother's screams, but it was too much. He'd heard about Nazi torturers, it must be something like that. But why was Mrs Wren torturing his mum? He couldn't listen any more. If Mum died they'd put him in a home and he'd had enough of that old lark when he was evacuated. They'd have to catch him first. He crept over to the cupboard and removed his mother's bag. The contents of her purse were disappointing, nothing he could lift without it being obvious. But somehow he didn't think his mum would be in any state to check her purse for a while, so he pocketed the two bob coin and replaced the purse. Ronnie slipped out, hoping to find the tea stall in Crucifix Lane still open. Two bob should get him quite a bit more than his usual arrowroot biscuit and strong brown brew.

Down in the courtyard, in spite of the late hour and the freezing cold, some of the gang were still hanging about. Among them were his best friends, Nutty Norman and Frankie the Fish. But Ronnie didn't want to answer any questions about his mum tonight and nipped round the back of the dust chutes to avoid the gang. He cut along the soot-caked railway arches, scooting from lock-up to lock-up, imagining himself on a secret mission deep behind German lines. He crouched low, sprinting along the ice-slick pavement, dodging from arch to arch, pressing himself into the dark shadows, holding his flick knife up, ready to plunge into any German guard who might challenge him. 'Hand yer hock!' he said out loud in a harsh German accent. But as he was passing one of the arches a figure came lumbering out of it in a sudden, blinding flurry of fresh snow. A German guard! 'Hand yer hock!' Ronnie screamed as the man crashed into him.

Ronnie felt the knife bury itself into flesh until it hit bone. He sprang back as the man fell heavily to the snowy ground.

'Effin' hell!' He dropped to his knees, shivering. He'd come out wearing only his shorts and jacket, but it was the thought that he'd killed someone that had turned every limb to jelly. He examined the man by the light of a single lamp hanging over the arch. He was squat, not much taller than Ronnie, and he lay curled like a baby, nestled in the soot-streaked snow. Ronnie shoved the man's shoulder. He knew he should feel a vein somewhere to check if he was dead, but he had no idea which one. 'Bloody hell, you don't half pen-and-ink, mate,' he muttered to the body as he turned the bony face towards him, trying all the while to keep his nose in the air. But as the smell of urine and dirt permeated his nostrils, he realized with a shock that he couldn't have picked a worse person to kill.

In the early hours of that morning, as Ronnie lay under the blanket, he stuck fingers into his ears to block out the groaning and crying and screaming which had gone on and on till he'd wanted to get up and stuff the scratchy blanket into his mum's mouth. After he'd killed the man, he'd run to the tea stand anyway; what was done was done and it wasn't every day he got two bob to spend on a hot jacket potato, a teacake and as much sweet tea as he liked. He'd hoped his mum would be cured by the time he got back, but the screaming had lasted all night. Now suddenly there was silence, which was even more scary than the noise. What if she was dead? Dead as the man he'd killed. Dead as Nan and Grandad and little Sue, dead as his dad. Then he'd be all on his own. But he didn't care. It felt like that most of the time anyway. His mum didn't know what day it was and sometimes she called him Vic, his dad's name. 'Come and give me feet a rub, Vic,' she'd say, 'I've been standing all day and me feet's so swollen I can hardly get the bloody shoes off.' He'd given up trying to tell her who he was. And besides, he preferred it on the bombsites. Some nights he didn't come home at all.

And then, when the other kids had gone home, he would stoke up the fire and get a dustbin lid to roast potatoes on, and there were always plenty of places, rain-tight and snug, that he could crawl into.

But the thought of his various camps reminded Ronnie of Pissy Pants, the man he'd killed, for he was another who'd lived in any hole he could find. Sometimes Ronnie had turfed Pissy Pants out of a nice comfortable bombed-out cellar. But he shouldn't have stabbed him. Ronnie broke into a cold sweat under the blanket and began shivering. His nose was so cold he thought it might fall off. That's what happened to liars, and he was one of those, for sure. Now he was a murderer too. And though Pissy Pants might seem like a tramp, his real name was Johnny Harper and the Harpers were the biggest villains in Bermondsey. Six brothers and two sisters, all hard as nails. One of those families whose name you spoke only in a whisper and when you found out a kid was related to them, you treated them very carefully, never nicking their conkers or marbles, never saying they couldn't play 'run outs' with you.

Lenny Harper, the eldest brother, was always trying to clean up Pissy Pants, or get him to live in a house, but Johnny preferred the ruins and his scavenging. They said he'd gone bonkers after they put him in Stonefield Asylum for nicking sausages out of Richmond's factory. After five years in the nuthouse he'd started pushing that old handcart around Bermondsey, collecting newspaper, rags, any old rubbish he could sell. And now he was dead and the Harpers would be after Ronnie as soon as they found out.

It was then that the welcome silence in the house was split by another cry, thinner than his mum's, a long high wail that ended in a choking sound. Ronnie crept to the bedroom door and pushed it open an inch. Mrs Wren was holding up a squashed-looking purple baby, covered in sticky white stuff that made Ronnie feel sick. She wiped its wet head, which was covered in curly black hair and then she wrapped the baby in a blanket, and Ronnie watched as Mrs Wren smiled and laid it on his mum's chest.

'You've got a lovely baby girl, Lou,' Mrs Wren said softly, and his mother answered, 'I know I have. Her name's Sue.'

He ran back to the kitchen and burrowed beneath the scratchy grey blanket. He didn't like to think about his little sister, Sue. He remembered the day his mum had brought them both home from evacuation in Dorset, because she missed Sue and because he hated it down there. Sue was a pretty little girl and she'd been picked by a nice family, but he was stuck in a kid's home run by bastards who half-starved him. So, after a few months, Mum said, 'You're coming home. If we get bombed out at least we'll all go together.' But one night Sue went to stay with Nan and Grandad in Spa Road and the house got blown up by a flying bomb. So Mum was wrong, they didn't all go together after all.

His mum was never the same after Sue died, and when Dad didn't come home after the war she took up with that feller Gordon, who ate all the grub and kicked him up the arse when she wasn't looking. When Gordon pissed off, Ronnie was glad, but Mum got even worse – started wandering round the bombsites, calling all their names, all the dead ones, Nan and Grandad's and Sue's, but never his. It was a right show-up, when everyone started calling her Loony Lou. That's when he went on the bombsites. He knew them all, all the good sites from Blackfriars to Tower Bridge, all along the river and over the other side, down the Old Kent Road and up Rotherhithe, all the empty warehouses and bombed-out factories and ruined houses. Sometimes he'd be missing for days and she wouldn't notice. Perhaps now she had a new baby, she'd start being happy again. Perhaps she'd even remember his name.

\* \* \*

Lou Payne looked at the baby and tried to make sense of it all. It couldn't be hers. Mina must have swapped hers with some other woman's baby because Lou knew for a fact her little girl had blonde hair. She looked at the scrunched-up face, eyes screwed shut, curly black hair. No. Her kids were born blonde and stayed that way. She pushed the child away.

'You take her, Mina, and give her back to her own mother. She'll be missing her daughter. Gawd knows she ain't mine, but I do think it's wicked of you, to take my Sue away and give me this one.'

Mina lifted the baby from Lou's chest. 'I'm sorry, love, but I never took her. Your Sue's been gone four years, along with your poor mum and dad.'

Lou heaved herself up from the bed and lunged at Mina, pushing her and the baby away. 'No! You evil cow, I'm telling you I'm not having that child anywhere near me. You wait till my Vic gets in, he'll be fuming…' Then Lou, exhausted beyond words, fell back on to the bed.

Mina had talked Lou round before. She retreated briefly, laying the baby in the bottom drawer she'd padded out with a blanket. Then she went to hold Lou's hand. She stroked it until the woman was calmer. 'When's Vic coming home then, Lou?' she asked gently, 'Is he due some leave?'

Lou looked round the room, barely focusing, her head moving this way and that in a searching motion that had become habitual. Her face lit up as she fixed her gaze on a framed photograph on the mantelpiece. The photo was of a man in army uniform and the frame was bordered with a black ribbon. Suddenly it was as if a fog lifted. As Lou seemed to stare into the stark reality of her life, the glare was too painful, and her face creased with grief.

'Vic ain't coming home on leave, is he, Mina?' she said in a hushed voice. 'And that poor little thing's not his… but it is mine.' And then Lou sobbed, great wracking sobs that made her wrap her arms around herself, while Mina waited until the shuddering grief had ebbed.

'Give her here,' Lou said.

She held the child and pulled open the blanket so she could see for herself. 'It ain't my Sue. You know what, Mina, I don't think I can look after this baby, can I?'

And Mina thought those were the sanest words she'd heard from Lou Payne in a very long while.

'I could find someone who'd take her, love, if that's what you want.'

Lou nodded her head wearily, 'How can I bring a dear little baby into this place?' she said, looking round the room as if it were only a matter of the dilapidated flat and not her broken spirit that prevented her. 'Truth is, I ain't got it in me to love another child. It's for the best, so long as she goes to a kind woman.'

'There's a lovely young woman I saw to last week, but her baby died. I know she'd take this little one, Lou, and she's got a good husband and family to help her. I don't think she'd want for nothing...' Mina said, looking down at the scrunched-up face and fists of the baby, which looked almost as if it were pleading to go.

'I'd rather give her away than keep her and something happen to her. I've not been meself for a long time, you see. I ain't capable. You take her.'

Lou held the baby one last time and kissed her on the forehead. As she offered her up into Mina's hands, tears trembled and spilled from Lou's weak blue eyes. But it seemed as if a heavy weight were lifting from the woman's stooped shoulders and she straightened up. 'I might have let down both my other kids, but as gawd's my judge I'm not letting down this one too...' She swallowed her tears and looked Mina firmly in the eye. 'Go on, quick, Mina, take her.'

# 4

## *The Alaska*

Hattie had to get out of Cissie's. Anywhere must be better than this. She'd been woken early again this morning from her elusive sleep by her mother's girlish giggles in response to Mario's enthusiastic advances. She thumped the hard cushion and coughed loudly, with no effect. She'd put up with Cissie's ridiculous behaviour while she'd been recuperating from her beating, only too grateful for a place to hide away and lick her wounds. She'd certainly been in no fit state to vent her anger at Cissie, but all the while she'd been seething inwardly. The woman had tricked her into coming home and she'd have to voice her anger soon or explode.

Hattie waited until Mario left for his work clearing bombsites, before she emerged from her lumpy nest of a sofa. The room was freezing and she hastily heated water on the gas ring, before washing at Cissie's marble-topped washstand. This was squashed behind the curtain, next to the bed, where Cissie now lay smoking a cigarette, watching Hattie. Without her make-up and with her red hair garish in the light of day, Cissie looked what she was: a fifty-odd-year-old woman who, after a lifetime of smoking and drinking to excess, had been reluctant to give up on her youthful good looks. Perhaps Hattie should tell Ciss she was fighting a losing battle – 'mutton dressed as lamb' was what other people said behind her back. But Hattie had a certain admiration for her mother's defiance in the face of those killjoys who would like her to be as grey as this morning's snow-blurred skies.

No, let her continue to dye her hair the same shade as her bright red lipstick.

Hattie finished hiding her visible cuts and bruises with pancake make-up borrowed from Ciss, and dressed carefully, still conscious of her battered limbs. She layered herself with vest, jumper and cardigan, but shivered as she went to peer out of the window, which had a thin film of ice on the inside. She could barely see the church spire for snow, and the whole square looked like a snow globe she'd seen in a Christmas market in Brussels. But appearances could be deceptive; her life was not pretty.

'I think I'll go up the council this morning about a place, Ciss.'

Her mother finally got out of bed and emerged from behind the curtain, a candlewick bedspread draped around her like a Grecian robe, falling to the floor in folds. She tripped over it.

'Blimey, my eyes is getting worse!' she said, squinting at Hattie, silhouetted against the window's pearly light.

'Well, at least you can see *something*. You wrote and told me you needed me to come home because you'd gone blind!'

'I've been blind as a bleedin' bat for years, you know that, darlin' – but I never really expected you to come home! You ain't exactly rushed to see me every leave, have you? Anyway, it was a moment's weakness, weren't it? My chap had just left me and I was fit to be tied. You know what I'm like without a feller. Just so happened Mario come along shortly after that...'

'Well, good for Mario. But I'm bloody furious with you, Ciss, and if I hadn't been in such a state when I got home, I'd have had my say then. I could have stayed on in the army!'

'What d'you want to do that for? You're better off home in Bermondsey, best place in the world.' Cissie hitched up the bedspread and lit another cigarette.

Hattie raised her eyes. 'Believe me, Ciss, I've seen a bit of the world and this is *not* the best place. It's a shithole, and if you had two working eyes in your bloody head you'd see that for yourself!'

'No need to get nasty, you cheeky mare. I'm your mother.'

Hattie let out a laugh of disbelief. Anyone less like a mother she couldn't imagine. But that was an old sore – she was no longer the ostracized little girl, ridiculed by the other kids for having a tart as a mother. She'd grown up.

'No, you'll never starve here, gel. Not with neighbours like ours.' Cissie was warming to her subject. 'I've known next-door have one lump o' coal in the bucket and give me half if I needed it. That's what I mean by best place in the world. Give me pie and mash over a bleedin' Belgian bun any day!'

Hattie shrugged. 'It's your choice to live here. I just don't appreciate being tricked. So, I'll be moving out.'

Finally Cissie's face softened into her version of maternal concern. 'I'm sorry, love, didn't you get much sleep? You look like a death-worn duck!'

'You mean "death warmed up", and thanks for the compliment, but no, I slept fine. It's just this place is too small for three,' she said truthfully.

'Well, you'll be lucky up the council. The waiting list's interminable. There's no places to be had for love nor money. Mrs Hill's son come out the army and they told him it'd be six years' wait for a council place, six years! Him and his wife's living with her mum in Sidcup now.'

'Perhaps Mrs Hill's son's used to taking no for an answer – I'm not,' Hattie declared, throwing on her coat and walking out of the door.

Cissie might have a talent for exaggeration, but after queuing for three hours at the town hall Hattie found her mother was right. Of course she could put her name down, the housing clerk explained, but there were thousands in front of her. She remembered the row of little white cubes she'd passed in Grange Road. When she asked about one of those, the clerk laughed out loud. A prefab was out of the question! Hadn't she heard that every single one of the nineteen thousand houses in the borough had been destroyed or bomb-damaged? She told him she'd seen that much for herself, but didn't it count for anything she was a returning servicewoman? No, he said, families had priority for prefabs and flats. As a single woman she'd simply have to make her own arrangements or, the clerk sniggered, she could try getting married and pregnant. A baby could boost your points. Hattie gave him a sour look and walked out with a flaming face and her housing number: seven thousand and fifty-three.

She stood on the town hall steps, wondering what to do. She was still waiting to hear back from two office job applications; if they didn't come up trumps she'd be out of options. Before leaving Belgium she'd applied for a dozen office jobs. Ten rejections later, she was fed up with hearing she was too old, under-qualified, or simply excluded because she was a woman and the job had been reserved for a returning serviceman. If she didn't hear soon from the bank in Gracechurch Street or Pearce Duff's offices, where she'd applied to be a clerk, it would be back to the Alaska for her. Perhaps it was time to visit her old friend Buster. If the Alaska was hiring he'd know and, if she needed it, she was sure he'd help get her old job back. But her other reason for seeking him out was that he had a flat in Grange House, not far from the factory. Perhaps he'd do her a favour and put her up.

The snow had thickened even more, so that passing vehicles already had their headlights on, smudged spots of brightness in the yellowish gloom. It was dinner time and she knew Buster would be in the Alaska canteen, housed in a low-rise building opposite the factory. It was only a short walk from the town hall and soon she was pushing through the canteen doors.

It was like stepping back in time. Her heart sank as she pulled the doors shut behind her, but not before a waft of icy air blew in with her. The canteen was a warm fug, thick with smoke from hundreds of cigarettes and the steam from stewing cabbage. She scanned the tables and heard Buster's distinctive rapid-fire lisp before she saw him. There he was, entertaining a group of women with his latest jokes, gesticulating elaborately to emphasize the punch lines. The foreman was popular with the Alaska girls, probably because they sensed he wasn't interested in getting anything from them. Buster, by his own definition, was 'camp as Christmas', but that hadn't stopped Hattie from being his regular dancing partner before the war. It suited them both, she got the best dancer in the factory and he got his decoy. But she liked to believe it wasn't merely convenience between them, and whenever she'd needed his help, he'd always come through.

'Buster!' she called, waving until he spotted her.

He was a chubby man of medium height with a round face and Brylcreemed, fair hair, swept back from his forehead in a quiff. He beamed a smile and hurried towards her, dodging nimbly between the crowded tables. He threw his arms round her. 'Hattie! Why didn't you tell me you was comin', love? You look rough! You been ill, darlin'?'

His extravagant embrace drew a couple of stares, but Buster didn't care if he was as flamboyantly out of place as a flamenco dancer in The Horns pub on a Saturday night. He'd made his way up the ladder in a world where men were tight-lipped and undemonstrative and that, at least, had earned him their grudging admiration.

'Want a cuppa, love?' he asked. 'Looks like she needs one.' He addressed the room generally. 'Bleedin' sergeant major, looks like she's been fighting the war single-handed! You come to sort us out? Gawd knows why you stayed on in the army all this time. Still, you're home now, come and tell Buster all about it.'

Hattie scanned the room, feeling suddenly awkward. There were some familiar faces, but she was surprised by how many of the women were new to her and she felt strangely out of place. This didn't feel like her world any more and she was glad of it. Perhaps seeing her unease, Buster took her elbow. 'Come back to my place. I've got half an hour before me shift starts.' But Buster could do nothing quietly, not even exit, and as he led her out he took her hand, twirling her round under his arm. 'Me old dancing partner's back!' He beamed at Levin the nailer, the most morose and foul-mouthed of her ex-workmates. Levin spent his days nailing fur pelts to boards to dry, stretching them tight as drums, then bashing home nails to keep them in place. It required great physical strength, accuracy and speed, and the nailers regularly suffered bruised knuckles and broken fingers; Levin eased his pain with liberal expletives.

'I effin' well know who she is! I might be getting old but I ain't gone bleedin' blind yet,' Levin said.

'Well, crack a smile for her, you miserable old git,' Buster ordered and Levin stared at her with his long sallow face, raising a corner of his mouth in a lopsided smile. 'All right?' he asked Hattie – the warmest welcome she would get from Levin after her long absence.

'But he really has missed you, haven't you, Levin?' Buster raised two fingers at the nailer.

'Don't know why you bothered coming back to this shithole, but welcome home anyway,' Levin said graciously. He drained his tea and pushed past Buster. 'Move your fat arse and make way for the workers.' As he passed Hattie he gave her a peck on the cheek. She was knocked back by the smell. Eight years' war service disappeared in one whiff of that old familiar work aroma, a powerful cocktail of leather, oily fur, hydrogen peroxide and tobacco.

Buster raised his eyes good-naturedly. He was used to abuse. 'He don't mean nothing by it, do you, Levin?' And it was true, Levin was kinder-hearted than he liked to show. There were others in the factory more open in their undisguised loathing of Buster, and one of them was bearing down upon them now. But he had spotted her. 'Look out, love. Axmouth's on the warpath.'

Hattie had never met Doris Axmouth, but Buster had told her the tale in one of his letters. Doris was a woman scorned. She'd set her cap at Buster when she'd first joined the firm a couple of years earlier, but had been sorely disappointed. When Buster made the mistake of telling her the truth about his preferences all her previous ardour had turned to repugnance.

As she passed them her face wrinkled in disgust. 'Don't waste your time with him.' She almost spat at Hattie. 'He's one of them.'

Hattie smiled innocently. 'One of what? A foreman?'

'A Mary Ann.' The woman curled her lip and gave Buster a wide berth, as if he were carrying some infectious disease. Buster ignored her and pulled on his camel overcoat; he would never be seen outside work in his foreman's blue overall. He always wore a shirt and tie, with a smart suit or blazer. Once they were out in the street he put a proprietorial hand on her elbow and steered her towards his flat in Grange House, a newish block of flats. His home was tiny, but warm and welcoming.

'You're better than me with a needle, Buster,' Hattie said, noticing that he'd made a decent job of the curtains using a couple of yards of parachute silk.

'Thanks, love. I did me best. You still can't get good material, not even down East Lane.'

He served them tea in bone-china cups. 'I'd make you a sandwich if I had any bread!' he laughed.

'Looks to me like you're getting enough under the counter.' Hattie prodded his paunch.

'At least you was getting well fed in the army. So, what's brought you home?'

'Everything was disbanding over there, but I could have stayed on. My evil cow of a mother begged me to come home, tricked me with some codswallop about going blind. Oh, Buster, I could have strangled her! Did you know she's taken up with a new feller?'

'Ciss don't change.' He chuckled and there was a mischievous look in his eye. 'But listen, I've got some news too. Didn't want to say nothing in the canteen 'cause there's always some mean bastard ready to shop you to the old Bill, but guess what, love? I've only got meself a chap!'

Hattie's heart contracted with a moment's intense fear.

'Don't look like that. We're careful, nothing in public.' His expression had turned serious, 'I'm not taking no stupid risks, not after the last time.'

She put a hand over his, for Buster had only narrowly escaped prison after a policeman had tried to tempt him into the public conveniences in Tower Bridge Road. 'I was just strolling round them, looking at the electric signs!' had been his defence at the time and though the health-education illuminated billboards were entertaining enough, she thought the judge was naïve to have believed Buster's main interest had been how to avoid TB. 'No, as far as anyone's concerned, Aiden is just me lodger.'

'He's moved in?'

Buster nodded happily, but his smile quickly faded. 'You don't look very pleased for me, Hattie... I'll still be your dancing partner!'

'It's not that... Thing is, Buster, I was hoping you could put me up for a while. Cissie's in one room now, so it's a bit crowded with the fancy man there...'

'Suppose that makes two of us!' He laughed, but when she didn't join in, gave her a long look. 'What else? It's not just having to live with Cissie the Red, is it?'

He made her smile with his wicked nickname for Cissie, which she'd earned not just for her preferred hair colour but because she'd been a fearsome union activist in her youth.

Hattie sighed. 'What Levin said – about me coming back. He's right. I shouldn't be here, Buster. The war's changed me. I've managed gun teams, run a records office in Brussels HQ. I've spent too long being in charge to go back to a factory floor, but it could come to it. I might need your help getting me old job back at the Alaska.' She felt almost embarrassed to be asking – but this was Buster.

''Course I'll help, darlin'! But it ain't so easy these days in the fur trade. They're still classed as luxury goods and we're nowhere near full production. Besides, Chris Harper's not going to make it easy for you.'

She'd had a run-in with the senior foreman shortly before she enlisted. Chris was one of the large Harper clan, most of whom were out-and-out villains, while others held down jobs but indulged in dodgy dealing on the side. Chris was one of the latter.

Hattie had once shared Cissie's socialist principles and she'd thought the Alaska needed a trade union instead of the toothless workers' committee. She'd been branded a Bolshie and Chris hadn't liked it, but he'd put up with it because at the time Hattie was engaged to his cousin, Lenny Harper. But it hadn't helped relations between them.

'For God's sake, Buster, we've been through a war since then. Surely that's all water under the bridge.'

'Well, Lenny might have something to say about it if Chris hires you...'

She made a gesture of impatience. 'Just because I dumped him! I hate this bloody place.'

The underside of Cissie's vision of Bermondsey's salt-of-the-earth neighbourliness was the Harpers. When she was engaged to Lenny, Hattie had resented their incestuous demand for loyalty and loathed their vicious treatment of all who stepped outside the bounds of their tinpot kingdom. 'I can't have Lenny Harper dictating what I do and don't do,' she said simply.

'Don't worry. If it comes to it, I still might be able to get you in under the radar – maybe on the bambeaters? Bessie Clutterbuck's always had a soft spot for you.'

Bessie Clutterbuck, more commonly known as Old Buttercup, was the bambeater supervisor and had been at the factory for as long as anyone could remember. She'd inhaled so much fur over the years that Hattie was convinced it had invaded her brain as well as her lungs.

Hattie groaned and pulled a face. 'Is Old Buttercup still going strong?'

Buster nodded. 'Old Buttercup's not that bad. She might be dim but she ain't vicious like Chris Harper. You'll be running rings round her, just like you used to.'

'Perhaps, but I don't want to spend my life stuck on the bam-beater, breathing in fur till I'm as senile and wheezy as her.'

'Well, beggars can't be choosers, Hattie. Anyway you might get transferred to shearing or grooving. You can always work your way up, like me,' Buster said cheerily. Hattie didn't want to deflate him, but a forelady at the Alaska wasn't what she'd dreamed of. The army had both made her and spoiled her. She didn't know where she fitted in now.

She finished her tea and got up. 'I'll let you know if I get desperate.'

Buster gave her a kiss. 'At least they've tarted up the social club now – gramophone, piano, the lot! There's a dance on Saturday night. Come as me partner?'

And Hattie smiled. 'So long as your chap Aiden won't mind!'

The social club met in the canteen building and on Saturday night she rediscovered the sheer joy of dancing with Buster. They quickly slipped into their old jitterbug routine, with Buster teaching her a few new steps along the way. He spun her round, swinging her to either side like a pendulum so that her red-gold hair brushed the floor and her dancing shoes pointed to the ceiling. Her battered ribs had improved but could still give her pain, which they did now. But she ignored it. Being whirled across the cleared canteen floor to the blaring gramophone record was the closest to home she'd felt since stepping back into Bermondsey. There still wasn't much drink to be had but a whip-round had produced a few crates of beer, so before the evening was out Hattie was tipsy and in high spirits – until she remembered where she was going to spend the night. She couldn't bear the thought of returning to Cissie's and, not for the first time, found herself longing for the army. The humblest Nissen hut from basic training days had begun to seem preferable to the lumpy sofa and the lovebirds.

Hattie left the canteen to a fresh fall of snow and she trod gingerly through its icy opaqueness towards the bus stop. The bus, when it came, was crawling along, keeping to the wheel ruts already scored into the icy road. It was escorted by the conductor, who'd got off and was waving an ineffectual torch to light the way for the driver. When she eventually reached the Square she had to feel her way round the low airey walls until she got to Cissie's on the corner. Or at least she thought it was the right house, but they were all so similar and she could barely see an inch in front of her. When she thought she saw a figure entering the basement, she realized she must be on the wrong side of the Square. Another circuit left her shivering, convinced she'd been at Cissie's all along.

It was only after she'd crept into the made-up sofa bed that she remembered the shadowy figure in the airey – it was just a fleeting glimpse of movement. Her mother had said the basement was running with rats and 'inunhabitable'. Desperate as Hattie was for somewhere to live, she was sure nothing would induce her, nor anyone else with any sense, to attempt to inhabit it.

*

Over the following week Hattie tried to stay out as much as she could. It wasn't easy with the Arctic weather freezing them in. She visited Buster or went to the pub, catching up with some of her old pals; she spent mornings in Spa Road Library, scouring the newspapers for office work. But the nights were inescapable, nights which Cissie and Mario made unashamed use of. Fear of the rats was the only reason she hadn't decamped to the basement. If she could just land a decent job she'd have half a chance of renting somewhere of her own. When both replies came on the same day she tore at the envelopes, certain one of them would be her salvation. The bank said she was under-qualified and Pearce Duff's offices had been instructed to give three per cent of jobs to disabled servicemen... the clerk's job was one of the three per cent. She crumpled the letters into a tight ball.

'What's the matter, darlin?' Cissie asked as she unpacked her shopping. 'I tell you, you can't get a packet of fags for love nor money, I'm induced to these.' She tossed a white paper bag of loose cigarettes on to the table. 'Have a gasper.'

Hattie took one of the five and sat smoking as her mother complained about the lack of food down the Blue. Eventually

Cissie remembered why she'd offered Hattie the cigarette. 'What you got that face on for?'

'Looks like I'll be going back to the Alaska.' She didn't expect Cissie to understand why her heart felt hollowed of all hope by the prospect.

'Life's full of disappointments, darlin'. Look at your father. I thought he was a good 'un. You just carry on, make the best of it. Sometimes these things is for the best… I wouldn't have had half so much fun if he'd stayed, I can tell you that!' She coughed on her own cigarette and began to heat a precious tin of Crosse & Blackwell's mulligatawny on the gas ring. 'We'll have a treat from our combustibles, eh, Hattie?'

Hattie bit her lip, hiding the smile at her mother's brave stab at an elevated vocabulary. Not for nothing had Cissie spent her youth in the company of Suffragists and Fabians at the Fort Road Labour Institute.

Eventually she'd had to give in and ask for Buster's help. She waited for him in the Alaska canteen while he manipulated whoever he needed to. It was usually enough for a foreman to give a recommendation, but when he returned to the canteen she could see from his glum expression that even Buster's charm had failed her this time. He sat down next to her and took a gulp of her cold tea.

'I'm sorry, Hattie, I couldn't do it under the radar. Chris Harper says he wants to interview you first,' he said.

'Interview me! Chrissake, I've got a ton of references from the army he can look at. He just wants to rub my nose in it.'

Buster nodded his head, his double chin wobbling. ''Fraid so.'

Hattie gave a small snort. 'All right. When's the interview?'

Buster looked at his watch. 'Now.'

'Now! Why didn't you tell me?'

'I've only just found out!'

She swallowed the dregs of her tea, wishing it had a nip of whiskey in it, and steeled herself to see Chris Harper again. She was glad in a way that she hadn't had any warning. It would have been too tempting to run, just as she had eight years earlier. For however much she liked to think she'd left to do her patriotic duty, that hadn't been the only reason she'd signed up.

She knocked once and walked into the tiny office, no bigger than one of the cubicles in Grange Road baths, but which Chris Harper inhabited with undisguised pride.

'Hattie!' Chris pretended to be pleased to see her. Lenny's cousin was a typical Harper, stocky, with a massive head and thick features. 'Come in! Sit down.'

The office smelled of petrol from the delivery vans in the yard, as well as the all-pervasive oily reek of sheepskins. He leaned back and smiled at her, his crooked canines crowding out a mouth full of large teeth. 'So you've come back to the fold! Buster tells me you want your old job back?'

'If it's going.'

He sucked on crowded teeth. 'Nahh, it ain't. We're only at half-production. Coneys, though, we got plenty of rabbits.'

'Bambeating?' she asked, choking on the word.

He grinned again. 'Let's get one thing clear. There's no trade union at the Alaska and there never will be, not while I'm in charge, got it? If you're still a Bolshie you can forget about it. But if you toe the line, well, I'll give you a chance.'

'Thanks, Chris,' she mumbled, imagining tying him to the mouth of an ack-ack gun before shouting 'Fire!'

He peered at her face. 'What's happened to your boat race, Hattie? You been letting some feller bash you about again? Carry on like this and people will think you like it.'

She instinctively put a hand to her cheek, wishing she'd applied a bit more pancake to hide the fading bruises. Her heart lurched as he fixed her with his small, sunken eyes, but she tried to keep her face impassive. 'Slipped on the ice.' She got up to go before she said something that would sabotage her chances.

'Oh, and by the way... our Lenny sends his love.' The tomb-stone teeth flashed and she knew he'd checked with his cousin first. Obviously Lenny approved of Hattie being back at the Alaska. She didn't know if that was a good or a bad thing...

On her first day back, Hattie shoved her card into the clocking-on machine and pulled down the brass handle, and it was as if the past eight years had been wiped away. She was an Alaska girl once more. Up on the bambeating floor, the machines were already in full swing and the noise deafening. Rows of bambeaters, each fitted with flailing bamboo rods, were bashing out dirt and dust and down from rabbit skins being fed to them by the girls. Snowy flurries of white rabbit down swirled around the machines and up into the high ceiling space, clogging the moving belts and rafters, edging the metal window frames with white fluff. It was as if the snowstorms outside had invaded the factory. She took a deep breath and choked, coughing violently. She'd forgotten that, on the bambeaters, mouths must always be closed and any talking was done with tight lips and elaborate gestures. They called it deedee. It was a language she'd used herself once and, as she waited for Bessie Clutterbuck, she read the lips around her: they were talking about her. She was breaking their monotony.

Bessie approached with her slow arthritic gait, feet turned out like an ice skater, sliding through the white down coating the floor. She beckoned to Hattie. 'I've got the boy to load your hopper up, love.' She gave Hattie a sunken-mouthed smile. Old Buttercup had never got on with her dentures. She gave Hattie a cursory explanation of what to do. But every girl who'd ever worked in the Alaska would know the mind-numbing, back-breaking, leg-aching task that lay ahead of them.

She plucked the first rabbit skin from the full hopper beside the machine and slipped the small silky pelt under elastic ties criss-crossing the conveyer belt. She pushed the red button and watched as the bamboo poles ranged along the belt began to beat their tattoo. Coney fur flew, coating her cheeks like snow, and dust stung her eyes. She attached another pelt and then another, watching as they ran the gauntlet of the bamboo rods, before passing under a perspex hood where ineffectual suction tubes drew the dirt and fluff away. The pelts came back round to her to be removed and dropped in the 'cleaned' bin. She put the pelts on, she took them off. That was her job for the next nine hours, with a fifteen-minute tea break and a half-hour off for lunch. This would be her life now – but not for long if she had anything to do with it.

That evening after work she couldn't face going back to the Square. Buster had said he'd meet her in The Horns pub opposite the factory. But when she arrived he wasn't there. At the bar she ordered a whiskey mac, and it was as she was looking for somewhere to sit that she spotted a face she thought she'd long forgotten. It was a fine-boned face, with a small nose and neat ears, pinned close to his head. He raised mocking eyes, beneath a brow too heavy for the delicate face, and she knew Lenny Harper had seen her. He was sitting alone at a corner table. Stubbing out a cigarette, he picked some tobacco from his lips and beckoned her over. She cursed Buster for not being here. But Lenny was not the sort of person it paid to ignore and she joined him.

He hadn't changed much. With none of the stocky frame nor the Neanderthal strength of the other Harpers, he had a well-proportioned elegance about him. He wasn't tall, but while his brothers lumbered about, Lenny was neat in all his movements and light on his feet. Perhaps the physical differences to the rest of his family were what had persuaded her he might be different in other ways too. He'd always been a snappy dresser, and she noticed the suit he wore now was far from utility. His hair was still cut short, but a rather high quiff had replaced the side parting of his younger self.

She set the whiskey mac on the table, noticing that the sculptured edges of his features were sharper than they'd once been, the planes of his forehead and cheeks harder. Other than that the only sign of age was a papery thinness around those mocking eyes.

He was the first to speak. 'How've you been, Hattie?' His voice was lower, hoarser than she remembered. He offered her a

47

cigarette and lit up another for himself. Narrowing his eyes, he took a long drag and then smiled at her. 'You've changed. You're looking a bit rough, Hattie.' He gave her a winning smile as he insulted her.

'Eight years in the army will do that for you.'

'I wouldn't know. They never got me, did they?'

She shouldn't have been surprised. She'd always imagined he'd landed a cushy number in the army stores somewhere, probably with a little black-market operation on the side. Her shock must have been obvious.

He patted his chest. 'Failed the medical, didn't I? Seems I've got a bad heart.'

'Sorry to hear that,' she lied, having no desire to antagonize him, but the irony wasn't lost on her. It was after all Lenny's 'bad heart' that had forced her into volunteering for a war rather than stay anywhere near its toxic influence.

'Thanks, but I'm not sorry. I made a mint out of me ticker during the war. Hired meself out as a stand-in for the army medicals.'

It was a common enough practice among those who wanted to fail the army medical to hire someone with a genuine illness to attend the examination instead. Hattie despised it. She tried to keep her face a blank, but failed.

'You can sneer all you like, Hattie. But you mugs that volunteered, what have you got to show for it? Doing well are you, Hattie? Good job at the Alaska, nice big house in the Square?'

So he had been bothered enough to track her movements. His smile looked as if it might be genuine, but she knew better.

'The Alaska's only temporary. I'm getting an office job soon.'

'Ohhh, really? Chris told me you was practically begging for a job in that dump.' He jerked his head towards the factory. 'You should have stuck with me, Hattie, biggest mistake of your life, walking out on me. His smile had faded and she told herself there was nothing he could do to her. She was as down on her luck as she ever hoped to be. She'd already been beaten and humiliated by a bunch of kids and she was back living with Ciss.

Besides, after eight years fighting Germans, he seemed less frightening than he'd once been.

'I think it was the *best* thing I've ever done.' She stood up as she saw Chris Harper and Buster come through the door.

'Here's your Mary Ann friend,' Lenny said. 'I don't want him sitting with me, can't have people thinking I'm an iron, can I?'

Chris came to sit with his cousin and Hattie got up without a word. She felt Lenny's eyes follow her as she joined Buster and she heard Chris say, 'Can't see what you ever saw in that cold bitch.' Lenny's reply was lost on her and she fell gratefully on to the bench next to Buster.

'What you talking to him for, you silly mare? You're meant to be steering clear of Lenny!' Buster said.

'Don't start. If you'd been here on time it wouldn't have happened.'

'Sorry, darlin'. Chris held me up. How was your first day?' Buster asked with forced cheeriness.

She shrugged. 'It's already driving me mad up there – I think I've got a fur ball stuck in me lungs!' She thumped her chest and coughed. 'Want another drink?' Before he could answer she got up and went to the bar. She needed another whiskey, whether she could afford it or not. When she came back Buster was folding a letter. 'What's that you're reading? Love letter from Aiden?'

Buster lowered his eyes, almost shyly. 'Shhh, Hattie,' he said, looking nervously around. 'No, it's from a young girl, needs her old job back even more than you do!'

'She must be desperate. Do I know her?'

Buster leaned forward and lowered his voice. 'No. She worked here during the war – after your time. Poor little cow hooked up with an Aussie serviceman and my God, Hattie, you'd think she'd married the devil the stink some of 'em kicked up about it – treated her like a leper.'

'Why?'

''Cause he was a coloured man – half Aborigine, apparently.'

Hattie nodded, needing no explanation. She'd read the outraged letters in the *South London Press,* calling those women who'd married black GIs sluts. 'So why would she want to come back here?'

'She sailed out on the bride ship to Australia – only last year. When she gets there, she finds out this chap's not much cop, by which time the poor girl's saddled with a baby. She was a lovely girl, Clara. No more than nineteen. Innocent, you know?'

Coming home with a failed marriage to an Aborigine soldier and a kid struck Hattie as excessively foolish. Why hadn't she just stayed in Australia? Hattie would have jumped at the chance of a new life in a new world, even with the encumbrance of a kid. Australia must surely have offered far more than the Alaska ever could. 'You're right, Buster. She sounds like she does need a job more than me. Give her mine for chrissake?' And as she took a gulp of her whiskey, she meant it.

# 5

# *Three Women*

*February 1947*

Clara told herself the basement wasn't so bad. 'We'll be fine, won't we?' she asked Martha, who gave a wide smile. 'All these old places are damp, darlin'. I know it's not Australia, but it'll do till I find something better for us,' she said in as bright a tone as she could muster. After their scary visitor had gone on that first night, she'd forced herself to pick through the pile of blankets, stuffing one into the hole in the broken windowpane to keep out the draught. But she knew she needed to get them some form of heat if they weren't both to freeze to death. She decided she'd have to risk lighting a fire. Coal was impossible to get these days but she had no money to buy it anyway. She'd spent her second day back in Bermondsey foraging the bombsites for wood. It was a meagre enough fire, and one she could only keep going for a few hours, but at least it lessened the aching chill of the damp basement.

Still, tiredness and cold froze her brain, so she could think only one step ahead, and the next step was how to keep clean and wash Martha's dirty nappies. After a few splutters the scullery tap had run with water that looked a little rusty, but at least she'd been able to give herself a cat's lick, splashing her face with one hand, while holding Martha in the crook of her arm. She'd also unearthed a battered zinc bucket from under the sink and filled it.

While Martha's nappies were soaking in the bucket, she fed her daughter, crooning to her and feeling guilty for what she had to do next. She was still waiting to hear from Buster Golding, but she had to believe she'd get her old job back at the Alaska. Without it, she'd certainly be forced to give Martha up. She dreaded going back to the factory and the tide of tittle-tattle and snide comments she'd had to face every day before she'd left for Australia. A few of the girls had stood up for her, but most had shunned her as a slut. Still, she'd willingly face all that, and worse, rather than lose her darling baby. There was a trade-off, however – she'd have to put Martha into a nursery. 'I'll miss you, darlin', but you'll be nice and warm and you can play with toys while Mummy's at work…'

Martha let out a high-pitched squeal of delight, raising her chubby fist to catch a weak beam of sunlight piercing the broken window. Clara hugged her tightly, trying not to think of the impossible: what if there was no job, no nursery, nothing better to live in than this? What would she do then?

After waiting for the upstairs occupants to leave for the day, Clara crept up the backyard steps and out of the side gate, carrying the baby and her case. She skirted the Square, avoiding her parents' house, and walked up Fort Road. She knew there was a little nursery in the street, set up by a local woman during the war when, suddenly, married women were again needed in the factories. It was only a small nursery located in an ordinary terraced house and she just hoped it wasn't full. She knocked on the door to be met by a woman with kind, tired eyes, who by the noise coming from inside already had her full complement of children.

'Hello, is it Mrs Flint?' Clara asked, and the lady scooped up a little girl who was squirming round her legs, trying to get out of the door.

'Yes, I'm Peggy Flint.' She glanced at Martha, and Clara was alert for the slight pause that her brown skin often caused in people they met. But instead Mrs Flint moved to one side. 'Come in, love. You both look perished!'

Mrs Flint handed the toddler to a young helper. 'Here, take

Pearl for me, will you, while I see to this lady?' She then led Clara to the back room, which was kitted out with babies' cots and cribs.

'This is the baby room,' Mrs Flint explained. 'Are you looking for a place for the little one?'

Martha gave Mrs Flint a winning smile and put her arms out to be held. Clara blessed her silently.

'Have you got one?' she asked hopefully, as the woman laughed at Martha.

'Can't really say no, can I? Not to someone as pretty as this.' She chucked Martha under the chin, and the baby gave a giggle. 'To be honest, it's a bit tight,' she went on. 'Kintore Way Nursery won't take babies, so we get more than our fair share here. But she doesn't look like she'll take up much room.' Martha placed an exploratory hand on Mrs Flint's cheek – it seemed Mrs Flint's heart was far more easily melted than Clara's own mother's.

The woman asked a little about her circumstances and explained the costs, including the few pence extra a day for Martha to be fed on formula milk. At least the nursery fees would be manageable, once she'd got her first pay packet.

'If you've just come back from Australia I don't expect you've got baby clothes suitable for this weather!' Mrs Flint looked out at the freezing grey day, and smiled as she began sorting through a cupboard. Soon, there was a little pile of baby clothes, nappies and other essentials laid out for Clara.

Perhaps every mother was treated so well, but Clara guessed the woman felt sorry for her. Still, she was in no position to be proud. Her next stop would be the Sally Ann in Spa Road, seeking more charity: a ticking mattress to go on the iron bedstead, some blankets that didn't smell of piss, and perhaps even a second-hand pram.

Mrs Flint finished wrapping the small bundle of baby clothes and handed them to Clara with a smile. 'Have you found some-where for you and Martha to live?' she asked. 'It's a nightmare these days.'

Before Clara knew it, the lie was out of her mouth. 'Oh yes, we're staying with Mum and Dad. They've been ever so good.' And she accepted the parcel gratefully, hurrying out with the untruth still burning her lips. Her father had brought her up never to lie, but God must have been looking the other way, for when she went to check at the factory on the way home, she heard the good news she was waiting for. Buster Golding told her there was a job on the bambeater for her, if she wanted it. If she wanted it! If she'd been bolder, she would have kissed him.

*

When the day came to return to the Alaska, however, Clara wasn't so happy. As she placed Martha into Mrs Flint's arms, she felt ashamed of her tears and was afraid to linger. If she once looked back, she'd be lost. Martha's crying followed her all the way along Fort Road and even as she entered the factory gates she swore she could still hear her sobs. She gritted her teeth and blotted out the sound, ducking under the small shelter next to the timekeeper's lodge. Her hand trembled as she punched her card, and she started as she felt a sharp tap on her shoulder. She'd rehearsed what she would do if the abuse started up again. She needed to put her fighting irons on, she'd told herself, and now she summoned a brazenness that wasn't hers, ready to fend off an insult. But her defensiveness was dispelled in an instant. The hand belonged to her saviour.

'You all right, love?' Buster asked.

She nodded, so grateful to see his friendly face that tears threatened to undo her bravery before it had even begun.

'Oh, Clara, love. Don't let 'em see you cry, for gawd's sake!' He shot a look at some girls who were whispering and giggling as they approached the clocking-on machine. Clara fell in with Buster.

'Just keep your chin up, and your head up, and everything else up, gel!' He chuckled. 'And don't take no old nonsense from any of 'em. It's only a few that stirs up the rest.' He lowered his voice as the girls overtook them and began clattering up the iron staircase to the factory floors. 'Like her – Dotty Axmouth over there. She's new since you left. Steer clear of her.'

Buster pointed her to the bambeating floor. 'You're up there.' He gave her an encouraging pat on the back. 'Littl'un all right?'

'Yes, thanks. I couldn't have kept her without this job. I'm so grateful…' But she couldn't express her feelings, not here in the bleak factory yard, in full view of the drivers loading their vans and the men in the electric shop, one of whom flashed her a cheeky, good-natured grin. Buster surprised her by blushing at her gratitude. 'Shhh, our secret… don't want anyone crying favouritism.' And as he hurried up the staircase with a surprisingly light-footed step, he called down to the young electrician, 'Oi, Alan, you behave yourself! She's one of my girls!'

Obviously Buster took his responsibilities as foreman of the Alaska girls seriously and perhaps he was as protective of all of them, but she doubted it. Still, Buster's advice about keeping her chin up wasn't so easy to carry out. She understood perfectly the deedee comments of the two women who passed now. One nudged the other and mouthed, 'She's the one went with an Indian…' And the other slid her a look and mouthed 'Slut!'

Bessie Clutterbuck led Clara to her machine, and out of the corner of her eye she saw the woman Buster had pointed out as Dotty Axmouth looking her way. She felt her face burning. In spite of all her resolutions to be brave, she knew she wasn't. Their slow progress through the lines of bambeaters began to feel like a walk of shame as the women stared openly or glanced up and deliberately turned away. The bamboo rods thrashed and thundered around her, till she felt like a rabbit pelt herself, bashed by these women's disapproving looks and their ill-disguised scorn. Bessie was agonizingly slow and Clara almost ran to the sanctuary of her machine when they reached it.

Contrary to Buster's advice, she kept her head firmly down. But at one point in the morning she couldn't resist looking up at the clock and immediately caught the eye of a tall, striking-looking woman with red-gold hair standing at the machine next to her. Clara thought she looked too glamorous for factory work. She had an oval face, pretty pointed chin and pale ivory skin, and was brave enough to wear bright red lipstick. It was a shock when Clara realized the woman was smiling at her. She raised her eyes and mouthed at Clara, 'Nearly dinner time! Roll on stewed cabbage, eh?'

Clara smiled back shyly and, not for the first time that day, felt tears of gratitude prick her eyes.

* * *

Hattie watched the young woman standing next to her. Clara Young's fine-boned, pale face was half hidden as she bent her head to her work. Occasionally, dark liquid-brown eyes would peep out from beneath the victory roll of her brown hair, which fell in soft waves to her shoulders. Hattie saw someone as uncertain of her place in this world as she herself was. But however shy and unconfident Clara appeared, Hattie was more struck by her courage. Surely it had been braver to come home than to stay away. Partly because Hattie was bored rigid on the bambeater and partly because she hated bullies, she decided to befriend the girl, intrigued by Buster's tale of someone who had been foolish enough to risk everything for love.

When the dinner-time hooter finally blew, Hattie was ready to tell Old Buttercup where she could stuff the next rabbit skin. The old woman had fussed around her as if she'd been crafting the Crown Jewels instead of attaching dead animals to a conveyer belt. Bessie Clutterbuck sucked in her old lips so far that Hattie though her face might turn inside out. 'No, gel, you're still too slow. Look at your gaps!' Bessie pointed with an arthritic clawed finger to the unevenly loaded conveyer belt. Hattie held her tongue and speeded up, but then her pelts kept detaching themselves and jamming the machine. Bessie hovered round her, pointing out every time she forgot to sort out the precious white skins from the black and brown, till she was ready to pick up the old woman and toss her into the bin too.

Buster had to get her out of here. At least in her old job of grooving, there had been a bit of skill involved. At the sound of the hooter, along with all the other girls, she gratefully pressed the large red button on the side of her machine. The bamboos stopped flailing, the fine fur ceased flying and the silence rushed around her so that she felt dizzy.

As the exodus began, women fell into groups, going to the canteen or home, or to Tower Bridge Road for shopping. Doris Axmouth perhaps hadn't noticed Hattie's sarcasm the last time they'd met, for now she approached her with a group of girls in tow and asked, 'Coming to the canteen? I've got a few stories I can tell you about that Buster!'

'Ohh, have you? I love a bit of gossip,' Hattie said mischievously, and then called, 'Clara, you coming to the canteen?'

Doris Axmouth stared at Hattie as if she were mad, then frowned and gave an obvious warning shake of her head, which Hattie ignored. Smiling broadly at Doris, she waited for Clara to leave her machine. But the girl blushed. 'Oh no, sorry, I can't. I've got to go and...' As she stumbled over her words, Doris and her friends were already walking away. Clara began unbuttoning her overall and when she looked up, seemed surprised that Hattie was still waiting for her.

'You're not letting them stop you going to the canteen, are you?'

'No, no, of course not!'

'You're welcome to come with me. I'm meeting Buster.'

Clara shook her head. 'Thanks all the same, but I'm going down to Fort Road... I've got a baby in nursery.'

'Oh yes, I know,' Hattie said, and could have bitten her tongue off. Of course everyone knew that Clara Young had a baby, and what colour it was as well. 'Buster told me!' she covered.

'Are you and Buster good friends?' Clara asked, obviously in a hurry as she was already pushing through the swing doors. Hattie nodded and walked with the girl to the narrow gantry outside.

They clattered down the iron staircase and Hattie explained how they had a saviour in common.

'Buster's such a kind man,' Clara said. 'I didn't know him that well before I left for Australia, but he always said hello and he was very civil to me, especially when some of the girls got nasty about Barry.'

'Barry, that's your husband?'

Clara nodded, and there again came the blush and a lowering of her liquid-brown eyes as she attempted to hide her face behind the soft shield of hair.

'Listen, love, as far as I'm concerned I don't care what colour your hubby is and I don't care if you left him or why. Marriage is not for everyone. I'm the last girl to be preaching to anyone about "till death do us part". I don't think I've ever had a feller longer than six months. Sometimes, when I've had two on the go, I suppose you'd have to say it was three months apiece!'

Clara gave a shy laugh which totally transformed her sad brown eyes, lighting up her delicate features with the sort of open-hearted warmth Hattie could see might well be taken advantage of by the wrong man. In the cloakroom she was surprised to see Clara pull out a small suitcase from her locker.

'Things for the baby...' the girl explained.

They walked to the factory gates together, and when they parted Hattie said firmly, 'Don't forget, tomorrow you come to the canteen with me and Buster!'

Clara nodded her thanks before hurrying off along Grange Road. As Hattie crossed the road to the canteen she had to wait for traffic to pass and, looking to her right, noticed that Clara was entering Grange Baths. She couldn't imagine that the girl was going for a swim in her short dinner hour: she was either going to have a bath or to do her laundry, or both. In which case she was probably living somewhere just as bad as Cissie's...

Buster was already sitting at a table with a small coterie of Alaska girls, along with Levin the nailer and a fair-haired, athletic-looking man in his early twenties she didn't recognize. There were many who had no time for Buster, but those who did give him a chance were usually won over by his humour and good-heartedness. As she approached, the other girls shoved up to make room for Hattie. Levin stayed exactly where he was. The young man had obviously just finished telling a joke, for everyone round the table was laughing, and now he broke off to give Hattie a welcoming smile. His long, thin face with its aquiline nose wasn't exactly handsome, but the crooked-toothed smile and twinkling eyes spoke of a sunny nature, which in itself Hattie found attractive. Buster introduced him as Alan Manners, one of the factory's electricians.

'Luckiest sparks alive, him.' Buster said, and Hattie obliged her old friend by asking why.

'Colour blind!' Buster said, tucking in his chin.

Hattie's eyes widened. 'A colour-blind electrician? Obviously a man who likes to take risks!' She laughed, putting down her tray.

'What can I say?' Alan grinned. 'I like to live dangerously.' He nodded towards her dinner plate. 'Looks like you don't mind taking a risk yourself!' he said, pulling a face.

Like all the food she'd had since coming back home, her dinner was unappealing and meagre, but at least as factory workers they got a few extra bread rations, and the canteen manageress, who was a friend of Cissie's, had piled up a few slices of grey national loaf and margarine on to her plate.

'Ooh, you've been introduced to cook's meatless meat loaf!' Buster said, as she sat down and tucked in. 'I tell you food's worse now than during the war.'

'Oh, stop moaning about the grub, Buster, and tell me about that poor girl Clara you're fairy godmother to,' Hattie said through her first hungry mouthful. There were a few titters from the girls, which she ignored. 'Fancy condemning her to the bambeater. Why didn't she stay in Australia? At least she'd be warmer – and better fed! The newspaper said the Aussie meat ration's seven pounds!' Hattie grimaced at the meatless loaf and made the other girls giggle. She tried the bread, which tasted and looked like soggy cardboard.

'You can't blame her for wanting to come home to her family, poor cow,' Buster said. 'She didn't know a soul out there and the feller turned out a bad 'un.'

'So, what happened?' Maisie, a skinny, pale-faced girl, asked. 'Didn't she like it, being married to a native?' And, lowering her voice, she asked, 'Did she have to join his tribe or something?'

Buster cracked her head with a knuckle. 'Stupid girl, Maise. He was a docker in Sydney before he joined up and his dad was Irish, no, Scottish, well, something Mac-ish, and when I asked her what went wrong she said she found out she didn't really know him.'

'Well, we can all say that about our old man, can't we?' Vera addressed the table in general. Hattie had worked with Vera when she was single. 'Once they get their feet under the table, it all changes!'

The other women chorused their agreement, but Hattie caught a lingering, rather sad smile upon Buster's face and she kicked his ankle. 'Men! More trouble than they're worth!' she said and winked at him.

After dinner, Hattie hung back with Buster. 'Listen, you've got to get me off that bambeater. I won't last another week. Don't they need any groovers?'

'Ooh, aiming high!' Buster joked.

She raised her eyes. 'I'm serious!'

Her old trade of grooving was a skill that turned a humble sheepskin into a 'beaver lamb', an imitation of a beaver fur that cost a quarter of the real thing. After the shearers had cut the sheep fur down to a short, straight nap, it was spray-dyed a rich brown, then it was up to the groovers to apply their artistry. Carefully painting black lines down the fur with a dyed resin, they gave the illusion of long narrow pelts of real beavers, sewn together. Hattie had liked to think with every stripe she painted a poor beaver was being saved from becoming a fur coat – the good old mutton had already been eaten anyway. Accuracy with the brush was paramount, the stripes needing to be dead straight and unbroken. As well as being more absorbing, it was a better-paid job, and if Hattie was to rent a place of her own she needed to earn more money.

'I'll do me best, Hattie, but there's nothing going at the moment on the other floors. Who's got money for furs these days? Besides, little Clara needs a friend up there,' Buster said.

'You can't keep me on the bambeater just so I can babysit her! What makes you think I'd want to be a fairy godmother just 'cause you are!'

'Oh yeah, you're hard as nails, you. But I know you won't take no nonsense from Dotty the bleedin' axe murderer up there! She'll eat poor Clara for dinner unless someone sticks up for her.' Buster looked exaggeratedly over his shoulder in case Doris Axmouth was still about, making Hattie laugh in spite of herself.

'To be honest, I've already gone out of my way to talk to the girl. But I'm busy enough trying to sort myself out, Buster. Just let me know if you're thinking of taking on any more waifs and strays – I want to know how long I'll be stuck up there playing nursemaid along with Old Buttercup!'

'Well, now you come to mention it—'

'No!'

'Just hear me out. It's me poor sister I need to talk to you about. While I'm helping everyone else, I think I'm entitled to do something for her.'

'I thought she was off work, pregnant.'

'She's had the baby... but I've just found out she's given it up,' Buster said, with an air of resignation.

'Oh, Buster, that's sad, but why?'

'Tell the truth, love, she's not been right in the head since she lost her little girl... you know, in the blast, with me mum and dad.' Buster's eyes welled with tears and for a moment he was unable to speak. He'd suffered his own tragedies during the war, but rarely spoke about losing his parents to a flying bomb.

'She had a little boy too, didn't she? What happened to him?'

'Ronnie? He's a lost bleedin' cause, love, gone to the dogs. But she lets him run wild, can't even look after an eleven-year-old, let alone a baby. Mina Wren, the midwife, come round to see me and she says to me as soon as Lou's on her feet you've got to give her something to do, Buster, or else she'll be chucking herself off Tower Bridge once she realizes she's lost another baby...'

They had just passed beneath the sad gaze of the Alaskan seal carved above the gates and Hattie stopped in the yard. She was hugging herself against the cold that seeped through her threadbare wool coat. The afternoon was already dark as dusk and above her the rows of factory windows began to glow as lights were switched on. 'If she's doolally, what makes you think she'll even be *able* to come back to work?'

'Well, you don't have to be sane to work a bambeater, do you, darlin'? Besides, I'll have someone up there looking after her now, won't I?' He patted her on the shoulder and hurried off towards the sheep-shearing building before she could object.

Hattie was used to being in charge of dozens of girls; she'd had no trouble issuing orders, or keeping them in line. She'd excelled at getting the best out of raw recruits, but she knew her girls hadn't loved her. The CO said her pastoral skills were poor. The only bad report she'd ever had was when she'd reprimanded a private for missing guard duty. The girl had just lost her fiancé in a plane crash over France and, even by army standards, Hattie was judged to have been too harsh. Yet she hadn't intended to be cruel. If it'd been her, she'd have wanted to be treated no differently from any other private that day. But her CO had told her most girls were not like her, which was why, of course, he'd recommended her for sergeant in the first place. For Hattie, being a leader was simply a talent like any other, like dressmaking or dancing. She might have discovered her talent late, but since she had, she'd wanted to use it after the war. Buster's little scheme felt constricting, condemning her to the role of nursemaid, for which she was totally unsuited.

It was as she was making her way back up the iron stairs that she heard someone's hesitant footsteps following, and looked back to see her charge. She knew instantly that Clara was deliberately dawdling, but Hattie was unsure why. She stopped and asked, 'How was the baby?'

Hattie waited for Clara to catch up. She didn't like subterfuge or games and she wanted to see what sort of a person Buster had put himself out to help. As she fixed Clara with her sergeant's stare, she noticed that the girl's shoulder-length hair was damp.

'I only got to see Martha for a few minutes – she seemed happy enough, but then she usually is.' She hesitated before confessing, 'Tell the truth, I had to go to Grange Baths, do some laundry and have a bath.' She blushed slightly before explaining unnecessarily, 'There's no bath where I am.'

Hattie smiled. Some impulse made her want to ease the girl's obvious embarrassment. 'Same here! I'm in one room with me mother and her chap. Next time you go to the baths, let me know and I'll come with you. Is the old dragon still rationing hot water?'

The baths attendant who regulated the water flow to each bath cubicle was famously stingy, and even before the war you were only allowed so much hot water per bath.

Hattie raised her eyes. 'I asked for more hot and she gave me cold, and they've put the price of a packet of pine needles up to sixpence!'

'Bloody diabolical – you could buy a whole bar of Wright's Coal Tar for that before the war!'

They were both laughing as they walked to their machines, so that Hattie hadn't registered that Doris Axmouth was staring at them until she'd started up her machine. Then she saw the woman mouth to her neighbour, 'No amount of soap'll clean up a scrubber like her – the black's probably rubbed off on her skin!'

Hattie didn't let the smile fade from her lips as she walked slowly to the end of the floor and grabbed a heavy bin full of rabbit furs. She rolled it towards her machine and as she passed Doris, gave the bin an almighty shove, sending it hurtling towards the woman, who had to hop smartly out of its path.

'Oi, oi, watch what you're bleedin' doing!' Doris shouted.

Hattie gave an insincere smile. 'Sorry!' She retrieved the bin, but in a low voice she said, 'My mate Buster tells me you're a right goer yourself, Dotty. You wouldn't want that spread round the canteen, would you?'

Doris pretended not to hear and said loudly, 'Just be a bit more careful in future!' She looked around to garner support and Hattie muttered, 'You too.'

★ ★ ★

Her first day at the Alaska hadn't been that bad. Hattie had wished her goodnight before rushing out as if her tail was on fire. She struck Clara as someone who wouldn't be content to stand still in life, especially not if the place where she was standing was a factory floor. Then there were the girls who were friendly with Buster. They had made a point of walking out with her, which she appreciated. But she was glad when they all went their separate ways. She had enough of a reputation already without everyone knowing she was destitute. She certainly didn't want anyone tagging along with her when she paid a visit to the Sally Ann in Spa Road.

She picked up Martha first, who immediately vomited down her only coat. 'She's not been too happy taking the formula today,' Mrs Flint explained as Martha began crying, a sound so mournful it wrenched Clara's heart. The child's normally sunny face was pathetically forlorn and if a baby could give an accusing look, Clara thought that this must be one.

'I'm sorry, my darlin', but Mummy's got to work... come here.' The child fell gratefully into her arms, nestling against her breast and falling almost immediately into a contented sleep. Peggy Flint looked on sympathetically. 'But she's been happy most of the time, really. She enjoyed watching the other children. They all love her of course... so do we.'

Clara loved the woman for her 'of course'; she only wished it were so cut and dried with her own parents. She took with her some powdered milk and a bottle from the nursery, and then carried the baby in her arms to the Salvation Army colony.

They'd already provided her with a ticking mattress and blankets for the bed, and had promised her she could pick up a second-hand pram and baby blankets today. All she had to do now was get it into the basement undetected.

The weather in this case was her ally. Still early evening, it had been dark since four o'clock and now the swirling snow flurries intensified the gloom. No one would see her, not unless they bumped into her. She stopped the pram outside the side gate, checking both ways and waiting for the smudged headlights of a car to pass before giving the gate a shove. It stuck, but she knew the odds were it was warped rather than that someone had locked it. In the Square, as in most Bermondsey streets, the front doors were left unlocked and keys hung on strings inside letterboxes so that children need never be locked out. Except, she thought ironically, her own child. Her parents had made it clear she would always be locked out.

She took in a deep breath, tasting snowflakes on her tongue, then with all her strength pushed on the old gate. It gave an inch, squeaked, then jammed, just as Martha began stirring.

'Damn it!' she hissed. She was tired and cold, and though the basement wasn't exactly welcoming it was all she had to call home. She summoned all her remaining strength and, hoping that the snow would muffle the sound, gave the gate a hefty kick. It was enough to dislodge the piled-up snow behind the door and it swung wide. She hauled the pram in behind her and eased the gate shut. The yard was at first-floor level, so now she bumped the pram down the few steps to the basement's backyard door, pausing on each step, checking for noises from Martha or from the upstairs occupants. Finally, she pushed the pram through the door and into the kitchen. She'd already decided it would be safer to live in the one room, easier to keep warm and with less chance of detection. She'd found an abandoned broom and some cloths and had cleaned as quietly as she could. There was little she could do about the water-filled scullery but tonight it was frozen solid anyway.

First she hung one of the old blankets up at the window, then lit a candle. As its thin light spread out in a weak circle, she realized she'd had another visit from the man who'd scared her witless on her first night. For as well as his pungent smell, he'd left on the table a pint of milk, a loaf of bread, a paraffin stove, a small can of paraffin and a teddy bear. She sat down on one of the rickety chairs, hardly knowing whether she should be pleased or scared. Her visitor obviously meant them no harm and she was touched by the teddy bear, though immediately thought of fleas. But she had her suspicions about who her benefactor might be, and if it was who she thought, then he was best avoided because of his family, for they were more than likely to accuse her of robbing their scavenger brother if they ever found out about this simple act of generosity. She feared her new friend could prove a dangerous one.

★ ★ ★

There was never any food in his house and even if there had been, Lou was incapable of cooking it. Ronnie hadn't bothered to go home since his new little sister had been born. What was the point? Today he'd rounded up two of the Barnham Street boys for a raid on the Borough market. All they needed was a fishing net, and his mate Frankie the Fish had the very thing. The son of the local fish-stall owner, Frankie could always get one of those for his father used nets to hoik out live eels from water buckets prior to chopping them into wriggling segments for Bermondsey housewives to take home for tea. Ronnie and his tribe had practised the operation so often it was seamless. The gates at the market were always locked at night but it was easy enough to climb up them, which Ronnie did with ease. Once at the top he dipped the net down into a convenient cage full of potatoes and began flipping them one by one up and backwards over the locked gate. 'Catch 'em!' he shouted to the boys on the ground, who ran up and down catching them like cricket balls until they had enough for a blow-out. They hastily stuffed their contraband into their jumpers and, clutching their lumpen stomachs, transported it back to the Spa Road bombsite. Soon Ronnie was sitting next to a small bonfire, baking potatoes in its white-hot heart and roasting peanuts on an upturned dustbin lid wedged into the fire's edge. The potato skins were turning nicely black and the peanuts giving off a toasty aroma, but his pleasure was dimmed as his mind turned to Pissy Pants, though his victim had never been far from his thoughts since that night. Confessing the crime to his closest confidantes, Frankie and Nutty Norman, had relieved the burden of it somewhat, but as he watched, irritated, as Norman tested the nearest potato with a sharp stick, he couldn't help feeling sick at what had happened.

'Leave off, Norm, it ain't done yet!' Ronnie batted his friend's stick away. 'You got to wait till they're really black and then they'll be nice and soft inside.'

'Well, they ain't black when my mum does 'em in the oven,' Norman said, eyeing the potatoes hungrily.

'Just have a bit of patience!' Ronnie said tersely. 'Or else we won't enjoy 'em.'

But the smell was driving him almost mad with hunger, for he hadn't found much to eat since the night the baby had been born.

'You've been a bloody misery since you done Pissy Pants in,' Norman said morosely. 'You ain't no fun no more.'

'Don't you think you should have checked on the body?' Frankie asked.

'Shut up about it, will you. There won't be no body, will there, because the police would have found it by now, you dozy git.'

But in reality Ronnie had been too scared to go back to the scene of his crime. He'd seen enough films to know murderers who did that got caught. But he was less afraid of the police than of the Harpers. There was a rumour that they sliced up anyone who crossed them and threw the bits into the Thames. He thrust the end of his own pointed stick into the nearest potato and, as he felt the flesh yield, shuddered. It reminded him of how the knife had slipped so easily into Pissy Pant's body. One by one, he flicked the potatoes out of the fire and Nutty Norman pounced on them. He'd earned his nickname for his over excitable nature and constant larking about, and now he tossed the black, hot potatoes up in the air, juggling them like a clown and yelping with pain every time he held one for too long.

'Giss 'em here!' Ronnie intercepted one mid-air and with hardened fingers began to peel away the black skin. But as he blew on the fluffy potato, he saw a figure approaching. Suddenly he found he had lost all his appetite. It was Dickie Harper, one of Pissy Pant's many brothers and he didn't look happy. Ronnie threw down the potato, sprang up and shouted, 'Leg it!'

His friends were a little slow in responding, as their backs were turned to the approaching Harper.

'Harper!' Ronnie shouted, before sprinting off. Frankie realized what was happening but Nutty Norman, obviously thinking the potatoes were worth risking the wrath of a Harper for, stooped to gather them all up into his jumper before following the other two boys.

'Oi, come back here, you little toe rags!' Dickie Harper bellowed. He was a muscular, stocky man in his thirties and he set off in pursuit with a lumbering run, but the boys were nimble and soon outstripped him, leaping fallen beams and scooting round collapsed walls until they entered a labyrinth of half-ruined houses. The basements had been blasted into one long tunnel, which Dickie didn't seem to relish entering.

'What you lot running for? What you got to hide?' His voice echoed along the basement walls to where the boys cowered behind a coal cellar door.

They sat, holding their breath, as the seconds passed. Then Dickie's voice came again. 'Oi, you with the knife. Ronnie. I know you're the one cut my Johnny! I'll be waiting...'

The cellar was a bolt-hole the Barnham Street boys had agreed on as a meeting point for all of them in case of trouble. There was another way out. It involved dropping down even deeper, into a crater beneath the basements, to where the remains of a huge concrete pipe led to some tanning pits in a ruined leather factory. They had no idea what it had been used for, perhaps as a drainage pipe for the noxious tanning liquors because it still stank to high heaven. For now, they huddled together in the coal cellar, panting with exertion and fear, until Ronnie said, dry-mouthed, 'Well, I ain't going home never now. He knows where I live!'

'Where you gonna stay?' Frankie asked.

'I'll stay down one of the pits.'

The abandoned tanning pits were good for hiding, though deep enough to be deadly without a ladder or a mate to help you out. But Ronnie had his secret way in and out – the concrete pipe. He hadn't thought beyond tonight. All he knew for sure was that the Harpers wouldn't easily forget that he'd killed their brother.

'But what about your mum?' Norm asked, handing him a cooling potato.

Ronnie paused for thought, stabbing the potato with his flick knife, remembering his dream that Lou would suddenly get happy and start taking notice of him now she had another baby to replace their Sue. 'She don't know if I'm there or not half the time. Besides, she's got herself a new kid. She'll be all right now.' He shrugged, squeezed open the potato and bit into it, remembering that he was ravenous.

# 6

# *The Huts*

*February 1947*

Hattie was beginning to think she would suffocate if she had to spend another week at Cissie's. Today she'd trudged the length of Southwark Park Road, looking at every room for rent. Those that hadn't already gone were either over-priced or not much better than Cissie's. The long, looping road led her through the Blue market and ended at the park. She was in need of open air and space, and in Bermondsey there were only two places to find that – the river or Southwark Park.

She'd always loved the park. It had been her first taste of freedom as a child and was nearer than the river, so she headed there now. All the railings were long since gone to build spitfires or bombs, but force of habit sent her to the Jamaica Road entrance. Though the gates were no longer there, she passed between the two posts all the same and walked the length of what had once been a handsome avenue of stately old trees. Now it was full of ragged gaps where ugly stumps, burned black by incendiaries, stuck up through the pillowy snowdrifts like broken teeth. Many chestnuts and oaks which once dotted the parkland had been felled deliberately to make way for allotments needed to boost food production during the war. The allotments were still there, in far greater demand since food prices had soared during peacetime. With food shortages much worse now, when even bread was on the ration and everyone she met was obsessed with food, the allotments were vital. Still, she resented that they took up all the open spaces she'd loved to range through and it was a depressing prospect when rows of cabbages and beets replaced lawns and flower beds.

She remembered those long childhood summers, when all she'd needed to be happy was a bottle of cold tea, a jam sandwich and a day to run free here with her friends. Today she hardly recognized the place. It was a wreck. The war had ruined it – like so much else in Bermondsey. Even its camouflage of snow couldn't soften the harsh scars of war.

After skirting a bomb crater, which was all that remained of the children's paddling pool, she came to the once grand boating lake. It had been commandeered as an Emergency Water Supply during the war. Now it was a dwindling stagnant pond, as the bomb craters on either side had been slowly leaching away its water since the Blitz. Hattie's heart contracted at its ruined beauty. The war had made everything ugly and the place which had once allowed her to breathe now seemed to suck the very air from her lungs. Perhaps it hadn't been such a good idea to come here after all.

She was heading for a large field called the Oval, the most open area of the park, which, during the Blitz, had become a heavy artillery gun site. Ack-Ack guns and rocket launchers had taken over from cricket, thundering fire each night, raining down shrapnel on Bermondsey, while desperately trying to deter enemy bombers from reaching the docks. Of course, the gunners had to be housed somewhere and it was their abandoned huts that now caught Hattie's eye. She had lived in similar barrack huts quite happily during her army days, and she wanted to get a closer look at these relics of the war.

The barracks were ranged along the southern boundary of the park. Typical long, low wooden buildings, three windows on each side and one at either end. Duckboards connected the huts to a wash block and a NAAFI hut. She could guess without looking what they would be like inside. Wooden floorboards, uninsulated wooden walls, pitched corrugated-iron roofs swallowing all the heat – the source of which would be a central stove set on a stone base.

She pushed on the door of the nearest hut. It appeared that the last gunner had left it padlocked. She searched around for a rock in a nearby pyramid of bomb debris. She knew these huts had come under fire during the war. Gunners had died on this very spot, the huts and the pitted earth and piled rubble now their only memorial. With two hands she hefted a sizeable rock and brought it down heavily, smashing off the padlock.

She stepped inside. Dust was piled into the corners and brambles infiltrated the floorboards, but the army had built the huts well. Looking up, she saw that the roof appeared watertight. She pounded the wooden walls – they were sturdy. In the centre was the square stone base with its tall, cylindrical stove and chimney. She'd had many cups of cocoa brewed on just such a stove. The memory of that camaraderie gave her a feeling of homecoming and that was when the idea occurred to her.

It wasn't original; she knew that thousands of homeless had moved into ex-military bases all over the country during the past year. The news had even reached her in Belgium about 'the Great Sunday Squat' last September, when homeless families had occupied an empty block of luxury flats in Kensington. The squatters were mostly ex-servicemen and their families, and only a few politicians risked being labelled mean-spirited by condemning them. Hattie could see nothing wrong in it. The huts were shelters, nothing more. Unwanted by all but the truly desperate, they could either be left to moulder or put to good use.

Of course, there were none of the comforts of home. But she didn't enjoy any of those as it was. She had nothing to lose, and a lot to gain – space and privacy being uppermost in her mind. The hut was freezing, but a bag of coal, if one could be found these days, would warm the space, which had once housed a dozen men. As her eyes adjusted to the gloom it seemed she could see them now, polishing buttons, spitting on boots, laughing at dirty jokes, writing letters home, dying in flames on their beds as the flying bombs hit. She shuddered. Were there too many ghosts here for her to make a home in one of these huts? She hunkered down beside the stone hearth, with her back to the stove. Almost asking permission of the dead. The answer came ringing back. Wouldn't it be better if this place became somewhere to live instead of somewhere to die?

By the time she left the hut night had fallen. She was carefully hooking the padlock back on the door so that it at least looked secure, when she was startled by a noise behind her. She spun round. Blinded by a torchbeam shining directly into her eyes, she shaded them with her hand. A man held the torch. He wore an army greatcoat and a commando-style woollen hat pulled low over his ears. For a moment her heart seemed to stop beating – was this one of those ghostly gunners? But then the man lowered the torch and stepped forward so that she could see his face. He looked to be about thirty, with a lock of floppy dark hair falling across his forehead, which convinced her this was no gunner ghost – the army would never have allowed such long hair. His darkly stubbled chin had a definite cleft and his full-lipped mouth seemed set in a grim half-smile. It was a handsome face, but two deep frown lines between his dark eyes gave it an air of seriousness. Even half obscured by the low cap, the face looked familiar to Hattie.

'Sorry I made you jump,' he said. 'I thought you were a kid up to no good.' He waved the torch in a vague arc. 'There's a gang of them like to come in after dark and play at smashing up the huts.'

'Oh, are you in charge of them?' Hattie asked, disappointed. If the army was guarding the huts, then they'd still have a use for them. It looked like her idea was a non-starter after all.

The young man gave a crisp laugh. 'No fear! I'm demobbed. The hat and coat are just to keep me warm. I'm staying over there.' He indicated a nearby hut.

'You're living in that?'

He nodded.

'Damn, you beat me to it! That was my plan too,' she said, miffed but not entirely surprised that the idea had already occurred to someone else.

'Well, you can't do that,' he said, with a finality which immediately set Hattie's hackles rising. More than anything, she hated being told what to do.

'Well, if no one put you in charge, then you don't own the place,' she said. 'Looks to me like there's plenty of huts to go round. What's to stop me just picking one and moving in?'

They stared at each other until he looked away, letting his gaze steal along the double row of huts.

'If you need convincing it's a bad idea, just come in and have a look round mine. You'll soon see it's no place for a woman on her own.'

She hesitated. He didn't seem too friendly and the park was deserted.

'It's getting late...' She was about to refuse, but then he took off his hat and pushed back the floppy dark hair. Now she remembered where she'd seen him. 'You work at the Alaska!'

He nodded briefly. 'I'm a chemist in the drug room.' He stuck out a hand. 'Joe Jerwood. I thought I knew your face.'

Bambeater girls didn't usually cross paths with the chemists, who were employed to develop new dyes and better curing liquors.

'You were in the social club the other night, with Alan.'

The young man nodded. 'He's a good pal. We're on the sports and social club committee. He was *trying* to organize the football team and asked for my help. Not that we got much done. You're the good dancer I noticed Buster Golding swinging around.'

'Buster can get carried away!' She paused, flattered for a moment that he'd noticed. Perhaps they'd got off on the wrong foot.

'Do you like dancing?' she asked.

'No,' he said, which for some reason annoyed her.

'What was that you said about cocoa? I'm perishing!' Hattie hugged herself and shivered.

'Cocoa?' He raised his eyes. 'I'll do my best. Follow me to the Jerwood residence.' He lit their way along the duckboard to the next hut. Inside, she waited for him to light the oil lantern he'd left by the door and as he held it up, she saw the stove. He went to stoke it, and she looked round while he boiled a billycan for the cocoa. There was a single cot-bed made up with grey army blankets, and a black trunk stood at the end. A camp table and an old armchair nestled close by the stove, and along one wall were some shelves on which sat cups, saucers, pans, a few books and a well-used Leica camera. It was sparse. But, even though she could see Joe's breath, at least it was warmer here than outside.

'See what I mean, not much is it?' he asked, following her gaze.

'It's... roomy.' She hesitated.

'You mean there's not much furniture.' He didn't seem insulted as he offered her the armchair and set down cocoas on the camp table. He pulled up a stool for himself.

'Well, I expect once you've been here a while, you'll get some bits and pieces,' she said, assuming he'd just moved in.

'I've been here since last August!' Joe said, frowning into his cocoa as a dark blush rose in his cheeks. 'I don't need much.'

There was an awkward silence as she searched around for something nice to say about his little home, but she gave up and began asking questions. After half an hour she'd found out that he'd moved in as part of the nationwide 'Sunday Squat' the previous year. Before that he'd been living in an overpriced B&B in South Norwood, travelling to the Alaska every day.

'I couldn't afford to go on paying for the train fare and the B&B, but there was nowhere decent near the factory, so when I read about all those thousands of squatters moving into old army bases I thought I'd do the same. I'm surprised it took so long for someone else to cotton on to these ones. They're very sound,' he said, looking up at the roof and then down at the floorboards. He seemed a bit awkward in her company and she was sorry she'd made him feel that his decorating efforts were sub-standard.

'I admire you. Taking things into your own hands like that.' She leaned forward, cupping the cocoa, inhaling its sweet warmth. 'That's what I want to do. And if no one's bothered to chuck you out in five months, I can't see them trying now. What's so off-putting about having a neighbour like me?' She flashed him an encouraging smile and sat back, waiting for him to respond.

'I can't stop you.' He set the mug down and stood up. 'But if you move in, I'll have to move out.'

'But why?' She was shocked, unused to being turned down by men.

He was shaking his head, his full lips compressed in a straight line. 'If you can't see why not, I don't think I can explain it,' he said.

'I'm not an idiot!' She flushed. 'I've got a brain in my head even though I work on the bambeater!' She slammed the cocoa down and stood up to leave.

'Hang on a minute. I'm not saying you're stupid. It's just I've got certain ideas when it comes to what's decent and, well, it wouldn't be right, a single woman living alone out here with a man...'

'Oh, for God's sake. Don't bloody flatter yourself.' She yanked open the hut door and felt a draught of icy air. 'If you're such a gentleman you can see me out of the park. I've got no torch.'

But before leaving the park she insisted Joe wait while she paced out her chosen hut and spent ten minutes working out what she would do with the luxury of so much space. Afterwards she'd persuaded him to show her the water supply, which was plumbed into the ablutions and NAAFI huts. He'd done what he could to lag the pipes, but he told her that in this weather they were frozen most days. There was even an unconnected electricity meter in the NAAFI, he pointed out. She patted it proprietorially, taking ownership. 'All mod cons if we can get this hooked up!' she said cheerfully. And she saw his face fall.

'There'll be no we,' he insisted.

He really was a wet blanket. 'Oh, you'll get used to me,' she said.

She returned to the Square with the sort of bubbling excitement she hadn't felt since her overseas posting. She recognized the feeling of optimism and, with regret, realized that it had once been her natural state. Surely it would be again, she told herself as she bounded up the steps to her mother's front door. She was still lost in working out the logistics of heating the hut, finding a bed and some furniture. She would make her hut far more homely than Joe's and was already imagining curtains; perhaps Buster could make them for her? As she reached inside the letterbox to pull out the key, she became aware of a scuffling noise coming from the basement. She stopped and cocked her head to one side. She'd heard noises down there before but had dismissed them as the wind blowing through the casements – Cissie always insisted she'd heard nothing. But as well as being short-sighted, Cissie was rather deaf. When Hattie asked Mario if he'd heard anything, he'd shrugged and said, 'If someone's down there, I pity them.' It was hard to fathom what Mario really thought about anything. He was an enigma – a handsome, well-built man, a good ten years younger than her mother. If Hattie had been looking at him and her mother from the outside, she'd have assumed he was using Cissie simply for bed and board and a bit of recreation. But he'd surprised her with his occasional impromptu thoughtfulness, bringing home for her mother a rare tangerine from the Blue, a bunch of flowers or an impossibly expensive non-utility frock. He might be genuine; Hattie hadn't decided.

Perhaps the basement had attracted a tramp. She should see him off. But then that impulse made her smile. What was she, if not a vagrant? And how would she feel about someone seeing her off once she was squatting? Still, she didn't want to risk an intruder coming upstairs to kill them in their beds that night, so she felt her way down the basement steps. The front door was wide open.

She stepped inside and was hit by a nose-wrinkling smell of damp and mouldy distemper. She peered along the passage, then poked her head into the front room where floorboards had rotted and the sash window was falling off its frame. She backed out of the room and again heard the scuffling sound. She turned just in time to see a shadow move into the passage from the kitchen. The figure seemed to be dragging something heavy. Fear clutched at her for an instant, but she clenched her fist and took a deep, calming breath. She had faced flying bombs and helped chase down fleeing German troops in France – how much harm could an old tramp do to her?

'I know you're there!' she said through a tight throat. 'You'll have to go now. It's not safe down here!' She tried to keep her voice steady. There was the shuffling sound again, a little like an animal rooting around in the earth. Then she caught the pungent whiff of an unwashed body. It was strong enough to make her recoil. She moved slowly forward, announcing her progress by tapping the Lincrusta on the lower half of the wall. Whoever it was, she didn't want to make them feel cornered, but she wouldn't feel safe letting them stay either. She had almost reached the kitchen when the shuffling sound grew louder and a low almost animal growl came from out of the darkness. All at once it sprang upon her, slashing with wild windmill arms, growling, 'Outta way, leave 'er alone, outta way!' The shape that materialized was definitely human, and as he whirled past he knocked her sideways, so that her head banged against the stair bannisters. She staggered and fell back on to the lino with a crack that knocked her out.

When she came round she noticed the lingering stink, but had no idea how long she'd been unconscious. She felt her forehead. Enough time had passed for a lump the size of a small egg to form. She groaned and propped herself up on an elbow. She was groggy but her mind was beginning to work at normal speed. Jumping up too quickly, she had to grab the bannister and wait for her dizziness to pass. Drawing in a deep breath, she wrinkled her nose. The man was gone, but his smell wasn't. She steadied herself, and was about to go up the hall stairs to Cissie's, when she decided to check the rest of the place, just in case the persistent smell was coming from a mate he'd left behind.

She crept forward into the little kitchen and nearly fell over a can of paraffin. Tattered blankets covered the window, but a chink of light allowed her to make out a table on which was a sight she hadn't seen in many years: a bunch of bananas. Next to them was a tin of milk with what, on inspection, proved to be a white five pound note tucked beneath it. She turned and saw a single bed. There was someone sleeping in it. But as she drew closer, she realized the figure wasn't that of a tramp.

Someone had placed a child's wooden rattle on the blanket. As a thin sliver of moonlight inched through the window and crossed the bed, it illuminated sweet, soft features that Hattie had only recently come to know. Her hand flew to her mouth.

'Clara!' Hattie whispered, and then, 'Oh, poor Clara.' As the baby lying on Clara's breast stirred, she nestled her sleeping head further into the crook of her mother's neck.

It was dawn when Hattie woke, stiff and cold. All night she'd sat beside Clara's bed, keeping vigil against the return of the tramp. But sleep must have claimed her at some point, for now she started up as something ran over her foot. She gasped as life shot like electricity through her cramped limbs. Last night she'd resisted the impulse to wake Clara. The girl had been in such a peaceful sleep and the baby looked so comfortable. In another time and place, the scene of mother and child sleeping contentedly would have been a heart-warming vision of everything that made life worthwhile. It seemed too cruel to wake them both into the mean reality of their surroundings. So she'd waited.

She rubbed at her stiff shoulder and became aware of a pair of eyes, staring at her. Calm, serious, almost pleading, little Martha's gaze was so expressive that Hattie thought she understood the child's questioning look. 'Can't you help us?' it seemed to ask. Hattie smiled encouragingly back and Martha broke into an unexpected smile, which ended in a giggle.

'I'm not making any promises!' Hattie said, and the child blew out a mouthful of bubbles.

Clara's eyes, on the other hand, were full of fear when they opened and lit upon Hattie. She sat bolt upright. 'What are you doing here?' she asked.

'I could ask you the same question. I live here.'

'So do I!' said Clara.

'What the bloody hell are you doing sleeping in my mother's basement? You told me you're at your mum and dad's! And do you know some stinking old tramp's been rooting around the kitchen while you've been asleep? Anything could have happened to you – or to the baby!'

Clara got up, hastily gathering her things. 'I'm so sorry, Hattie. I didn't know this was your place. I had nowhere to go and it was empty… and…' Clara stood in the centre of the kitchen, some of Martha's clothes in one hand, fumbling to open her small suitcase with the other. Hattie could see her fingers were trembling on the catch.

'Chrissake, Clara, calm down.' Hattie realized she must have sounded angrier than she felt. 'It's all right. Don't cry. I'm not cross with you. I just got such a fright finding you with that tramp. I've been sitting here worried sick all night, not knowing why you were here.'

'I'm not crying. You should have woken me up.' Clara went on packing Martha's few things, not meeting Hattie's eye. 'It's only temporary… Mum and Dad wouldn't have us staying with them. They put me on the street the first night I come home, but they only live across the Square, and I was lucky I found this place. I'll pay your mother the rent.'

Hattie took hold of Clara's hands. 'Stop that. Cissie doesn't own the place! I'd ask you to stay with us, but we're all cramped into one room up there. You go and see to your baby. Have you got any tea? I'm gasping.'

Hattie found the tea and picked up the tin of condensed milk on the table, sending the five pound note fluttering to the floor.

'What's that?' Clara asked as she shifted the baby on to her breast.

'Your money.' Hattie picked it up, wondering how Clara had managed to save a fiver out of her meagre wages.

'It's not mine. It's his.'

'Whose?'

'The one you frightened off last night. He brings me presents when I'm asleep.' Clara pointed to the bananas. 'Those are from him, and these.' She reached down for the teddy bear and the rattle, showing it to Martha who, still sucking, made an expert grab for the colourful toy. 'He's never left money before, though.'

Hattie was amazed at Clara's matter-of-fact tone. 'Do you think you ought to be encouraging him?'

Clara soothed Martha with a soft croon and sighed. 'I don't do anything. He was here the first night and I think it must have been his camp – so I suppose if I've got a landlord it's him!'

'Clara, do you know who he is?' Hattie asked, though she already knew the answer.

The girl nodded. 'It's Pissy Pants. But I don't think there's any harm in him. He just leaves things. It's like he's taken me under his wing.'

'Smelly wing,' Hattie said, and was glad to see Clara break into a shy smile.

The girl looked up from her veil of hair. 'You get used to it after a while – the smell.'

Hattie hadn't known her long, but she found herself admiring the girl's lack of self-pity. She'd noticed Clara could be brought quickly to the edge of tears, by unkindness or even tiredness, but she always managed to resist them. Perhaps that's what happened when you had a baby – your own needs and feelings just melted away. Hattie was damn sure she could never do it.

'Well, he's a Harper, however harmless, and the less you have to do with that lot the better. Beside you shouldn't need to get used to his smell, nor to living in this hole. Have you tried the council?'

Clara nodded. 'They put me on the waiting list. Six years.'

'Same here. Did you tell them about the baby? The housing

clerk reckoned the only way I'd ever be offered a place was if I got myself up the duff and I wouldn't do that – not even for a council place!'

Clara kissed the top of her daughter's head. 'I had Martha with me in the council office.' The veil of hair fell across her cheeks. 'Didn't make no difference. Perhaps she was the wrong colour.'

'No... surely not?'

'You've seen the way the girls treat me, and I get worse than that. I've had people look in the pram and spit at me.'

She saw Clara swallowing her tears.

'Well, sod them and sod the council. This place is a wreck. We need to get you out of here and into somewhere a bit decent.'

The baby gurgled her agreement, but Hattie only noticed the 'we' after she'd said it. It seemed Buster had known her better than she had herself.

\* \* \*

Cissie was almost as enthusiastic as Hattie about the squatting plan, even offering to help with the organization. Part of her keenness might have been down to Hattie cramping her style. Cissie's maternal instincts had a distinct limit.

Hattie was sitting on the sofa, holding a pencil stub over the scrap of paper on her knee. 'So, I can have one of your old iron bedsteads from upstairs, but it'll need a new mattress. Mario's offered to put up shelves and clothes hooks. I can get a table from bomb salvage and blankets from the Sally Ann. What else?'

'I think you'll need some company.' Her mother nodded sagely.

'Don't tell me you want to come?' The idea of her mother and Mario joining her in the huts filled her with dismay.

'We'd liven the place up a bit for you!' Then Cissie laughed and choked on her cigarette. 'Your face! No, what I mean is there's strength in numbers. I learned that when I marched with Eliza Gilbie in the 1911 women's strike. Thirty-odd years ago! Gawd, I'm getting old! Back then, you was lucky to get six shilling a week...'

Hattie headed her off before her mother could launch into the oft-repeated tale of how she'd come to be called Cissie the Red.

'Well, I was sort of hoping for a bit of peace and quiet, Ciss... a bit of my own space, you know? Besides, there's Joe.'

'Oooh, Joe, is he handsome? I daresay you just want him all to yourself!'

Hattie raised her eyes. 'He's not my type.'

'No? Anyhow, it's about time someone put a squib up this Labour council's arse. They need to get a move on and build some proper houses. You got to organize the troops, love. That's what your army training's for...'

Hattie carried on making her list, but Cissie's words had struck a chord. Perhaps the very reason she'd liked army life *was* the company. She'd spent years living cheek by jowl with a host of strangers in camps from Barkingside to Brussels, and apart from the odd personality clash she'd enjoyed it. As an only child who'd often been ostracized for her mother's failings, she'd always felt somehow set apart from the crowd.

The army had replaced all her youthful socialist ideals with a feeling of camaraderie and a sense that they were all fighting a common enemy. She wasn't ready to launch a squatting campaign. She just wanted a home of her own and Cissie was right, she wanted company.

Clara in the basement was the tip of the iceberg. Thousands of people would find army huts a better prospect than the places they called home at the moment. There was too the added bonus that the ridiculously proper Joe would have nothing to complain about and she wouldn't have to feel guilty about turning him out of his home.

'Cissie the Red, you're a genius!' she declared and gave her mother a rare kiss.

*

The following week she put the word out at the factory that she knew of some spacious accommodation at a very cheap rent.

She didn't mention the squatting. In the army she'd learned the delicate art of getting someone to volunteer. By the time she'd finished with anyone who took the bait, they'd think squatting was their idea.

The other reason she wouldn't make her invitation too specific was that her mother had warned her not to. 'Cissie the Red' knew a bit about civil disobedience. She'd once occupied the offices at Southwell's jam factory and she'd tutored Hattie through her own brief foray into union organizing at the Alaska. She assured Hattie that squatting wasn't a criminal offence – the most she'd be accused of was trespass – but they could throw the book at her if she seemed to incite anyone else to trespass. It had to appear to be their idea.

In the social club after work that evening, she sat at a table near the bar with a whiskey mac in front of her and a clipboard in her lap. If anyone asked, she wasn't recruiting; she was socializing. But Buster joined her and snatched the clipboard.

'Give us it back!' she barked. 'I don't want everyone seeing it.'

'Yes, sir. Permission to speak, Sergeant Wright?' He gave her a sloppy salute. 'Are you bonkers? Alan's mate, Joe Jerwood, told us what you're up to. You can't live in those huts, Hattie. They've been empty over two years! Who knows what's crawling about inside them.' He gave a visible shudder. 'It's all right for a bloke, but…'

'Oh, a *bloke*! Buster, will you make me some curtains?' she asked, batting her eyelids and dropping her voice.

'She's not listening to a word I'm saying, Al!' Buster complained to Alan Manners, who had just joined them at the table. He sat down, crossed his long legs and gave her one of his disarming cheeky grins, but she wasn't to be won over.

'Alan, if Joe Jerwood's sent you to put me off, then you're wasting your time,' she said firmly.

Someone had put a record of Bing Crosby singing 'Blue Skies' on the gramophone.

'Blue skies! If only.' Alan smiled wistfully at the song, ignoring her comment about Joe. 'I reckon the last time I saw a bit of sun was when I was in Australia with the marines.' Hattie thought he looked too young to have served in the war, but then, they'd all been too young.

'They say the weather's getting worse… more Arctic blasts.' He paused, 'What are you going to do for heating in the huts?'

Hattie saw his remark as a challenge and readied herself for a battle. 'I know Joe Jerwood's your friend, but I've just spent eight bloody years making sure it's a free country. I'll do what I like.' She set her jaw in a way that had never failed to quell a cheeky recruit.

But Alan simply laughed at her. 'I think the best thing is to find out if the coalman would deliver to the park once a week. What do you think?'

At first Hattie didn't understand. Then when it dawned on her that Alan wasn't trying to dissuade her, but actually offering to be her first co-squatter, she gave him her broadest smile.

'Ah, see, Buster! Someone with a bit of faith in a woman,' she said, nodding towards Alan. 'My first volunteer! It's your idea, Al, so you ring the coal yard tomorrow, OK?'

'He'll be lucky, they're sending it all abroad!' Buster scoffed, and then gave up the fight. 'Oh, all right then, I'll make your curtains. You got any coupons left for material?'

'Not enough. I'll need another month's at least.'

'Surely not!' Buster did a quick calculation. 'You won't need that much material!'

Hattie conjured up the hut in her mind's eye. 'Well, there's six… no, eight windows, counting the ones at each end.'

'How big's this place, for gawd's sake?' Buster asked.

'Bigger than your flat. Are you tempted?'

'Nooo, you'd never talk me out of my little flat. Come and find me when you've finished. I've got a new dance to show you.'

Buster glided off, holding an imaginary partner, leaving Hattie with Alan. There was a moment's silence before he grinned and asked, 'Looks like it's just you, me and Joe then for the country estate?'

'Did Joe talk you into it?' she asked.

'No, he didn't need to – but it struck me it would kill two birds. You get a chaperone, Joe can stay where he is and I get to leave Mum and Dad's! It was a bit of shock going home after shifting for myself in the war. Mum even wants to know what time I'm getting in of a night, and if it's after eleven I'm in trouble!'

Hattie laughed at him. 'You're frightened of your mum! I thought you told me you liked to live dangerously?'

He heaved a sigh. 'If you knew my mum…'

She gave a wry smile, feeling a sense of kinship with the young man. 'No shame in wanting to escape your mother, Al. That's what I'm doing! Anyway, we'll need people who want to shift for themselves. The coal's a good idea, but it'd be even better to have electricity. You're an electrician – do you think you could hook us up?'

Alan's blue eyes lit up and he gave her his twinkling smile. 'I'll hook us up any time you like,' he said with a wink.

'Careful, sparks might fly if you do!' she said, flattered. Alan was popular around the factory. With his fair hair and lean athletic build, she knew he was the object of quite a few of the Alaska girls' affections. He played for the firm's cricket and football teams, could tell a joke and play the piano at a party, and what's more he had the sort of confidence which had nothing to prove. She did wonder, however, if she was more attracted to his popularity than to him. He was about to reply when Maisie, looking thinner and paler than ever, sat down beside her. The young girl's pasty complexion reddened as she glanced at Alan, revealing her not-so-secret crush.

'These places you're on about, are they prefabs?' Maisie asked, overcoming her confusion. 'Only my family's crowded out where we are and Mum said she'd give anything for one of them.'

'Prefabs?' Hattie struggled with her conscience. 'Well, yes, sort of… but you'd better come and see one before you get your mum's hopes up, Maise,' she said, honesty winning out, for she had to admit, compared to the huts a prefab would seem like a palace.

# 7

## The Squatters

It was the worst of times to make the move. A bitter wind was blowing from Siberia and Hattie feared the whole enterprise would be ruined by the Arctic weather. That week Joe called an emergency meeting of the squatters' committee, which sounded grander than it was, as it consisted only of Hattie, Alan and Joe. Buster offered his flat as their HQ and taking his duties as their host seriously, he'd acquired a bottle of brandy under the counter and set them all up with winter warmers.

'It's now or never,' Joe said before she could even ask what the emergency was.

'But we agreed not to move in till the weather gets better,' she objected.

'I think he's right, Hattie,' Alan said.

She raised her eyes. Their inclusion of Joe Jerwood on the committee had been Alan's idea and though Hattie hadn't liked it, she'd agreed in order to get him on their side. But she always seemed to find herself at odds with him.

'Just hear him out,' Alan persisted.

'I wouldn't suggest it if it wasn't necessary.' Joe frowned. 'But the council's got wind of our plans.'

'Oh no, that's all we need! How the bloody hell did they find out?' she said, almost accusingly.

'I bet it was Vera's husband,' Alan suggested. 'Brian's always got a bit too much bunny when he's tipsy.'

'We can't know that for certain,' Joe said. 'But whoever it was, I've had a couple of housing officers snooping around for the first time since I started living there. They went into the ablutions hut, said the place was unsanitary.'

'Damn.' Hattie downed the brandy, wishing, not for the first time, that she'd just picked up her bag and moved in alone. But then she remembered Clara and Martha. She could never have left them to moulder in that basement.

'They said they'd turned a blind eye to a single ex-serviceman living there, but they wouldn't tolerate it when children's health and safety was at risk.'

'So, if they know that families are moving in, they must have found out everything. Cissie warned me to take possession before the rumour mill started. "Possession's nine-tenths of the law" she told me!'

Alan laughed and a rare smile lightened Joe's habitually serious expression.

'Well, I agree with Cissie the Red,' Buster chipped in. Although he wasn't joining the squat, his advice was always welcome. 'You should move into them huts and make sure the *South London Press* knows about it. The council won't want photos of homeless kids being dragged away through the snow plastered all over the front page!'

'Buster, you can be our press officer,' Hattie said and then, before he had a chance to object, added, 'Call the paper, tell them a dozen homeless families are going to take over the army huts this Sunday, and if the council tries to stop us they'll have a fight on their hands!'

\*

Hattie picked her way down the snow-covered basement steps, her feet sliding from under her. Her rubber-soled bootees had very little tread left on them. But though her footwear might not be the best, in this weather she realized there was at least one advantage of working at the Alaska – fur offcuts and imperfect garments could be got cheaply. Today she wore a black Cossack hat and a detachable collar, both of which she'd made herself from rejected astrakhan offcuts. She'd also lifted a pair of the ex-service-issue sheepskin mittens the Alaska had made throughout the war for use in the North Atlantic, and had lined her bootees with some strips of soft white coney. But the cold was still intense enough to penetrate her hands and feet and freeze her ears till they ached.

Down in the basement Clara had readied her few pathetic belongings. A single suitcase, blankets and baby things were packed up in the pram around Martha, who was swaddled like a little Eskimo in a miniature parka which Hattie had made from sheepskin rejects. Clara's slight still frame was perched on the edge of the lopsided chair, a picture of patience. But as soon as she saw Hattie she sprang up, gripping the pram handle with a determined look on her face. The girl had quailed when Hattie first told her they might have a fight on their hands, but she looked ready enough for battle now.

'Hold your horses!' Hattie said, clapping her mittened hands together for warmth. 'Wait for Alan. We'll let him lug the pram and all your worldly goods up the stairs.'

Clara put a dummy into Martha's mouth, though there was so little of the baby's face visible beneath the fur-trimmed hood that Hattie wondered how she found it. The child's eyes reflected weak daylight piercing the dingy basement kitchen. Now they fixed Hattie with a sombre stare. Hattie pulled a funny face and was rewarded by a smile so broad not even the dummy could mask it.

'You're easy,' she said, wandering over to the pram to tap the flat little nose. 'You've got to make people work for that lovely smile!' she said, and the child laughed. She wouldn't admit it to anyone but Martha had begun to wear away at her normal indifference to children, and no one had been more surprised than herself.

'They only smile like that so you won't put them out on to

a cold hillside and let them be eaten by wolves, you know,' she said to Clara, to counteract her own secret softening.

'Really? Ask the Spartan babies how well that worked out.' The voice came from behind her and she spun round, surprised to see Joe there instead of Alan.

'Oh, look out, here's the other little bundle of joy!' she retorted. 'Where's Alan?'

'Dealing with a crisis upstairs. Maisie's brother brought the budgie and it's not coped very well with the cold... the boy's sitting in the snow, won't move.'

'And the budgie?'

'Exactly the same!'

They manoeuvred the pram down the dark passage and Hattie noticed Clara looking back towards the kitchen. 'You surely can't be sad to leave it?'

'I was just thinking about – him, you know. Whether he'll come back and wonder where we've gone.' There was a half-apologetic look on her face. 'I know I've got more to worry about than that, but he was good to us, a lot kinder than some ...'

Normally Hattie would have been impatient with such sentimentality, but she could not find Clara irritating. The girl had endured enough to earn her respect. She tried to reassure her. 'He'll know where you've gone. This is Pissy Pants we're talking about – he lives all over Bermondsey. He'll probably end up in one of the huts himself!'

There were a dozen families due to gather in the Square that morning, everyone so unhappy where they were living that they welcomed the prospect of exchanging it for a wooden hut. Organizing them all hadn't been as easy as she'd imagined. They were worse than a bunch of raw recruits. Maisie's family were initially under the impression that the huts would be done up for them by the council and had nearly backed out when she'd told them it would be a case of DIY. Vera and her warring husband Brian could agree on nothing. If Vera said yes to the moving date, Brian would find an objection. Levin the nailer had surprised her by introducing a surprisingly demure wife and five children, who were all living in a tiny flat in Monarch Buildings, a crumbling Victorian tenement next to the Star cinema. A couple of other Alaska girls and their families had thrown in their lot: one of them was bringing her elderly parents and the other had a husband and two children. By far the easiest person to please was Clara, the one who truly had nothing to lose.

By the time they'd consoled Maisie's brother about the budgie and waited for the rest of the squatters to assemble with their belongings, the snow had started to fall again, thin biting granules, soon turning to flat sticky flakes, coating Hattie's black Cossack hat in seconds. Cissie came to the door. Standing at the top of the steps, wrapped in the green candlewick bedspread and knitted scarf, she looked like an ageing Boadicea. She sent them off with a regal wave while singing 'We'll keep the red flag flying high' in a tremulous off-key voice.

'Go in, Ciss!' Hattie shouted through the snow. 'You'll catch your death!' But as the little band set off she looked back to see her mother still standing there, with Mario's muscular arm firmly round her. She was waving a little red flag.

They traipsed the length of the Blue, but with no shops or stalls open due to the ever-thickening snow, few people were out in the street to witness their raggle-taggle procession. Some of the squatters pushed prams and handcarts containing their belongings and these snaked tracks in the pristine early morning snow, but the majority left only their footprints, carrying all that they owned in cardboard suitcases. The families who followed Hattie had accumulated little enough over the years and then had lost most of it during the war.

When they reached the park, she was panting for breath; it had been hard-going carrying all their possessions through the resisting snow. She paused at the gateposts to let the children and older ones rest. The unrelenting snow of the past weeks had gradually softened some of the scars of war. Bomb craters were filled to the brim with its billowy whiteness, burned tree stumps were buried and splintered branches were laced in sparkling ice. Some drifts were almost too deep for the smaller children to traverse, so Alan and Joe hoisted them on to their shoulders and backs, while other kids perched on prams or the handcart being pushed by Vera's bull-like husband, Brian. Hattie and Clara turned Martha's pram round and pulled it like two huskies attached to a sled while Martha sat up overseeing them with an excited alert look in her dark eyes, her golden cheeks reddening in the cold.

'She really does love the snow!' Clara gasped and flashed Hattie a smile.

'Well, I've never seen this much!' Hattie replied between laboured breaths.

It was as they approached the Oval that she spotted a handful of men dressed in heavy overcoats and trilbies, chatting to two bobbies, both wrapped warmly in their long, blue coats.

'Company halt!' Hattie shouted in her sergeant's voice, and was surprised when the chattering which had accompanied their march was silenced and the crunching of feet on snow ceased.

'Hold up, they've spotted us,' Alan muttered to her.

'Someone's blabbed again,' Hattie said angrily looking around and catching Joe's eye as he handed down a child from his shoulders. 'And I think I know who it is...'

'What are you looking at me like that for?' Joe blushed. 'This isn't my doing!'

'You're the only one it benefits...' she snapped. 'They said they'd turn a blind eye to you on your own, but not if there were kids here ...'

She was interrupted as a council official approached with one of the constables.

'Cecil Worth, housing officer,' he introduced himself. 'Now, we don't want any trouble.' He addressed Joe, even though she was at the head of the little column. 'But you can't occupy these huts. The council hasn't sanctioned it and they're unsanitary.' He gave the group a little shooing gesture, as if they were a herd of sheep, which only made Hattie dig her fur bootees deeper into the snow.

'*Everywhere's* unsanitary!' she said, furious at the man's smug tone and his assumption they would comply. She pointed to Maisie's family of six. '*They* live in two rooms, no kitchen, outside toilet shared with five other families. *She*,' pointing at Clara, 'lives in a bombed-out basement, no electricity, broken drains, outside lav, rats – so where do you suggest they should go? If you can give them a sanitary house we'll "move along", but if not then we're staying put!'

She was surprised but touched to hear a rousing cheer coming from the squatters crowding closely behind her. The other policeman and officials joined them. A short man who said he was from the public health department peered through round, horn-rimmed glasses into Martha's pram. He jumped back with a start as she excitedly struck him with Pissy Pants' rattle. He stood up, rubbing his nose, and shot a look at his colleague.

'We know from other councils' experience that squatting camps attract riff-raff of all sorts, vagrants and gypsies and women with questionable morals...' He looked at Martha, who began threatening him again with the rattle.

Suddenly Brian pushed to the front. 'Oi, oi, less of your bleedin' cheek. We're all respectable working people here. Just 'cause Hitler bombed our homes don't make us immoral – and you can stop looking at her like she's scum an' all!' His balled fist was raised and ready, but might not have struck anything if the nearest policeman hadn't made the mistake of grabbing his arm. Brian, who was a drum 'boy' at the Alaska, had the job of hauling heavy pelts in and out of huge revolving drums filled with bleaching liquor, which had pickled his massive fists to the hardness of a cricket ball. Now he clenched one and smashed it into the little health official's face, knocking his glasses to the ground and causing an alarming quantity of blood to stain the snow red. One bobby jumped on Brian and the three fell back in a tangle into Maisie's dad's handcart, scattering blankets and sending the birdcage with its dead budgie hurtling into a snowdrift. Maisie's brother set up a howl, just in time for the *South London Press* photographer, who came at a run, eager not to miss the shot of two policemen harassing a homeless child in the snow.

'Can you tell us why you're manhandling these ex-servicemen, when other councils in the country are encouraging them to occupy unused properties?' The reporter puffed along, pulling out his pad. 'What comment would the housing office or the public health department like to make?'

The bloody-nosed council official was in no fit state to make any comment. He'd escaped Brian's grasp and had his face buried in a handkerchief. But Hattie called to the photographer. 'I'm ex-ATS.' She pointed in turn to Alan and Joe. 'They're ex-marines, ex-army, them girls worked day and night to make sure our fighter boys had sheepskin bomber jackets, and she,' indicating Clara, 'used to clean the blood off 'em when they got sent back damaged! What's our thanks? No homes, no food, no coal!' She felt the spirit of Cissie the Red running through her veins. 'All we want is a disused hut or two to live in. The council should be ashamed, sending their bullies to keep us out!' Shouts of agreement rang out, and now a little crowd of people who'd been out enjoying the snowfall in the park gathered round too. Fathers with children on home-made sleds stopped to see what the commotion was about, a couple of elderly churchgoers started to heckle the officials, and a crowd of young men out for a snowball fight muscled in, closing the group into a tight circle.

'Get Brian off the bobby,' Hattie muttered to Alan, unsure which way things would go, for crowds were fickle and Brian didn't look as if he were being bullied. But suddenly Joe stepped forward and, in a voice which reached to the back of the gathering crowd of onlookers, said, 'These council men have let me live in the huts for nearly *seven* months and now they want to bully homeless women and children. They threatened to turf me out if I helped them!' The crowd began to jeer, and after a hasty consultation the head housing officer put up a pair of placating hands. 'We're not bullies. We all have a job to do and ours is to oversee rehousing in Bermondsey—'

With a jeer, one of the young boys threw an icy snowball which knocked the officer's hat askew, and a woman in a headscarf and worn coat shouted, 'What rehousing? We're all living in slums while you lot sit in the town hall drinking cups of tea!'

The crowd erupted and, swelling the ranks of the squatters, surged forward, pushing past the bobbies and setting the council officers running, the photographer snapping all the while. It wasn't the orderly arrival that Hattie had hoped for, but once at the perimeter of the army huts the families spread out to claim their new homes. They all knew which hut to occupy and the padlocks had already been removed the previous night by Brian.

With the housing officers gone, the two constables seemed to relax. They sauntered over to where Hattie and Clara were unpacking Martha's pram.

'Here y'are, love,' one said, taking Clara's suitcase. 'We'll help you in with that. Tell you the truth, neither of us wanted this job. Don't tell the chief, but if it wasn't for my police flat up Abbey Street I'd probably be joining you. But you can't tell that bunch of office civvies nothing, can you, Sarge?' He smiled at Hattie before giving her a smart salute.

Families got settled while children chased each other from hut to hut, thundering along duckboards, darting in and out of the NAAFI, before ploughing through drifts and rolling down the snow-filled crater nearby. Hattie stood for a moment, listening to their laughter as it rang, like muffled bells, reverberating from the snow-filled pit. Similar laughter had come from the paddling pool, years before it had become a bomb crater, and she marvelled at how children could always ferret out the potential for joy, however unpromising the situation. Her thoughts returned to the straw-haired little hooligan who'd attacked her on her first day back in Bermondsey. He seemed to be the unredeemed exception. There had been no joy in his haunted, pinched face.

She wondered who the mother was that he'd so fiercely defended and, as she surveyed her own new domain, why he'd seemed so territorial about that bombsite in Spa Road.

⋆ ⋆ ⋆

Clara was surprised. She was actually glad to be sharing a hut with Hattie. She doubted they'd ever have been friends before the war. Hattie was the sort of girl everyone noticed, not in a loud-mouthed way, but just because she seemed to have a style all of her own. She wore bright colours to work when everyone else was still making do with wartime drab, she didn't seem to care about what people thought or said about her, and what's more, she was confident and brave. Just the opposite of Clara, who was always glad to disappear in a crowd and felt fear waiting for her every morning when she awoke. Why Hattie had been kind to her she didn't know. But she'd befriended Clara in a way that somehow seemed natural and, more importantly, hadn't made her feel like a charity case.

Eventually they would partition the hut, Hattie said. There was ample room for two bedrooms, a little nursery for Martha, and a sitting room-cum-kitchen, but the need to move in quickly meant that for now the long, bare hut was furnished only with two camp beds, the pram, their suitcases and a stove. Now, following the afternoon's excitements, they sat together beside the stove, which was giving out a blessed amount of heat after the cold of her basement. By the light of two oil lamps Hattie brewed tea in a kettle of water drawn from the NAAFI and, after opening up the stove, began toasting bread in its flames.

'Cosy enough for you?' she asked Clara, with her broad smile. Even today, she'd managed to looked beautiful, her red-gold hair coiled up beneath the black astrakhan hat.

They had been arranging their few belongings in silence and now spoke in hushed tones, so as not to wake Martha.

'It's like a palace,' Clara whispered.

'Are you having me on?'

But Clara was serious. 'Well, compared to the basement it is... and besides, it's just nice to have somewhere of your own to call home.'

Hattie gave her a quizzical look. 'You've got a bloody good imagination. But I know what you mean. One day it'll be home. We'll make it home.'

She handed Clara her toast and nodded to the window, 'Snow's falling again.' Then she asked suddenly, 'Do you ever regret leaving those blue skies down under?'

'No,' Clara answered, though it wasn't entirely the truth. She regretted the blue skies, but not the leaving.

'Really? But why did you come back from Australia when you knew your mum and dad wouldn't have you back? Why not just try to make a go of it out there?'

Clara didn't mind the question. In fact it was a relief, having someone ask her about her choices instead of simply condemning her for them.

'Funnily enough I liked it there, the country, the people, the sun, but I had to leave... because of Barry. What he did to me. I didn't even want to be breathing the same air as him.'

'Did the bastard break your heart?' Hattie asked.

Clara's first shy impulse was to evade the question, but Hattie's gaze held concern, not the curiosity she'd got from the few other girls who'd asked her about Barry. They'd wanted to know what it was like being married to a black man, as if the heart bore any colour other than red. Again Clara felt that sense of relief.

'Yes, he broke my heart, but he wasn't a cruel man.' Clara saw Hattie beginning to scoff. 'No, it's true. If anything, he was too kind really. He didn't like upsetting people.'

'Funny way of showing it!' Hattie said.

'Do you know, when we fell in love, I didn't even realize he was a coloured chap. I just thought, well, he's Australian and they're all suntanned, and he told me his dad was Scottish – he didn't say nothing about his mother. My dad always did tell me I'm a bit slow on the uptake.'

'When did you find out?'

'Only when I took him home for tea. Dad had a blue fit and me mother couldn't get Barry out the house quick enough before Dad said something. It was horrible, I thought they'd be pleased for me. Still, I didn't care. We were in love and Barry thought he was going abroad the next month to die, and he knew I wanted to get married. So he asked me and I didn't even think twice about upsetting Mum and Dad.'

Clara stared into her cup and felt a familiar constriction round her throat. She hadn't relived her early days with Barry for a very long time. She couldn't: she'd needed anger to get herself away from him and back to England. She'd needed to hate him. But it had been hard for her. Turning all that overflowing love into hate hadn't come naturally. She could so easily have forgiven him for herself, but not for Martha.

'So what went wrong?' Hattie interrupted her thoughts.

'He didn't die,' she said simply, and Hattie let out an awkward laugh. 'If he'd died,' Clara went on, 'I never would have gone out on the bride ship to Australia, and I never would have found out after being there six months that he already had a wife living round the corner from us.'

Hattie took in a sharp breath. 'Oh, Clara, you poor thing. I've picked a few bastards in my time, but your'n takes the cake. So, what did you do?'

'It was one of the women I'd gone out with on the bride ship told me about Barry's other wife and I went round there to see for myself. He opened the door, and when he saw it was me standing there he just started crying.'

''Cause he'd been found out.'

Clara shook her head. 'I told you, he loved me, or he thought he did. He cried because he knew I'd leave him and take Martha with me. Tried to persuade me to stay, said he'd divorce her. As if I'd let Martha grow up with a dad who'd do that to her. No. I took her that night and I didn't know where to go. So I just went to where the boats left, down the docks. I got a room, only a bit better than the basement! Then I waited till I could stow away. I didn't have a penny for the fare.'

'My God, Clara, you act all soft, but you're a million times tougher than me. I couldn't have done that.'

She shrugged. 'You'll do anything for your baby. I had no choice. I just wanted to get us home and never go back there, but like you say... the blue skies... I miss them and I think Martha does too. She wasn't born to this.' Clara gave the snow-filled windowpane an anxious look as she went to check on Martha's sleeping form, swaddled in the pram.

'I don't like babies usually,' Hattie surprised her by saying, but quickly followed with, 'But I like Martha. She smiles with her eyes.'

Clara was pleased. Her child had received few enough compliments since they'd returned. 'You noticed. Barry had smiling eyes.' And there again came that constriction in her throat. Hattie had asked if he'd broken her heart, but she never felt the pain there, it was always here, in her throat, as if fate had decided she shouldn't ever again tell anyone that she loved them. She'd loved him so much, too much. So much that she'd given up her life without a qualm, and let him trample over all her pristine, unloved self, just as the kids had scrabbled the snowy field around the huts. She hadn't even tried to protect herself; she'd thought that loving someone meant you trusted them.

'I didn't even ask him why he'd done it. I think it was the war.'

Hattie gave a disbelieving snort. 'Men don't need wars to be bastards, Clara.'

'Tell me about yours then,' Clara said, sitting down again, holding her hands up to the stove.

'Too many!' Hattie's laugh echoed round the bare boards of the hut. 'But there was only one I let hurt me... never again! I took on all the bad boys after that and it was always me that walked away without a scratch.'

Clara believed her. It wasn't boasting, but she was curious about the one that had managed to pierce Hattie's defences.

'So who was it broke your heart?' she asked softly, enjoying the feeling of confidences shared in the closed circle of light.

'Broke my heart? Perhaps he did, but he broke my collarbone too.' And Hattie tilted her neck to expose the fine bone. Clara could see it was slightly deformed. 'Lenny Harper – oooh, he had a sweet tongue and a vicious right hook. But back then I was like you, love. Silly as a sackload of monkeys and head over heels. He only did it the once, though, and I was gone.'

'Lenny Harper!' Clara was shocked.

Hattie nodded. 'That's why I don't think you should worry about Pissy Pants not visiting you any more. Believe me, the less you have to do with the Harpers the better.' And Hattie fingered the part of her collarbone that had been bent out of shape by the man she'd loved. Perhaps, Clara reflected, they were not so different after all.

# 8

## *Three Men*

### *March 1947*

Hattie soon realized it would take more than mere effort to make her hut into the home she'd promised Clara. But everything seemed to be conspiring to make the enterprise a failure, from the merciless Arctic weather to the country's grim economic situation. As the winter extended its icy grip into the first days of what should have been spring, the country's coal supply ran out and the Alaska, which had never reached full production since the war ended, was forced by power cuts to cut back even further. They were all given notice that the factory was now on a three-day week, the worst possible news for Hattie, who desperately needed to earn extra cash.

She determined to swallow her pride and supplement her income with an early morning job, cleaning the Alaska's sales offices across the river in Upper Thames Street. It seemed ludicrous that she had to be interviewed for a cleaning job, but she'd arranged to see the supervisor before her shift and to get there in time she had to leave when the early morning was still dark.

The snow spun in intense sharp flurries outside the hut. She'd woken early and by five o'clock was dressed as if she were setting out for the North Pole: two vests, long woollen stockings, two jumpers, a woollen skirt and her beaver lamb, which she'd bought before the war at staff discount. It was her best coat, but the only thing that would keep the cold from penetrating her bones. She'd finished off her outfit with the astrakhan Cossack hat. At least she'd look the classiest cleaner in Upper Thames Street. She was checking herself in a mirror the size of a postage stamp, which some gunner had left tacked to the door, when she heard a pitiful scream.

She turned to see Martha's face poking over the edge of the pram. Most of her face seemed to be mouth, a gaping maw from which was coming a bloodcurdling sound. Clara had gone to the NAAFI to fetch water for steeping the nappies and Hattie stuck her head out of the door. Swallowing a snow flurry, she called, 'Clara! Quick, something's happened to the baby!'

Clara, struggling with her bucket, dropped it at Hattie's call and dashed to the hut, coming to a halt by the pram.

'I've not touched her!' Hattie said as the screams grew louder. 'What is it?'

Clara looked calmly from the baby and back again to Hattie, who couldn't understand why she wasn't more panicked. Martha was obviously in great pain.

'Hattie! She's *hungry*! Don't you know what that cry means by now?' Clara laughed and picked Martha up.

Now Hattie felt foolish. 'Don't laugh at me! I don't know anything about babies. It sounded as if someone was murdering her!'

'What's all the commotion – who's being murdered in their beds?' It was Alan at the door.

'That's what I thought,' Hattie said, feeling vindicated as Clara turned away to feed the baby.

'I'm on my way out,' Hattie told him, stepping outside.

'Oh hello, gorgeous!' He smiled. 'Going anywhere nice?'

'I've got a date with a zinc bucket and a bar of carbolic. Jealous? What are you doing here so early?'

'I just wanted to let you know I've hooked up the electric.' He waved a screwdriver at her to emphasize the point.

'Al! That's great. It'll make all the difference,' she said, still wondering why he'd chosen five o'clock in the morning to tell her.

'Oh, and there's another thing,' he said casually. 'I was wondering if you wanted to come to the dance with me tonight?'

'You don't mess about!' She shooed him out on to the duckboard and into the snow. 'Move yourself, we're letting in all the cold air.'

'Well?' he persisted, and she was about to answer when Maisie scurried up, hugging herself in a blanket, trying to smooth her tousled hair at the sight of Alan.

'Hattie, don't tell me you're leaving already! I need your help. Mum's gone office-cleaning and I'll never get ready for work in time if I don't sort me brothers out. They're hollering the place down!'

The sound of Maisie's little brothers' crying reached her ears. 'For God's sake, not more dying children. I'm not cut out for this, Maise. What's happened to them?' she said, leaving Alan behind as she ran to Maisie's hut. She found the boys writhing around on the bed they shared, screaming like cats in a fight. Maisie explained above the din that the boys had spent the previous day playing in freezing snow, and against their mother's advice had insisted on planting their feet over the stove to warm them. Now Hattie was looking at chilblains as bad as any she'd seen in the army.

'You're meant to rub your feet warm!' she said sternly. 'Not toast them!'

The boys' screams turned to whimpers. 'Got any onions, Maise?' Hattie asked.

The girl ran to a cupboard made of old orange crates, which passed as their kitchen, and came back with a sprouting onion. Hattie took a knife and sliced it.

'Old army trick! Sit still and let me rub these on your feet,' she ordered the boys.

'No, we don't like onions!'

'Do you want the pain to stop or not?'

Frightened into silence by her commanding tone, they submitted to the procedure. Then one of them muttered. 'But we'll stink.'

'So will I, but you don't hear me complaining, do you?'

'Will you be all right on your own now, Maise? I need to get going.'

The girl nodded, applying the onion with concentration, trying hard not to set her brothers wailing again.

Hattie was surprised to find Alan still waiting for her outside. 'See – this is why I always avoid kids,' she said, and then added casually, 'All right, I'll come.'

And as she began trudging through the snow, he called after her. 'By the way, you're a born mother!'

After a freezing wait at the bus stop, she sighed as she got on the bus, wriggling her own chilblained feet in her boots and feeling a little more sympathy for Maisie's brothers now her own feet were ice-bound. Had she really wanted to say yes to Alan? He'd caught her off-guard, what with rushing to the new job, then Maisie's silly crisis. That was the only reason she'd said yes, wasn't it? She prided herself on managing her love life as efficiently as she'd managed her gunner teams. It was just a matter of plotting and trajectory. She simply calculated the maximum amount of fun to be had from any connection and developed an 'attachment radar' that never let her down. If the chap or, more seriously she herself, showed signs of becoming overly serious, she gave him the elbow. She found it easier to do this if she had a couple on the go at once. Talking about Lenny with Clara had given her an uncomfortable insight into why she so rigidly policed her affections. And Clara was a prime example of what she wanted to avoid – trusting someone so completely that all your defences came tumbling down.

Lenny had been her first love, and also her last. Like a fly in a spider's web, she'd been caught by his charm before she'd even realized what was happening, and she'd paid for it in a broken bone and bruised confidence. Only the war had saved her from Lenny.

Still, she was sure she'd got Alan's mark – he wasn't the type to get too serious. He had a sportsman's casual grace and she suspected he would be a good dancer. She hoped he wouldn't mind sharing her with Buster. No one could move round the floor like Buster. Besides, she wouldn't let her old dance partner down. He was the constant, after all, and Alan the passing fancy.

She was still lost in thought, picturing herself dancing with Alan, when she entered the lobby of the Alaska's City offices, a smile playing on her face. A dark-haired man held the door open for her and she felt herself staring into his cool blue eyes for longer than was polite. He was dressed in a suit that looked considerably more expensive than the utility demobs most men wore these days, a fine, navy pinstripe, cut in an elegant style that showed off his well-proportioned figure to perfection. Any non-utility clothing cost a fortune, but this looked like Savile Row. His close-shaved cheeks glowed with the sort of rude health that was rare these days. So many people she encountered looked haggard, gaunt, with bad teeth and skin like old fag papers. She caught the whiff of an expensive cologne that hung about him as he stopped and with an easy smile revealed perfect, white teeth, asking, 'Can I help?'

He was so different from the men she worked with day by day that she found herself answering his dazzling smile with her own. 'I'm looking for the personnel department,' she said, the lie taking her by surprise. There was no way she would tell this suave man that she was going in search of the cleaning supervisor.

'You're an early bird!' He laughed. 'Personnel won't be at their desks at this hour!'

'Oh, thank you. I'll come back later.' She waited for him to leave so she could ask the porter for directions, but the debonair man stood, one hand in his trouser pocket, an amused look on his face.

'There's a Kardomah just round the corner, you could go there to wait. Better still, let me take you – I'll treat us to a coffee!'

He had an easy charm that sprang from innate confidence and she felt alarm bells ringing – her attachment radar was working already. He was definitely one to avoid.

'Oh no, I can find it. I don't want to put you out!' She back-tracked through the entrance doors and he gave a small laugh. 'Turn right, then it's second on your left... oh, and before your interview, a dab of perfume might not go amiss.' And he lowered his voice: 'Instead of *bouquet d'onion*!'

She hurried down the street, her face burning, and then stopped suddenly. He had set her running. 'Sod that for a lark,' she muttered to herself. After Lenny, she'd vowed never to run from a man again. Besides, she needed this cleaning job and she wasn't going to let that charmer frighten her off. She turned on her heel and marched back into the lobby, scanning it quickly. He was gone.

This time the porter directed her to the basement, where she found the cleaning supervisor.

'You sure you come for the cleaning job?' the woman asked, looking doubtfully at her beaver-lamb coat and astrakhan hat. When Hattie assured her she had, the woman asked her a few cursory questions about her cleaning experience. Hattie had plenty of that in the ATS. The job was hers. On the bus back to the factory, she blocked out the sight of hoards of early morning commuters streaming over London Bridge with alternate dreams of the suave man in the pinstripe suit and Alan. The part of herself she called 'the Cissie half' reckoned she might easily manage both. But her more cautious side told her Mr Savile Row was the more dangerous and should be avoided at all costs.

But that night at the social club dance she forgot all about him as she was whirled round the canteen floor in Alan's arms. After three dances he leaned in close. 'I'll sit the next one out. I'd better let poor old Buster have a go. He's been mooching about like a lost puppy, waiting to dance with you.'

They made their way to one of the canteen tables, which had been pushed back against the walls to make room for the dancing. Buster was waiting with a beer in one hand and an eager look on his face.

'You'd better watch out, Buster, he's not bad!' she teased,

sitting down. She turned to Alan. 'Where did you learn to dance like that?'

'Streatham Locarno before I was called up.'

With the lights dimmed and the gramophone blaring, her imagination could just about transport them to the Locarno.

'But don't worry, mate,' Alan said, patting Buster on the back. 'I'm leaving the fast dances to you. You're fitter than me.' He winked at Hattie.

Buster excelled at the jitterbug, the jive and the Lindy hop, but she was sure Alan could easily have handled more than the smoother ballroom dances. He was just being thoughtful.

'Be back in a minute,' Alan said suddenly, heading off in the direction of the bar. When he returned with a supply of under-the-counter gin, she began to feel even more fond of him.

The gin flowed liberally all night and she couldn't deny she was having fun with Alan. He chatted easily at the table they shared with Buster and the usual crowd, not seeming to need to monopolize her. He made her laugh with a seemingly endless supply of jokes and he even finished the evening with a sing-song at the piano. When he walked her home she waited, expecting him to put his arms round her, but instead he kissed her on the cheek. Nothing more, which had amused and pleased her. He was just what she needed at the moment, light, fun, keen and uncomplicated.

Next morning at the Alaska she found something to be irritated with Alan about – his liberality with the dodgy gin was responsible for the headache from hell. Now the thud of a hundred bamboo rods was marking time with the thumping in her head. Before this morning shift on the bambeaters she'd already suffered through her first stint of mopping duties at the City offices and the headache was like a hot iron vice round her temples. Of course she blamed Alan. She was grateful that the early morning cleaning job hadn't required much attention. Cleaning was the same the world over, and she'd done enough fatigues in her early ATS days to know the necessities – hot water, carbolic and elbow grease. She'd been assigned the regular job of mopping the canteen floors, a monotonous task, and she deliberately stopped halfway through. Army fatigues had also taught her the importance of pacing yourself. It was no good finishing too early; she'd only be landed with another job and her head couldn't take that today. She lingered by the staff notice-board, where her eye was caught by a poster featuring a pretty young woman in a silver squirrel coat, striding along a catwalk. *Models Required*, the poster read. It seemed there was to be a fashion show for trade buyers and the sales department wanted in-house volunteers to model the firm's products. There would be what the poster described as a *small remuneration*, which made Hattie's eyes widen. It was double her weekly wage. Of course, the poster was aimed at office staff, but it occurred to her that only yesterday morning Mr Savile Row had mistaken her for such.

Written applications, with an accompanying photograph, had to be sent to a Mr Crosbie, the sales manager, who would be holding a group audition. There were a thousand things she could buy with the extra money, but she laughed softly to herself when she realized the first that sprang to mind was a proper cot and quilt for Martha. She'd so prided herself on never being lured into domesticity by a man, yet it seemed Clara's little charmer had ambushed her into it without even trying.

Now, with the din of the bambeaters almost too painful to bear, she half closed her eyes, veiling the silvery light making its way through frost-filled factory windows. The bambeaters were in the newer factory block, where large windows reached almost from floor to ceiling. Today she could have done with less light. Even through half-closed lids she could do her job easily, but she hadn't spotted Buster approaching and when he tapped her on the shoulder she jumped, opening her eyes.

'Dreaming of your Alan?' he joked, mouthing in deedee to combat the noise of the machines.

She gave him a sour smile. 'One date's a bit early to be marrying me off!'

'I like him. He let me dance with you.'

'*Let!*' She raised her eyes. 'I dance with who I like.'

He saluted. 'All right, I know you're always in charge! But listen, I've got a favour to ask. Remember I made you *nursemaid*?' he mouthed, giving a slight nod towards Clara.

She nodded, quickly checking to make sure their lips were hidden from Clara at the next machine.

'Come down to the end of the floor. I need a new bin,' Hattie said. It was true her bin was almost empty of rabbit pelts, but it would also be easier to talk when they were away from the noisy bambeaters. Buster followed Hattie.

'Just to let you know, the other one I told you about, my Lou, she's starting,' he said, helping her to pull out the heavy trolley. 'Don't turn your nose up like that. If I don't get her back to work she'll end up in the nuthouse. Thing is, her boy Ronnie's gone missing, as if we didn't have enough to worry about.'

'Gone missing, when?'

'Couple of weeks ago.'

'Weeks! Have you told the police?'

Buster shook his head. 'He's done it before. He can look after himself.'

'In this weather?'

'He's hard as nails that kid.'

She wondered what sort of little monster the boy must be to strain even Buster's good nature. She couldn't help noticing her friend looked drawn, his normally cheerful expression, obscured by worry lines.

'I don't know what else to do for Lou. At least if she's here I can keep an eye on her.' He paused. 'She's lost everything and all I can give her is a job on the bambeater. Don't seem much...'

'No. It's not much. Poor cow.' She paused. 'Oh, all right then, get Old Buttercup to put her next to me.'

To show his gratitude he pushed the trolley load of pelts back to her machine and gave her an extravagant kiss, which didn't go unnoticed. 'Oooh, watch out, Hattie!' one of the girls called out.

Then she heard Doris Axmouth snort, and say for all to hear, 'She'll be safe as houses with him!'

She doubted she would be picked for the audition – it would come out she was just an Alaska girl eventually. But to have half a chance she needed an up-to-date photograph. The only decent one she possessed had been taken in Belgium by a GI she was seeing at the time. The light was certainly flattering and her figure had been more voluptuous back then when she hadn't been on the starvation rations that passed for normal these days. But the photograph showed her in uniform, looking almost fierce. There was a challenging determination in her face that she was sure the sales manager would find off-putting.

She decided to ask Joe. He belonged to a photography club and she'd seen him trudging off with his camera and tripod to take photographs of the snowy park. She'd been feeling guilty about accusing him of tipping off the council. It had emerged pretty soon after they moved in that Alan had been right all along. Brian had said too much one night in the pub to a mate who worked on the council. Vera had been making him pay for it ever since. Hattie hadn't yet managed to apologize to Joe and besides, he seemed to be avoiding her. But this evening she would be sure to see him at the squatters' committee meeting.

The committee, which now included Vera and Brian, assembled in Joe's hut, still the most habitable. Hattie and the others were working every spare hour to help families with children to get comfortable. She had put Brian in charge of the work detail, which involved frantically replacing missing boards, patching holes in roofs, mending broken stoves and keeping the water pipes in the NAAFI unfrozen. But in the end they were still just living in a collection of wooden huts. Tonight, they were discussing how Alan would link the electricity supply from the NAAFI to the huts. They also needed to persuade the coalman to deliver into the park. Coal was a constant worry, and not just for the squatters. At the moment all they could get hold of was a mixture of coke, slate and dust, but even that was hard to come by.

'I'll talk to my mate about it,' Brian said.

Vera jumped in. 'No, you bleedin' well won't! Your big mouth's got us in trouble enough already.'

'No, this geezer's all right. He works for a coal merchant. They might want the business.'

'I think that's a good idea, Vera,' Hattie said. 'And I think it's about time we let Brian off the hook about tipping the council off. He wasn't to know his friend would blab.'

Vera didn't look convinced, and out of the corner of her eye Hattie noticed Joe raise his eyes. She felt a fresh pang of guilt that she'd made him the scapegoat. She'd have to eat humble pie, which wasn't a dish she found easy to stomach.

After the meeting, she wandered over to the stove where Joe was brewing cocoa for them all. 'Need some help?' she asked.

'No, I'm fine.'

She began spooning the dark powder anyway. 'It's better if you make a paste first,' she said, adding a little water to each mug.

'I was going to do that,' he said, taking the mugs from her and topping them up with boiling water.

As she added condensed milk she stole a glance at him. A small muscle in his jaw clenched and unclenched. She took a deep breath. 'I've been meaning to say sorry, Joe, for accusing you of—'

'You don't have to apologize,' he interrupted, pushing back the floppy strand of hair that fell across his forehead. He didn't look at her. 'You don't know me, so why would you trust me?'

It wasn't the response she'd expected. So, he hadn't been blaming her, and now she was put off-guard.

'You're right, I didn't trust you. But that's not because I didn't know you. I don't trust anyone!' she gave a sharp laugh, which caused him to look up.

'Why not?'

She shrugged. 'Experience. But that's no reason why we can't be friends. Fresh start?'

Joe stirred the last cocoa almost ponderously, making her wait. 'What can I do for you?' he asked finally, and she felt like a Heinkel caught in a searchlight beam. She might not know him, but he had come perilously close to knowing her. She supposed she deserved it.

'Nothing, forget it.' She gave up and turned away, ready to hand round the cocoa. But he stopped her.

'Sorry,' he said, 'but I can be a bit blunt sometimes...'

'That makes two of us. But you weren't wrong. I wanted to ask a favour...'

*

The following Sunday when Joe came to her hut for the photo-shoot, he suggested they go outside into the park, saying he knew the ideal spot.

'Outside? I want to look chic, not like Nanook of the North!' she protested.

'You always look chic actually. Wear your beaver-lamb coat and astrakhan hat.'

She shot him a look of surprise. Perhaps he'd taken more notice of her than she'd imagined. 'Where are we going?'

'Follow me,' he said.

He led her to an ancient gnarled tree that had escaped the bombs. Its snow-draped branches were twisted into great black knots. A large round hole in the trunk exposed the hollowed-out bole. 'It's called the fairy tree,' he said. 'Stand underneath it and I'll get the snowdrift in the background. The light's just right.'

She still wasn't convinced that an outdoor photo would give the right impression, but acquiesced. He had after all extended the olive branch, or rather the fairy-tree branch, she thought, smiling to herself.

He said he'd need to use the darkroom at his camera club, so she was forced to wait until after his next club night before he could show her the printed results. She was enchanted. The dark fur of her coat and the black branches stood out starkly against the wintry backdrop. The light seemed to have collected around her face, framed as it was by the black astrakhan hat and upturned fur collar.

'Joe, these are brilliant. You've made me look like a Russian princess instead of an Alaska girl. I look almost glamorous!'

'Ah, I don't think that's down to the photographer,' he said, peering intently at the photograph. 'That's all you.' His tone was brisk. He was obviously a man who couldn't take a compliment, nor was he particularly adept at giving them.

'Well, whoever gets the praise, I'm grateful for your help. I think you might even land me the job!'

Over the days her confidence in the photo's power faded and, now, sitting outside the City office boardroom with the other applicants her confidence was somewhat dented. They were all pretty, with an average age of sixteen, and she was sure that their wars had not included nights on exposed gun emplacements or mornings washing in mugs of frozen water. They still had the bloom of youth which, at twenty-seven, Hattie knew had been dulled in her by all the years of war. Still, Cissie had donated a box of pre-war Atkinsons finest Black Tulip face powder and an almost new spare red lipstick, which Hattie had applied as expertly as she could. Who knew, this sales manager might just value experience over innocence.

They were shown to a small office, which was to act as their dressing room and were each given a different fur to model. Hers was a full-length mahogany mink. Her height gave her an advantage and when she slipped the coat over her shoulders she naturally arched her body, letting the back sway out. But the mirror revealed a too-gaunt face. She pulled up the collar, so that her red-gold hair nestled into the fur and fluffed up around her cheeks. *Better*, she thought and, when called, she glided confidently into the boardroom where the auditions were taking place.

Her eyes met the cool, appraising gaze of Mr Crosbie, the sales manager, who stood arms crossed, dressed in the same immaculate blue pinstripe suit she remembered from their meeting in the lobby that first day. Of course, it would have to be him – Mr Savile Row himself. But he'd given no hint of recognition 'Please, Miss Wright.' He indicated that she should do a circuit of the room.

She took a deep breath, threw back her shoulders and walked. She pointed her toes as she knew models did and, at the head of the room, whirled round effortlessly as if she were dancing with Buster on a Saturday night. She put a hand on one hip, so that the long fur fell open, revealing her slim legs. As she passed Crosbie, he nodded his head.

'Excellent. Thank you, Miss Wright,' he said, then inclined his head and grinned. 'Who could resist such a magnificent – mink! You'll be a marvellous ambassador for the Alaska. My secretary will give you the fashion show details.'

He turned away and she assumed she was dismissed, but as she went back into the dressing room she heard him say, 'And the perfume's a definite improvement on *bouquet d'onion*…'

When Lou first appeared on the bambeating floor, Hattie was struck by her almost ghostlike pallor. She couldn't have been more than thirty-five, yet she looked ancient, with straw-coloured hair so pale you could see her skull beneath it, the deeply hollowed eyes and cheeks, skeletal in their effect. She was wrapped in the same green overall they all wore, but it swamped her stick-like frame. She seemed a figure hewn out of grief, and the other girls shrank from her as Old Buttercup led her to the bambeater. Hattie felt a rush of compassion and an almost simultaneous burst of anger at Buster. He knew she would feel responsible as soon as she saw his poor sister. The woman didn't belong here and would certainly end up catching her hand in the vicious rods of the bambeater.

'Hattie's looking after you today, Lou. But it'll all come back to you,' Old Buttercup quavered, patting Lou's arm and placing her at the machine. She shuffled off to her chair by the doors, where she sat observing the workers like a bumbling queen bee.

Lou didn't move. She fingered the edge of the machine and Hattie was about to leave her station to show her what to do when, with a sudden firmness of purpose, the woman reached into the bin of rabbit furs and plucked one out. She examined it briefly for flaws, pushed the red button to start up the bamboo rods and, once they were at full speed, attached the small fur to the belt, then bent for another pelt and then another. Hattie looked on in amazement. Vera had told her that Lou had once been the fastest worker in the factory, working her way up to supervisor in an unusually short time. Some memory of the job must have embedded itself in her wasted muscles, for the automatic movements came quicker and quicker until she was outstripping Hattie in the number of bins she was getting through. After a single morning's work, Loony Lou had proved to Hattie the truth of what Buster had said. While working at a bambeater all day could drive you nuts, you really didn't have to be entirely sane to work one in the first place.

However, it wasn't long before Hattie realized that Lou wasn't earning herself any friends on the floor. She was so productive that some of the other girls had started to whisper at the amount of bins she was getting through. After all, on a three-day week there was only so much work to go round.

Hattie heard Doris Axmouth stirring up the girls with her usual venom. 'She ain't doing 'em right!' Doris complained to Old Buttercup. 'They're all crooked on the belt, look! They'll only have to come back to us to do 'em over again.'

Old Buttercup rose from her chair. She approached in a sort of zigzag, which was all her arthritic legs allowed. She looked the length of Lou's bambeater and sorted through the cleaned pelts, before nodding.

'Getting on all right, Lou?' she asked unnecessarily and then, lifting her wobbly old chin, she said in a tremulous voice to

Doris, 'She's showing you up, Dotty. She'll be earning twice what you do this week.'

Hattie's impatience with Old Buttercup evaporated in a second as the whisperers were silenced, and when the dinner-time hooter sounded Hattie was happy to lead Lou down to the canteen. They found places at Buster's table and Hattie gave him an encouraging nod. 'She's doing fine,' she whispered.

There was no choice at all in the canteen today. They all had identical plates of cubed, grey-looking fish called Snoek, which tasted as bad as it sounded. The accompaniment was a single potato and a spoonful of over-boiled cabbage. Hattie wrinkled her nose but was hungry enough to try anything after her long morning's work. Lou pushed the food around for a few minutes, before tipping hers on to Buster's plate.

'He'll eat anything, my brother. He's a right gannet,' she said, covering her mouth as she spoke, which Hattie had noticed was a habitual attempt to hide her bad teeth. She took it as an invitation to talk to Lou.

'So, how have you found it, coming back to the Alaska?' she asked.

Lou hesitated. 'Not too bad.' She looked at Buster, as if for approval, before turning her eyes towards the canteen window and the falling snow. There was an awkward silence.

Clara stood up. 'I'm going to the nursery to see my Martha. She's only six months,' she said to Lou. 'She misses me…'

The woman gazed at Clara, an expression of haunting incomprehension on her face, and said, 'I think mine's six months.' Then she looked at her brother for confirmation. 'That's right, ain't it, Buster?'

Buster's face clouded with sadness. 'No, Lou, you're getting mixed up,' he said.

Clara gave Hattie a puzzled look, which she answered with a small shake of her head. Whatever fog Lou existed in obviously came and went, for the woman who'd worked so efficiently up on the factory floor seemed to have disappeared completely.

* * *

Ronnie woke with tears frozen on his cheeks. He'd been dreaming about his sister Sue and the time their mum fetched them home from where they'd been evacuated. Dad had come home on leave too. He'd brought them this massive bar of chocolate, more than Ronnie had seen in his whole life and their Sue had never even eaten chocolate. They all stood round gawping at her, waiting till she'd tasted it, and then this great big smile spread across her face and she'd crammed the lot in, till Mum said she'd be sick and took it away. Sue had chocolate plastered all around her gob, and that's where he'd been in his dream – laughing at her little pink tongue trying to lick all the chocolate off her own chubby chops; it just wasn't long enough, and the more frustrated she got the more he'd laughed, and then she'd started crying so he gave her some of his. That was the best time he could ever remember. Before everything got blown up – Sue and Nan and Grandad in their house in Spa Road. Before Mum told him Dad wouldn't be coming home on leave no more. He'd been laughing in the dream, but suddenly Sue had turned into one of them china dolls with its face all smashed. Then he'd woken up crying like a baby, the tears cold on his face, wishing he could have stayed in that happy place, but he couldn't. He didn't have nothing nice to dream about no more. He was pretty sure all the happy times were gone for good.

He was living mostly on the Spa Road bombsite in the shell of a house that had been somewhere near Nan and Grandad's. The windows were all blown out and half the walls were gone, but he'd done up one room pretty good. Found rusty nails and boards to patch up the smashed windows and some plywood to make new walls. The days weren't so bad. At least the place gave him some shelter from the bitter wind. He could climb up the half-shattered staircase to the first floor and keep a lookout for Dickie Harper. But at night he preferred to decamp to the safety of one of the tanning pits near Grange Road. There he made a nest of old roof felting and a pile of leather pelts he'd found. They stank, but he felt safe enough with the escape tunnel should Dickie Harper ever come looking. But the last couple of nights had been bitter enough to freeze the pelts stiff and this morning his fingers were so cold the pain made him yelp. Nutty Norman had smuggled out his dead grandad's old coat and bobble hat. They were a bit big for him, but Ronnie had rolled himself in the coat each night and had managed to keep out the cold, until now. Snow had piled into the stone tanning pit and, this morning, icy air was scraping at his lungs.

He was hungry all the time. His mates sometimes brought him grub from their mums' kitchen cupboards, a bit of bread or a potato, and Frankie would fetch him cooked fish from his own tea. But they couldn't risk taking too much or their mums would notice the empty spots in the larders. Today him and the Barnham Street boys were going to the river, to raid barges for peanuts. They'd build a fire and roast them on an upturned dustbin lid. He could almost taste the sweet, burned flavour of the nuts, still hot from their shells. But peanuts wouldn't be enough to keep him going for another day. He needed to move on to somewhere warmer and he needed to get some proper food.

There was somewhere he could get grub – but he never liked going there. It wasn't too bad in the summer, but in brass-monkey weather it was no soddin' joke. You had to take your clothes off, and it was too bloody cold to be standing about stark naked while the man smiled and smiled, pissing about taking photos. It wouldn't be so bad if he just took one, but no. Move here, move there, sit on the stool, lay on the sofa. And then there were the other things he had to do, which he didn't like at all. Not that the smiling man had ever touched him, and if he did, Ronnie would kick him in the nuts and run for it. No, he just took the photos and afterwards he'd give Ronnie a handful of sweets. The geezer must be getting them under the counter 'cause his ration never seemed to run out. When Ronnie started getting so skinny that his ribs stuck out, the man gave him money instead, told him to go down the café for Spam fritters and chips, said the punters didn't want kids looking like they come out of Belsen. God, he could do with some Spam and chips right now. But that smiling bastard give him the creeps and he didn't want to go on his own. Nutty Norman and the others who used to come with him in the summer said it was too cold, and they wouldn't go and freeze their arses off. Well, they had mums and dads who made sure they got enough grub, so they didn't have to, did they?

His stomach grumbled and pain gripped it, migrating to his throat, till even his jaws ached for food. 'Sod it, I can't get no colder than I am now.'

He scrunched his body into the drainage pipe and slithered along its freezing length till he emerged into the cellar of the Spa Road bombed house. He could never tell now where exactly his grandparents' place had been, but he'd once uncovered an old china pot on the bombsite which he was sure had lived under Grandad's bed. It had something written on the inside, which he could never make out, but it used to make Grandad laugh. Sometimes he came across chunks of wall covered in a flowery wallpaper that he knew used to be in his nan's kitchen. Mum went to all the bombsites looking for Sue, but she always ended up back here, in Spa Road.

Though they all called him 'the smiling man', Ronnie knew his real name was Wardick. He'd once sneaked a look at an envelope addressed to him. The house was in a bomb-damaged terrace down by the river and usually Wardick couldn't get Ronnie in there quick enough. Today was different. When the smiling man opened the door there was no smile. His round podgy face looked shocked instead, and behind him Ronnie could see a woman. The smiling man shifted his position to block the woman's view and he hissed at Ronnie, 'Sod off!'

'Don't you want to take no photos today?' Ronnie asked, perplexed. He'd never been turned away before.

The man grabbed his jumper. 'Clear off, you little tyke. I've got company.' And he slammed the door shut.

Ronnie kicked it in disgust. 'Shit!' he thought, a cramp of hunger almost doubling him up. There was nothing for it. He would have to go home. He'd be taking a risk – the Harpers might be looking for him there. But the thought of his mum spurred him on. He wanted to see her looking happy again. Perhaps she'd even be smiling at the new baby? He wasn't jealous. He just wanted Mum to look up at him when he walked through the door and say, 'Hello, Ronnie, love, where you been, you street raker?' Just like she used to.

He made his way via back streets, then across another vast stretch of wasteland along the river to Barnham Street. He crept round the back of the buildings, where the huge square bins beneath the dust chutes were overflowing with rubbish that smelled worse than Pissy Pants. Barnham Street always seemed to be last on the list for the dustcart, but it was much worse since the snow had kept the carts in the depot. As he scooted round the big bins he tripped and speared his knee on a pile of smashed beer bottles. He pulled out a shard and, ignoring the pain, made a dash for the stairwell. Snow puffed up around his pounding feet. He prayed the Harpers had no spies out and threw himself up the icy staircase. His heart was banging against his ribs as he reached the third landing, but now that he was sure he'd evaded Dickie Harper he was desperate to get indoors.

He pulled up the key through the letterbox and crept in. Careful not to wake the new baby, he made his way through the front kitchen to his mum's bedroom. She was sitting with her back to him, staring out of the window at the brick wall of the railway viaduct only feet away. It struck him that there was nothing at all to look at. Perhaps she'd fallen asleep. He touched her shoulder and she turned slowly. Her face was red, her eyes puffy. She'd been crying.

'Oh, Vic, thank gawd you're home. I done a terrible thing,' she cried. 'I lost another baby!'

Ronnie had been shivering with cold before, but now something burned in him, white-hot like the heart of one of his best bonfires. 'You effin nutty old cow, I'm not Dad, I'm *me*!' he roared and pushed Lou so that she fell to the floor. He ran to the chest of drawers. The lowest drawer was still pulled out and lined with a blanket for the baby, but the drawer was empty. He didn't know which to hate her for more, that she'd lost the baby and the chance for them to be happy, or that she still didn't know his name.

'What you done with our baby, you stupid mare?' He kneeled down beside her and shook his mother hard, so that her head wobbled and banged on the lino flooring, and then her eyes rolled back in her head and she went floppy, so that he couldn't rouse her.

'Oh Jesus, no, don't tell me I've effin' well killed her too!' he wailed.

# 9

## *Lost Mothers*

### *March 1947*

Martha was crying. Clara lay there for a second; she was so tired and the effort required to get out of the bed seemed almost beyond her. But with Hattie sleeping only feet away and having to get up so early for office cleaning, it wasn't fair she should be woken up. Clara swung her legs out of the bed. Martha still woke for a feed in the middle of the night and sometimes it felt as if the baby was draining her lifeblood, not just her milk. When she'd first returned from Australia she'd been living on high alert, just to keep them both alive. But now they had friends, shelter and food, however meagre, it seemed some tightly coiled resolve was loosening, replaced by a lassitude which made it hard to keep up the daily toil at the Alaska as well as these nightly demands. Perhaps the weather played its part. Every element of her life had seemed frozen since she'd been back: her heart, her hopes, her dreams, everything except Martha, who was full of movement and change and warmth. She could never resent her demands, and sometimes she thought that Martha was the only thing in her life that was truly alive.

Saturday afternoons and Sundays were spent on hard physical work, but she'd come to like the routine of it. They'd all agreed on a rota for common tasks. Hers were to organize the children into wood-collecting and cleaning teams. Then there was the repair work on their own hut to manage. Hattie's new job had provided money to buy lino, which they had laid themselves, struggling to cut and fit it with fingers numb from cold.

Now, she dragged herself up, cold seeping into her bones. She swore they creaked as she lifted Martha from the cot, which was something else that Hattie's new job had supplied. Clara didn't know how she'd ever repay her. But whenever she offered, Hattie simply shrugged and said that some day she might need help herself, which Clara couldn't believe. Nothing seemed to daunt Hattie.

Clara took Martha into her own army surplus bed and wrapped them both tightly in the old grey army blankets, remembering another such narrow bed, the one she'd slept in aboard the 'bride ship'. It had been filled to the gunnels with girls such as herself, going out to meet their servicemen husbands in New Zealand or Australia, half a world away.

Now the whistling wind blew unseasonal flurries of snow against the windowpanes, telling her how far she'd come from the blue skies of Australia. Here she was, lying in bed fully dressed, swaddled in jumper and coat, Martha nestling into her, snoring gently after her feed. Half asleep, Clara felt herself drift away to the bride ship, feeling again the damp warmth of a hundred other sleeping bodies around her, rocked in the bed, with the rise and fall of the ship's deck beneath her, a deck which had, in the ship's former incarnation as a luxury liner, once been a well-sprung dance floor. But they'd been warned this would be a strictly 'austerity cruise', all vestiges of opulence stripped from the vessel in order to cram in as many women as possible.

Her quarters had been in the old ballroom, now a maze of canvas partitions, giving each woman minimal privacy with scant space for a bed and suitcase. Somehow the central glitter ball of the old ballroom had escaped the bride ship conversions and still swung high above her bed. Each night she'd stared up at it, imagining pre-war days of glamour and ease, couples circling the floor in a romantic haze. She could even remember the thoughts that arose as the waves rocked her. She would dream of the day she'd see Barry again, her vision firmly focused on her own romantic future.

Leaving everything behind hadn't been hard. He'd so quickly made himself her whole world that she'd wanted no other. They'd been married only briefly before he shipped out from England so she'd only ever known the bright, sparkling, mesmerizing excitement of being in love. That was the glitter ball that hung over every experience, even her father's disappointment when he saw the colour of Barry's skin, or her mother's disgust as she told her they were to be married. She had been hypnotized by that spinning light and somehow, like the glittering ball in the centre of the room, it had survived. She'd kept it in her heart, through the rejection at home and the long voyage out, and all the unknowns ahead of her.

She smiled in her half-sleep at that feeling which was still able to warm her heart. But then another scene flashed across her vision. The Sydney dockside coming into view, herself and hundreds of other girls crushed against the side rail, waving at men they loved but whose faces were indistinguishable from one another. And though she hadn't spotted Barry she'd waved at nothing, out of sheer joy at the thought of being reunited with him, the dream so near, she could reach out across the narrowing strip of water and touch it. And then she'd landed, and all around women had flung themselves into waiting arms, lost in kisses that seemed to last longer than all their separations combined. The girls she'd come to know during the voyage gradually dispersed with their men and new families, to catch trains and boats and buses, to spread themselves the length and breadth of Australia, while she stood as if frozen to the dockside, waiting. When she'd realized he wasn't coming, the glitter ball crashed to the floor and her eyes jerked open.

Why hadn't she got on the next boat home? He hadn't been there to meet her. That was surely all the warning she needed. Yet the ties were already too tight, the dazzle too bright. She went looking for him. Betty Almond, the other girl from Bermondsey on the bride ship, took pity on her and invited her to stay with her new husband's Australian family. Barry had worked in the docks before the war, she knew that much, so Betty's father-in-law put the word out. It wasn't hard to find him, and for Clara it wasn't hard to forgive him. He'd been called away, he said, out of the city to where his mother had been taken dangerously ill and had later died. Clara mourned with him and loved him more than ever, knowing that she'd done the right thing, coming here to meet the other half of herself. Barry's father was long dead, so now she would be everything to him. It was only after Martha was born that she discovered that her new husband wasn't as alone in the world as she'd believed.

He'd often been away on labouring jobs, supplementing the dock work so they could have a proper home instead of their two rooms in a tumbledown house. At first, she flatly refused to believe it when Betty Almond told her the rumours about Barry's 'other wife'. It was beyond Clara's comprehension how some people could gossip so wickedly. But his absences grew longer and his pay packet never seemed to increase for all the 'extra work' he was doing. With her baby in her arms, she followed him one weekend – a few streets away, not far, but by the end of that journey her world had shifted on its axis.

She saw him kiss the woman who opened the door before they went inside. It was the sort of lingering kiss he gave her after an absence 'working'. She'd needed no more convincing. She marched over with the baby and knocked on the door. And when he saw her, his face crumpled, his smiling eyes shedding so many tears they fell like a little waterfall down his full cheeks. She walked away, ignoring his pleas for her to stay, and all she could think of was how far away she was from home. She needed to get back to Bermondsey. However harsh her parents had been in their judgements, they surely wouldn't turn her away when they saw the child.

*Stupid little girl...* that's how she thought of herself now. She groaned at her blindness, at the ease with which she'd thrown herself away and the foolish hope which had brought her home. Martha stirred, whimpering, her lower lip trembling as if at some bad dream, and she hushed her daughter. 'Shhh, Mummy's here, Mummy's always here,' she murmured, knowing that she'd done it again – given her heart away completely.

Perhaps Hattie had heard the cries or her groan, or the snow plopping from the corrugated roof had woken her, but Clara saw her sit up in bed.

'Are you OK?' she whispered. 'Is Martha all right?'

'Hmm,' Clara replied. 'I can't sleep.'

'Shall I light the lamp?'

They should be saving oil, but Clara didn't want to be alone with those feelings that had been keeping her awake. 'All right.'

She heard Hattie get out of bed and watched as she lit the lamp, the spreading golden light immediately making her feel warmer.

'Why can't you sleep?' Hattie was back in bed, sitting with the covers drawn up under her chin.

'Oh, I don't know. I was thinking about Barry.'

'Does it still hurt?'

'Yes. But that's not really what keeps me awake. I worry about Martha. She's never going to have a dad and she'll never have it easy here. I look at her when she's asleep, and I love her so much – that's what hurts. To think people don't see her at all – they just see her brown skin. I wish I could protect her.' She felt tears prick her eyes. 'Hattie, do you think you can love a child too much?' she whispered, afraid of the answer.

'You're asking me? I'm the worst person to ask about kids, love. Most people would say no, of course you can't love a child too much.'

'But what do *you* say?'

Hattie was silent for a while. 'Honestly? I think you can... Look at Lou, poor woman. She's gone mad because she loved her Sue so much she couldn't bear the pain of losing her. And look at your mum and dad...'

Clara was taken aback. 'What's Mum and Dad got to do with

it? They don't love me at all!' Martha stirred and she lowered her voice. 'What do you mean?'

'Imagine that's you.' Hattie pointed to Martha. 'There she is, the apple of your eye, and don't you think your mum and dad was the same with you? Making up all the stories about what you're going to be and how you'll always love them, and then you grow up and disappoint them and that's that. You're the ungrateful child who threw it all right back in their loving faces... 'course they chucked you out.'

Clara had got used to Hattie's blunt way of talking. 'Thanks, Hattie. That's cheered me up no end.' She felt sick, perhaps because she recognized the kernel of truth in what Hattie had said.

'Why don't you try again, with your mum and dad? Go and see them,' Hattie advised. And for an instant the glitter ball started turning and the hypnotic lights brought memories to mind, days when her father's face had lit up whenever she'd come into a room, times as a child when she'd skipped along by his side, her hand firmly held in his. Perhaps Hattie was right and they had simply loved her too much.

*

Clara struggled to push the pram along the icy pavement where old snow falls had frozen into ruts and mounds. It had been hard to avoid passing her parents' house in the Square when she was living in the basement; she'd had to walk past it practically every day on her way to the nursery in Fort Road. Sometimes she managed to keep her eyes fixed firmly ahead, but more often she would sneak a look at her old home to see if someone were looking out of the window. Her parents had the first floor, and now she carefully bundled Martha in blankets and carried her up the front steps. They were coated with ice, and she'd noticed her father had sprinkled salt on them to try to break it up. Even so, her feet slipped from under her and she stumbled. For one breath-stopping second she thought Martha would fall, but she righted herself. At the front door she paused. Perhaps this was a sign that she was riding for another fall. It was stupid to have come back. Why had she listened to Hattie?

In any case there was no answer to her knock on the front door, and she was about to leave when she saw the front curtain twitched aside then quickly fall back.

'Mum! Ain't you goin' to let us in? She's your only grand-daughter!' she called, knowing she could be heard.

Whatever Martha did in the future to disappoint her, she knew she could never treat her like this. Her parents weren't at all like her. She was finished with them. She picked her way back down the treacherous steps and on to the icy pavement. But one of the pram wheels became stuck in an icy pile that someone had shovelled to one side, and as she tried to push through it her feet skidded away from her. She grabbed at the pram, which came tumbling down with her as she fell to the glassy pavement. Martha shot out of the pram on to the icy street. Her daughter's wail ripped through Clara.

'Oh, my baby, no!' A wave of nausea gripped her, the blood in her veins ran colder than the ice she kneeled upon. She shuffled forward on her knees, ignoring the ice burns, desperate to get to Martha. 'Please God, let her be all right.'

She fumbled for her child, but before she could reach her two hands grasped Martha and lifted her from the ground. Clara looked up with a smile of gratitude which froze on her face.

'Give her to me!' She held out impatient hands, getting to her feet. 'I don't want you touching her.'

Her mother hesitated. 'I wouldn't wish the child any harm.'

Martha's screams had continued as Clara examined her head and tested limbs while her mother looked on.

'What are you talking about, you wouldn't wish her any harm? You sent us away into the night. We had nowhere to go, *nowhere*!' As Clara's voice rose, her mother looked nervously up and down the row of houses. 'It's not what I wanted... it was your father... you know what he's like if I cross him.'

'Codswallop! I'm a mother now, don't forget, and I'd leave

any man in a second if he didn't treat my child right… and that's exactly what I did. So don't try and blame Dad.'

All the while Clara had been talking she'd been rocking Martha, but her raised voice had only exacerbated her baby's distress. Checking that there was no physical damage done, Clara quickly tucked her back into the pram and pushed it into motion. 'Don't worry, Mum, you won't have to worry about upsetting Dad no more. You won't be seeing me or my child again.'

'Don't go like that, Clara…' she heard her mother calling, but it was not a plea that convinced her, for she noted it was quiet enough not to disturb the neighbours.

When Clara got back to the squatters' colony, Hattie was trying to choose what to wear for the Alaska fashion show. But as soon as she saw Clara's face, she put down the dress and went to her. 'Whatever's happened? Did you fall over?'

Clara nodded and, letting the tears fall, explained what had happened with her mother.

'That's my fault,' Hattie said. 'I shouldn't have encouraged you to go there.'

'It's not your fault. It's hers. But that's it, Hattie. I've got no family now. It's just me and Martha. I'm better off on me own.'

'And me… you and Martha have always got me,' Hattie said, almost tentatively.

'I don't want to be ungrateful, Hattie. But you don't owe us nothing.'

'All the same,' said Hattie, 'I'm here.'

\* \* \*

Ronnie had run from his dead mother, out into the wind, his long straw hair flying, sleet pellets biting his face and stinging his ears. He knew he was crying because warm rivulets streaked his cold cheeks and then froze solid. His only defence against the snowstorm came from his too-small school blazer and a threadbare jumper unravelling at wrists and elbows. His legs beneath the grey shorts were frozen to white marble. He skidded round corners, plimsolls sliding on icy pavements. At kerbs he sloshed through snow till his feet burned with cold. He ran in unthinking panic with no idea where to go. There was nowhere. His mum was dead. They were all sodding dead. Nearing the end of Crucifix Lane he came to a halt, his chest heaving, wincing with every breath as ice crept down into his lungs. He doubled over, holding his side, then fell to his knees. Curling into a ball, burrowing deep into the snow, he laid his cheek on its chill pillow and scrunched into the lea of the railway viaduct.

It was in this very spot that he had killed Pissy Pants. What did his Sunday School teacher used to say – *an eye for an eye, a tooth for a tooth*. He'd never really understood what she was going on about until now. He had to pay. And it wouldn't be such a bad thing to die here.

'Sorry,' he whispered into the snow. 'Sorry about Pissy Pants.' And then he sighed. It would be just like going to sleep, and when he woke up Mum would be there, with Sue and all his family. Ronnie's thin blue lips settled into a smile and he closed his eyes.

⋆ ⋆ ⋆

Hattie arrived early. She poked her head through the door and saw that the entire ground-floor sales room had been cleared for the show. She walked into the large showroom, which took up almost the entire ground floor of the building. Normally the space was filled with long rails full of fur coats, but these had been rolled back against the walls, leaving room for rows of chairs arranged either side of a raised central catwalk. She skirted the edge of the room, brushing past the rails of coffee- and champagne-dyed minks, chocolate musquash and silver squirrels, then skimming her palm over the near-black sables and curly astrakhans, and burying her fingers in the blue fox furs and chestnut-striped beaver lambs. It was hard to believe that all the smelly, oily, dirty pelts piled high in the Alaska factory, passing endlessly from drum room to dyers, nailers, bambeaters, shearers, groovers and knifers, had anything to do with such sleek, shining elegance. Yet they were the product of countless hours of hard graft, which Hattie felt daily in her aching back, her sore finger bones, her throbbing feet.

A fortune in furs lined the room, ranked in all their luxurious glory. But she knew the truth was very far from the appearance – this was all pre-war stock. The government still insisted on imposing a luxury goods tax and wartime austerity measures on the fur trade, even though the chance of Hitler rising from the grave, or turning up in South America eager to start World War Three, were slim. This fashion show was part of a plan to get the factory stocked with orders, ready for the day when the ban on luxury goods would be lifted.

She made her way behind the curtain to the screened off dressing room, where some of the girls were already in an excited huddle, touching up their make-up and checking for ladders in the precious nylons that had been supplied by the company. Hattie had avoided chatting too much to them at the rehearsals. They were all office girls and she didn't want any awkward questions from them about which department she worked in. She only had to keep her secret from Crosbie until the fashion show was over. Once the cash was in her pocket, she'd revert to Alaska girl. By the time she'd finished her make-up and put on the new nylons, she could hear a rising chatter coming from the sales room. The buyers were arriving.

Hattie went to the curtain and peeked out. The audience of buyers had been carefully selected; it was even rumoured the royal furriers were to be present. The factory staff committee had suggested it might be good for morale if some of the Alaska girls were invited to the show, and there in the crowd she spotted some workmates, but noticed it was only a hand-picked few, she guessed those deemed pretty and presentable enough not to stand out as such. Three young girls from shearing were there and a couple of her old mates from the grooving room, as well as Maisie and Clara. No Old Buttercups, no Lous, but she was furious to see Doris Axmouth walk in with her friend Marjie and pointedly ignore the spare seats next to Clara. No doubt Doris would find fault with her performance, but Hattie wasn't bothered what tales the acid-tongued woman told at the factory about the show. She was, however, beginning to feel more nervous now. What if she tripped up? She shuddered at the memory of the long mink catching in the heel of her shoe during a rehearsal, but just then Maisie waved at her excitedly and, instinctively, she waved back.

She felt a hand circle her waist and pull her away from the curtain. Surprised, she turned to find herself uncomfortably close to Crosbie. As the curtain swished closed, she noticed he didn't let go. 'We don't want to draw attention to the little factory girls out there! The buyers are here for a touch of class and glamour...' He let his hand fall a little lower, and grinned. 'So am I for that matter.'

He was attractive but he knew it too well, and though her instinct was to slap the self-satisfied smile from his face, she couldn't afford to make a scene. Instead she concentrated on the two weeks' wages she'd be getting for one afternoon's work and how Clara had to get out of her freezing bed every night to feed the baby, her teeth chattering louder than the baby's cries. The money would help to fund insulation materials for their hut.

She put her palms on his shoulders and fixed him with wide eyes as she slipped out of his grasp.

'Don't worry, Mr Crosbie, I've heard that Bermondsey girls are known for their smartness. Besides, didn't you only invite the pretty ones?'

He laughed, showing teeth white as a film star's. He whispered in her ear, 'I'm sure the Alaska girls are a credit to the factory, but not a patch on you. You've set the standard very high...' And he turned away to round up the models into their order of appearance.

She felt flustered by the encounter and uncomfortable, pretending to be someone she wasn't. She wanted to get by on her merits, just as she had in the army. But the Alaska was never going to allow her that. Perhaps playing the game with Crosbie might not be such a hardship and who knew where it might lead? She shrugged on the mink coat, feeling its gold silk lining slip elegantly around her figure. The weight and the warmth encompassed her, and as the curtains parted and she walked on to the catwalk, she tried to imagine herself the owner of such a garment, instead of just its maker.

She kept her gaze firmly fixed about a foot above the audience, focusing on the door at the far end of the room. She paused at the end of the catwalk and, as she'd practised, put one hand on her hip, opening the coat to reveal its shining underside. She put the collar up and spun round, before gliding back, toes pointing slightly outward. Crosbie had been quite a task master, insisting they comport themselves like real models. Out of the corner of her eye, she saw Doris smirking and Maisie giggling. Clara's pale oval face was full of encouragement, but Hattie stopped herself from smiling at her. Back behind the curtain, Crosbie pulled her to one side.

'I need you to go again, now! The silly girl with the sable has just been sick as a dog – stage fright. Here...' He helped her off with the mink and slipped a Russian sable over her shoulders. There was a stirring in the audience at the pause; perhaps it seemed to them as if the show was over. 'Just go on like that, you look stunning...' he said hurriedly, giving her a little push, and she realized it was the first time she actually believed anything he'd said to her.

She looked back as the curtains parted, aware of his ice-blue eyes fixed on her, and she blanched, while his gaze held hers for a moment too long. She knew in an instant what was happening, but if she was falling, she was determined to break her fall as soon as she left the catwalk. She strode out into the lighted room and let the expensive black fur trail behind her, to gasps from the audience. Enjoying the profligacy, the sheer wastefulness, the immoral extravagance of dragging hundreds of pounds' worth of fur coat along the floor, she swung the coat up and walked back with it over her shoulders. She saw smiles and inclined heads from the buyers. She saw them bend over their programmes to make notes. Crosbie came out to escort her from the catwalk and said under his breath, 'Well, I think you may just have landed us a few buyers out there. I'm off to grab some of those orders, but we do need to discuss your position within the company. Come and see me afterwards...'

She watched him go, elation at her triumph quickly giving way to frustration and fear. How had he found her out? No doubt she'd be in big trouble for letting him believe she worked in the office. She'd already explained to Maisie and Clara why she couldn't acknowledge them and had seen them leaving. But as she turned towards the dressing room, she bumped into the remaining group of Alaska girls filing out, with Doris Axmouth and her friend Marjie at their head.

'Ohhh, look, Marjie, it's "Miss mutton-dressed-as-lamb 1947" ... see you back on the bambeater tomorrow!' Doris deliberately raised her voice and Hattie felt her face burning as she glanced across the room at Crosbie, who was holding up a silver squirrel bolero for an interested buyer. She stifled her normal quick retort and gave the two women a bold smile. 'I've got the rest of the day off.' She kept her voice low, smiling all the time. 'Models are invited to the after-show cocktail party,' she said, sweeping past them, still with the Russian sable draped over her shoulder.

The cocktail party was a figment of her imagination. The firm could afford no such extravagance. Besides, finding the ingredients would have been quite a challenge. But she did have the rest of the day off, which was good enough. She thought she might take her 'small remuneration' down to the wood yard near Southwark Park and order some sheets of plywood for the hut. She was about to leave the offices when Crosbie came hurrying after her.

'Not so fast, Miss Wright. Don't run off – I told you to come and find me!'

'Sorry – rushing for a train...' She pointed at an imaginary watch.

'Tomorrow then, my office, ten o'clock?'

'That's too late for me,' she said and was flustered when, not to be put off, he came back with, 'Eight then, eight sharp.'

She picked her way along the well-worn snow ruts in Upper Thames Street, caught in the lunchtime crush of office workers seeking sandwiches and teas. She pushed against the tide of bowler hats and overcoats and brass-buttoned messenger uniforms, only able to breathe when she was on London Bridge. Halfway along the bridge she stopped, and leaning her elbows on the parapet, she looked down at the swift running oily waters. Rubbish, tipped from wharf sides or barges, bobbed and churned around the bridge pilings along with chunks of floating ice. She felt her life beginning to swirl from her grasp. What on earth was she thinking? She'd almost believed it herself, this stupid pretence that she was something other than a factory girl, but if Crosbie wanted to talk about her position in the company he'd obviously got wind of her subterfuge. If he got nasty and reported her to management, she'd probably get the sack from the factory and then where would she be? Her only hope was to miss the appointment tomorrow and pray he just forgot all about her. It was annoying; he annoyed her. But much as she needed the money for herself and Clara, she'd just have to pack in the cleaning job tomorrow and leave well before she was due to see Crosbie at eight. It wouldn't be difficult to avoid him. In an uncertain world, the one thing she could be sure of was that the paths of Crosbie and those of the early morning office cleaners would never cross.

# 10

## *Lost Children*

### March 1947

Hattie stowed away the mop, bucket and scrubbing brush in the basement broom cupboard and went in search of the cleaning supervisor.

'Sorry to let you down, but I've got to pack the job in,' she explained.

The cleaning supervisor shrugged, unconcerned. 'You didn't last long. Too much like hard work?'

'I can't do the early mornings any more,' she lied, all the while resenting Crosbie for her loss of income.

It was still only seven o'clock and if she slipped out by the basement exit, she would be long gone before he turned up. She bundled up in her beaver lamb and Cossack hat. This morning she'd felt like a rubber ball, she was wearing so many layers of vests and jumpers. Once out in the early morning City street she gave herself up to the cold and began to enjoy the skyline of City churches all coated with an icing of snow. She crossed to the river side of Upper Thames Street and, passing Mansion House, she came to the snow-spattered river, where barges and lighters were weighed down by cargoes of snow. She was hurrying, head down, when she collided with a passer-by and looked up into the amused blue eyes of Crosbie.

'I believe you're going the wrong way, Miss Wright!' he said, grasping her elbow and turning her round. Before she could protest, he'd frog-marched her across the road, weaving through the opaque blur of snow, avoiding slow-moving cars and steering her down a side street.

'Sorry, Mr Crosbie, I couldn't stay for our appointment,' she protested, but he ignored her.

'Not a problem,' he said. 'I'll buy you that coffee I promised you the other morning. You look like you need warming up.'

In minutes they had reached the Kardomah coffee house. He pushed open the door and a warm blast of roasted coffee-bean aroma hit her. She thought of the unheated factory floor waiting for her at the Alaska and gave in. If she was going to lose her job, then at least she'd get a coffee out of it. 'I can't stop long... just a quick one.'

'Always in such a hurry! You must have a very important job to be so in demand...' He smiled broadly and her heart sank. He was playing with her. She was obviously his morning's little amusement.

The place was packed, but he was the sort of man who would always find a seat in a crowded café. When they had cups of steaming froth in front of them, Hattie sipped the strong brew, expecting fake chicory, but was astonished to taste the real thing.

'Is this what I think it is?'

He inclined his head to the pretty girl making the coffees. 'Under the counter. Young Julia always gives me the good stuff – for a price, of course.'

Hattie took a deep draught of the rare bitter-sweet blend. 'Yes,' she said, lifting her eyes from the cup. 'I suppose there's always a price.'

He propped his elbows on to the table and leaned forward. 'Sometimes it's worth it.' He gulped the steaming coffee. 'Now, do you want a job in the sales office or not?'

'A job?' Her mouth hung open and, uninvited, he reached over to wipe foam from her top lip.

'Yes! Working for me. Partly in the showroom with clients, partly admin. What do you say?'

She'd wanted something like this so badly, an office job, a

chance to escape the factory. And yet now it felt impossible, the burden of secrecy spoiling the prospect already.

'What's wrong? I thought you'd jump at the chance.'

'It's taken me a bit by surprise, Mr Crosbie. To be honest, I thought you were going to get me the sack, not offer me a job!'

'Why?'

It was now or never. She saw her dreams of an office job evaporating as the confession was forming in her mind, but he interrupted her before she could speak.

'Listen, I don't give a damn what your current position is.' He stretched out his hand. She noticed his nails were perfectly clipped and buffed. He lifted her own hand for inspection.

'You're a beautiful woman, but I've worked in the fur trade long enough to know the hands of a factory girl. These told me everything you didn't. What is it, grooving, shearing?' His index finger stroked hers, checking for callouses. 'The knifer?' He turned her palm over. 'Surely not bambeating?' He had a teasing smile on his lips.

Hot with embarrassment, she pulled her hand away. 'I'm not a bloody horse for you to inspect. Keep your sodding hands to yourself.' He had made a fool of her and she was about to march out, not caring if she got her cards that day, when he clutched at her hand, pulling her back down.

'Oh, sit down!' He laughed. 'I didn't peg you for the sensitive type. Listen, I'm offering you a *new* job! One where you can keep these lilywhite.' He rubbed a thumb across her hand and his smiling mouth snapped shut. 'Just say yes, and we'll get on fine. None of this needs to get back to Chris Harper. I'll manage him and arrange the transfer.'

Still she hesitated.

'The wage will be four times what you can earn on, what is it, the bambeater? Interested?'

Four times! She could buy new boots and decent off-ration dresses that didn't fall apart after a few wears like the horrible utility clothes she was forced to wear at the moment. She could buy enough black-market coal to keep them warm until the summer finally arrived, she could do up the hut like a palace. She might even one day become a manager herself. Could she put up with Crosbie for all that?

'It's the bambeater, and yes, I am interested,' she said finally. And Crosbie patted her hand, satisfied.

*

Hattie had known the hardest part would be telling Buster, but she hadn't anticipated this long-drawn-out tussle. They'd been arguing for over half an hour and still he refused to accept it.

'You can't leave and that's that. I need you here!'

'Don't you want to see me get on in the world, Buster?'

'Of course I do, but I've seen the way that Crosbie feller carries on and I don't like him. Last year we had a joint factory and office staff Christmas party – morale boosting and all that. He was all over our young girls, kids of fifteen, sixteen. It was a bloody disgrace. 'Course he gets away with it.'

She put on her world-weary face. 'I'm not sixteen any more, Buster, haven't you noticed? Besides, I've fended off worse than him in the army!'

Buster turned down the corners of his mouth. 'I'll miss you though.'

She hugged him. 'But I'll be in the social club every night, love, so you won't get a chance to miss me. Still my dancing partner?'

She grabbed Buster and forced him to give her a reluctant twirl round.

'The only thing I'm worried about is leaving Clara and Lou to the wolves… or the she-wolf. Can't you get them off bambeating? Then at least they won't have to face Dotty Axmouth every day.'

Buster promised he would try and Hattie went back upstairs to the bambeating room to break the news to Clara and Lou. Clara's unfeigned look of delight was refreshing after Buster's damp response to her new job. But Lou wasn't at her machine and Clara hadn't seen her at all that morning. Lou had been drifting disconcertingly between periods of lucidity and lostness recently, and there was never any warning as to which she might be.

'I'd better tell Buster she's not come in,' Hattie said. 'For all we know, she's been on her midnight wanderings again and not come home. God knows how her boy manages to drag himself up.'

That dinner time Hattie and Buster went to Barnham Street to check on Lou. However well Lou had done on the bambeater, Hattie still thought the woman wasn't fit to be at work.

'It's just as well you didn't put her on the knifer or she'd have no fingers left by now,' Hattie said as they crunched through the snow, icy breath streaming behind them. Buster grunted; he still hadn't forgiven her for her proposing to leave him. When they walked into the courtyard of Barnham Street Buildings she looked up at the high, soot-blackened tenement walls and shuddered. The smell of rotting food and uncollected rubbish from the chute bins penetrated the freezing air and nearly knocked her off her feet.

'Good God, Buster, you've brought me to the armpit of Bermondsey. Does Lou live here?'

Her friend nodded grimly. 'Lovely, ain't it? I think they condemned it in 1913 – been promising to pull it down ever since!' he said.

Icicles dripped from the landings where frozen pipes had burst, and they dodged through a gang of kids hurling snowballs hard as rocks. One hit Buster on the back of the head.

'Oi, sod off, you little git,' he shouted at no one child in particular, which brought a rain of missiles on both their heads. They dodged into the stairwell and Buster led her to Lou's flat. They found the front door ajar. Buster's annoyed expression turned immediately to one of alarm. 'I think you're right, Hattie. Lou's gone walkabout.'

They checked the kitchen first, but there were no signs of life. It was Hattie who found her fast asleep in her bed.

'Buster!' she called quietly. 'She's here.'

They stood at the bedroom door, looking at Lou. Her face was pale and her breathing shallow. But when Hattie approached the bed she saw a few spots of blood on her pillow. She shook her gently. 'Lou? Lou? Wake up!'

The woman's eyelids flickered, and with great effort she opened her eyes.

'Are you all right, Lou?' Buster came closer. 'What's happened to you, love?'

Lou's hand moved to the back of her head and came away bloody. 'I think my Ronnie done it,' she said, remembering her son's name for the first time in a very long while. 'But don't be cross with him, Buster. Don't be cross...'

Buster's face turned white and, as Lou's eyes closed again, Hattie saw him clench his fist. 'Don't be cross?' he said to Hattie in a low voice. 'I'll effin' well kill him.'

He turned away and when he reached the door he said, 'Look after her, Hattie, and keep her awake.'

'Buster, don't do anything stupid!' she called after him, but it was too late. He had already gone.

Hattie looked around for the sink. She needed to clean and dress the gash on Lou's head, which was small but deep. There was blood on the fender by the kitchen fireplace. Whatever had happened, it looked to Hattie like some force had been used and Lou's head had come off the worse for it. She found a small range, but no water supply, and then she realized that the filthy, cracked sink they'd passed on the landing must serve all the flats. She swore to herself and took a jug out to the sink, praying the tap wasn't frozen. As the icy water sputtered into the jug, Hattie found herself overcome with an unaccountable sadness. Poor Lou. This was her home. Not because she'd been bombed out, not because of any housing shortage, but because this was deemed good enough for the likes of her and her son. She wanted to weep, but didn't. Instead she went back and bathed Lou's wound.

After settling her back against the pillow, she sat with Lou, holding her hand, jostling her gently every time she slipped into sleep. As an hour passed and Buster still hadn't come home, Hattie made the woman sit up, giving her hot sweet tea and gradually coaxing from her the story of her son's return.

'I don't think I've seen my Ronnie for a long time. I think he might have been in the country – evacuated. I know he wasn't happy there. He didn't get a nice family. They put him in a home and they wasn't good to him. But I said to my Vic, we'll have the kids home. Well, when I see our Ron today I never recognized him, he'd got so big. But I had to tell him about losing the baby... her name was Sue.' Lou paused and it was as if the stopped clock of her life had suddenly restarted. 'No, not Sue, she's gone poor love. I meant my new little baby. He was in such a rage when he see I'd lost her too. It wasn't his fault.' She put a hand to her head. 'You don't think Buster'll hurt him?'

Hattie stroked Lou's hand. 'Buster wouldn't hurt a fly. Don't worry, Lou, we'll find Ronnie. He has been away, but he's back home now and he needs you.'

Lou nodded, looking round at her bedroom. 'Look at the state of this place. It's a disgrace. My Vic was so particular about his home being clean. He'd have a right go at me he would, very particular, very smart, my Vic.' Lou tutted at herself and reached over to pull a finger through thick dust on her bedside table.

'How's your head, Lou? Shall I get you an Anadin?'

But Lou didn't have any Anadin, and on closer inspection Hattie realized she didn't have much of anything else. She felt a pang of guilt, ashamed that she'd moaned about having a lowly factory job when this woman looked like she'd been living on air for months. Hattie wished she'd known but as Buster had said, it was hard to help Lou, for however often he made sure she had her rations for the week he couldn't make her eat them, and when he went back to check, what little food there was had either gone off or been eaten by mice. He'd long ago written off his nephew. The boy was as wild as a young wolf, he said, and after seeing the gash on Lou's scalp, she could believe it.

But something about that bang on the head must have been beneficial because Lou seemed more lucid now.

'I think I'll get up and have a wash,' the woman said suddenly.

'Hang on, Lou, you might still be woozy.' Hattie held her gently by one skeletal arm.' You sit there and I'll bring you a basin of hot water.'

From the jug she filled a kettle and had a look round the kitchen while she waited for it to boil. There were touches here and there that made her feel this had once been a proper home – a knitted tea cosy on the teapot, a grey but once decent embroidered tablecloth, the tarnished brass fender round the fireplace. She kneeled to peer into a built-in cupboard next to the fire. The door was warped and hard to prize open. Inside was a small, heart-breaking collection of toys. Not Ronnie's by the looks of them. A rag doll, a miniature doll's cradle, a small, pink cloth bag, the sort that a little girl might like to store treasures in, and a miniature pair of heeled shoes with red sequins sewn on to them, the shoes of a tiny princess. The objects brought unwanted tears to her eyes. She knew Sue had been four when she'd died, and from the dust on the toys it looked as if the cupboard hadn't been opened since her death.

At the kettle's whistle she got up, noticing the open bottom drawer lined with a blanket. Hattie prided herself on her tough, unsentimental nature, but now she shook her head and took a deep breath, as if to banish the sadness that had once again caught her unawares. She'd heard some vicious tongues at the factory talking about Lou's collapse as if it were a crime, a weakness. It was true everyone had lost something precious in the years of war, but Lou had lost more than most – her parents, her husband, her child. And now she'd had to part with another baby. No wonder Lou spent her nights wandering the bombsites.

When Buster got back, his clothes were snow-crusted and his chubby face was pinched with cold.

'Lou!' he said, teeth chattering. 'What are you doing up?' He shot Hattie an accusing look.

'She wanted to, didn't you, Lou?' Hattie smiled encouragingly at the woman, who was sitting by the fire, washed and changed and seemingly in her right mind.

'I could only find a few lumps of coke, so poor Lou's lost one of her kitchen chairs.' She pointed to the glowing remnants of chair legs which she'd chopped up to fuel the fire.

'Better to sit on the floor than freeze your arse off, eh, Lou?' Buster said, and Lou smiled at her brother.

'Did you find my Ronnie? You didn't jaw him, did you?'

Buster shook his head. 'He must have gone to one of his mates' houses. He's never stayed out in this.'

And Lou nodded. 'I think he's got some nice little friends,' she said, seeming content with Buster's explanation. But when Hattie went to make him tea, he joined her and voiced his worry in a low voice.

'I know most of Ronnie's mates, but I went to all the street rakers he hangs about with. He's not with Nutty Norman or Frankie the Fish or any of the others. Just have to hope he's found somewhere warm, the little bastard.'

'Don't say that, Buster. If you was a kid, would you have wanted to be home here with Lou all day?'

'I know, I know. To be honest, I'm feeling bad I never done more for him. The boy's not had it easy. But he's such an ungrateful little git. If I tried to help him I just got a mouthful of abuse, or he'd nick whatever he could from me flat.' Buster shook his head. 'But whatever he's done, Lou seems to have turned the corner. I'll have to give him another chance – if only for her sake. I just wish you wasn't leaving. You seem to be able to get through to her...'

She ignored his attempt to make her feel guilty too. But seeing Lou's life up close had made her even more determined to pull herself up out of this hand-to-mouth existence. Sometimes she wondered if they'd really won the war at all.

★ ★ ★

Ronnie woke to a red light which hurt his eyes. A burning glow pulsed from a creature with dozens of smouldering eyes; flames spewed from its head into the dark cavern. The smell was foul. A thunderous roar shook the walls and vibrated beneath his body. Panic gripped his chest; terror stifled the scream in his throat. Mum had told him Sue was an angel in heaven and that he'd see her again when he went there. But this couldn't be heaven. He'd come to the wrong sodding place! He struggled to throw off foul-smelling covers that restrained him, while his feet and hands throbbed with pain as heat surged through them. Flames shot higher from the glowing fiery creature. Out of the lurid light came a hulking misshapen figure, stopping in front of him.

'Oh Jesus, save me!' Ronnie cried out, realizing all at once that if he was in hell, then Pissy Pants must have got there first. For he recognized the shuffling unkempt figure immediately.

As he wriggled to escape, Pissy Pants grasped his ankles and held on tight. Nutty Norman had once told Ronnie that if you went to hell, demons would tear you apart then eat you up.

'Don't eat me! Don't eat me!' Ronnie pleaded.

Pissy Pants sat on him, preventing him from wriggling.

''Ungry, 'ungry,' said Pissy Pants.

Ronnie screamed and thrashed beneath the rag-shrouded scavenger, who now bounced up and down on Ronnie's stomach, knocking the remaining fight out of him until he lay exhausted and panting for breath. As Pissy Pants' hand reached for him, Ronnie screwed his eyes shut, waiting to be torn apart, but instead he felt leathery fingers patting his cheek. He opened one eye and saw that the hand bore an unhealed cut that oozed puss. He looked up into vague blue eyes, not the red eyes of a demon.

''Ungry?' the scavenger asked and pulled from inside his blanket a white paper bag, which he stuck under Ronnie's nose. 'Doughduts...' He shoved the grease-streaked bag closer and Ronnie smelled vanilla and sugar and warm dough.

'Edwards's?' Ronnie asked wonderingly, naming the bakery in Tower Bridge Road which made the best doughnuts in the world.

'Edwuddsis,' Pissy Pants replied.

Ronnie smiled. He definitely wasn't in hell and more importantly neither was Pissy Pants, which meant Ronnie hadn't killed him after all!

The scavenger sat on the floor watching Ronnie intently as he stuffed the doughnut into his mouth. As he ate Ronnie looked round the tunnel-like space, recognizing the regular, thundering drumming noise coming from steam trains overhead. He must be in one of the railway arches that spliced Bermondsey. Before he was evacuated he'd sheltered under them with his mum during the raids. Arch 61 had become more like home than their two rooms in Barnham Street Buildings and he preferred it. With hundreds of people packed in every night, there were sing-songs and games and tea and buns. He didn't worry about the bombs, not until Sue got blown up. The oily smell told him this one had probably been used as a garage at one time, but now it seemed that Pissy Pants had commandeered it. He licked the sugar from his fingers and Pissy Pants shook the bag. Ronnie took another doughnut.

'Sorry,' Ronnie said between mouthfuls. 'About your hand… it was an accident. I thought I'd done you in.'

Pissy Pants seemed to find this funny and gave a brown-toothed grin. 'Johnny not dead!' He thumped his broad chest.

'Your brother's been after me…' Ronnie said.

Jonny Harper held up his injured hand. 'Dickie said pay you back…'

It was a trap! Ronnie jumped up, looking round for Dickie. He launched himself towards the doorway, ready to fly back out into the snowstorm, but Pissy Pants stuck out a foot and sent him sprawling. Johnny's deep, booming laugh echoed in the cavernous arch. 'Y'all right. Dickie not here.' Johnny shuffled on his backside nearer to the perforated oil-drum fire that Ronnie had mistaken for a flame-spewing, many-eyed demon. Ronnie moved closer too and they sat in companionable silence, enjoying the warmth and finishing off the doughnuts. When his belly was full and the blood ran warm again in his veins, Ronnie remembered his mum. His eyes brimmed with tears, which he staunched with his blazer sleeve.

'Why you cryin'?' Johnny asked. 'Dickie not coming.'

Ronnie sniffed back his tears. 'It ain't your brother I'm worried about now. I banged me mum's head on the floor and she didn't get up. I think she's gone and died.' He dropped his head on to his knees, feeling more lost and far from home than in all the years he was a vaccy. Pissy Pants gave him a heavy pat on the back. 'Johnny not dead.'

'No, you ain't dead,' Ronnie said, trying to feel the relief of it. He leaned his head on Johnny's smelly shoulder, not even minding the stink, and in the heat of the fire his eyes began to droop. Eventually he fell into a deep sleep, while the snow fell steadily and a drift grew so high it almost blocked the entrance to the arch.

Hours later, when a snow-muted dawn light filtered through the arch entrance, Johnny Harper got up. He studied the still sleeping form of Ronnie. Then he bent to scoop up the boy's bony body in his thick strong arms. He pushed through the snowy curtain that filled the doorway. He had a pram which he used to transport all manner of scavenged goods, from old newspapers to enamel stoves, and now he lay Ronnie in the pram like an oversized baby. After throwing a blanket over him, Johnny pushed the pram down a canyon of snow that had formed between the viaduct and the buildings opposite. He passed under the dark road tunnel and Ronnie slept on, swaddled in Johnny's blanket. Sometimes he seemed about to surface, only to sigh and descend into sleep once more. Johnny turned into the deserted courtyard of Barnham Street Buildings. The landings above him, normally a gallery of gossiping women, were silent and empty. Everyone had been chased indoors by the vengeful cold. Here the snow was three feet deep and trammelled only by the tracks of a few stray cats. Johnny bent like an oxen to pull the pram to the stairwell, and then he carried the still sleeping boy up three flights of stairs to his home.

When Ronnie woke later that morning he turned over in bed and stretched, enjoying the feeling of sheets and a soft feather mattress beneath him, until he registered where he was. He turned over and found himself lying next to his mother. Lou's face was whiter than the snow outside. She looked just as if she were sleeping. How had she got off the floor and into her bed? How had he? He reached out a stealthy hand, placing it on her skinny ribcage. It rose and fell. He waited. Again, it rose and fell.

Relief flooded him and a sob escaped from deep inside his chest. He bit down hard on his own fist, before stuffing it into his mouth. Being careful not to wake Lou he kissed her lightly on the cheek. 'I'm really glad you ain't dead, Mum,' he whispered and slipped out of the bed. He knew it was a miracle. He felt reborn. His only purpose in life now would be to make Lou happy again. Although he was still fully dressed he shivered. Pissy Pants had removed his shoes before putting him into the bed and now the lino froze his feet. He went to the kitchen. Lou hadn't collected this week's rations, so all they had was a cube of mouldy cheese and a wedge of stale bread. He remembered the cooked breakfasts Dad used to make them. What if he could do the same for Mum? He had an idea. There were other places he could get grub besides the smiling man's. Families had moved into the old army huts now and on reccies with Nutty Norman and the gang he'd spied women cooking up stuff on their stoves. They had bacon or sometimes even a sausage sizzling away. It drove him and Norman mad sometimes, the smell was so good. The squatters had a kitchen in the NAAFI hut, with a big food safe. It would be easy, like taking sweets from a baby.

* * *

They'd set up a communal kitchen in the NAAFI hut, which had a bigger stove with a proper oven. There was also a large food safe with a close-meshed grill to keep out the mice. It was possible to cook on the small flat-topped cylindrical heating stoves in the huts, but for anything other than simple fry-ups the women would come and cook together in the NAAFI. On Sundays the squatters had begun to club their meagre rations together to make as near a Sunday roast as they could manage for the whole camp. It had become their first community tradition. On Sunday morning when Vera went to the NAAFI to start preparing the roast, she discovered that there had been a burglary at the squatters' camp. She ran out of the NAAFI, banging on hut doors. 'Some mean bastard's only gone and nicked our grub!' she shouted, waking anyone who had managed a Sunday lie-in.

Clara turned over in bed and groaned. 'What's all that row, Hattie?' she asked groggily. Typical, the one night when Martha had slept through till a decent hour, and someone was banging on their door. The morning light was enough to tell her that Martha had slept at least an hour longer than normal.

'Tell Vera to pipe down, she'll wake the baby,' Clara whispered.

Hattie threw a blanket over her shoulders. She'd slept with her clothes on over her pyjamas, and now she hopped in stockinged feet to the door. She opened it a crack and a vicious wind whipped snow into the hut

'Jesus, it's March and it's still freezing!' Clara muttered. Raising her head, through the open door she saw other squatters emerging from their huts.

'Sorry!' Hattie whispered. She stuffed her feet into fur-lined bootees. 'Sounds like we've had another burglary. I'll go and see what's happened.'

Clara turned over gratefully, though it was worrying to hear they'd had another break-in. Alan and Joe had even suggested they set up a night patrol since the huts were obviously being targeted by thieves as an easy option. Not that the squatters had much to steal. At first they'd put down the pilfering to wandering gangs of kids or opportunistic villains. They'd stolen an odd array of things, from pens and comics to some photographs of Joe's, though oddly none of his camera equipment had gone. But food was a precious fuel they could not afford to lose. It was a particular blow when they'd been working so hard physically all week in their factory jobs, and after work in freezing conditions trying to make the huts weatherproof. But of late the thieves had been taking more of what was most valuable, their precious coal and paraffin, along with off-ration items, mostly clothes, especially boots. There had also been some mean thefts of personal, sentimental valuables which had survived the bombing raids.

It felt to Clara as if the country she'd left only a year earlier had become a more mean-spirited place. Perhaps her own treatment at the hands of her former workmates had tainted her view of things, but during the war at least it had felt as if they were all in it together. She had done her bit, working day and night trimming thousands of sheepskins for airmen's jackets, and she'd felt proud to be part of a team that worked while bombs fell and fire rained down. Now she just felt like an outcast. Sometimes it was too much of a change to comprehend.

Martha was unusually quiet. She'd been snuffly of late, and breathing like a little steam train at night, choking on her phlegmy cough. Not surprising that she'd caught a cold in the seemingly endless Arctic weather which had engulfed their thin-walled hut. Clara forced herself to get up. But as she leaned over to lift Martha from the cot, her mind turned blank as the white field of snow beyond the frosted window. She felt encased in ice, her heart frozen mid-beat. Her baby was gone.

# 11

## A Bad Heart

### March 1947

Clara stood immobile for a second, refusing to accept the evidence of her eyes. 'No!' She tore aside the blankets in a wild hope that her baby might have wriggled to the end of the cot. It was empty. Her body seemed to melt away and she was left with only a scoured emptiness at her heart. From somewhere, she found the strength to run from the hut on legs barely able to support her. Aware of her heart pounding, her mind whirling with every possibility, she sped along the duckboards to the NAAFI and yelled, 'Hattie!'

'I don't think it was mice.' Hattie was examining the broken padlock on the food safe. It was kept locked, not because anyone thought a fellow squatter would steal from it, but because rats and mice could burrow up under the wooden floorboards and into the huts. 'But the wry smile vanished when she saw Clara.

'What's happened?'

'It's Martha – she's gone! I thought she was still asleep... she's not in her cot! Someone's taken her – did any of you take her?' Clara looked from one to the other. Their faces showed only incomprehension. Why weren't they understanding her? Why didn't they move? 'My baby's *missing*!' she shouted, louder now, so they would understand. 'Help me find her... someone, please.' Her mouth was so dry it was hard to speak – perhaps that's why it was taking them so long to understand. But then she felt Hattie's arms round her and the whole hut erupted into movement. 'We'll find Martha. Don't worry, Clara,' Hattie was saying. 'It's probably just one of the kids, taken her out in her pram.'

It wasn't uncommon for the little girls to wheel Martha around the camp, playing at mothers. 'Did you see the pram?'

No, she hadn't noticed if the pram was missing too.

'Her teddy was gone,' she said as Alan came to her side. 'She loves her teddy... Johnny gave it to her.' She remembered how the scavenger had watched over them in the basement. Perhaps if they'd stayed there this wouldn't have happened. She knew he used to keep guard, sometimes she'd wake to hear him shuffling about in the other rooms, but after that first night she'd never been frightened of him.

'We'll search the huts and send someone out to round up the kids. One of them's got to have Martha,' Alan said. But his voice lacked its normal jaunty lilt, and when she looked into his eyes what she saw did not reassure her.

Joe came to join them. 'Of course we'll find her,' he repeated, but with a decisiveness which made her believe she'd been stupid to think the worst.

'I'm coming too.' She took a heaving breath, and found her legs really wouldn't support her. As they buckled, Alan caught her.

'Stay in your hut, Clara – just in case one of the kids brings Martha back. Maisie'll sit with you,' he said.

'I'm all right, really, Alan.' She pushed herself up out of his arms as if she were a drowning woman coming up for air, but she knew he was right. Someone needed to stay at the hut, yet it was impossible for it to be her.

'I can't just sit around doing nothing. Maisie can wait at my hut. I'm going with you.'

Before the search began she went with Hattie to put on warm clothes. The first thing she noticed was the pram. Why hadn't she registered it was still there? A surge of irrational hope flooded her and she ran to pull back the hood. She covered her face with her hands, shaking her head. 'I'm so stupid, so stupid, as if she could have flown out of the bloody cot. I'm too stupid to be a mother. I've messed it all up...' She had never known such pain, not even Barry's betrayal or her parents' coldness had caused her such paralysing agony as this. Hattie came to stand beside her. 'You are *not* stupid,' she said with deliberate emphasis, which managed to penetrate Clara's guilty confusion. 'You couldn't know! Anything's possible – I might have moved her in the night... It's not a question of being stupid. You're her mum and you've got to keep hoping. That's your job now, Clara. I don't think you should be out searching—'

'I've got to, Hattie. I can't keep still.' And it was true, not an inch of her body was at rest, from her trembling limbs to her pounding heart and her heaving lungs. She knew for certain that she would never rest until Martha was back in her arms.

They searched in twos. Clara and Alan, Hattie and Joe, Vera and Brian, and any of the others who were able-bodied enough to brave the freezing weather. First they found out where the squatter kids had gone to play that morning. Maisie said they had planned to go to the allotments, where sometimes the owners would let them work for payment in potatoes or turnips. But there were over a hundred of the wartime allotments still being worked and they could be at any one of them. No one could say for sure if the kids had taken Martha, but they all treated her like a little sister and could have simply assumed it was all right to go off with her.

Clara and Alan set off for the allotments, while the others spread out to search the huts and to sweep the Oval, planning to spiral the search out from there. Hattie and Joe headed to some deep concrete air-raid shelters near the Jamaica Road entrance to the park. Built too late in the war to save many lives, the shelters had since been left undisturbed by all but tramps or the odd brave child who wasn't scared of their echoing depths. Clara shivered as she watched the two of them go. The idea that her baby might be in one of those dark bunkers chilled her heart.

When she and Alan reached the allotments there were only a very few hardy gardeners tending to them. This spring frost had ruined all the tender buds and the ground was still iron hard. Alan pointed to an old man slowly uncovering sacking from an area he'd tried to protect from the snow. They went over to ask him if he'd seen any children about. The old man eased himself up, hand on his back, seeming glad for a chance to interrupt his work.

'I chased off some little buggers yesterday, trying to nick onions out of my store. Some of your lot come over this morning looking for work, but there's nothing you can do in this.' He stamped the icy ground.

'Were there any young girls with a baby?' Clara asked. 'My baby's gone missing.'

The old man shook his head. 'I'm sorry, love, I did see two little girls, but no baby. I'll keep an eye out.'

They thanked the man and began combing the rest of the allotments, looking for other gardeners to question. But only a few had ventured out and none of them had seen the squatter kids.

'This is useless, Alan,' Clara said, knowing somehow that Martha was not nearby. 'What about the lido?' The outdoor swimming pool was a far cry from the 'Riviera of Bermondsey' it had once been. Though it had served as an emergency water tank during the war, cracks from bomb damage had drained it of water and the splashes and laughter of long summer days were distant memories. But the squatter kids had still found a way to make it into a playground, and Alan agreed they should at least try there.

They found Maisie's brothers and the others engaged in an engineering feat, building an igloo of sorts in a dug-out area of the snow-filled lido. Clara spotted some of the girls smoothing the ice walls and, jumping into the snowy pool, ran to them.

'Have you got my Martha?'

The girls looked guilty as Clara gripped the smallest by the shoulders. 'Where is she? You shouldn't take her without asking me!' Clara shook the little girl, whose lip trembled.

'You're not in trouble, love,' Alan said, quickly hunkering down in the snow next to her. 'We can't find the baby and sometimes you take her for a walk, don't you?'

The little girl nodded. 'Not today we ain't. It's too cold out for a baby.'

By now the other children had gathered round, eager to help.

'Has anyone else seen her?' Clara asked.

'No, but we can help search,' Maisie's eldest brother, Roger, offered, and Alan sent them off to look round the bandstand area. 'Only there, and once you're finished go back to the huts. We don't want to lose any more kids today,' he called after their retreating figures. He looked guiltily at Clara, realizing what he'd said.

'She's not lost.' He put an arm round her shoulder. 'We just haven't found her yet...'

But as Clara watched the little tribe leave under the direction of Roger, she felt her stomach turn. She'd told herself Martha would be with them, and as that hope drained away so did her strength. She twisted out of Alan's grasp, slumped to her knees and retched into the snow.

'I'm sorry,' she sobbed, 'so sorry.' Her hands and knees trembled as he lifted her up.

'No need to be sorry, you're just worried. But you're not staying out in this state. I'm taking you back.'

'No, you're best to carry on looking, Al. I'll make me own way back home, I'm just holding you up. You go...' She gave him a small shove. 'Go and find her for me?'

He nodded. 'If she's in this park I'll find her.' He hesitated. 'But if she's not, I won't come home without going to the police, OK?'

'OK,' she said, and turned away before he could say more.

The snow and her weak legs allowed only slow progress back to the huts, and with each passing second a new hope arose, yet with each hope came a new pain, for all the stories she told herself of a happy conclusion seemed so thin. But she felt her heart would stop beating if she let herself imagine the worst.

As the little girl had said, it was too cold out here for a baby, especially her sun-born Martha. She should have stayed in Australia, that was where Martha belonged, not here in this grey-cloaked, ruined world. She stamped down each fear as she trudged back. But the snow clawed at her legs and tripped her up as, leaning forward, she tried to plough her way through. By the time the huts came into view, her courage failed. What if Martha was not back in her cot? What then? If she went back, she'd have to face that news. And so she stayed where she was, leaning her back against the gnarled old fairy tree. After a while she slid her back down its trunk and hunkered down, hiding herself in the womb-like, hollowed-out bole. Perhaps she would freeze here and never have to hear the bad news she dreaded.

★ ★ ★

'The bomb shelters? But the kids are all too scared to go down there...' Joe was trying to persuade Hattie to look first in what remained of the children's play park. Bombs hadn't spared slides or swings and the pitted surface was far from safe, but there were other far more perilous playgrounds in Bermondsey these days, as Hattie had witnessed on her first day home.

'Maybe, but I've seen them climbing up the entrances to the shelters and I bet some brave jack lairys will be sliding down them in this snow.'

She'd seen kids scaling the ten-foot high wedge-shaped brick structures, which formed the entrances to the vast underground bunkers. Whatever Joe thought, her experience of the terrifying bombsite gang on her first night home had convinced her that these war-born children were fearless. But Joe still seemed reluctant to waste time on the shelters. She had noticed he could be stubborn and she was in no mood to argue the point. 'I'll go on my own,' she said and saw him raise his eyes. 'Well, we're almost there!' She pointed to the shelters as they came into view. 'I think it's worth a look.'

She pushed on, not caring if he followed. The wedge-shaped

entrance buildings were now snow-covered humps, and if the children had been using them as snow slides then the evidence must have been hidden by the last snowfall, for they were pristine. Undeterred, Hattie made her way to the door of the first shelter. The lock was broken and she pushed open the metal door. She descended a flight of stairs but the light soon faded to impenetrable blackness. She could hear Joe following, but couldn't see him when she looked back.

'Wait a minute!' His voice echoed to her as she reached the bottom stair. 'Let me get my torch out.'

There was a click and a circle of light illuminated a large concrete chamber. Joe played the light along its length, which seemed to go on forever. Two tiers of wooden bunks lined the walls and in places there was wartime graffiti. Cartoons of Hitler and the ubiquitous roughly drawn 'Wot, no potatoes?' character peering over a wall.

'Doesn't look like anyone's been down here recently,' Joe said, shining his torch on the bunks.

Hattie shivered. Though its purpose was to save lives, the place felt like a tomb. She moved further along the row of bunks. Then she sniffed. It really did smell like death, and despite the cold she felt herself break into a sweat. 'Joe, come here!' He had been peering into a side tunnel, but was with her in a second.

'Have you found something?'

'No, but I can smell something. Give me the torch.' She felt in the dark for his hand and registered its softness. Of course, he was a chemist. No hard graft had turned his palms to leather. He relinquished the light, which she now shone over the nearest bunk. Bundles of newspapers were stacked on top to form a mattress, and a heap of worn blankets were rolled at its foot. The stench coming off them was as good as a signature.

'Pissy Pants!' she said, and then with a terrible certainty she knew what had happened to Martha.

'Who?' Joe asked, revealing that his origins were not in Bermondsey.

'Johnny Harper, you must have seen him. He's a totter. Goes all over the place collecting scrap and newspapers. Poor sod went barmy as a kid, after they locked him up in Stonefield Asylum for stealing half a pound of sausages.'

'Pissy Pants? Because of this smell then?' Joe wrinkled his nose.

'I don't think the kids have taken the baby, Joe. It's him, Pissy Pants. He was obsessed with Clara and Martha, when they lived in the Square. Used to leave them food and toys for the baby. And the day we left the Square Clara said to me, "I wonder if he'll miss us"…'

'So you really think he'd take the baby? Sounds like he wanted to protect them, not hurt them.'

'Who knows what's in his mind? Perhaps he's harmless but he's unpredictable. We used to tease him as kids and he could turn nasty – mind you, we did make his life a misery. He'd chase us away… But there's another thing I never told Clara. I've seen him in the park a couple of times since we moved in. I called out to him once and he ran off… Oh, I don't know, it's just a hunch.'

'So you think if we find him, we find Martha?' Joe asked and she nodded.

'But it'll have to be soon. How's he going to look after a baby, especially in this weather?'

'If he's living here, surely all we need to do is wait for him to come back.'

'It's not that simple. He lives all over the place, dosses down in bombed-out buildings or railway arches. There's plenty of ruined houses he can take his pick of.'

'Do you know where?'

'Not really, but I know someone who does.'

They decided to return to the squatters' huts to warm up, and Hattie needed some dry clothes before she set off on her mission to find Johnny Harper. She hoped that she wouldn't have to do it, that Martha would be back safely already. But a discovery convinced her otherwise, for as they approached the Oval she spotted a small arm poking out of the snow and, as she drew closer, a tiny furry head. It was Martha's teddy bear. She bent to pick it up. It was frozen solid.

'It's been here overnight. Feel,' she said, handing the toy to Joe, who felt its stiff limbs.

'Why take the teddy bear if you were going to harm her?' he asked.

'Perhaps it'll be best if we don't show this to Clara yet,' she said.

And he stuffed the teddy inside his greatcoat. 'You're right. What good will it do? She'll only make up more stories about it.'

Hattie was struck by the insight, and for the first time began to feel curious about Joe's life. She'd only ever seen him as the awkward sitting tenant. And he'd always been so tight-lipped about his own desperation, which she knew must be hidden somewhere. For they were all desperate, those who'd come to live in the huts. Perhaps he had lost something once, equally as precious as Martha, and had made up stories of his own to ease the loss?

'OK, we'll keep quiet about it, and another thing she shouldn't know is that I'm going after Johnny Harper. We'll tell the others, but not Clara. She's such a trusting soul, and she'll only blame herself once she knows he's taken Martha.'

But Clara and Alan weren't yet back and Hattie was grateful that she didn't have to lie to her friend about where she was going. In the NAAFI, Vera was busy serving vegetable soup to squatters as they returned from searching. She gave Hattie a questioning look.

'No luck,' Hattie told her, shaking her head as the woman handed her a bowl of soup. 'But we did find something. Don't say anything to Clara, but it looks to me like it's Pissy Pants took her.' And she told Vera about their findings in the shelter and the teddy bear.

'It's time to go to the old Bill then,' Vera said.

'I suppose so. But I think I can find him quicker.'

'What you going to do, sniff him out?'

'I'm going to see Lenny Harper.'

'What! For gawd's sake, what's the matter with you? You don't want to get mixed up with him. He'll knife you soon as look at yer. No, let me send my Brian over to Rotherhithe nick.'

'OK, but I'm still going to see Lenny. He won't hurt me,' Hattie lied. For Lenny Harper had already proved he could do that. Perhaps he'd mellowed in the eight years since he'd broken her collarbone, but she doubted it. She tried to remember them back then, both eighteen and she with some romantic notion about him being so different from the rest of the Harpers. Even Ciss with her questionable taste in men had begged her to steer clear of him.

'I know a mean bastard when I see one, gel,' she'd warned, and when she'd been proven right Hattie had been less disappointed in Lenny than she had been in herself for being fooled by good looks and sweet words. Still, she was grateful to Lenny in a way, for he'd taught her a valuable lesson: if it howled at the full moon and had long sharp teeth, it was probably a wolf, no matter how many sheepskins were draped over its back.

When she arrived at the big three-storey Victorian building in Southwark Park Road, she was surprised to find the Harpers' house still standing; so many others in the long winding street were not. Great tracts of land had been flattened all around it but for some unimaginable reason God had spared the Harper house, perhaps because of its proximity to the mission hall. It was Dickie who answered the door. Short and muscular like all the Harpers except one, he looked well fed. Austerity was obviously not yet biting in the Harper household.

'Sod me,' was all he said, in his gravelly voice.

Hattie took that to mean he recognized her.

'Is Lenny in?' she asked, and all the years in between disappeared in an instant. She was eighteen and breathless with excitement, standing on Lenny Harper's doorstep, peering along this very passage waiting for him to appear with his jacket slung over his shoulder and his hair clipped clean over his neat ears, his fine eyebrows drawn into the most delicate of frowns which always dissipated when he saw her. Now Dickie closed the door in her face and she felt as disappointed as that silly eighteen-year-old to have lost the vision of Lenny as he was then, at the exact moment she'd fallen in love with him.

She waited, feeling herself blush at her own stupidity, until she heard Dickie's heavy footsteps and the door reopened.

'Lenny said you'd better come in.'

Dickie led the way to an empty front room with high sash windows, where he left her alone. She stood looking out at the bombsite opposite. Hardly a brick stood of the row of houses, which had once each housed three or four families. Where had all those people gone?

She smelled him before she heard his light footstep. He always smelled of some sweet soap, Imperial Leather she seemed to remember, and he'd obviously found an under-the-counter supply. She wondered how he stood the stink of his brother, but he'd never shown the slightest distaste in Johnny's presence. In fact he'd always been powerfully protective of him, perhaps another thing that had masked his true nature from Hattie.

'I hear you're looking for me, Hattie,' he said, with a cool smile.

She turned away from the window to face him. 'I'm not. I'm looking for your brother Johnny.'

'Johnny?' Suspicion clouded his smooth brow. 'What do you want with him?'

She took a deep breath. 'It's about a friend's baby.'

He interrupted her with his deceptively pleasant laugh. 'There's no way you can pin that one on our Johnny. He wouldn't know how to!'

'Not that. The baby's gone missing and I think Johnny can help find her—'

'Are you fuckin' saying what I think you are? He's not like that – he wouldn't hurt a fly!' He paused for effect and grinned at her. 'Not like me, eh?'

'I'm not accusing him of anything. He helped out my friend… gave her food and other stuff when she needed it. He was good to her and the baby. I'm not saying he'd hurt anyone.'

'Well, you'd better not be.' He leaned forward and ground out the cigarette he'd been smoking. He seemed about to leave and she hadn't yet got what she wanted.

'I'd really appreciate your help, Lenny. I've only come to you because I wouldn't want Johnny getting into trouble – the other squatters are talking about going to the police, but if I could find Johnny first, he might have seen something that can help us find her… without bringing in the *police*…' She deliberately repeated the word that she knew would get his attention.

He took in a deep breath, and his nostrils had a pinched look that bore out the army doctor's diagnosis of a bad heart. 'I can't keep track of him, you know that. He goes where he wants to and I can't make him live in a proper house… but I don't want Johnny getting in no trouble. Last I knew he was dossing in one of the arches – Crucifix Lane.' He stood up. 'But anything bad happens to my brother over this and it's down to you, get me?' He drew his fine-boned finger along his collarbone, 'I'll be honest, I was surprised to see you back here again, Hattie. I reckon you'd have been better off keeping *right* away from Bermondsey… and from me.' And the smile he gave her had no warmth in it at all.

He left the room without another word and she wasn't sure if he'd threatened her or simply been giving her some good advice. Lenny was like that. He would keep people second-guessing themselves and pounce when they least expected it.

He'd been the doting lover until one day he hadn't. She'd questioned him over something so small, about a purse of hers that had gone missing, and he'd lashed out with the force of a coiled spring released. With Lenny you never saw anything coming.

She let herself out and walked almost in a daze towards Jamaica Road and then down to the river. She stood on the ruined Cherry Garden Pier for a while, looking out over the steel-grey

Thames, noting her trembling limbs and the deep breaths that filled her lungs but left her gasping for air. With a sick feeling in her stomach, she remembered why she'd preferred rushing off to join the army to staying in Bermondsey, and she wished more than ever that she'd never come back.

But the feeling didn't last. By the time she'd walked to the railway arches in Crucifix Lane, she realized that fear for Martha's safety was so much worse than her fear of Lenny's fist.

*

Johnny had his back to her. His humped shoulders were covered in a moth-eaten blanket and he was sorting out a pile of paper. She'd walked along the railway arches and let her nose lead her. It hadn't been long before she came to Johnny's arch.

'Johnny,' she called out from the doorway, not wanting to startle him into running away.

At the sound of his name, he spun round, his low forehead creased with fear. But when he saw who it was, fear turned to anger.

'Go way!' he growled. 'You took her!'

He gathered up whatever he was sorting out and stuffed it into his coat, though the garment was so tattered it appeared to be held together by crusted dirt and grease.

'Took who, Johnny? Took the baby?'

'Baby gone, my girl gone, you took them away. Don't like you.'

She walked slowly into the arch, blasted by the smell and the heat rolling off an oil-drum fire.

'I'm looking for the baby, Clara's baby. I didn't take her. Do you know where she is?'

Johnny stood up, waving his arms in the peculiar windmill action he used when agitated. 'In the park! Baby's in the park!'

Fear gripped her. Had he left her in the bunker all along? 'In the shelter? Did you leave the baby there?'

'Not me!' he roared. 'You took her and Johnny can't see her no more. Sad.'

He controlled his waving arms, folded his hands under his armpits and sat on the barrel. 'Little baby, my friend,' he said, and began to cry.

Hattie stifled her own gagging and moved closer. 'Johnny, I need your help. The little baby, someone else took her from the park... not me!' She edged back as his hand whipped out towards her. 'And her mummy is very sad. You wouldn't want Clara to be sad, would you? Someone came and took the baby from her, last night. Someone nicked some food from our NAAFI and whoever did that, we think took the baby. I saw your camp in the shelter... were you there last night, did you see anyone take her?'

The watery blue eyes gave her a look of surprising intelligence and for an instant she wondered if he wasn't as simple as he appeared. Then he nodded. 'Johnny seed someone.'

# 12

## The Wrong Baby

### March 1947

Ronnie had broken the padlock easily. There hadn't been much in the food safe, not to feed all them people, but it had been better than nothing. He'd put their bacon and a sausage and a bit of other meat he didn't recognize into a big bowl that was still half full of dripping. There'd been some bread and some cheese that he'd stuffed into his pockets. He'd intended to take it straight back to his mum, but outside the wind was howling like a pack of wolves and the snow had stung him, like he'd been pushing through a swarm of bees. He'd sheltered in the lea of one of the huts, debating whether to go back to the NAAFI or push on. Everyone must be asleep by now, but peering through the hut window he'd seen a paraffin light still lit. It had been turned down low and its glow spilled out from a little table. He'd seen a woman holding a baby, its head resting on her shoulder, and she was patting its back gently, pacing up and down. She'd turned her back to him and Ronnie had seen the baby's face. Round, with large dark eyes and a head of black hair, thick with tiny ringlets. The baby had seen him too, and her little head had craned to keep him in sight as her mother walked up and down. When he'd smiled at her through the window, she'd smiled back as if she knew him. The woman had turned again and Ronnie had ducked out of sight. He'd hunkered down against the wooden hut, shivering and trembling with joy at the same time. He'd found Mum's baby, the one she'd lost! It was definitely her. He remembered all that black hair from the night she was born, and she knew him! He'd promised he would do everything he could to make Mum happy again. And now God had given him this chance.

By the time he'd reached the Jamaica Road entrance he'd been almost crawling, the cold was so intense. He'd always hated them bloody shelters, they was spooky. He knew there was a tunnel leading from one of them straight to the Paradise Street nick. The tale was that before ever it was a nick, it belonged to a doctor, a body snatcher who'd built the tunnel to bring back dead bodies from St Olave's Workhouse graveyard. He was just like Frankenstein and it gave Ronnie the shivers. But it was the only place he could think to get out of the biting wind. He'd needed to wait until the weather cleared before he could go back to the huts. He'd pushed open the metal door and let in a flurry of snow. After feeling for the matches and the candle hidden in a niche behind the door, he'd descended the stairs one by one, his knees still trembling from the effort of ploughing through the snow and the shock of finding his baby sister.

He hadn't expected Pissy Pants to be there. It was one of the scavenger's camps, but not his favourite. Johnny was warming his hands by a small spirit stove where a billycan was boiling up water. Ronnie had deposited the bowl of food in front of his fellow vagrant. 'Fancy a fry-up?' he'd asked and Johnny grunted a yes.

Johnny had made camp coffee in a mug for them to share, and then he'd fried up the grub on a small black pan. Ronnie had spread dripping on to hunks of bread and soon they'd been feasting on the best food Ronnie had tasted in a long time. He'd smiled so much that sometimes he couldn't chew the next mouthful. He couldn't remember when he'd last been so happy. He'd wanted to tell Johnny about the miracle of finding his sister, but he would never understand. It was enough that the miracle had happened and that it would change everything.

Later, in the early hours, when dawn was tinting all the snow pink, Ronnie had crept out of the shelter and made his way back to the baby's hut. The door hadn't been locked and it had been a simple matter to slip in quietly, creep to the cot and lift out the sleeping child. She was heavier than he'd thought, but he'd held her as he'd seen the woman do last night, close to his chest, with her head resting on his shoulder. It was very quiet outside, the wind had died down and the humped snow muffled every sound. Icy breath plumed from his open mouth as he'd trudged steadily across the park, witnessed only by a rabble of hungry starlings, skirmishing in the snow for scraps. They'd scattered as he approached, their hard cries disturbing the baby. He hushed her and nestled her deeper inside his coat. But his arms were already aching and as he'd shifted her weight she'd almost slipped from his arms. Quick as one of the noisy birds he'd dipped and scooped her up before she could land on the frozen ground. Her eyes had stayed fast shut, her dark lashes tipped with lacy snowflakes. He'd have to hurry before the snow started falling again. He couldn't remember their Sue being so quiet, but he'd been just three when she was born and seven when she had died. He did know she used to scream blue murder, Mum said, because she was a hungry baby. Perhaps this one got enough to eat.

He was out of the park and heading along Jamaica Road when she'd finally stirred, her mouth opening in a round pink yawn, her little fist rubbing her sticky eyes. When she'd opened them she'd stared placidly at Ronnie, who'd given her an encouraging smile. An uncertain look played across her face and then she'd begun to cry. He'd reached for the teddy he'd stuck into his pocket on the way out of the hut, but it was gone.

'Shhh, shhh, I'm taking you home,' he'd crooned, but her cries had only grown louder, attracting the attention of a passing milkman who was dragging his crates along on a sled.

'All right, son?' he'd called and Ronnie waved.

'Just me little sister! Cold!'

Through the deserted early morning streets he'd trotted, increasingly alarmed at the baby's cries – he couldn't afford any more unwanted attention. But eventually the motion had rocked her to sleep and she'd fallen silent. When he'd reached the buildings it was fully light, but only old Granny Stout on the ground floor was up and about.

''ere Ron, run us an errand?' she'd called from her front door, holding out a screw of paper with some money in it.

'No!' he'd yelled.

'Get us a packet of Weights, son, I can't get out in this.'

'Later, I'll come back later,' he'd said, trying to hide the baby.

'What you hiding there? You been tea leavin' again?' the old lady had said in her trembly whiney voice.

He'd ignored her and stumbled up the stairs, pulling the key from inside the letterbox and letting himself in. Mum was asleep and he'd laid the baby on the pillow next to her. The little thing had a funny-coloured skin, which he hadn't noticed on the night she'd been born. And she had a fat neck too. But her hair was the same as he'd seen, black as his nan's old cat, and the way she'd smiled at him in the night – she had to be his sister.

He'd watched his mother and the baby sleeping, his excitement bubbling up like an unstoppable spring, so that he couldn't wait any longer. He'd shoved Lou's sleeping form till she stirred. When she saw him she smiled sleepily. 'Hello, Ron, you little street raker, where you been?' she'd said and he'd smiled back. She'd remembered his name.

'Here, Mum, look who I've brung home.' He'd lifted the baby so she could see her. 'It's the baby you lost!'

Lou had jerked up, wide awake. 'Oh, Ronnie, love, what have you done? This ain't my baby!'

His smile had faded. ''Course it is, you're getting all mixed up again. Look! She's got black hair just like our baby's, and brown eyes. And she knew me, she smiled at me!' He'd pushed the child towards her. 'Don't start all that again, Mum. You know this is me, don't you?' He stabbed at his own chest. 'Well, *this* is *her*!'

★ ★ ★

When Lou took the child from him it was as if a sunbeam crossed her frozen heart. The warmth and weight of the child felt so familiar that, even knowing it wasn't hers, Lou felt comforted. She nestled it in the crook of one arm with its chubby legs dangling over her forearm. One fat little hand grasped her nightgown as the child inspected her with a puzzled smile, seeming to know she was a stranger, yet prepared to be friendly. It was a beautiful brown-skinned little girl. Lou rested her lips on the baby's head and for a moment inhaled the smell of baby hair, so new, so sweet. Perhaps she could keep this one. The thought had insinuated itself before she could check it, bringing the old sadness rushing back. It was so tempting to go back into that semi-dark dream world where nothing was as it really should be. But something about the child's appearance had forced her to dismiss the beckoning dream. The poor little thing wasn't well. It was obvious to her. And if it was what she suspected, then the baby might not be long for this world. The mere thought of some other mother's approaching grief galvanized her and she got up, still holding the child.

'Now listen here, Ron. This baby ain't mine and she ain't your sister neither. Your blonde sister's in heaven and the new one, the dark-haired one, I didn't lose her, I give her away – to a young couple whose own little baby had died.'

Ronnie shook his head. 'You lost her – you never give her away! Why would you do that?'

She struggled for a way to explain. 'Because I couldn't look after her, you see. I couldn't even look after you, son, so how could I take care of a tiny baby?'

Telling Ronnie the truth of it seemed to dissolve the weight of guilt. She'd done it for love, that was all, and it left her mind clearer somehow.

'Now tell me honestly, Ron, where did you find this baby? We've got to get hold of her real mum.'

'She was in the park,' he said dejectedly.

'In the park? What, out in the snow?'

'No! In one of them squatter huts.'

Now she guessed who the baby belonged to – that poor little cow Clara.

'We can't keep her, love, she ain't ours.'

Ronnie's face suddenly creased into tears and Lou remembered her son was still a child himself. She shifted the baby on her arm and put the other round Ronnie.

'You know how sad I was when I lost our Sue?'

He sniffed a yes.

'Well, that's how this baby's mum is feeling right now. We can't do that to her, can we?'

'Please, Mum, can't we just keep her? I'll help you look after her and then it can all be like it was when Sue and Dad was here…'

She kissed the top of his head. It smelled bad, so different from the baby's, and yet she could remember Ronnie's own baby hair, spun fine-gold like an angel's. Now stiff with dirt and grease, she wondered how she'd not noticed it before, and his clothes stank to high heaven, as if he'd been living in a sewer.

'Listen, boy. This little mite's not well. Dry your eyes – here.' She offered him the cuff of her nightgown. 'Now run round the doctor's and bring him here. Don't take no excuses about it being too early – tell him it's an emergency.'

\* \* \*

Johnny Harper had been as convincing as his limited vocabulary would allow. Sausages and bacon he'd said, and a pot of dripping. He'd known exactly what had gone missing from the NAAFI and he'd known the name of the burglar too. Hattie had been certain that the food thief and the baby thief were one and the same, but Ronnie, Lou's son? Why would he take a baby?

She knocked hesitantly on the flat door. What if she was wrong? But Lou answered almost immediately, her eyes alive in a way Hattie hadn't seen before. She practically dragged Hattie inside.

'Don't worry, love, you've come to the right place. Clara's baby's here.'

'Oh, thank God, thank God, Lou, we've been out searching all day. How did she get here?'

'I'll tell you later. But listen, Hattie, I've had to call out the doctor. He's inside with the baby now.'

Lou led her to her bedroom where the doctor was still examining Martha. He looked up and Hattie's elation melted away at the sight of his worried expression.

'Are you the mother?' he asked and Hattie shook her head.

'I'll have to make the decision without her then. This child is dangerously ill. She has diphtheria. I'm afraid if she's to live through the night I must get her to hospital. Can you inform the child's mother?'

Hattie nodded. 'Yes, of course.' The words stuck in her throat. How on earth could she tell Clara her baby might be dead by tomorrow morning? She walked over to the bed. Martha was almost unrecognizable from the sunny child who had so easily stolen Hattie's heart. Her neck was swollen to twice its normal size and her breathing came in painful rasps. Her bright eyes were closed and a sheen of sweat covered her face.

Hattie felt tears sting her eyes. 'Oh no, not our little Martha,' she whispered to a God she did not know. 'Please, not our lovely baby.'

She leaned over Martha, willing her to open those bright eyes, and for that heart-stopping smile to light up her face again. But the child slept painfully on as the seconds ticked away. Lou put a comforting arm round her shoulders. 'She was like this when my Ronnie brought her in. She must have had it for a while. Didn't anyone notice?'

'No, we never thought it could be diphtheria. It just seemed like a bad cold. It's bitter in the huts at night and the walls are so thin,' Hattie said. 'We tried to keep her warm...'

'It's not always easy to spot,' the doctor interrupted. 'You shouldn't blame yourself. Fortunately, this lady here recognized

the symptoms. Her prompt action might make all the difference.'
The doctor hurried back to his surgery to telephone for an ambulance, leaving that 'might' hanging heavily in the air between the two women who stood watching over Martha, until Hattie broke the silence.

'How did you know?' she asked.

'Her neck, her breathing...' Lou explained. 'My Ronnie had it when he was tiny, but they caught it in time.'

'Do you think we've caught Martha's in time?'

Lou looked at Hattie with pitying eyes. 'It's bad, love. Poor Clara's had enough trouble for a lifetime, but she might have to face worse than all that put together now.'

It was only after the doctor had returned and they were waiting for the ambulance that Hattie thought to ask the question.

'Was it your Ronnie that took her?'

Lou's grief-lined face clouded with sadness. 'It's all my fault, love, not his,' she said in a low voice. 'You know I give me own baby away? Well, he thought that this little girl was mine. He thought it'd make me happy if he brung her home to me. Poor little sod, he feels bad now.'

Lou sat down on the chair next to the bed and let her head drop into her hands. 'I'd never live with meself if what he done robs that young girl of her baby...'

Hattie took the woman's hand. 'Don't say that, Lou. If he hadn't brought her to you we'd still be thinking she had a cold. Perhaps you've given her a chance.'

'Gawd's good, darlin'.' Lou looked anxiously towards Martha, who had begun to whimper. She stretched out a hand to pat her. 'Shhh, babe. Your mummy's coming soon.'

'Lou, I must go back and tell Clara we've found her. She's worried sick. But when the ambulance comes, will you go with Martha for me? Clara wouldn't want her to be on her own.' Hattie dropped to her knees beside the bed. 'Poor baby, her mum's not here...' Hattie stroked the child's cheek. 'She shouldn't be alone, not when she's so ill.'

Lou came to sit on the side of the bed. She lifted Martha, expertly cradling the sick child in her arms. 'She ain't on her own, love.'

Ronnie had kept out of sight in the kitchen, but as the ambulance drew up Lou grasped Hattie's arm. 'They won't let the boy on to the ward. Will you do me a favour and look after him? I've give him the gypsy's warning – he won't be no trouble.'

From what Hattie had heard from Buster she doubted that, but she hadn't the heart to say no. 'I'll take him with me to the squat. He can stay with us till you get home.'

Lou nodded. 'He'll want to say sorry, to Clara... I'll get him.'

Hattie could only put Lou's rosy-coloured view of Ronnie down to the fact that she'd been absent in mind if not in body while he'd been running wild over the bombsites of Bermondsey. She kissed Martha one more time, trying to remember every detail of what the doctor had told her, looking for hope in the baby's appearance, something she could give Clara to hold on to. But all she could see was that Martha's glowing brown skin had turned putty-grey and the normally springy dark ringlets lay plastered to her head, while the nostrils of her tiny flat nose strained to take in enough air to keep her lungs pumping. She turned away from the bed just as Lou came into the room with her son.

'Hattie, this is Ronnie,' she said, giving him a slight push forward.

The pinched feral look and the spikey straw hair were unmistakable. Ronnie was the boy who'd attacked her on her first day back in Bermondsey.

At sight of her he bolted. Hattie lunged, grabbing him before he could escape, while Lou looked on open-mouthed. Hattie held fast to the unravelling sleeve of his jumper and answered Lou's uncomprehending look. 'Me and Ronnie have met before.'

'Ron! Don't show me up.' Lou's surprisingly stern order stopped him from wriggling. He stood up straight, and she was surprised to see him glance nervously at his mother and then back at her, with a little shake of his head which seemed to plead for Hattie's silence.

She realized the boy was less worried about his own predicament than his mother's fragile state.

She smiled. 'You were the boy who helped carry my case on my first day back in Bermondsey!' she lied. 'He'll be all right with me, Lou. You go. I'll bring Clara as soon as I can.'

She watched Lou follow the ambulance man, who was carrying Martha swaddled in a red blanket.

'Stay with her!' she called, hardly crediting that she was trusting the woman known as Loony Lou with Clara's precious child. But something had changed in Lou, and whatever Ronnie had hoped to achieve by stealing Martha he had at least brought his mother back to some semblance of her former self.

When they were alone she turned to Ronnie.

'And you, you little git, I don't want to be saddled with you any more than you want to be with me, but I won't say nothing to your mother if you behave yourself. All right?'

He nodded, drawing his thin blazer sleeve across his runny nose.

'Is that all you've got to wear?'

'Suppose so.' Ronnie shrugged.

'Let's have a look.'

She went to the flimsy wooden wardrobe. There were a few of Lou's frocks and a red fox-fur jacket, with a detachable fox stole complete with head and brush. All the Alaska girls acquired at least one fur in their time at the factory, and Hattie couldn't say she thought much of Lou's choice.

'Here, put this on,' Hattie said, handing the jacket to Ronnie.

'I ain't going out in that. It's a bloody girl's coat!'

'It's warm. Put it on, pretend you're Davey Crocket or something.'

Ronnie pulled a face but shrugged on the jacket. 'If me mates see me in this they'll take the piss rotten.'

Hattie flicked his hair and wished she hadn't; she wasn't too sure if she'd seen something move in there. She made a concession to his pride and removed the stole with its grinning fox's head.

'And when we get to the park, you're going in the tin bath. Come on.'

'You ain't me mother,' he grumbled.

'No, but I am in charge!' she said in her sergeant's voice.

She wasn't sure why she hadn't told Lou about Ronnie's attack. The little sod had hurt her and humiliated her, and she'd often dreamed of bumping into him so that she could clip his ear when he wasn't surrounded by mates or carrying an iron rod. But that had been when he was just another anonymous street urchin; now she knew it was Lou's son who'd headed the welcome home committee she couldn't feel the same anger. The woman's tragedy was just as much his; it had seeped into his young life staining it like blood on snow. Buster had done his best, but he'd had no chance. The bombs had ruined the boy just as surely as they'd killed his grandparents and little sister.

He trailed behind her for the entire length of the Blue. She made a point of ignoring him. Only occasionally did she shoot a look behind her to make sure he was still there. The fox-fur jacket reached to his knees and he looked deeply miserable, his head perpetually lowered, no doubt hoping to avoid recognition.

The depth of snow prevented her from running, but she wanted to. A few stallholders had optimistically braved the weather and set out their wares along the Blue. People still had to buy bread and whatever fruit and veg was available – though there was little enough on display. She'd read that there were no green vegetables left in the entire country, and most butchers were only opening for a couple of days a week. Unfortunately for Ronnie, the fish-stall owner had been one of the hardy ones and seemed to have plenty of merchandise. Hattie recognized the young boy helping his father set out wings of skate as one of Ronnie's sidekicks. At the same time the boy saw Ronnie, and he gave a long wolf whistle.

'Oi, Ron, you don't half look gorgeous in your fur coat!' he called.

'Shut yer cake hole, Fish-face!' Ronnie lunged across the stall to grab the boy, scattering skate wings in the snow.

Hattie yanked him back by his fox fur and marched him off at her side.

'I haven't got time for this,' she said, smiling secretly to herself. It was revenge of sorts.

Once in the park she broke into a trot, sticking to some icy ruts, eager to get to Clara. She ordered Ronnie to keep up. In between guarding her charge she had been agonizing over how to tell Clara the best news of her life along with the worst. She still hadn't figured it out when she spotted her. Blue-faced and bundled up in her sheepskin flying jacket, she was pacing up and down outside their hut. Hattie drew in a lungful of freezing air and increased her pace. Clara ran towards her, flinging herself into Hattie's arms. 'I was hoping you'd bring her back... Oh, Hattie, we still haven't found her!' she sobbed.

Hattie felt Ronnie's fox fur brush her hand. She clutched his arm. 'Stay with me,' she said, and looked down at his filthy face, seeing fear in his eyes. Then she turned to Clara.

'I've found her, love...'

Clara's hand flew to her mouth. 'Oh! Thank God! Is she all right? Where is she?' The young woman's face was still taut with anxiety and her hand trembled on Hattie's arm. 'What's happened to her? Tell me, Hattie, I knew! I could tell it was bad news from your face.' She gripped Hattie so tightly it hurt.

'She's in Guy's – it's diphtheria.'

'Jesus, no.'

'Ronnie, catch her,' Hattie ordered as Clara staggered.

'Listen to me, love, she's all right.' Hattie spoke slowly, choosing her words carefully. 'She's in hospital. I found her at Lou's. She was the one spotted it was diphtheria. Ronnie ran for the doctor and he sent her to Guy's. She's in the best place.'

'Yes, that's good,' Clara answered, in a daze. 'But you found her at Lou's? I don't understand.'

'Ronnie here's got something to say to you.' She gave him an encouraging nod.

'I'm sorry, missus, but I took your baby,' he mumbled.

'So this is our culprit, is it? Not Johnny Harper then?' The male voice startled them all and they turned as one. Hattie hadn't noticed the police constable approaching. She shot an enquiring look at Clara.

'Joe said you thought it was Johnny Harper took her, so that's what we told the police.'

'Yes, madam.' The constable interrupted. 'We were informed it was a case of child abduction, and that the Harpers were involved. We've sent someone to speak to them.'

Hattie groaned inwardly. 'No! It's nothing to do with the Harpers. I was wrong.' If the police turned up at Lenny's asking questions he would certainly blame her.

'So are you now saying this boy is responsible?' The constable gave him a stern look.

'The baby was at our workmate's all the time,' Hattie covered quickly.

'So, the missing child's been found with a friend?' The constable was writing carefully in his pad, but the expression on his face called her a liar.

'Obviously, your workmate's son had no permission to take the baby. We'll need to speak to him at the station, along with his mother. We take child protection very seriously.'

Ronnie fixed his gaze upon Hattie, his normally sharp eyes wide with fear. She almost wanted to laugh. Child protection? Where was child protection when Ronnie and his mates were hopping the wag for weeks on end, risking their lives playing in Bermondsey's ruins? The stench rising from Ronnie's dirty clothes reminded her of Pissy Pants and she realized Johnny Harper had once been an ordinary, mischievous boy like Ronnie, until his love of sausages had landed him in a madhouse, for want of anywhere else to put him. These days it would be an approved school not an asylum, but she wasn't sure they were much better, and surely Ronnie deserved the chance of not becoming another Pissy Pants?

'Does it need to come to that? I'll stand as character witness,

Constable. It was all a misunderstanding!' she said quickly. 'The boy thought the baby was his own sister and took her home. As soon as his mother realized the mistake she would have brought her back… it's just that the baby was ill and she got a doctor out instead.'

Hattie held her breath, hoping that Clara wouldn't ask any awkward questions in front of the policeman.

'I suppose I should be grateful,' Clara said, holding Hattie's gaze, 'that Lou knew to send for the doctor.'

The constable didn't look convinced, but she hoped she'd said enough to avoid a charge.

'We'll still need to interview the boy and his mother. Sounds like she doesn't have much control over him if he's out in this weather stealing babies from their cots.'

When he'd left Hattie found herself prising Ronnie's hand from hers. He'd been holding on so tightly that her fingers were white. She let herself breathe again.

'What's going on, Hattie, and why is he here?'

'Let's go inside.'

Once back in their hut it took seconds to explain. Clara knew Lou's story. 'But I still don't understand. Why would you think she was your sister?' Clara asked Ronnie.

The boy had shed the ridiculous fox-fur jacket and stood, scraping the toe of his wet plimsoll across the wooden floor.

'I'm really sorry, missus, but our baby had black hair just like your'n. I did only see her for a minute when she was born, though. When I see your baby through the window, I thought it was her and that you'd took her from me mum, so I was only getting her back, weren't I? I should've known when I see her brown skin it was the wrong baby…' His habitually hard expression was softened by disappointment and remorse.

Clara took his chapped hand. 'You shouldn't have taken her, Ronnie, but I know you just made a mistake and you looked after her for me, didn't you? You took her teddy so she wouldn't feel alone, didn't you?'

'Sorry, but I lost the teddy,' he said.

Clara went to Martha's cot and produced it. 'We found it, and when I go to the hospital I'll give it to her, shall I?'

Word had got round the little colony that Hattie had returned and soon their hut was full of people. The main topic of discussion was getting Clara to the hospital quickly, and Alan surprised Hattie by offering to drive her.

'I thought you'd used up all your petrol ration?' Hattie said.

Alan shot Clara an anxious look, his normal bright expression softened by concern. 'I have, but poor Clara needs all the help she can get. I'll get petrol somehow – there's a friend who doesn't always use his...'

Hattie knew there was always a 'friend' to be found in Bermondsey who could supply extra rations for the right backhander. It would cost him an arm and a leg, and she was touched that he'd stepped up to help Clara get to her baby more quickly.

'Thanks, Alan,' she said, kissing his cheek, grateful that if she couldn't be with Clara herself, at least he would be.

The others gathered round, giving Clara hugs and good wishes. And when Alan was ready to go, Hattie held her friend tight. Clara looked so fragile and young herself, and yet her wide dark eyes seemed ancient, heavy with the terror of every mother whose child was in danger.

'I wish I could come with you, but I promised Lou I'd look after him.' Hattie nodded towards Ronnie. 'Martha will be all right, I promise.' But she was promising herself, just as much as Clara, a dark sliver of guilt taking hold. Perhaps she should have left them in that basement after all, instead of bringing the child to a hut in the middle of an Arctic winter.

Clara gave her a brave smile.

'Look after her!' Hattie called to Alan as, with a protective arm round Clara, he led her away to his car.

When she turned back from the door she realized that Joe hadn't left. She'd noticed him hanging back during all the excitement, but his gaze had frequently returned to Ronnie. The boy was sitting close to the stove now. His eyes had begun to droop as soon as he'd received Clara's forgiveness.

'Why do you always have to go against everything I ask?' she hissed at Joe, who didn't appear in any hurry to leave.

Joe looked taken aback. 'What do you mean?'

'I thought you agreed not to tell Clara about the bloody teddy and you had to go and ignore me.' It might seem unimportant to him, but she was fed up with his contradictory ways. After holding herself so rigidly controlled for Clara's sake, she suddenly wanted to be angry at someone, and it couldn't be Ronnie.

'Vera told her,' he said, leaving her feeling foolish. But he seemed more interested in Ronnie than in her wrongful accusations.

'Do you know him?' Clara said, keeping her voice low so as not to wake Ronnie.

Joe shrugged. 'He seems familiar. I might be able to tell if some of the dirt was removed.' He gave her one of his sudden smiles.

'Well, you might get a chance. You can fill up the tin bath for me and chuck him in. I promised his mother I'd look after him, but he's not sleeping in this hut until all his little friends have been scrubbed away,' she said, scratching at her own hair.

Ronnie must have had one ear open, for he sat up. 'I ain't havin' no bath in front of you!' he said.

'Not me. Joe's supervising. I don't trust you to give yourself more than a cat's lick!'

Ronnie looked at Joe. The boy's skin beneath its dirt seemed to pale. 'Well, I ain't soddin' well taking off me clothes in front of him neither!' And he made a run for the door.

Hattie stuck out a foot, sending him sprawling, but as Joe picked him up he thrashed his bony legs and arms like a bird caught in a cat's mouth. From nowhere came a flash of steel and Ronnie's flick knife slashed across Joe's knuckles.

'You little sod!' Joe yelped, but held on fast to his wrist and with a well-practised grip forced the knife from his hand, sending it clattering to the floor.

'Ronnie! What's the matter with you? We're not going to hurt you. It's a bath, for God's sake. Haven't I just got you out of all sorts of trouble with the police?'

Ronnie's head drooped, then he seemed to make a decision. 'You're all right,' he said, 'but I ain't going nowhere with him.'

Hattie gave Joe a puzzled shrug. 'Seems Ronnie's not keen on you. Let's forget the bath. We'll be all right now.'

Joe held his injured hand. 'So long as you're sure.'

Ronnie sidled closer to Hattie's side and she held out her hand for the knife, which he'd pocketed. He relinquished it meekly enough. 'I'm sure,' she said.

Joe gave a quick nod. 'Any trouble, you know where I am.'

And Hattie watched him go back to his hut, dripping blood along the snow-covered duckboard as he went.

It was an agonizing night for Hattie, alone except for the boy asleep in her own bed. She'd taken Clara's bed, for although she'd made Ronnie wash his hair and have a good wash, she hadn't wished to visit any lingering infestation on Clara. She couldn't imagine what her friend was going through. But at least Clara had Lou with her, who'd been through the same thing herself. She remembered how Clara had asked if it was possible to love a child too much, and right now Hattie understood why she'd answered yes. The thought of Martha not being here tomorrow was too much to bear. And Lou must have once prayed for the delinquent in the next bed, exactly as Clara was praying for Martha now. When had he stopped being the blond-haired little angel? Wars weren't good breeding grounds for angels. When all he'd known was destruction, why should they expect anything else of the boy? Hattie stared at the corrugated roof above her bed and seemed to hear the weight of snow creaking and sliding down it. Was this the long-awaited thaw?

'You awake?' Ronnie whispered, startling her.

'You should be asleep.' It was too dark to see him, but she felt he was sitting up.

'So should you. Do you think the baby will be all right?'

'I don't know, Ron. We can only pray.'

'That never did me no good before.'

'There's always a first time. Your mum seems more herself.'

'Yeah. Back to nagging me.'

'Ronnie, why don't you like Joe?'

There was a silence and for a moment she thought he'd gone back to sleep. Then he said, 'He's in that camera club.'

She almost laughed, wondering how he even knew. 'It's his hobby. What's wrong with that?'

'Nothing, I suppose. It's just I don't like his type. They're …' He searched for a word. 'They think their better'an us, think they can do what they like, order us about. Well, they can't…'

'Joe's all right, when you get to know him.' It seemed odd that she was defending him, but the truth was she didn't know him. 'Anyway, you'll be home tomorrow and you'll never have to see him again.'

'I'm sorry about the baby. I did say a prayer.'

'I know. So did I.'

'Why didn't you grass me up to the copper?'

She hesitated, not really knowing the answer. 'I felt sorry for your mother.' It was only half a truth, but the other half she was not yet willing to admit.

# 13

## Wolves and Lambs

### March–April 1947

Clara had never known such fear. It seemed to invade every cell of her body, as relentless as the snowstorms that had besieged them, blanking out everything but Martha's next breath. Every out-breath was a prayer, 'Don't let her die', and every in-breath a piercing anxiety that her prayer wouldn't be answered. She felt it was somehow wrong to be breathing herself while her darling baby was drifting between life and death, when, like the most fragile of snowflakes, it would need only a change in temperature to dissolve her existence.

She was allowed too brief a time at her daughter's bedside and though she protested, the sister ushered her out after half an hour. She sat in the corridor outside the ward through the long night, with Lou on one side and Alan on the other. Alan soon dropped off to sleep, but Lou, whose nights had usually been spent wandering the ruins, was an ever-wakeful, comforting companion. She didn't need to speak. Sometimes her hand grasped Clara's and she would whisper, 'Gawd's good, gel. Gawd's good.' But mostly the woman sat silent and stoical; her son, Ronnie, all the evidence she needed that even in a life like hers, which had seen so much loss, there had once been a miracle.

There was no question of Clara sleeping. Awake and alert to every rustle of a nurse's skirt, every cough coming from the ward, every imagined breath behind the screens, she felt that her concentrated love alone could keep Martha alive. And if she didn't survive, then Clara doubted she'd ever find the comfort of sleep again. Eventually, the morning routine of the hospital began, with the banging of tea trollies and flurries of starched uniformed nurses coming on and off duty. She felt a stab of fear as the ward sister approached. Her expression was a professional blank – calm and unemotional. Clara held her breath.

'Well, my dear. Your daughter is still with us. Doctor says it's a miracle she survived the night.'

Clara's sob caused Alan to jerk out of sleep. Lou gripped her hand as the sister went on. 'We administered the anti-toxins just in time…' Here the sister nodded at Lou. 'Thanks to this lady's prompt action.'

Clara thanked God and the sister and then thanked Lou, who in the end asked her to stop for the sister hadn't yet finished.

'But I must warn you, my dear, she's not out of the woods yet. We had to put a tube down her throat to help her breathe, and we don't know yet if there has been any permanent damage.' The sister waited for what she'd said to sink in.

'Damage?'

'It's only a possibility. Sometimes we see paralysis or heart damage, but it's too early to say… Try not to worry.'

The woman was asking the impossible. Until a second ago, Clara had wished for nothing more than Martha's survival, but as quickly as the euphoria of that miracle had arisen it was replaced by this new anxiety.

'Can I see her?'

The sister nodded and Clara followed the swish of her starched dress into the ward.

Martha's eyes were still closed. The tube in her mouth dragged down the tender, blue-tinged lips. But apart from the paraphernalia she looked more like herself; her neck wasn't as swollen and her skin colour had lost its blue-grey tinge. Clara sat beside her until she was gently asked to leave again. And yet to leave was almost as painful as the long waiting through the night.

Now the pain was more active, more insistent. Martha was alive. But when would she be back with them?

'You and Lou stay here while I go and crank up the car, get it warmed up,' Alan offered. And when she started to protest, he insisted. 'The last thing you need is a chill. You'll have to be fighting fit for when Martha comes round.' He fixed her with an encouraging smile, softer than his normal cheeky grin, and she was taken aback. This was not the flip, jokey Alan she'd come to know, and she found herself warming to this new side of him. She was grateful for his optimism, even if she didn't share it.

As Alan drove her and Lou through the London Bridge traffic Clara gazed at the ice-bound world, which was beginning to melt. Cars skidded on roads that were turning to dirty slushy pools. People who'd got used to the feel of ice beneath their feet were sliding on the slush and tumbling over banks of melting snow piled against each kerb. The car crawled along St Thomas Street, where the railway viaduct rose like a sheer iceberg from a sea of melt water. She silently berated herself. This snowbound place had been to blame – no, *she* was to blame. Her Martha had been born under blue skies. She should never have brought her here. It had been her wounded pride and her broken heart that had sent her fleeing back home, and it had cost her child dear.

\*

In the weeks that followed, the snow that had bound them for so long almost disappeared and the world began to melt, with the Thames threatening to burst its banks and swallow them all up. And through it all her child simply slept on.

'Clara, love, you've got to eat something. Clara?' Hattie's voice startled her. She looked down at the untouched plate of food and began pushing it around with her fork. She had been trying to banish the images of an empty hospital bed and the pitying face of the nurse as she told her Martha had died. They were imaginings that plagued her before every visit.

'Eat? I can't, Hattie, it sticks in me throat,' she said, shoving the plate away. 'I don't know why you keep making me dinners. Besides, I'm not putting anything into the kitty now I'm not at work.'

'I've told you not to worry about that.' Hattie sighed and began clearing away the tea things, when a knock came at the hut door.

'That'll be Alan,' Hattie told her. 'He's offered to drive you to Guy's tonight.'

'He shouldn't,' Clara said. 'He should be taking you out somewhere nice, not spending his evenings ferrying me backwards and forwards.'

'Don't be silly, love. He only wants to help. Besides, it won't be long and we'll be able to dance every night away – once the baby's better.'

Clara recognized the tone that Hattie used when she was trying to lift her spirits. For her friend's sake, she tried to believe all the positive things she said.

'Yes, 'course we will!' It was Alan, smiling as he spoke. He gave Hattie a brief kiss and turned to Clara. 'Are you ready? I brought some sandwiches, thought you might need something to keep you going while you're up the hospital.'

Hattie gave an approving nod.

Every evening he came to drive Clara to the hospital, every evening he brought her sandwiches and every evening she didn't eat them. 'You shouldn't have, Alan.'

'Yes, he should!' Hattie insisted in her sergeant's voice, and Clara wondered if Hattie was missing him. She felt she'd been monopolizing his evenings.

'I don't deserve such kindness,' Clara said, forcing back tears.

'Stop that, Clara,' Hattie told her sternly. 'You're not to keep blaming yourself. You're a good mum, you didn't do anything wrong.'

But Clara didn't believe her.

★ ★ ★

As Hattie punched her cards and contemplated her last day as an Alaska girl, a gush of snow melt poured from a broken gutter on to her head. Typical. This place wasn't going to let her desertion go unpunished. Crosbie had been as good as his word, and despite her transfer being slow in coming through he'd arranged everything with Chris Harper, though she still had no idea how Crosbie had won him over. But there was a cloud dimming her happiness at escaping the factory. It had been almost three weeks since Martha had been taken into Guy's and she was still no nearer coming home. What's more, poor Clara had got it into her head that it was all her fault, that her baby was pining for 'home'. This was impossible, Hattie argued, as she'd only been on Australian soil for a few months of her life. But Clara wouldn't listen. Hattie brushed at her hair as she negotiated the iron stairs, which were slick with water pouring from every gutter. Just one more day to get through and tonight she'd walk out with her cards and never look back. Clara hadn't been at the Alaska since Martha's illness and Hattie could see the strain was beginning to tell on her. Her pretty face was gaunt and hollow-eyed. It wasn't just worry about her child. Clara was running out of money, but the girl would rather starve than accept help.

In the squatters' colony it was usually easy to help each other out. Food from their allotment was shared with all who worked a stint on it, including the children. Then they had what they called their ration bank, where those who hated cheese but needed bacon could swap rations with each other. If there was a pressing need it was usually noticed and someone would step in with an offer of coal or some precious coupons. When Clara stopped eating, she insisted it was because she couldn't stomach anything. And when Hattie offered to buy her a new blanket – to replace the one which had been topped and tailed till there was nothing of the original left – Clara assured her it was warm enough and instead filled empty ginger beer bottles with boiling water to supply the heat that the blanket no longer gave her. It was almost as if she were punishing herself. Hattie knew her friend was spending what little money she had on medical bills. If only the government had moved themselves and got their much vaunted National Health Service up and running by now, it could have saved Clara a world of worry. But disease didn't run to the government's schedule, no more than the trains or the buses or the mines or anything else in this broken-down country did.

Her dampened mood had made her irritable. When she got to her machine and Lou innocently asked if there was any news of Martha, she snapped a curt *no* and instantly regretted it.

'Sorry, Lou. Take no notice of me.'

'It's just the worry getting to you, gel,' Lou replied, without taking offence.

Since Lou's long vigil with Clara, Hattie had got into the daily habit of exchanging news with the woman. First Lou would ask about Martha, then Hattie would ask about Ronnie. For the police hadn't dropped the matter of the abduction, and Hattie had promised to be a character witness when Ronnie appeared before the juvenile court. 'You're right, I'm worried about Clara. She's always been thin, but now she's disappearing! Her arms and legs are like sticks and her clothes are falling off her. She's not getting a penny from the welfare, not a penny from this place, and she won't accept any help from me...'

'What about from me?' Lou asked.

'You?' Hattie had seen Lou's house, and if anything she was in a worse state than Clara.

'Not just me...'

Hattie noticed that the supervisor, Bessie Clutterbuck, aka Old Buttercup, was approaching at glacial speed – no doubt she had some fault to find with Hattie on her last day. Hattie had been surprised at the old woman's reaction to the news of her going – the supervisor had acted as if it were a personal betrayal. Now some of the girls were leaving their machines and joining Bessie.

'We had a whip-round for Clara. Here, you give it to the poor little cow,' Old Buttercup quavered, and her liver-spotted hand shook slightly as she gave Hattie the envelope, which was heavy with coins.

'Oh, girls!' Hattie exclaimed, genuinely touched. 'You're diamonds.'

'It was Lou's idea,' Bessie said and Lou looked vaguely surprised to be praised.

A woman who'd been one of the most vociferous condemners of Clara left her machine and walked deliberately over to the group. Hattie was expecting some abuse, but to her surprise she leaned over and put a shilling into Hattie's hand.

'I didn't get a chance before. Tell Clara we're thinking of her,' she said, a little shamefaced.

'I'll try to give it to her. But she's so independent, she won't take no help,' Hattie explained to the women.

'If she won't take it for herself, tell her it's for the baby,' Lou said.

Hattie felt a lump rising in her throat. She knew many of these women had little enough themselves, with too many children or husbands out of work. There were some who could have shown Clara more sympathy in the past, but a child was a child, and it didn't take much imagination to realize what Clara was going through. She felt less ashamed of being an Alaska girl now than she had when she'd clocked on this morning.

'Oh, and this is for you,' Old Buttercup added, drawing a little package from her overall pocket. 'Leaving present, though if it was up to me you'd get sod all for deserting us.'

'She just means we'll miss you,' Lou said. 'Open it then.'

The little package contained three bars of Pears soap. 'My God!' She lifted them to her nose and inhaled the long-forgotten tangy scent from the translucent amber ovals. She couldn't remember when bars of soap had gone missing from the shops, but it was long enough ago for her and Clara to have started saving leftover pieces to press into a new bar. 'Where did you get these?' she marvelled.

'Don't ask,' Vera said. 'No names, no pack drill!'

From this, Hattie gathered that Brian had been under the counter again.

'All right, this ain't getting the rabbit skins cleaned. They ain't payin' us for standing around doing sod all,' Bessie said, ushering them away.

Hattie noticed Doris, stony-faced, pointedly not looking up. She and her best friend Marjie were the only ones who had continued to sit feeding rabbit pelts into their machines. Hattie shrugged. It was piece work, and they refused to lose a penny for someone like Clara, but as Old Buttercup passed them she dipped an arthritic hand into Doris's bin.

'Dotty, your rods ain't working properly. Look at the dust still in that.' She rubbed her misshapen thumb along the white fur. 'You'll have to come off that machine till I can get it fixed.'

'Well, what am I supposed to do? I'll lose me piece rate!' Doris was flushed, no doubt realizing there was nothing at all wrong with the machine.

'Help the boy sweep up the floor,' Bessie told her, with a wave of dismissal, before swaying back to her chair.

'I ain't a bleedin' cleaner!' Doris snapped back.

It took the forelady several seconds to turn round. 'I'm docking your pay for foul language.'

'What! When did that rule come in? You'd have to dock the whole bloody factory—'

'I'm a bit deaf, love, I don't hear half what people say. But funny enough, I heard you.'

Hattie had never loved the toothless old tartar, but today Old Buttercup had become her heroine.

Buster had at long last grudgingly forgiven her for leaving, especially after he'd heard how she'd tried to protect his nephew from the police.

'You coming for a leaving drink, Hattie?' he asked after work.

'No, not tonight, Buster. I want to get back to Clara.'

'Baby's no better then?'

She shook her head, feeling the return of a sickness in the pit of her stomach. Martha, though she was now breathing on her own, wasn't waking up, and what the doctors were telling Clara sounded suspiciously like a preparation for the worst.

'Every day Clara goes up to Guy's and expects to get her baby back. It's heartbreaking, Buster, and I don't know what to do for her.'

'What can you do, love? If I'd got the answer to that, I would have been able to help me poor sister, but I couldn't. Makes me glad I'm never going to have kids.'

'Me too.' But Hattie thought Buster looked the opposite of glad. 'How's Aiden?'

He shook his head. 'No good, darlin'. He never wanted to settle down, too young. Pissed off with a feller he met in Soho.'

'Oh, Buster, you never told me!'

'You got your own troubles, Hattie. Besides, you're heading for pastures new...'

Her workmates' kindness and Buster's obvious sadness had its effect, and though she still desperately wanted to get out of the factory, she did begin to wonder if she'd made the right choice. For all her sense of difference, these were girls she'd grown up with, their families had gone through the same privations as hers, their streets were her streets. What did she have to do with the likes of Crosbie, and what did he see in her? The answer was obvious and was perhaps another cause for her hesitation. She guessed she would have an almighty fight on her hands with Mr Crosbie and his ice-blue eyes.

How Crosbie had found out her status she didn't know. Perhaps he'd noticed her rough accent or her rougher hands, but she suspected he'd known from day one and had strung her along for a little while for his own amusement. She remembered a stupid joke he'd made at one of the rehearsals about keeping her housemaid's knees covered, and she realized he must have been laughing all along at her attempts to fool him into believing she was an office worker. She would have to be ten steps ahead of Crosbie.

The hardest thing about becoming an office girl had been finding something decent to wear. All her clothes were either threadbare or five years out of date. The only thing that would do was a summer frock she'd last worn in Belgium. She paired it with a cardigan she'd found in the Sally Ann, and when she got to the office in Upper Thames Street she exchanged her fur bootees for high heels. It felt so strange to be without her overall. It was ugly, certainly, but also a great leveller. Beneath the drab green coveralls, who knew if your frock was falling to bits?

She presumed she had to report to Crosbie's office. There was an outer office where a couple of typists and young office girls had already started the day's work, and as she passed through it she drew some curious glances. She knocked at Crosbie's door and when there was no answer pushed it open. She was immediately caught off-guard when he didn't look up. She was expecting him to be as overly charming as he had the last time she'd seen him.

'Oh, Miss Wright, good,' he said, intent on a typed document. 'I'll want you along with me this morning. A meeting of potential buyers in the boardroom, and afterwards you'll be modelling the lines they're interested in. I'll come and collect you.'

He went on scrutinizing the letter and she was left standing in the middle of the office, unsure what to do. She retreated to the outer office and after putting her coat and hat on to the stand in the corner, she sat at the nearest desk and waited. The other girls pretended to be oblivious to her. One tapped at a typewriter, another was struggling with a huge ledger and a third was filing her nails. Hattie wasn't going to ask what to do.

'That's Diana's desk,' the girl with the nail file said. 'You can't sit there.'

'Do I get a desk?'

'Ask him.' The girl inclined her head towards Crosbie's door. 'He's the one that hired you. He can show you what to do.'

Hattie shrugged. She didn't care if her appointment had ruffled a few feathers. She wasn't here to make friends. 'I'll just sit here till Diana gets in then.'

But she didn't have to wait, for Crosbie came out at that moment and this time gave her a charming smile. 'Our clients await, Miss Wright. Follow me.'

Her duties were easy: making tea and coffee for the buyers while Crosbie gave them his sales pitch in the long, high-ceilinged showroom, then afterwards modelling whichever coats they'd shown interest in. The morning flew by, and after the buyers had left she was hanging a long musquash coat on the rail when Crosbie came up behind her.

'Excellent first morning's work, Miss Wright.'

She felt herself pushed into the rack of furs. Making a grab for the rail, her hand sank deep into the musquash but could get no purchase, while the other hand slipped down the length of a chestnut-coloured beaver lamb as his hand encircled her waist, ostensibly to save her from falling. He spun her round to face him.

'Oops! We can't have you injuring yourself on your first day, can we? You're going to be a real asset, Hattie. Honestly, I couldn't keep my eyes off you.' He grinned and she felt his hand move down to squeeze her behind. Her face burned and about now she would normally have brought up a knee and then given him a right-hander. But she only had to think of the pittance she'd been getting at the Alaska since the three-day week, or remember her fingers aching from cold after the daily power cuts had left the factory like a cold store, and she knew a few tussles with Crosbie would be no hardship. If she wanted to keep the job, she had to keep him on her side.

'I'll take that as a compliment, Mr Crosbie, but I think you should move your hand off my arse, just in case someone comes in. I wouldn't want you to get into trouble,' she said, moving his hand away and stepping to one side.

He laughed, wagging his finger at her. 'Watch that factory girl mouth of yours, darling. It might well get *you* into trouble one of these days.'

She had encountered many men like Crosbie, who thought any pretty woman was fair game, and she was confident she could deal with him. As far as Hattie was concerned, he was fair game too.

Fortunately, for the rest of that day Crosbie was occupied in meetings and she spent the afternoon in the office, being patronized by the other girls who looked no older than twelve. Obviously, word had got round that she'd migrated from the factory, for they seemed unable to believe that Hattie could master a telephone or a typewriter. It struck her as ironic, for by the war's end she'd been number one in a gun team in Belgium, with the Germans still mounting a fierce resistance only a stone's throw away. After VE day she'd run a department of twelve in the communications HQ in Brussels, yet none of that seemed to matter now the war was over. To these people she was what she'd always been, a factory girl from Bermondsey. It was irritating, but life was full of irritants and she'd swallow this one – for now.

When her first day came to an end she didn't feel like going straight home to the squat. She needed to shake off all the petty problems of her day before she saw Clara. For some reason, the young woman believed her when she promised that Martha would certainly recover fully. Hattie would keep her voice calm and steady, praising the skill of the doctors, the renown of Guy's, the resilience of children. She used a tone she'd learned in the army, which she called her 'calm under fire' voice, and luckily it worked every time on Clara. But tonight Hattie was shaky herself and would be no good to her friend. She went to see Cissie instead. If anyone could give her advice about predatory men, it was her mother. But Cissie, it appeared, was in the midst of her own man troubles.

'I've sent him back down the basement,' she announced, after adding a drop of her precious brandy to Hattie's tea.

'Ciss! You can't do that to Mario. He's been so good to you.'

'Don't talk to me about him. He gets on me nerves. I like a bit of a challenge, and he's like a great slobbery puppy.'

Cissie had recently applied a fresh coat of red lipstick and her newly dyed hair was particularly zesty. 'Matter of fact, Hattie,

I'm going out with someone else tonight, so I'll have to get a move on. Everything all right with your new job?'

'Oh, fine,' Hattie replied.

'Don't sound fine.' Cissie was peering closely into the mirror, patting down her red halo.

'It's just the boss is already after me. Well, he was after me before he gave me the job.'

Cissie carried on pulling. 'Well, if I ain't taught you nothing else, I've taught you how to deal with fellers.'

Hattie would get no sympathy here. 'You're right, you didn't teach me much else,' she answered.

'Cheeky cow. What d'you reckon?' Cissie spun round for inspection.

'Gorgeous,' Hattie said, resigning herself to getting no help from her mother.

She drained the tea and brandy and they left the house together, Hattie helping Cissie negotiate the front steps, which she knew were almost invisible to her without her glasses.

'Mind how you go, Ciss. Don't fall arse over tit before you get to your date!' she called, and Cissie raised two fingers as she turned into Fort Road.

Once Cissie was gone, Hattie went down to the basement. Mario's eyes lit up when he answered her knock.

'Hattie! Did my Cecilia send for me?' he said, and she hated to disappoint him.

'Sorry, Mario, she's gone out, but I wanted to see how you were?'

He shrugged, trying to hide his disappointment. 'It's a place to live. I have had worse.' He showed her in. Nothing had changed. The same oil lamp lit damp-encrusted walls and the smell of drains was as putrid.

'My mother's a blind fool, Mario, and I've tried to tell her she couldn't find better than you...' She paused, looking round at the grim place he had now to call home. 'But I reckon you could certainly do better than this!' she said.

When she and Mario at last approached the park there was a sudden power cut. Every street lamp and house light was extinguished. Warm glows from pub windows vanished and the world was cloaked in darkness. During the worsening fuel crisis everyone had been on their honour to use only a few hours of electricity per day. Most people had kept to it, but the government had begun enforced power cuts, and they'd become used to being enveloped by the dark without a moment's notice.

'This is worse than the blackout!' Hattie said, digging into her bag for her torch. But as she switched it on, the bulb flickered and died.

'It's no problem,' Mario said. 'It's just like home. My village, it's in the mountains. No electricity, lots of trees. I like it here!' Mario's teeth flashed white in the darkness and she was glad to take his arm as they pushed on through the slushy Oval towards the darkened squatters' colony. It was only as they came to the outer huts that they heard the commotion. Raised angry voices, feet thundering along the duckboards, and then the unmistakable scuffling of a fight. She broke into a run, but was soon outstripped by Mario. They came upon a scene of chaos outside the NAAFI, with a group of squatters holding spades and lumps of wood ranged opposite a gang of young men. At their head was someone she recognized instantly, the neat, stylishly dressed figure of Lenny Harper.

Hattie sprang between the two groups, noticing that Joe had put himself at the forefront of the squatters. 'What are you doing here?' she demanded of Lenny, carefully planting herself out of his reach.

'Your mates ain't very friendly, Hattie,' he said. The velvet collar of his well-cut overcoat was turned up and at his throat he wore a silk scarf. His hands were casually plunged into his pockets. But she knew that in one would be a flick knife and in the other a knuckleduster. A cigarette hung from his lips and his demeanour was unperturbed, in stark contrast to the angry faces of the squatters. Only Joe matched his coolness. He fixed

Lenny with a cobra-like stare from beneath the stray strand of hair falling across his forehead. Joe didn't move a muscle, but stood holding a stave of wood like a latter-day Little John of Sherwood Forest.

'They're trying to muscle in,' Joe said, his eyes never leaving Lenny. 'We've told them nicely they need to be approved by the committee, but they're not having any of it.'

Lenny's hand moved from his pocket and she saw the flash of steel, whether a knife or a knuckleduster she couldn't tell. 'This camp don't belong to you. We're homeless, same as you lot, and we'll take whichever huts we bloody well like.' Lenny held his impassive expression and didn't raise his voice, but the pitch became slightly higher. A small change which perhaps none but Hattie would notice, but which signalled that he was about to make his move.

'He's got a knife,' she yelled just as Lenny lunged at Joe. 'Mario, help him!' But she needn't have worried. Before Mario's great physique had even lumbered into action, Joe moved so quickly his hands were a blur and Lenny was on his back, spread-eagled in melting, dirty snow. He looked far from elegant now and with a gash oozing blood.

The Harper gang surged forward, surrounding Lenny, who flipped back on to his feet in one fluid motion, ready with the knife. Joe pushed Hattie behind him as Mario joined him, with Brian and Levin either side brandishing iron crowbars. They made an impressive-looking quartet. With the other men backing them up and even some of the women standing ready with saucepans, she saw a flicker of hesitation cross Lenny's face.

'Go now, Joe,' she whispered urgently.

He gave a small nod, raised the staff, and charged straight at Lenny, while Mario caught two other gang members with a couple of sharp left-hooks. Levin hobbled another with a crowbar and Brian rugby-tackled another.

'Follow me!' Hattie called to Vera. She grabbed a frying pan from Maisie, joining in the chase as the Harpers retreated. She managed a satisfying swipe to Dickie Harper's broad buttocks and heard a few yelps from others who'd been slapped with fish fryers or hit by hurled colanders. They chased the Harpers clean off the Oval. But before the darkness could quite swallow him, Lenny turned, running backwards. He wagged his finger at her and called across the churned-up slush. 'Next time, Hattie!' Then he skipped lightly beneath the ruined avenue of trees and trotted out of sight.

Joe came up beside her. 'Who is he?'

'That's Lenny Harper.'

Joe grunted. 'He seems to know you pretty well.'

Hattie turned away. 'He did once, a long time ago, but not now. I do think it's my fault he's here, though.'

After the squatters had dispersed to their huts, the committee met in the NAAFI, which was freezing cold as the government had banned coal fires till the autumn, and all their supplies of wood were too damp to use. The large hut was lit by a single oil lamp. Vera handed her some cocoa that she'd painstakingly brewed on a small spirit stove. Hattie blew on it and cupped the mug in her hands.

'So what are they up to?' Joe asked, looking at her.

'Of course they're not homeless. Lenny and his brothers still live with their mum in Southwark Park Road and none of the others are exactly down on their luck. Lenny's just looking for some quick money.'

'How?' Joe asked.

'Setting himself up as a landlord. People are so desperate he could charge whatever rent he liked, and all he's got to do is take over a few of the huts, same as we did.'

'But that's why we've got the committee, to keep out any old rough,' Brian said. He was rubbing his knuckles, which had done a considerable amount of damage to the jaw of one of the Harper gang.

'If he wants money, perhaps we should just pay him off,' Vera suggested.

Mario stirred. He'd been allowed into the meeting as it hadn't yet been decided where he could stay, though he passed his entrance interview when he knocked out one of their attackers' front teeth. 'Men like him, you pay them once, they come back again,' he said. 'They only understand one thing.' Usually the most gentle of men, Mario suddenly smashed his great fist down on to the trestle table, startling Hattie, so that she spilled her cocoa.

'All the army boundary posts are still here. I could build a bloody good fence round the camp in no time!' Levin the nailer offered.

'A fence has never kept Lenny Harper out before,' Hattie said. 'It'll be a waste of money and effort. He'll jump over it and take our homes while we're sleeping. We'll have to fight him.' She'd been almost musing to herself, and when she looked up from her cocoa she saw Joe staring at her.

'I'm with Hattie. We said we'd start a night patrol after all the burglaries. Let's do it now. These Harpers are more likely to come at night. We could patrol in groups on a rota system. At least we'll be ready for them next time.'

'I'm in,' Brian volunteered.

'You would be, you old bruiser,' Vera said. 'Anything for a scrap.'

'But we'll need a bit more discipline than for a pub fight,' Hattie told them.

Brian turned his nose up. 'No fear, I don't want to go back in the army!'

And Hattie realized suddenly that she did. 'I was a bloody good sergeant, but we'll need a captain.'

'That's easy.' Brian gave Joe a salute. 'Him. You was a captain, wasn't you, Joe?'

Joe nodded. 'In the Chindits.'

'That's settled then,' Hattie said. 'But don't expect all of us to go around saluting you.'

'So long as you do as you're told,' he said, straight-faced, and she couldn't tell if he was joking or not. He really was an enigma – not like Alan, with his open ways and bright smile.

As they shut the NAAFI door behind them and walked back to their huts she couldn't help grinning. 'Alan and Clara missed it all!'

'He took Clara to visit Martha.'

'He's been a very good friend to her,' she said, suddenly realizing just how little she'd seen of Alan over the past weeks, since he'd been ferrying Clara to and from the hospital. Joe gave her a rare smile. 'Yes, Alan's a decent chap.'

'The best,' Hattie agreed, smiling back.

# 14

## Secrets and Smiles

### April–May 1947

Clara held her breath. Had she seen a movement? No, Martha's curled eyelashes seemed firmly closed now. As the weeks had passed and still her daughter hadn't woken, she'd imagined such a movement countless times. No doubt she'd imagined that small tremble this time too. But then she saw another. The baby's eyelids definitely flickered. Clara jumped up from the chair at the bedside, as they opened into a wide-eyed stare. She cupped her child's face. Leaning close, she whispered, 'Martha? Martha? It's Mummy.'

But her daughter's normally eloquent eyes showed no flicker of recognition and she jerked her little head to one side, her gaze roaming the room as if Clara were not there.

'It's me, babe, it's Mummy!' With one gentle finger, she turned Martha's face towards her. 'Hello, my darling!' She smiled, but something in her heart flinched from the unknowing gaze that met hers. She waited with sickening hope for her child to come back to her. She smiled brightly, in spite of her fear. 'Look what Mummy's brought you.' She held up Johnny Harper's gift, the once-loved teddy bear. Martha's gaze shifted and fixed on the glassy eyes of the toy. Then, as Clara waggled the bear's head, a quicksilver flash of knowing lit her daughter's eyes. They crinkled into a smile, and then a little chuckle escaped her lips as her fat fist reached to grasp the teddy. Martha looked up into Clara's eyes and gave her the longed-for sunny smile.

Clara wiped tears from her cheeks as relief surged through her. 'Thank God, thank God,' she repeated over and over as tears and laughter mingled into one wet outpoured prayer of thanks. She had her baby back.

It was late when she left the ward. Sister had developed a soft spot for her and when she heard the good news about Martha she'd relaxed the rules, letting Clara stay long after visiting hours. There might be no buses running, but even the prospect of a long walk home couldn't lower her spirits tonight. She was desperate to get back and tell Hattie. Martha's illness seemed to have hit her friend hard. It had touched Clara, for Hattie so often boasted she had no interest in having children of her own.

But once outside the ward, she was surprised to find Alan waiting for her. 'What are you still doing here?' she asked. 'You must have been hanging about for ages!'

'I thought you'd need a lift.' His own smile of greeting faltered. 'What's happened? Is it Martha?'

She swallowed back her tears of joy. 'It is, but it's good news, Al. She's come round and she knew me!'

He threw his arms round her, squeezing her so tightly she couldn't breathe. 'That's the best news ever.'

'It is.' Clara felt her smile might split her face. 'The best news ever.' And she realized she was glad he was here to share it. 'Thanks, Alan. You've been so good to me.'

'It's been no hardship, Clara.' He still had her in a tight embrace and, as his eyes held hers, she saw something more than friendship reflected there. For a moment she had the ridiculous feeling that he might kiss her. The thought of Hattie caused her to pull away. Should she have seen this coming? She hadn't looked for it; she hadn't wanted it. She'd thought that Barry's betrayal had scoured her clean of all desire, yet now, in Alan's arms, it was here again and she was ashamed. She blushed and turned away.

'I need to get the hut ready for Martha!' She brushed at more tears, grateful that he seemed oblivious to the awkward moment. He'd certainly done nothing wrong; he'd only been happy for her. He drove her slowly back to Southwark Park, throwing spray up from the water running in rivulets along the roadside as the windshield wipers struggled to clear the streaming rain. Every now and then Alan slowed to a crawl and leaned forward to peer through the windscreen. It was good he was so occupied, for it covered what might have been an awkward silence for her. She tried to convince herself she'd imagined her feeling. Hadn't it simply been their shared joy at knowing Martha was awake and alive? But as they finally pulled into Slippers Place where Alan parked his car, he turned off the ignition and the silence seemed to roar between them. He didn't move to open the door, but instead turned to face her and reached for her hand.

'I'm so happy for you, Clara,' he said, and his eyes were like twin stars in the darkness. 'You don't deserve all the hard times that've come your way. Maybe Martha getting better, it's just the start...' He paused and smiled. She'd never noticed before how sweet his lopsided smile was. 'I actually saw a patch of sun today!' he went on. 'I reckon it's a sign.' Still smiling, he sang the first few lines of 'Good Times are just around the Corner'. And she had to return his smile, even though her mind was focused on his hand holding hers. She knew she had to move now but seemed transfixed by those eyes. He saved her by abruptly relinquishing her hand.

'Sit there. Wait till I come round and get you,' he ordered, and she sat with a beating heart, aware that she'd escaped a complication that she didn't want or need. She ducked beneath the umbrella he'd produced and took his proffered elbow, sheltering with him as the fat drops of rain penetrated the avenue of trees leading to the squatters' huts. It was hard to keep her footing on the slick path and sometimes she had to lean heavily on his arm. But when they neared the camp, the rain petered out and the sky cleared to an inky gloss sprinkled with stars.

'Look at that clear sky. I told you the weather's changing. Summer's coming.' When she didn't reply he said, 'Don't be worried about Martha, Clara. Tonight's a night for being happy!' And he let go of her arm to do a little Charlie Chaplin-style dance along the path, skidding and slipping till he forced a laugh from her.

The huts were all in darkness. 'I'll walk you to your place,' Alan offered. It was only a few yards along the duckboards, but she appreciated the gallantry. They stood outside Clara's hut, saying goodnight, and his face held a determined good humour.

'Remember what I said: "Be happy!"'

'I don't think I'll ever be unhappy again,' she said, unable to resist brushing his cheek with the lightest of kisses.

\* \* \*

Hattie had to shake Clara to wake her, she was sleeping so soundly. As her friend came round, she handed her the mug of tea she'd just brewed on the stove.

'You were late back last night. Did you get home OK?' Hattie asked.

She sat on the edge of the bed, already dressed and ready for work, as it was a much longer journey to Upper Thames Street than to the factory in Grange Road. Besides, with the flooded roads, any journey these days could turn into a marathon and it was better to start out early.

'Yes,' Clara answered groggily. 'Alan waited to give me a lift home – I was late leaving.'

'Oh, love, I've not even asked you about our little Martha. How is she?'

'She's awake, Hattie! She can come home soon!'

Only now did Hattie realize what a weight of anxiety had been dragging at her. 'Clara, I'm so happy! I told you! I knew our Martha was a fighter... just like her mum.' She gripped her friend's hand. 'And now we'll have to make bloody sure she's got a decent home to come back to. We're putting up that insulation and the partitions and we'll make it so cosy for her...'

But even as she pictured their bright future, the thought of the

Harpers crossed her mind like a dark cloud. They'd not returned, but she knew they wouldn't give up that easily.

*

Hattie had longed for spring, imagining the park alive with pink and white blossom, green shoots in the allotments and mild nights when they could make strides with turning the huts into homes. But when spring had finally come, the thaw was almost as bad as the snow. The first weak rays of sun at first had little impact, but rising temperatures had soon turned the squatters' camp into a mud bath. Mud clogged shoes and stuck to clothing. It was impossible to keep the huts clean and, as craters became overflowing pools, the whole Oval flooded. The colony of huts turned into an island.

She supposed she should be glad, for the floods had proved an unlikely defence against Lenny Harper, who, she suspected, didn't want to get his two-tone oxfords ruined. Whatever the reason, the Harper gang had paid them no more visits. But they'd instituted the night patrols and Levin the nailer had begun repairing the old army fencing that surrounded the camp. She knew Lenny would come back, but at least they would be ready for him.

Meanwhile she turned her mind to the other fight she had on her hands – keeping Crosbie at bay, but keen enough to retain her on the payroll. She didn't flatter herself he'd hired her for her brains and she desperately needed this new job. The extra wages would pay to insulate the hut and partition it into three bedrooms with a small sitting room-cum-kitchen. She'd also been able to afford some of the 'new look' dresses, their fuller skirts giving her tall slim figure a more curvaceous silhouette.

She knew she was good with clients and she enjoyed the modelling, but Crosbie had justified her full-time salary by adding some extra tasks to her day – even he couldn't get away with having her there only for his private amusement. He'd given her a list of telephone numbers and told her to drum up new foreign business. She was sure he'd no expectations she would do any such thing, but just wanted her to look busy.

When she arrived at Lower Thames Street, Crosbie beckoned her into his office. She grabbed an order sheet from her desk and hurried in.

'I've managed to line up some Belgian clients!' she said, eager to talk about her latest success. 'I had a contact from my army days in Brussels, a smart shop near HQ, and they put me in touch with the buyer.'

Crosbie looked doubtful as he read over the order, then he looked up with a smile. 'Good work, Hattie! You're a fantastic saleswoman, keep this up and you'll go far. But you haven't forgotten about tonight, have you? It's important,' he said, giving her new frock an appraising look. 'That's charming, but any factory girl can buy one of those. You, darling, deserve sophistication. Come with me.'

She wanted to enlighten him about a factory girl's wages, which she knew for a fact wouldn't stretch to the new dress she was wearing, but she bit her tongue and followed him down to the sales room. Here, along with coats and stoles, were a number of fur-trimmed dresses. He ran well-manicured fingers along the rack and paused at a midnight-blue, tight-waisted velvet dress, with deep fur cuffs. Holding the dress against her, he pressed blue velvet over her hips and bust. She didn't flinch. It was her daily battle, as much a part of her job as drumming up orders. His attention was flattering, but it had its drawbacks, for the more glamorous she looked the more insistent Crosbie became. He took it as his due to grope her whenever they were alone, and sometimes even when they were not. At the factory, the men's language might be filthier but at least they kept their hands to themselves.

'Will I do?' She matched his cool stare.

'Fantastic.' He smiled innocently as she disentangled herself from the dress and his hands.

Her strategy with Crosbie was deflection, but it could be hard work and sometimes she wondered if she shouldn't just give in. However handsome, charming and generous he was, she knew he hadn't the slightest interest in a real relationship and, in a way, that would have suited her. He reminded her of herself. Yet what about Alan? Up to this point their relationship had been flirtatious fun and she'd never promised him he would be the only one. But he was a decent, funny and kind man. Surely for him she should break her rule of keeping at least two men on the go?

To go with the dress, Crosbie picked a Russian sable coat. Not a good choice in her opinion since the weather had begun to warm, but tonight Crosbie was taking some Parisian buyers to dinner and he wanted her along to show off the ostentatious garments. It was a far cry from the still muddy squat, and she suspected he would be horrified if he knew where she lived. But he never asked.

Later, at the restaurant, she played her part – a mannequin who could speak enough French in an accent the buyers would find attractive, but who said nothing of any importance. She was grateful for the good food, but this wasn't the part of her job she enjoyed most. It turned out she was good at cold calling, and the buyers they were seeing tonight were only there because of her initial phone call.

By the end of the night Crosbie had secured an order to supply a chain of French furriers and, heady with wine and success, he draped the sable over her shoulders, leaning in to nuzzle her neck.

'What's that delicious perfume, Chanel?'

She smiled in the darkness of the restaurant lobby. 'Yes.' It was actually Atkinsons Californian Poppy, got from a friend of hers who worked at the factory in Southwark Park Road. Crosbie obviously wasn't as discerning as he made himself out to be.

'We should celebrate. I'll take you to a little club I know in Soho.' He put a hand round her waist and steered her into the street.

'I really wanted to pop back to the showroom and put the sable away safely.'

'Nonsense, you can be trusted with it for tonight.' He whistled for a black cab and one slewed up almost immediately. She jumped back so that the fur coat wouldn't be splashed with dirty water.

'See what I mean! No, I really should go back to the office.'

'All right. Hop in.'

She slipped inside the taxi while Crosbie leaned into the cabbie's window to give him instructions. Crosbie kept up his flirtatious chatter. 'You charmed them tonight… me too.' He edged in closer and his hand fell casually over hers. 'I wish you weren't so cold, though,' he whispered.

'Oh, I'm not cold. I'm too hot really – I'm wearing the sable!' She beamed at him and he laughed, flashing the white teeth. His cologne was heady and certainly far more expensive than her Californian Poppy. She looked out of the window and realized they were heading away from the river.

'The cabbie's going the wrong way,' she said.

Crosbie gave her an innocent look. 'Oh, is he? I think you're right. I do believe we're almost in Soho.' He laughed. 'Come on, Hattie, socializing's part of the job – if you want to get on in sales. A cocktail or two, and we could talk about my plans for expanding your role. Of course, if you don't want to…'

And understanding his meaning only too well, she let her head fall back against the leather seat, exhausted.

The club was a private one in a typical Soho back street. A narrow, four-storey house, with a rather battered front door and lopsided sash windows. Inside, it was a cavern of red-plush booths and smoke-wreathed tables, with a small dance floor in the centre. The jazz band was playing a song that happened to be a favourite of Hattie's and, after Crosbie ordered the cocktails, he looked pointedly at her tapping foot.

'Dance?' he asked.

It certainly wasn't the Lyceum and the cramped floor allowed for only close, slow dancing. Crosbie pulled her tightly to him and she felt herself giving in to the swaying rhythm. As they circled the floor, she pictured the long journey back to Southwark Park, and the wooden hut that awaited her. She'd left her boots and day clothes in the office. How could she walk across the muddy Oval to the camp in these high heels, and what would happen to the hugely expensive Russian sable as she trailed it along the grass? She felt like the sad-eyed seal sitting atop the Alaska gates. The sculptor hadn't included the hunter approaching with stealthy feet and hefty club, but the exhausted seal could see him all the same.

After too many cocktails and more than one dance, Hattie let Crosbie kiss her neck and lay his cheek against hers, and when he suggested they go back to his flat, she said yes.

★

Hattie woke to the sound of running water. Crosbie's pristine person was not kept that way by adhering to the government requests to bathe no more than once a week in four inches of water. As Hattie could never face the tin bath at the squat and her only bathing took place in Grange Road baths where the water flow was strictly supervised, she never had the chance to break the four-inch rule – perhaps she would this morning. She thought of poor Lou carrying her washing water from the cracked sink along the landing. And then she remembered Ronnie.

'Bugger it! Oh, bloody hell, no!' She leaped out of bed and began scrabbling around for the discarded clothes of the previous night. There would be no bath for her. She couldn't believe a night with a lothario like Crosbie was all it had taken to make her forget. When she was dressed she threw the sable over her shoulders and headed for the door, but before leaving she stopped outside the bathroom. The water was no longer running and she could hear Crosbie splashing about.

'Sorry, I've got to leave!' she called. 'Forgot I'd taken today off. See you tomorrow!' She hurried to the front door and heard him shout. 'Wait!'

But she didn't.

This was why she never wanted to have children. She would certainly be just as bad a mother as Cissie had been. It wouldn't be fair on the kid. Look at Ronnie. If ever a child needed an adult he could rely on, it was Ronnie, and he'd ended up with her as his character witness. Poor little sod. Fortunately, Crosbie lived not far from Charing Cross, and as she left the flat she saw a number one bus pull up at the nearby stop. If she could catch it, she might just about make it to Tower Bridge Magistrates' Court in time. She ran as fast as her high heels would allow her, staggering in an ungainly run-up, and, with a long-legged leap, just landed on the running board in time to hear the conductor ring the bell. She drew admiring stares from other passengers and she threw her shoulders back, walking as if she were on the catwalk to the very end of the bus. The conductor called her 'madam' as he turned the handle of the ticket machine, and she marvelled at the power to dazzle of a fur coat that would cost more than most people earned in a year.

At Tower Bridge Road she got off and dashed to the court, her feet sliding from under her, making her long for the old fur bootees. She arrived red-faced and panting for breath; the sable, which had been ideal for the Arctic weather, was torture in these balmier temperatures. Then she spotted them. They were sitting outside the mahogany-panelled courtroom: a nervous-faced Buster, checking his watch, and an unnaturally clean Ronnie, wearing a shirt and tie, and what looked like a new pair of grey shorts and long socks. There was nothing that could be done about the worn school blazer, but at least, Hattie thought, it would give the impression that Ronnie actually went to school.

Ronnie stood up when he saw her. 'Blimey, miss, you give us a heart attack. Didn't she, Buster?'

Buster flicked his ear. 'Uncle Benny to you.'

'Looks like someone didn't go home last night. You could have made a bit of an effort to get here on time.' Buster tucked in his chins and gave her a disapproving look.

'Don't talk like that to miss,' Ronnie said, and he actually blushed.

Hattie was bewildered. 'Why d'you keep calling me "miss"?'

"Cause you look like a miss, don't ya?' Ronnie said, and Buster gave a small chuckle.

'If she's a miss, I'm Charles Atlas. And get that sable off, Hattie. You look like a Russian bear.'

'I'm sorry, Buster, really. But I'm here now!'

She knew he was only being tetchy because she'd ignored his warnings about Crosbie and he was worried about her – and about Ronnie, though he'd never admit to that.

'Where's Lou?' she asked, looking around.

Buster took in a deep breath and raised his eyes.

'She's gone doolally again,' Ronnie said.

Hattie groaned and shed the heavy sable. The court wouldn't look too favourably on a boy whose mother couldn't be bothered to turn up.

'We think she's gone to Weymouth,' Buster told her.

'Weymouth? Why?'

'Well, it ain't cos she fancied a nice effin 'oliday,' Ronnie said, drawing another flick round the ear from Buster.

'She's gone to look for Sue… Weymouth's where the kids was evacuated.'

'Right shit 'ole, Weymouth,' Ronnie said, and Buster grabbed him by the collar just as the clerk called them into the court.

The charge of kidnapping was read out and the evidence from the policeman heard. The three magistrates huddled and whispered over the report of the welfare officer, who had already visited Ronnie at Barnham Street Buildings. When the woman stepped forward, Hattie feared that all was lost for Ronnie.

'The home situation is unsavoury to say the least. He and his mother live in two rooms in Barnham Street Buildings.' The three magistrates exchanged looks. 'The mother is obviously unable to control the boy, witness the fact that she has decided not to attend court today,' she continued, and Hattie hated her for not knowing Lou, for not even wanting to understand how much she had lost.

'It would seem that for the boy's own protection a custodial sentence in an approved school is warranted. But I believe we have a character witness present?' The magistrate looked over his glasses and pretended not to see Hattie. But she was pretty sure that in her midnight-blue velvet cocktail dress, with the Russian sable draped over her shoulders, she'd already been noticed.

She stood up. 'I would like to speak for Ronald, sir,' she said in her sergeant's voice, which didn't go at all with her outfit. 'He's struggled since losing his father, grandparents and sister during the war, but I can vouch for his good character. I know his mother is prone to bouts of illness but he has a devoted uncle, who's here today.' Buster half rose from his seat. 'I can also vouch for the fact that the whole incident was simply a misunderstanding. The boy believed he was being helpful by taking the child to be looked after by his mother…' She smiled and waited for the three magistrates' stern faces to soften.

'Hmmm,' came a long sigh from the chief magistrate. 'We'll hear from the boy.' And Hattie's stomach did a somersault. She bent to whisper in Ronnie's ear, 'Button your filthy tongue or you're going away.'

'What have you got to say for yourself, young man?'

Ronnie had an awed dumbstruck look about him, which she'd never seen before. She'd certainly never seen him lost for words.

'Speak up!'

'Please, miss, I'm sorry but I never meant to do nothing wrong. I only took the baby 'cause me mum was meant to be looking after her, and I thought it was too much for her, to walk all that way in the snow, miss.'

Hattie saw a smile ripple the stony surface of the chief magistrate's face.

'You may address me as sir, or your honour, but you most certainly may not address me as "miss".'

'Yes, miss… sir,' Ronnie said.

Hattie bit hard on the inside of her cheek. A dim school memory must have convinced Ronnie that when in doubt anyone who looked in charge was to be addressed as 'miss'. But he'd at least been polite.

'Very well. The boy is obviously simple, but because of the character witness and if the uncle can promise to stand as a father figure, the court is minded to give him a chance. I sentence him to one year's probation. The probation officer will be in touch to arrange a home visit.'

There was no argument, no persuading them otherwise. The decision had been made. At least it wasn't approved school; at least she'd saved him from becoming another Pissy Pants.

As they walked the short distance to Barnham Street, Hattie asked Buster, 'What makes you think she's gone to Weymouth?'

'She left a note – to Vic. Gawd knows how she'll get there – she couldn't afford the fare. I don't know what I'm going to do with Ronnie. If the probation officer finds him living on his own they'll put him away.'

'Buster!' Hattie thumped his arm and nodded towards Ronnie, who though lagging behind had heard their conversation.

'No!' Ronnie protested. 'I ain't going in no home.'

She put an arm round his shoulders. 'You won't have to. We'll find your mum. She'll be back home long before the PO comes round, I promise.'

The courtyard of Barnham Street Buildings was awash with a stinking mixture of drainwater from a burst downpipe. Her shoes were already ruined, but they tiptoed round the edge of the yard to the staircase, waving to Granny Stout at her window as they passed. She was at her front door in seconds with a screw of paper in her hand.

'Run us an errand, Ron. Go and get us a couple of bottles of stout and a packet of ten.' Granny Stout's real name was lost in the mists of time, but as her most frequent errand request was a bottle of stout, this served as well as any other.

Ronnie ducked his head and marched on. 'Can't, Granny Stout, busy!'

'I'll give you a fag!'

'Don't teach the boy to smoke, Gran, you'll stunt his growth,' Buster called back.

'What you talking about – he was the one taught me!' The old woman cackled and retreated indoors.

Ronnie ran up the stairs, his expression tight with anticipation. But once inside his face fell.

'She ain't come back. I'm going out.' Buster grabbed the back of his collar, while Hattie picked up the note on the kitchen table and read it silently.

DEAR VIC,

I've gone to Weymouth to get the kids back. I think its wicked leaving them down there, away from their mother and I can't stand it no more. Don't be angry with me. If it's our time to go, then at least we'll all go together.

Love always,
YOUR LOU

Hattie sat down. She looked at Buster, and the boy beside him straining like a dog on the leash. Her own concerns seemed petty now. She wished she didn't have the smell of Crosbie's cologne on her skin.

'Listen, Ronnie, we're not letting you roam the streets. Are we, Buster?'

'No?' Buster looked slightly puzzled. After all, the streets were where Ronnie mainly lived.

'No. You'll stay with your uncle until Mum gets back.'

'No, I ain't,' Ronnie said, wriggling from Buster's grasp.

Buster didn't look too disappointed.

'Yes, you will, you awkward little sod. The court said he's to stand in for your dad.'

Ronnie showed his sharp little teeth and, though he might be cleaner now, beneath the surface she saw that the boy who'd attacked her on that first night was still there. He picked up a poker from the cold fireside and brandished it at Buster. 'You

214

ain't me dad, you Mary Ann!' He swiped at Buster's forehead with a wild blow that sent him sprawling heavily to the floor.

'Ow!' Buster cried. 'If I get my hands on you, you little effer, I'll kill you!'

Hattie hurled herself at Ronnie's legs and rugby-tackled him to the ground. They were all writhing around on the floor, Buster holding his head and Hattie holding on to Ronnie, when a knock came at the door.

'Hello? Hello? Is anyone at home?' a male voice called through the letterbox. They obviously hadn't heard his knock in the melee. But the door was ajar and, as Hattie pulled Ronnie into a headlock, she looked up to see a middle-aged man with a round pleasant face and a broad smile standing in the doorway.

'Need any help?' he asked

She felt Ronnie freeze in her arms. Then, with the force of an arrow let loose, he shot forward, head down, straight into the soft belly of the man. He swayed slightly under the impact and caught Ronnie in a bear hug, holding him fast so the boy's head was buried in his chest, And all the while, the smile never left the man's face.

# 15

## Empty Shells

### May–June 1947

'Hold your horses, young feller,' the man said. 'I'm not going to hurt you.'

Buster helped Hattie up. He had a bruise like an egg on his forehead, and Hattie's velvet dress was covered in ash from the fireplace. The man who held Ronnie captive was dressed in a tweed jacket and grey flannels. With his round tortoiseshell glasses, he had the air of an avuncular school teacher, before whom she and Buster stood like naughty children caught in a playground fight. She was surprised that Ronnie had stopped struggling. He was staring at her in a way that she'd come to recognize as a mute appeal. Ronnie would never ask for help, but sometimes his eyes did.

The man smiled unctuously at Buster. 'No mother present?' he asked, looking around. It was clearly a mild rebuke. 'Mr Wardick, the probation officer.' He shook Buster's hand and then hers. 'I've been appointed by the court to Ronald's case.'

'You didn't waste any time!' Buster said, wincing as he patted the egg protruding from his forehead.

'I happened to be in court this morning. But it seems I've not come a moment too soon!' He gave Ronnie a playful shake. 'The usual procedure is for me to interview the child with the parents present. The mother's absence could be a problem...' He made a clucking sound as if he was flicking through a card index of possibilities in his head. He seemed to come to a decision.

'I believe the court has made you both temporary guardians?'
Hattie nodded, holding her breath.

'Very well. It won't be necessary for me to mention the mother's dereliction to the court, so long as this young scamp agrees to a few rules.'

He let go of Ronnie, who licked his lips and eyed the door.

'First, no absconding! Second, you'll come with me now for a little walk and a friendly chat in my office, and each week at the same time you'll report to me there. Do you think you can promise me that, young feller?' The man gripped Ronnie's shoulder.

Ronnie swallowed hard. None of the usual abuse escaped his lips, only a barely audible 'Yes, miss... sir.'

'Then we'll say no more of police or judges or approved schools, will we? Just a friendly chat *every* week to see how you're getting on.' He reached out his pudgy white hand to ruffle Ronnie's hair; she only hoped he didn't encounter any of the usual inhabitants in the process.

To her surprise, Ronnie left with the man without a word of protest. She was astonished that such a mild, unthreatening character could have cowed him so easily.

'I reckon he's scared stiff of going to an approved school, probably reminds him of that home he was evacuated to in Weymouth. Maybe the threat's all he needed?' Hattie said to Buster once they'd gone.

'Good job an'all.' Buster gently probed the egg.

'For chrissake, Buster, leave that alone.' Hattie wasn't as happy as Buster at Ronnie's sudden change of heart. 'I'm worried. How are we going to keep an eye on him without Lou? If he messes up this probation he's had it.'

'Hattie, he's my problem, not yours. I don't expect you to do any more. You got him off the bleedin' hook and that's enough. Besides, you've got your own problems, haven't you?'

She looked around at Lou's sparse kitchen, remembering the well-stocked cupboards and American-style fridge in Crosbie's flat. He must have a raft of black-market contacts; he was the sort of customer who made the Lenny Harpers of this world into rich men. She opened the tea caddy – there was barely a spoonful left.

'Ronnie won't be back for at least an hour. Shall we go to the pub?'

In the dingy, smoke-wreathed Waterman's Arms at the end of Barnham Street, Hattie sat drinking her whiskey mac while Buster downed a pint of Guinness. Foam sat on his top lip and she wiped it away with the deep fur cuff of her dress.

'You'll ruin it!' he said, pulling away.

'It's already ruined. Besides, it belongs to the Alaska. Crosbie asked me to wear it last night.'

Buster's face darkened. 'That's why you were late. I thought so. Tell me you didn't jump into bed with him, Hattie.'

'Fell more like! I'd had a bit too much to drink – he's very generous.'

'Yeah, with the firm's money. You silly cow, Hattie. He's got no interest in you. And what about Alan, he's a lovely feller. I'd have thought you'd have a bit more pride in yourself after all you did in the army...'

His words stung. Buster was more than just her dancing and drinking partner. He was the sort of friend who was always on her side. But now he'd made her feel ashamed and she snapped, 'Well, if you think Alan's such a lovely feller you can have him yourself for all I care.' And she turned her head, pretending to be looking out of the Waterman's grimy windows. But there was nothing to look at – no one ventured from Tooley Street into Barnham Street unless they absolutely had to. 'And you can talk! You flit from one chap to the next. You couldn't even hold on to that Aiden, and he thought the world of you.'

'He left me!'

'Only because you was ashamed of him.'

'What?'

'Hiding him away in the flat all the time.'

Their voices had got steadily louder, but now Buster whispered, 'It was you told me to be careful!'

'Careful in public, yes. But you could have introduced him to your friends – to me – as if he was actually someone that counted! No wonder he sodded off.'

Buster was about to say something but then shut his mouth. After a while he said, 'You think he thought the world of me?'

She gave the briefest of nods.

'We never argue, Hattie...'

She took in a deep breath. 'It's only because I feel so stupid. I let Crosbie get exactly what he wanted and he'll probably give me my cards tomorrow.'

'Don't give him the chance then. You jack it in first.'

'Perhaps I will.' She looked at the clock. It was almost two. 'Nearly chucking-out time. Shall we go back and wait for the boy?'

They walked amiably arm in arm along Barnham Street, as soot specks from trains thundering along the viaduct completed the ruin of her dress. She was thinking not so much of Crosbie, but about Alan. She suspected he was getting serious. He'd been quieter of late – always a bad sign – and sometimes she caught him gazing at her after an evening out, with a lingering, almost sad smile. Nothing like the normal happy-go-lucky chap that had attracted her in the first place. And now she had offered him to Buster, in anger, but partly in truth. 'Have him for all I care,' she'd said. And she felt sad that it was true. She really did deserve all she'd got from Crosbie.

They waited in the flat all afternoon. Ronnie didn't come home, but Lou did.

'I've been to Weymouth,' she said, with a wan smile. Her glazed eyes slid from Hattie to Buster. 'Brought my boy home, but could I find my Sue? I couldn't. I'll go back next week.'

Lou sat down wearily. It was as if all that Hattie had come to know of the woman when in her right mind had simply drained away. All the grit and presence of mind she'd shown with Martha, all the skill she demonstrated at the factory, it simply wasn't there. She was an empty shell. Lou examined her swollen legs.

'That's from all the walking I done. It ain't half a long bleedin' way to Weymouth!' She gave a bright laugh. 'But I got my Sue these.' She placed a small packet of seeds on the table. There was a picture on the front – a mixture of blue and yellow flowers. 'She loves her grandad's garden, so I think I'll make her one meself. See?' She shook the pack at Hattie. 'Forget-me-nots and marigold and heartsease. Look lovely they will… Make us a cup o' tea, Buster. I'm gaspin'. Such a bleedin' long walk to Weymouth.'

Lou let her eyes close and her head fall back against the chair. Buster rubbed at the egg on his head and kept his hand there like a shield, hiding the tears that fell for his ruined sister.

\*

When Hattie finally got back home, dusk was hanging over the squat like a pale green and rose tapestry. She kept her eyes on the horizon, tracing the gilded lace of trees that bordered the Oval. She didn't want to see the mud at her feet, which squelched up to her ankles. She wanted to pretend she was a woman who could afford a black sable coat and live in a house with acres of grounds surrounding it. She wanted to forget the squalor of Barnham Street Buildings and the sad sight of Buster putting his sister to bed so that she could find some rest in sleep. It was because her eyes were so firmly fixed on the horizon that she hadn't seen Joe approaching. Nor had she realized the fur coat had been dragging along in the mud ever since she'd entered the park.

'My God, that's a Russian sable she's wearing!' Joe said almost to himself.

'And why are you so surprised? Don't I seem the type to have one in my wardrobe?' she asked, still half in her dream.

'All I know is that's certainly going to take some cleaning up!' He pointed to the three inches of caked mud hemming the black fur.

'Bloody hell! Now I *know* I'm getting the sack.'

'Not yours then?'

Hattie felt sick. 'No! Crosbie, the sales manager, asked me to wear it – for a sales meeting yesterday.'

'Crosbie? Oh, I've heard of him.' Joe looked unimpressed. 'Well, you look like you've been in a rugby scrum.'

'Full of compliments, you are, Jack Blunt!' she said, sweeping past him.

'Hold on, I can get that clean for you...'

She stopped and spun round. 'You can?'

'I've been trialling a new cleaning fluid. But I've not tried it on a sable. I could use another good test subject.' He looked pointedly at the muddy coat.

'I wouldn't want to put you out,' she said stiffly, still feeling peeved by his damning assessment of her appearance.

'You'd be doing me a favour... really.' He held out his hands for the coat. 'I'll take it into the drug room tomorrow – it might take a while, though...'

She slipped the sable from her shoulders and he caught it. 'I'd be grateful – doesn't matter how long, just so long as you get it clean,' she said wearily.

'That must have been an important sales meeting if it lasted two days!'

'It wasn't so much the work, it was a dinner really...'

'Where did you stay last night?'

'What's it got to do with you?' she said defensively.

He looked taken aback, and then she thought she saw a flicker of understanding cross his face.

'You're right, none of my business. I just wondered if the firm had put you up somewhere nice. Sometimes they can take advantage... You shouldn't let them,' he said pointedly, and she knew it wasn't the firm he was talking about.

'Sorry,' she said, 'to be so tetchy. It's been a long day. I've been in court – with Ronnie. Then Lou went walkabout again, and the court's put Ronnie on probation and made me a guardian. Oh, I don't know what to do for the best.'

They were walking along the duckboards and now they stopped outside his hut. 'You look worn out,' he said.

She leaned heavily on the doorpost. The weight of her tangled relationships with Crosbie and Alan bore down on her, and she found she appreciated the sheer simplicity of being with Joe. He was so plain-spoken and uninterested in impressing her that she felt free to be herself.

'Come in for a cocoa?' Joe asked her, and then quickly added, 'Unless you just want to go home and put your feet up...' He looked down at the caked grey mud covering her feet and ankles like little bootees.

'Don't suppose you could take these into the drug room and clean them up as well while you're at it?'

He laughed, his normally serious face brightening, and he pushed open the door for her to go in.

Over cocoa, she explained more about Ronnie and the terms of his probation.

'But he never came back this afternoon. I reckon he'll have just gone off to the bombsites again. I don't know why I'm so worried about him... he's not my kid. But Lou can barely look after herself and it's his last chance, Joe. He really looked terrified by this probation officer. He seemed a friendly enough bloke, even though Ronnie did headbutt him in the belly and knock his specs off! I can't fathom the boy. He just takes against people. Look at the way he was with you.'

'Only when he found out I was in the camera club. He didn't seem keen on photographers.'

'Was it about the camera club? I never noticed.'

Joe nodded and handed her the cocoa. 'Actually, it might be an idea to let the boy stay here – just till his mum gets better.'

Hattie looked up sharply, surprised at his suggestion. 'Well, you've changed your tune – actually *inviting* someone to live at the huts!'

'Hmm, it was just a thought. What were you saying about this PO whatsisname? He seemed a good chap?'

'Wardick? A bit oily, but OK.'

'Can't be an easy job.'

She finished her cocoa. 'Not if they're dealing with the likes of Ronnie every day!'

It had been good to unburden herself to someone other than Buster, and she found that Joe, when he wasn't being insulting, was easy company. But she always ended up talking about herself and never him.

'So, are you used to having neighbours now? Not that I ever gave you much choice.'

He brushed the lock of hair from his forehead and gave her a half smile. And held her with his earnest, rather intense gaze. 'If you want the truth, it's been hard having you around.'

'Ha! Just me? Or all of us?'

He ignored her question. 'I spent a lot of the war on my own.'

'I thought you were in Burma, with the Chindits.'

'I was. But I got captured by the Japs, put in a POW camp in Rangoon. They seemed to object when I tried to blow up the place with a home-made incendiary. I was lucky they didn't execute me. Sometimes I wished they had… Instead they put me in a hole for a year. No windows, nothing but a dirt floor and a tin roof, much worse than this.' He looked up at the corrugated roof of the hut. His tone was matter-of-fact, as though he were describing his old B&B in South Norwood. 'You get used to your own company.'

'Yes. I reckon you'd have to,' she said, quietly, wanting him to go on.

'In fact, you end up preferring it, being alone… seems easier, more peaceful.'

Now she understood why he'd been so against her coming to live in the huts. She must have threatened to end whatever peace he'd managed to bring home with him from that POW camp.

'But now?' His expression brightened. 'Well, I'm getting used to having you here.' He gave a small smile. 'You're not as much trouble as I thought you'd be.'

And this time she knew from the mischievous glint in his eye that he was talking about her alone.

* * *

It had been like a physical pain, bearing down in the centre of her chest, this long separation from her baby. Clara had gone to bed with it each night and woken with it each morning. Hattie had done her best to distract her and had spent all her hard-earned wages on turning the hut into something resembling home. The partitions that Levin and Mario put up meant that Martha had her own nursery to come home to. Buster had made pink curtains and a matching quilt, on which she and Hattie had sewn appliqué figures of bunnies and lambs and ducks. Vera had made a rag rug and Alan had constructed a toy chest. Everything was ready. All that was needed was for the doctor to tell her Martha could come home.

Today she would find out. She'd seen a moment's hesitation on the doctor's face at her last visit, when he realized the baby's home would be an army hut. She'd left the factory early. It would mean losing half a day's pay, but she was determined to be there when the doctor decided if Martha could be discharged. She couldn't live with any more delays. She had to have her baby home. It was early afternoon when she walked across the yard to the factory gates, and she was surprised when Alan emerged from the electrician's shop. He wasn't wearing his overalls.

'Clara!' he called, and dodged through the lorries waiting by the weighbridge. 'Hang on, I'm taking you!'

'Alan, no. You can't lose any more time for me. I'll get a bus.'

'And what about when you bring Martha out?' She'd told everyone at the squat that this was the day. 'You don't want to be getting on a bus with her. No arguments, come on. I've got the car parked round the corner.'

As it was, she was glad to have him with her when the doctor did his rounds. She'd found from experience that if Alan was beside her at the hospital, the doctor would address him and give far more information than when she was alone. If it was just her asking the questions, he seemed more inclined to treat her like an over-protective mother who needed reassurance rather than hard facts about her child's health.

'Yes, she's made a remarkable recovery,' the doctor said, looking at Alan. 'But the welfare officer has some concerns about the home situation. An army hut, I believe?'

'Not really,' Clara said. 'We've converted it, haven't we, Al?'

'Fully insulated, hooked up to electricity,' Alan confirmed.

'Sanitary?' the doctor asked. 'What are the arrangements?'

'We have running water and a kitchen,' Clara said, not mentioning the shared latrines and NAAFI, or that the water had to be collected from a standpipe.

'We're mostly ex-servicemen and our families...' Alan said. 'Respectable. It's not our fault Bermondsey's lost all its houses. We've got a committee and everything.'

Clara waited. Martha had been sleeping, but now she woke. When her sleep-fogged eyes cleared and focused on her mother, she gave an excited squeal and put out her arms. Clara swept her out of the bed and into an enveloping hug. If the doctor said no now, she felt she might simply run away with her child.

'So, we can take her home?' Alan said, his tone firm. But she could see his Adam's apple rising and falling as he swallowed, a sure sign he was as nervous as herself.

'Ex-servicemen, you say? Very well. I'll discharge her into your care,' the doctor told Alan, as if he would be the one to feed her, clothe her and rock her to sleep every night. But Clara didn't mind. All she wanted was to walk out of the hospital with Martha in her arms and never let her go again.

She was wrapped in a blanket that Maisie had crocheted specially, with a matching hat that had two flaps to tie over her ears and a little bobble on the top. Clara practically ran from the ward. Alan kept up with her at a half-trot, and she only slowed long enough to negotiate the slippery stone stairs down to the lobby. Once outside, a combination of fresh air and elation hit her, and she swayed slightly. He caught her and she let him hold her steady, as she held Martha tightly to her and began to sob quietly.

'It's all right, Clara,' Alan said softly. 'We can just wait here a minute. There's no rush now. You've got her.' She nodded, unable to speak, overwhelmed with gratitude that the long wait was over and she was taking Martha home. She felt a small hand patting her wet cheek. Martha smiled up at her and Clara's tears dried as Alan steered them gently towards the waiting car. While they drove home Martha fell asleep in Clara's arms, and when they arrived at the park she was still sleeping.

'Shall we just wait here a bit, let her sleep?' she asked.

'Why not?' Alan turned off the engine and they sat in silence, listening to Martha's steady breathing. Sometimes she caught Alan looking at the child, and then they would smile at each other, appreciating the miracle of her just being there.

After a while Alan spoke in a soft voice. 'Clara, I've been waiting for Martha to get better before I said anything, but something terrible's happened.'

Her heart lurched. What had they been keeping from her? She knew all the squatters had been treating her with kid gloves, almost as if she were already as lost in grief as poor Lou.

'What is it, what's happened?' she asked, dry-mouthed.

She saw him swallow hard. 'I've fallen in love with you.'

Clara was stunned into silence. She'd tried to ignore her own feelings for Alan, but she'd betrayed herself at every meeting with either a racing heart or a surge of excitement when she saw him. It was a while before she could respond, but when she did it was not herself, nor Alan, who was uppermost in her mind, but Hattie.

'There *are* terrible things in the world, Al. I've just had to watch my daughter fight for her life, and that's a terrible thing. Love's not a terrible thing, but betraying someone you care about *is*. I've had it done to me, and I can't do it to Hattie. I'm sorry.'

He dropped his head. 'I suppose that's what I meant about it being terrible. But I just don't think I love her and I'm pretty sure she's not in love with me.'

When Clara had been swept off her feet by Barry, her heart had been young enough to feel that being in love outshone everything else in the world. She'd suddenly known what her life was for. You found someone you couldn't live without and then gave them everything. For Barry, she had ignored her family and left her country, and would have given more if it had been asked of her. But her heart had aged a century since then, and now it knew better. 'That might be true, but I'm Hattie's friend. I'm not going behind her back.'

He nodded as if to himself. 'I thought you'd say that, but I just couldn't keep it to myself any more.'

She opened her mouth to speak. She wanted to tell him there wasn't a hope in hell that she'd be ready for another romance. That ship had sailed as surely as the bride ship itself.

'Don't say nothing now, Clara. I just wanted to be upfront with you... And I will be, with Hattie. I'm finishing with her.'

'It's up to you, Alan. But I can't promise you anything.'

'I don't want any promises,' he answered, a rare seriousness eclipsing his easy bantering manner.

Martha stirred. 'She's awake,' Clara said.

'Don't think badly of me, Clara,' he said after a while.

She squeezed his arm, feeling sorry to have caused him any pain. He was always so happy-go-lucky, and she felt she'd knocked the shine off all that light-heartedness.

'You're the most thoughtful, generous man I know, Al. I could never think badly of you. I'm just sorry I can't—'

'No, don't be,' he interrupted her. 'Don't be sorry for nothing, just be happy you've got her home.' And he pulled a funny face for Martha, who giggled and expected more.

Once back at the hut she dressed Martha in her best frock, with a bow pinned into her dark ringlets, and attempted to keep her tidy until Hattie came home. Martha was exploring the new nursery, pulling at the brightly coloured strands of Vera's rug when Hattie came in.

'Martha!' Hattie's smile lit her face, which Clara thought had been looking too careworn of late.

Her child looked up, with a grin of instant recognition, and crawled at surprising speed across the rug to be picked up and swung round by her aunt Hattie, who threw her up into the air, just to hear her squeals of laughter. Their shared delight in each other was all Clara needed to convince herself she'd done the right thing. She would never hurt Hattie. Alan must do what he had to, but her feelings for him would just have to disappear like the snows of winter.

* * *

Crosbie wasn't happy that Hattie hadn't returned the Russian sable, but it had already been a couple of weeks and she couldn't put him off any longer. In fact the coat was still in the drug room with Joe, who'd been full of apologies when his boss had dumped another job on him. Crosbie had been magnanimous about the dress. It was hers to keep, a perk of the job, he said, though she wondered if it were more a perk of spending the night with him. But the sable was worth a fortune, and she could see suspicion in his eyes as he grilled her on why she hadn't yet returned it.

'I haven't flogged it, if that's what you're thinking! It's just this warm weather. I couldn't very well wear it on the bus, I'd swelter in a fur like that! I'll bring it back tomorrow, I promise,' she stalled.

'Well, make sure you do, darling, before someone misses it.'

He made a sudden grab for her and she shot a look behind her at the girls in the outer office, who appeared to be concentrating on their typing. She knew they weren't.

'Keep your hands to yourself!' She slapped him away.

'You're not worried about them, are you?' Crosbie laughed. 'They're only jealous.'

'Don't kid yourself. You're not that much of a catch.'

'Well, they've all had their chance.' He chuckled again. 'What about you, want to try your luck again tonight?'

She hesitated. Who knew, perhaps there was a slim chance she'd still be able to keep the job. But she doubted it. She rushed on before she could think better of it. 'Mr Crosbie—'

'Peter!' he insisted.

'Mr Crosbie, I made a mistake that night. I don't think it should happen again.'

He looked stunned. 'What? Are you crazy? It was bloody marvellous. *You're* bloody marvellous!'

She didn't know if he was being sincere, but she knew she was. 'No. I'm not crazy. I'm just not sure we should be mixing up our personal lives with work. I've decided I want to keep the job, but not you.'

Perhaps she could have been a little less blunt, but it was said now.

'Oh. *You've* decided you want to keep the job, have you?' He flashed his charming smile at her. 'I expect you do, it pays much better than the bambeater.' He pointed to the girls in the outer office. 'They'd all like the chance of your job, instead of tapping away all day.'

'But they wouldn't be as good as me. Look at the clients I've landed already.'

He pulled at his lower lip. 'It's true, you're an excellent saleswoman, but now I'm wondering if it's good for morale to have you around, Miss Wright.' His lips were set in a tight pale line.

'But that's ridiculous. The other girls' morale won't be affected if I keep the job!'

He pushed his chair back on to two legs and held her with those cool blue eyes. 'They haven't taken to you – jealousy, office politics. I'd hate to think you'd suffer because of it but... perhaps factory girls and office girls just don't mix.' He pulled a mock sad face.

So that was it. Crosbie's interest in her had stretched just as far as the bedroom and no further. But she needed the job; she wanted it.

'Well, perhaps we could make it work... somehow.' She gave him a false smile and left the office, smarting at her humiliation. Buster had been wrong. It seemed that her army days hadn't given her enough pride in herself to resist being used by, or using, the likes of Crosbie to get what she wanted. She went where she always did when she had got herself into a mess with a man.

But when she got to the Square, Cissie was in no state to listen to her woes.

'I've made a bleedn' big fox pass, letting my Mario slip through me hands.'

'It's a *faux pas*.'

'Too bleedin' right it is. I need help getting him back, darlin'. Can you have a word, tell him I wouldn't be adverst to him coming back here?' Cissie took a long drag on her Park Drive and flicked ash into the saucer. Her mother's roots were showing and she obviously hadn't felt up to enhancing her thin lips or white cheeks with the normal scarlet and vermilion.

'You're meant to be helping me with my man problems, not the other way round!'

'Oh, that's not a man problem. You don't give a monkey's about that Crosbie. It's a job problem you got there, love. If you want to keep the office job you got to string him along, sweetheart. Have you had efficient?' she asked, holding up the last square of bread pudding, which was all she'd had in the cupboard for tea. Mario had been the cook and Cissie's bread pudding, made with stale national loaf, was heavy as lead and just as tasty.

'Yes thanks, Ciss. But I don't think I *can* string him along. I think I've lost my touch.'

Cissie looked at her suspiciously. 'You in love?'

Hattie laughed and flicked her own cigarette. 'Do me a favour. Alan's a decent chap, but he's too young for me ... ' She paused. 'And too nice.'

'Someone else?'

Hattie shook her head. 'No one else.' But for the first time in many years, she found herself wishing there was someone special. In fact, the only person who had really touched her heart since she'd been home was Martha. The love she felt for the child demanded no return, apart from those easily won smiles. But now she probed the nagging pain around her heart and found it was more of an absence, a hollowness. The sight of Lou sitting in her kitchen, holding out the packet of seeds for Sue's garden came back to her. She had pitied the woman, but perhaps she wasn't so different herself. The war, after all, had left behind so many empty shells.

# 16

## *The Walls Came Tumbling Down*

### *June–September 1947*

Ronnie felt sorry about miss. She was all right, but he would have to let her down. She'd tried to help him, but once the PO turned out to be the smiling man, Ronnie knew he had no chance. That first day when they were meant to be at Wardick's office, they'd gone to his house instead. Wardick gripped Ronnie's arm with his podgy hand all the way, steering him there, pretending to be his friend, smiling and chatting about the probation rules as if he cared.

When they arrived at the house, the smiling man gave him ginger beer, which he gulped down, burning his throat. It didn't take long for Wardick to get down to real business.

'You've cleaned yourself up, Ronald!' Wardick's cheeks dimpled with an approving smile as he tousled Ronnie's clean hair. 'You'll look much better in the photos now.'

'That's not down to me,' Ronnie muttered. 'It was Uncle Buster.' His mum had called it a 'good fallamoostrin', when Buster had scrubbed his neck with Wright's Coal Tar till it stung.

Up till now Wardick had always kept his hands to himself. But today, after Ronnie had finished the ginger beer, the smiling man's pudgy hands started crawling all over him and Ronnie just froze. Once he'd have kicked Wardick in the nuts, but now there was too much to lose. So he put up with it, kept his mind busy thinking of all the ways he could kill the smiling man, and that's when he got the idea for the bomb. It was what you did to your enemies. The Germans had bombed them and the English had bombed the Germans, and now he would bomb the smiling man. It seemed fair.

'So what you gonna do?' Nutty Norman asked.

Ronnie made a sound like a heavy explosive and smashed his fist against his thigh.

'Make a bomb and stick it up his arse, that's what.'

Nutty Norman greeted the idea with enthusiasm. But Frankie, ever the realist, suggested it would be easier to just blow up the smiling man's home – with him in it.

'All right,' Ronnie said. 'We'll blow him to smivvereens! Giss that shell case.'

Of all the currencies they traded in, from coconuts nicked off barges to conkers shaken from trees, whole shell cases were the most precious, for they contained black gold – gunpowder. The boys were huddled in a redundant Anderson shelter in the back-yard of a ruined house down by the river. It was a good hiding place and here they stored their various treasures: shell cases, shrapnel from ack-ack guns, bits of downed German planes, bullets from strafing raids and – most precious of all – the gunpowder harvested from shell cases.

'Giss that lamp here, Fishy.'

Ronnie took the proffered lamp and dipped one of Norman's old shoelaces into the paraffin to make a fuse. Frankie's hand shook visibly and Ronnie froze, 'Hold it steady, bone'ead, you'll blow us all up!' He waited until Frankie had removed the lamp to a safe distance before he began to assemble the bomb.

'When can we do it?' Nutty Norman asked. Unbridled eagerness glinted in his eyes. Of all the Barnham Street boys, Nutty Norman took the most risks, whether climbing down into hazardous abandoned water tanks or scaling precarious walls. Ronnie was generally more cautious.

'It's got to work first time, otherwise he'll guess it's me done it. I ain't going back there every week for a year!' He shuddered and the two boys looked down at their feet. They all knew what had happened. They had all been 'models' for the smiling man at one time or another and at first the sweets had been worth it, but when he'd progressed from photographing to touching them, and later to suggesting other things which made them feel sick with fear, they had all run home as fast as they could, and found reasons never to return. But now, Ronnie couldn't run home. He would have to return to the probation office every week or face approved school. He had been caught well and truly in the smiling man's net. The weekly visits would make the next year a torture.

'I got to do it soon, but I got to do it right,' Ronnie said firmly.

The smiling man lived in a bomb-damaged terrace near the river. All the houses except his had either been condemned as unsafe or completely destroyed. The house immediately to his right was a pile of rubble with the adjoining wall left exposed, covered in the neighbour's wallpaper, with shelves hanging at odd angles, cupboards and even a picture still hanging on the wall. Wooden props and 'S'-shaped metal straps were all that kept it from falling down.

'D'you reckon this'll be enough gunpowder to do it, though?' Frankie asked, peering at the half-filled shell.

'Nah, we'll need more,' Ronnie said. 'Giss the ammo box.'

Frankie hefted a dented metal box from the back of the shelter. Ronnie opened the lid and scooped out more gunpowder, packing it carefully into the shell.

'That should do it!' Ronnie said grimly, before laying the bomb carefully on to the dirt floor. 'This'll wipe the smile off his bleedin' face.'

They finished making the bomb, using all the gunpowder they had, and stored it in the ammunition box. Then they went out to celebrate. They built a fire, well away from the Anderson shelter, and roasted the apples they'd stolen from Borough market earlier. While the apples cooked, Nutty Norman stood on a little mound of rubble and, in the flickering glow of the fire, did his party piece. He sang in a voice strident as a stray cat's, but what it lacked in tunefulness it made up for in power.

> OOOH, *when I was a lad just ten years old*
> *as fine as a feller could be,*
> *I sung for me supper and I sung for me tea and*
> *I sung for the fiddlers three,*
> OH APPles *red and yellow won't you come and buy?*
> APPles *for your* APPle *tart and for your* APPle *pie!*

With each mention of apples Nutty Norman slapped his thigh and did a little jig, sometimes turning on a circle. He sang till he was red in the face and the apples were black, with all their fluffy sweetness oozing out. The boys clapped and cheered and fished out the scalding fruit with sticks. Ronnie liked to listen to Norman's singing, it made him believe he too could run away and sing for his supper, just like the boy in the song, and never have to see the smiling man again.

Norman and Frankie had started going to school again, and the court had ordered Ronnie to return there as part of his probation, so it wasn't until the following evening that they could put the plan into action. Ronnie and Frankie carried the ammunition box between them and Nutty Norman ran ahead as lookout. They hadn't far to go from the Anderson shelter. The flattened house next to the smiling man's still had an intact basement, albeit open to the sky. Ronnie dropped into it, then waited as the others passed down the ammunition box before jumping down themselves.

They completed their preparations ready for when the smiling man came home from work at six, but just to be sure he wasn't going out again, they waited in the damp basement until it was fully dark. Charred floor joists above them cast slanting shadows across the moon-washed floor. There was just enough light to reveal Ronnie's trembling fingers as he lit the match and held it to the fuse. Sulphur and paraffin caught flame with a small hiss.

'Leg it!' Ronnie ordered, and the boys scrambled up from the basement, Ronnie hoisting out Frankie, who was the smallest. They sprinted away without looking back. The fuse was a short one and as he ran Ronnie covered his ears. The blast would not be so loud as the heavy explosive that had killed Sue, but it would be loud enough for them to hear a couple of streets away. They ran till they were out of breath and Ronnie finally had to stop, with his chest burning and his hearth thudding. He leaned his back against a brick wall and prayed softly. 'Dear God in heaven let him die, let him die, let him die.' Over and over, he whispered to himself the mantra that he hoped would save him. Until it came – a low boom. Ronnie fell to his knees and pretended to cover his ears. He wasn't going to let Norman and Frankie see him crying. But he couldn't help it. Often he'd heard his mum saying 'Gawd's good. Gawd's good,' and for once in his short life he agreed with her. Wardick was dead and God was good.

Nutty Norman was whooping like an Indian brave and Frankie the Fish was thumping Ronnie on the back. 'You're free, mate!' Ronnie felt he could have floated up like the barrage balloon they used to tether at the end of Barnham Street. He felt an over-powering desire to smash something else tonight. 'Come on, boys, let's get the gang together and go on a raid!'

They clattered through the dark streets, hurtling into the court-yard of Barnham Street Buildings, yelling 'Bundle, bundle!' Soon Ronnie was surrounded by all the gang members, including Betty and Bonny – the twins known as 'Ribbons'. Micky Driscoll, the lanky black-haired hardnut from the top floor, suggested the target. 'Let's get the Vine Lane Boys!'

Vine Lane was just the other side of Tooley Street and its near-ness suited Ronnie, who was aching to put his fist into someone's face or a brick through a window right now. He felt like a kettle boiling dry when someone had forgotten to turn off the gas. He knew the shrill whistling sound in his ears wouldn't go away – not until he'd destroyed something.

The gang pelted across Tooley Street, dodging traffic, barging into passers-by, until they reached the forbidding tenement blocks where they were met by the Vine Lane gang. It was almost as if they'd been warned by the thunder of feet coming towards them. The clash was immediate and noisy. Screams and thuds filled the courtyard. Handy missiles – bricks and bottles – were hurled at windows, so that tenants ran out on to their landings, complaining loudly about the noise but only increasing it. A woman emerged on the landing, dressed only in her nightdress, and threw a bucket of water over the landing, soaking Ronnie. He simply shook himself like a muddy dog and scampered after his next target. The fight was brief, lasting only until the police arrived with their whistles and truncheons, scattering the gangs like rats into the maze of back streets and alleys leading down to the river.

Ronnie, Nutty Norman and Frankie tore along the cobbles, laughing and breathless, following the river back to the Anderson shelter where they gleefully re-enacted the battle and their individual victories. When Norman and Frankie finally had to go home, Ronnie didn't feel like going back to Barnham Street Buildings. Lou wouldn't notice. For a while he thought she'd stopped being a nutter, but no. Now she was worse than ever. She'd started to dig up the bombsite near Spa Road in her dinner times. She said she was making a garden for Sue. Well, a garden for Sue didn't do him much good. It didn't cook his dinner or wash his clothes. It didn't make him feel missed at all. He lingered by the river, slipping like a shadow between warehouses and slithering down dark river stairs to the exposed Thames mud. Skidding pebbles across the moonlit low water, he couldn't say he was happy, but the piercing whistle inside his head had stopped. Someone had turned the gas off at last.

He stayed there until pink and gold streaks appeared above Tower Bridge. He was ravenous. He'd run a few errands for Granny Stout earlier, so he felt flush and now made his way to the tea stand at the end of Crucifix Lane. At this hour, the tea stall was frequented only by the very old who couldn't sleep and the very young who didn't want to sleep. Gathered round the steamy stand, with its single oil lamp, was Mr Notcutt, the old man from number twenty-five, cradling his mug of tea and chewing a rock cake with his gums, along with a couple of young chaps, dressed up to the nines, pissed as puddings by the looks of them. Then there were those who simply had nowhere at all to sleep, like Pissy Pants. Ronnie wasn't surprised to see him at the tea stand. He nodded as the scavenger shuffled up to him. The others wrinkled their noses, but Ronnie wasn't to be put off ordering his celebration tea and toast.

'Hello, Ronnie,' Pissy Pants said in his nasal voice, 'y'alright?'

Ronnie smiled and nodded. Over Pissy Pant's shoulder he'd seen the news vendor setting up the morning papers. The *South London Press* front page read 'Buried Wartime Bomb Explodes in Bermondsey'.

'Good as gold, mate,' Ronnie said. He doubted that the man would understand, but he had to share his triumph with someone. 'That was me!' he whispered gleefully, pointing to the paper stand. 'That bastard won't touch me no more!'

Pissy Pants followed his gaze. 'Notta UXB?'

Ronnie was shocked. 'You can read?'

A secret smile spread across Johnny's heavy-boned face and he put a finger to his nose. Lou had once told Ronnie that Pissy Pants was 'silly-on-his-own-side', and it seemed that she was right about some things after all.

On the following Monday Ronnie decided the best thing would be to go to the probation office as usual. He practised acting very upset when they told him about Wardick being blown up in his bed. With what was left of his errand money he had got hold of some sweets on the black market and if his mouth hadn't been full of them it would have dropped open. As it was, the gob stopper saved him from looking as if he'd received the shock of his life. For it was the smiling man who opened the door, very much alive and obviously waiting for him, his face spread with a smile so oily you could have fried a panful of chips in it.

'Ah, Ronald, come in, young man.' He put a hand on Ronnie's back. It was warm but not gentle. He gave Ronnie a shove and shut the door behind them. 'I see you've managed to find another supplier for your sweeties.' He squeezed Ronnie's shoulder. 'Now, young man, I hear that you've been on a few wrecking sprees. Vine Lane buildings, among other places! I'm struggling with my conscience – shall I mention this to the court?' He tilted his head to one side, as if the question were a real one. 'I should think it will mean a few more months of my company, what do you think I should do?'

'Bastard,' Ronnie mouthed, but the gob stopper prevented his lips from moving.

*

From that day, when he'd learned their home-made bomb hadn't been been powerful enough to bring Wardick's house down, Ronnie started picking away at the wall of the basement adjoining Wardick's. It somehow made the sessions with the smiling man bearable, to remove each brick – slowly, carefully – taking pleasure in imagining that as the wall came down, he was escaping from a prison, breaking free of Wardick's captivity. It was peaceful in the ruined basement at night and he would scrape away quietly so as not to alert the sleeping Wardick next door. Sometimes Ronnie even slept down there himself and only emerged with the dawn. But it wasn't long before his friends found out about his new plan and insisted on joining him.

Their deconstruction began with the adjoining wall of the basement in the flattened house, near to where they'd planted their bomb. The old Victorian mortar was friable, and, loosened by their home-made bomb as well as the original wartime heavy explosive, it trickled away like sand in an egg-timer. They scraped at it with their knives, beginning in the middle of the wall, loosening first one brick then another. With the release of each one, it became easier to prize more out. All along one course they went, excluding the corner bricks, then back along the course above, until they had a hole big enough to squeeze through into the smiling man's basement. There they started to demolish the other walls of Wardick's basement. But Nutty Norman was impatient to see results. He urged them to remove even more bricks.

'Not too many too soon!' Ronnie warned. 'It'll all come down on top of our bleedin' heads! It's got to stand until we're ready to take out the corner bricks. They're holding the bloody house up. We don't want to kill ourselves.'

'Nor no one else,' Frankie added reasonably. 'Only him.'

'Only him,' Ronnie repeated, and Nutty Norman nodded his agreement.

It took them all summer and into the autumn. He would have liked to go more quickly, but they had to work in the hours when Wardick was at home and they had to work cautiously, silently. Each weekly visit to the probation officer provided Ronnie with new reasons to carry on destroying the smiling man's house, but this latest visit was the worst. Wardick took him home and gave him sherry to drink. It was horrible sweet stuff that stuck in his throat, but Ronnie drank it down, knowing it would make it easier to move his mind to another place. It felt odd to be in Wardick's dingy front room, knowing that beneath them only a few brick piers prevented the weight of the whole house from crashing down on them. Ronnie was sweating. What if the bloody lot went now? Wardick misinterpreted his nervousness and sat him on his knee. 'Come on, young chap, surely you know by now I'm not going to hurt you!'

Hurt him? Ronnie hardly knew what hurt was any more and he sent his mind to the other place. Always it was that last happy time, when Dad was home on leave and Sue had tasted chocolate for the first time. And when Wardick finally let him go, Ronnie was actually smiling at the memory.

Wardick was pleased. 'There, Ronald, I knew you liked it really,' he said, and Ronnie kept the smile fixed on his face.

★ ★ ★

The muddy morass around the huts had retreated and the colony was gradually freed from its island state. The grass of the Oval dried out and the sun baked the allotments hard. Rotting vegetables were raked out and new seeds planted. Spring had passed like a faded watercolour, then one morning Hattie had looked out of the hut window to see the trees finally heavy with lush green. But her heart wasn't as light as she'd imagined it would be when this moment finally came. At least the snow and then the floods had given her something to fight against, but now that things were getting easier at the squat she was forced to admit her new job hadn't made her as happy as she'd hoped. The trade-off with Crosbie had been costly. She couldn't bear the thought that it hadn't been worth it. There was also the guilt she felt about Alan. He was such a good, kind bloke. She knew she should either be serious about him or give him up. And she'd decided she needed to be serious about someone.

She and Clara shared the cooking and it was her turn to make them tea. Hattie was taking a Spam shepherd's pie out of their second-hand electric stove when Clara walked in with Martha. Her friend didn't look happy.

'What's the matter? Is Martha OK?'

Clara nodded. 'Just tired. I'll take her straight in to bed. Give her a feed in there.'

It was unusual to see Clara down in the mouth. Her fragility was deceptive. She had reserves of strength that had amazed Hattie, and she'd met hardships with cheerfulness and grit. But tonight she looked irritated and worn out. Hattie put it down to a hard day at the Alaska and a wakeful night with Martha, and began to set the table. Soon she heard Martha's protesting cries subside. The baby usually put up a show of resistance at bedtime, which Clara won over with her favourite lullabies. Eventually she came out of the nursery and sat at their small table, not meeting Hattie's eye.

'Has someone upset you? Dotty Axmouth stirring it again?' Hattie asked, dishing the shepherd's pie on to two plates. The pink cubes of meat were few and far between, so the dish was mainly potatoes, onions and tinned tomatoes. It tasted better than it looked and was Clara's favourite, but now the younger woman pushed the food around, looking close to tears.

'No, not Doris... it's you!' she blurted out. '*You've* upset me, Hattie – how could you do it?'

'Do what?' Hattie asked through a mouthful of too-hot Spam.

'The girls were full of it today. Dotty Axmouth said you've been sleeping with that Crosbie. They say he's always groping the girls when he comes to the factory and that you've jumped into bed with him just to get out of the factory.'

The roof of her mouth was burned, but it was the accusing stare of her friend that smarted more. 'It's none of their business.' She threw her fork on to the plate. 'And it's none of your'n neither! You of all people shouldn't be listening to the tittle-tattle of those evil cows.'

Clara seemed to quail at Hattie's fierce response. But she persisted. 'How could you go behind poor Alan's back?'

'Clara, what's brought all this on? He's always known I'm not a one-man type of girl – and so have you!'

Clara looked away and the silence was strung like a taut wire between them.

'It's silly us falling out over it,' Hattie continued. 'It's just like you to think of Alan, but really, Clara, that's up to me to sort out. And if you must know, I was only thinking today that he deserves someone who's serious about him. I've decided to give Crosbie the elbow and make a go of it with Alan. Satisfied?'

'Really?'

Hattie nodded, waiting for Clara to respond more enthusiastically. 'Well? What do you think?' Her friend still seemed hesitant. 'What's wrong now? Don't you think I've got it in me to settle down? I think I can with the right bloke. And Alan's funny. He makes me laugh, he's a great dancer, likes a good time like me...'

It was sounding to her own ears as though she were justifying her choice. 'Can't you at least be pleased I'm giving it a go?'

Clara smiled suddenly. 'Of course I'm pleased for you, Hattie, I'm just a bit surprised. You deserve to have someone special, someone you love enough to want to stay with forever. That's how I felt about Barry...'

Hattie wasn't sure that he was a good example to hold up before her. Besides, the word 'forever' had never even occurred to her when she thought of Alan, but perhaps that was a good thing if Clara's experience of enduring love was anything to go by.

A lightness settled over Hattie that night. It all seemed so simple. She'd made a choice. Cissie was wrong; it wasn't a job problem. It really was a man problem and once she'd chosen Alan she didn't need to stay with Crosbie. She'd missed VE day here, but she'd seen the liberation in France and Belgium, and she'd seen the crowds flinging hats into the air, embracing strangers in the streets. And that was how she felt when she threw the last of her orders on to Crosbie's desk later that week.

'Here's three new clients for you. Oh, and by the way, I'm handing in my notice.'

He barely reacted. 'I think we've been here before, sweetheart. I'm not naïve enough to think it's my charms you find irresistible – you're an ambitious girl...'

'No. I'm not. I just made the wrong choice. I thought I wanted this –' she waved a hand round the office – 'more than anything. But I was wrong.'

He raised his eyes, and shrugged. 'What a waste. Maybe I'll see you on the bambeater then, next time I'm visiting the factory... that's if I recognize you in your overall, darling.'

It was better not to reply. Perhaps she'd regret it, but the months of being part of the squat and her growing attachments to Clara and Martha, even to that little savage Ronnie, had overturned all that she'd thought might make her happy. All she knew was that she would rather go back to the Alaska than be jerked around like Crosbie's puppet for a minute longer.

Later, when Hattie told him the news, Buster said, 'I'm not sorry.'

'I'll miss the money, but nothing else,' she said, which was untrue. She'd miss the feeling of making use of her brain as well as her charm.

They were in Buster's flat and she was meeting Aiden for the first time. Buster had taken her advice to heart and asked him to come back. The young man was now making a lot of noise in the little kitchen, cooking their meal. Buster's first show of making good on his promises to Aiden had been this evening with Hattie. And Aiden had been a surprise: though much younger than Buster, he seemed far more level-headed. He'd greeted her with a warm kiss on the cheek and a whispered 'I know it's you I've got to thank, he listens to you.'

The clatter of saucepans and the steam escaping through the kitchen door told her she still had time to broach the subject of work with Buster. 'So, can you get me back in?'

'I thought you wanted an office job.'

'Don't rub it in. I thought I did – but not at any cost. You're trying to make a go of it with your chap, why shouldn't I try with mine? I just need a job to tide me over.'

'Well, you're in luck. We've lost our best groover. You can start tomorrow if you like.'

Hattie smiled. 'Not the bambeater? Thank God for that.'

Aiden came in with their plates piled high with thick golden chips, mushy peas and fish cakes he'd made from tinned tuna.

'Thanking God for what?' he asked, putting the plates in front of them.

'Only work,' Buster said.

'No more of that,' Aiden ordered. 'Tuck in.'

When they'd finished their meal and conversation turned to Ronnie, Hattie found she liked Aiden even more.

'Why don't you have Ronnie here?' Aiden asked Buster. 'He might as well sleep on a camp bed in our kitchen – it's no worse than what he's got at home. At least you'd be able to keep an eye on him.'

She could see Buster beginning to squirm. He simply couldn't handle Ronnie.

'It's not that simple,' she said, saving her friend. 'Ronnie goes where he wants. The only reason he's toed the line with the probation visits is because he's scared of being put away. We do what we can, don't we, Buster?'

He nodded. But they both knew it was little enough.

\* \* \*

Hattie worked out an awkward notice at the sales office in Upper Thames Street, keeping out of Crosbie's way and returning to work at the factory with a surprising sense of relief. In the Alaska hierarchy, if the bambeaters were its scullery maids, the groovers were its princesses. The resinous dye painted in unwavering stripes down the length of the fur could make a humble sheepskin look like an expensive beaver or mink, imitating the joining of their narrow pelts on the real thing. The quality of their work could maximize profits, but any mistake on the part of the groover would ruin the fur, which had already gone through countless shearing, cleaning and dying processes. Their steady eyes and hands were well worth the extra money in their pay packets. No doubt the dye fumes were stripping her lungs, but Hattie liked the job, partly because the girls had to be so concentrated on their task that there was little opportunity for deedee gossiping. This was a particular relief to Hattie, as it appeared her affair with Crosbie had become the latest grist to the gossip mill. Mostly she liked it because she could lose herself in the challenge, which required so much focus that all other thoughts were banished, and a sort of quietness descended as she completed stripe after stripe. It was calming and quiet. The grooving room had the peace of a church after the cacophony of the bambeaters.

But this morning its peace was suddenly ripped by a shrill wail. Out of the corner of her eye, Hattie saw the girl on the opposite bench whirl round, causing the brush in her hand to deposit a splodge of dark paint in the middle of the fur. Hattie took a deep conscious breath, and her hand barely trembled as she held the brush steady until she reached the bottom of the pelt. Then she lowered it to the wooden bench, and turned to see Lou standing a few feet from her. Lou's hands were gripping the pale hair on each side of her head, and she tugged and pulled at it so that tuft after tuft came away, drifting to the floor like so much rabbit down. All the while, a wordless howl reverberated round the room until every woman had put down her brush and turned to watch the spectacle unfolding.

'Dead and buried! And I've not seen him! He's gone, Hattie! My Ronnie. Dead and buried. Just like my Sue and Vic and Mum and Dad. Under the ground and I'm still here. Gawd's good, pray God he takes me soon, Hattie.' And she crumpled into a heap on the dirty, dye-stained floor. It was almost as if the hushed quiet of the grooving room had been tainted by a demon possessed. The expressions of the women were almost disapproving. Who hadn't lost someone? Who hadn't suffered want and privation? Who hadn't been driven from happiness into terror during the dark storm of war? Why bring that into the peace? Hattie knew their thoughts; she'd often shared them. Now was the time to enjoy life, wasn't it? They'd survived it all. Yet Hattie knew that Lou hadn't survived. She'd ridden out the war, only to be shipwrecked by the peace, just as Clara had, just as Hattie had. Lou was still living, but she certainly hadn't survived.

She dropped to her knees beside Lou and then the other women, following Hattie's lead, moved as one to surround the grief-stricken woman. Some wept and didn't know why – perhaps it was for their own losses. But only slowly did Hattie coax an explanation of how Ronnie had died and been buried all on the same day.

A building had collapsed. It was in a terrace of houses where a small UXB had exploded recently. Hattie had read about it in the paper and now she assumed the foundations had succumbed to the accumulated damage of war and the latest bomb. They were in the factory sick room, where Hattie had taken Lou after she'd prized her from her foetus-like curl on the grooving-room floor. She made her drink water and lie on the cot in the tiny, airless cubicle reserved for those hurt on the job. Now she stroked the woman's boney, thin-skinned hand.

'Lou, listen to me. How can you be sure Ronnie was there? You haven't seen him – that's what you said.'

'I ain't seen him, but he's told me.'

For an instant Hattie feared Lou thought she'd seen the ghost of her dead son.

'Who's told you?'

'Pissy Pants. He comes round the buildings, saying my Ronnie's been sleeping in a basement in that street. He's a wicked liar, I says, my Ronnie's been sleeping in his own bed. He's been a good boy lately, you know that, Hattie, don't you? But Pissy Pants won't have none of it. He says Ronnie and his mates been pulling the place apart, gawd knows why. And now me boy's dead and buried.' She broke into sobs that shook the narrow iron-framed cot, and Hattie held her hand tightly.

'You can't go on Johnny Harper's word! You can't. Ronnie might have been there, but until we know for sure you've got to believe he's still alive,' she pleaded.

A faint glimmer of light appeared in Lou's pale eyes. 'What, like I done with our Sue?'

Hattie had no answer for her. Instead, she took her to Buster and together they decided to go straight to the collapsed building. But the street was cordoned off, and it was obvious that it hadn't just been the one house that had collapsed. Half the street was already a cleared wartime bombsite, but the other half now looked like a row of crumpled dominoes, with each house toppled at a drunken angle, crushed by its neighbouring house. The place was alive with activity, and a demolition gang were picking through a mountain of bricks from what had once been the central house in the street. Hattie moved the *Danger* sign to one side, and they walked through choking clouds of dust to where a little group of onlookers had gathered. A policeman came to usher them away but when Buster explained who they were, he allowed them to stay. There were other gang members' parents gathered in the street. Word of Lou's visit from Pissy Pants had got round, but no one knew exactly which of the Barnham Street boys were involved, so anyone with a child who hadn't yet come home had congregated there. The policeman kept a respectful distance while the parents whispered to each other about the last known whereabouts of their children.

'Do we know which cellar the boys were in?' Buster asked a shortish man in his late forties, who it turned out was Nutty Norman's dad.

'The middle one, we think. The others was all empty, condemned, so at least no one else will have got hurt.'

Hattie kept an arm round Lou, feeling the small tremors and jerks that ran through her body whenever a shout went up from the clearance gang.

'I'm sure my Norman was with him,' the man said. 'It'll kill his mother. He's our only one.'

'Our Francis will be there too,' Frankie's mother added. 'My husband's still packing up the fish stall. Pray God they're alive.' And she began weeping into a screwed-up handkerchief. 'They was all thick as thieves, them boys. But what I don't understand is why they'd be doing something like that?'

'Devilment,' Norman's father said. 'They don't know how to play, our kids. They only know smashing things up.'

Hattie felt oddly defensive about the children who'd welcomed her back to Bermondsey with a beating. She remembered their fierce young faces as she'd seen them that night, defending their territory – Ronnie's most of all – illuminated by firelight, hardened out of all semblance of childhood.

'It's no wonder, not when all they've got to play in is bombsites,' she said, and felt her heart quail as she looked towards the destroyed house. 'Ruin's all they've ever known.'

She felt Lou's body shudder beneath her encircling arm as a

shout went up. 'Got something! Steady, boys.' All the men on the brick mound stiffened and Hattie's keen eyes picked it out, before either Buster or Lou did – a white hand protruding from rubble.

It felt like an eternity before she drew her next breath, but when she did she saw that Buster had followed her gaze. His face had turned whiter than the dust clouds that were rising as the crew began disturbing debris around the unmoving hand.

'Take her home, Buster,' she whispered. He began to protest, but she knew that this was no place for her soft-hearted friend. She had seen far worse than this, when her battery had moved across Europe. She knew she was stronger than him. 'Quick, before...' And she inclined her head to Lou, who was beginning to register the change in activity on the ruined house. He nodded. 'Let's come back later, eh, Lou? It'll be a while before they get all this cleared...' And Lou let herself be guided away by her brother. She glanced back once and her gaunt face, with its sunken cheeks and hollow eyes, had taken on the calm look of death.

# 17

## *Love Can't Wait*

Hattie stayed until the body had been uncovered completely. She saw the look of relief on Norman's dad's face as the stretcher bearers passed. Then she heard Frankie's mother scream. Hattie turned away, feeling an interloper there, as the woman was surrounded by friends from the buildings. Norman's dad went home soon after, to see if his son had returned, and the search of the rubble went on until the light failed and powerful arc lamps illuminated the devastation. Eventually the little crowd of onlookers dwindled away as family members arrived with reports of this child coming home from school, or another child found playing in a friend's house. But Buster didn't come to relieve her and so she stood, the last remaining hopeful face, watching an increasingly weary crew clearing the site. Eventually the policeman went off duty and the crew went home. The last of them stopped.

'You may as well go home, love,' he said, the creases of his face thick with grey dust. 'We'll start again in the morning, but we'll have to work slow, just in case there's anyone else under there. You waiting for one of the boys?'

She nodded mutely and he touched her arm. 'Your boy might be still out playing somewhere.'

She nodded, but in her heart, she didn't think he was.

He left her standing in the deepening darkness. She wasn't sure why she couldn't move – perhaps because she feared going back to Lou and seeing that calm, deathlike mask, which had seemed to prophesy that there would be no good news tonight. She was about to go when she heard footsteps behind her. She spun round, a surge of hope catching her off-guard. 'Ronnie?' His name was on her lips before she realized the foolishness of it. The figure was certainly that of a man, and as he came nearer she realized she knew him. He was dressed smartly in a grey tweed jacket and grey trousers, with a trilby shading his forehead.

'This is my fault,' he said.

'What? How's this got to do with you?' she asked fiercely, wanting someone to blame.

But as Joe moved closer, she saw his stricken face beneath the low hat brim. It melted her anger. Whatever he'd had to do with Ronnie's death, she realized he was already paying the price.

'I've come too late. If I'd only done something sooner...' he said, his voice heavy with regret.

'What could you have done? We all tried to help him... but he was already ruined, just like all this.' And she glared at the devastation wrought by the war.

'I know what Ronnie's been doing here, and I know why. I just didn't find out soon enough. Is it certain he's under there?'

She shook her head. 'They've given up for tonight, got to search the whole terrace. They've only pulled out one body so far.'

'Was it Wardick? God, I bloody well hope so.'

Now Hattie was confused. 'Wardick? The probation officer?'

'That's what he called himself. I call him a predator, a wolf that preys on all the lambs we'll give him.' He took off the hat, and shoved back the stray lock of hair from his forehead. It had been one of those autumn days that harks back to summer, catching out those who'd already migrated to their winter clothes. Joe's dark face was flushed, but she knew instinctively it was anger, and not the lingering heat of the day or the wrong suit of clothes, that was the cause.

'Look, Joe, I don't know why you're blaming yourself. But if you can tell me anything that could help us find Ronnie, I need to know it.'

'You look exhausted, Hattie,' he said. 'Let's find you some-where to sit down.'

He took her to the Angel, a pub by the river, leaving her at a table on the outside deck that jutted over the inky Thames. She was glad of the breeze from the river. The slap of waves and their receding tinkling over the exposed shingle of the foreshore was somehow calming. Joe came back with drinks and for a moment they were silent, looking out to the lamps strung along the far Wapping shore and the bobbing lights of barges and lighters moored nearby. She had learned it was best never to rush Joe; he did everything in his own time. He liked to think before he spoke, a trait that she sometimes wished she had herself.

'It was when he took against me, just because I was a keen photographer. It seemed an odd reason not to like someone. But I just put it down to that awkward age, you know? But then I started to think, what if it's not photographers in general, but one specific photographer, and then I remembered the photos...'

'Which photos?'

'Photos I'd glimpsed once, in the camera club's developing room. I should have done something then, but I just wasn't sure enough of what I'd seen, and it's a bloody hard thing to accuse someone of. But when you mentioned his name, that's when I put two and two together. Wardick – he belongs to the camera club and it was him left these photos in the developer. I only got a brief look. He came back in sharpish and took them when he realized what he'd done.'

'Joe, what did you see? Were they photos of Ronnie?'

'Not him, but other kids. I thought at first, he's their dad, taken photos at bath time. But there was something about them that made me suspicious. The poses weren't... natural let's say, and the faces of the kids, well, none of them were smiling...'

Joe didn't have to explain any more. 'Oh no, poor Ronnie. We thought we were helping him...' She remembered how she'd exhorted him not to miss his appointments, how pleased she was when he'd knuckled down, gone there every week without complaining, and all the time, just like Joe said, she'd been throwing him to the wolf.

'But why didn't you say anything?'

'I didn't have any evidence. I was waiting to get hold of his photos again, and I did.' He pulled out a manilla envelope full of prints and she flicked through them, with growing unease.

'I was going to take them to his boss today. They would have been enough to bring him down, but it looks like Ronnie couldn't wait. He beat me to it…'

'What do you mean?'

'That mountain of debris? Used to be Wardick's house.'

'You think he did it on purpose?'

Joe nodded, and there was almost a look of admiration in his eyes. 'I wouldn't be surprised if the damp squib of a bomb that went off here was his doing as well. No one else was coming to rescue him, so he did the only thing he could think of.'

'Like you in that Jap camp?'

He nodded silently.

'It didn't do you much good, though, did it?'

'Oh yes, it did. They might have slammed me in a hole for a year, but the minute I set that bomb off I was free.'

'Really? And then you come home and choose to live all alone in a hut…' she said tartly.

'I didn't say it lasted, but I was free for that moment, and I think that's what Ronnie wanted.'

'Poor little sod. Wherever he is, I hope he found it.' She felt her throat tighten and her eyes brim with tears. She was grateful that Joe stared into his pint, pretending to ignore her distress. 'So, what do we do now?'

'It all depends who's still under there.'

'I want to believe it's not Ronnie… I suppose that makes me as loony as Lou.'

'You've really got attached to him, haven't you?'

She shrugged. 'I know what it's like to be the kid who's mum everyone takes the piss out of.' But whatever she might say, she knew it wasn't just fellow feeling. It was the way he'd grabbed her hand when the policeman came out of the squat that day, the way he'd gravitated towards her in the court. He'd adopted her and she found she didn't mind at all.

'I think we just assume he's alive somewhere, and until we know he's not, we'll look in all the places he could be,' Joe said.

'And what if Wardick's dead under there?'

'Then good. But if he's not, then I'll hunt him down.' Joe's dark eyes glinted like two black flints and she saw a flash of the ex-Chindit who'd survived the prison camp.

'And if it's Ronnie?'

'Then he's free.'

They left the Angel and went back to Lou's together, and on the way stopped off at some of Ronnie's favourite riverside bombsites and hidey-holes, or the ones Hattie knew about. There would be many more, but Buster would have to find those out from the Barnham Street boys. When they arrived back at Barnham Street, the courtyard and landings were full of people. They hadn't retreated into their own homes, but had already banded together in search parties for the kids who were still missing. Hattie spotted Norman's dad, but his earlier look of relief had been wiped clean away. 'He still ain't come home,' he explained as Buster, with Lou in tow, hurried up to her.

'Nothing,' she said before he could ask, 'and we've looked all along the riverside bombsites.' Buster looked questioningly at Joe. 'He's here because he knows why this happened.'

As she explained quickly about Wardick's involvement, Buster's chubby face hardened. 'I'll kill the bastard,' he said.

But Joe put a restraining hand on his arm. 'Ronnie might have already done that, but if Wardick's not dead under the rubble we can deal with him later. The important thing is to find the boy.'

Buster attempted to shake Joe off, but his grip was unyielding. 'One thing at a time, Buster,' he said, and Hattie nodded her agreement. They left Lou with Norman's mother, and while

Buster went off to look in the haunts he knew of, she and Joe made up their own search party of two.

'If the boy knows what's happened, it might be that he's too frightened to surface. Where's the place he's most likely to go to ground if he's not under all that rubble?'

They tried the Spa Road bombsite, the ruined tanning pits and a drained emergency water tank nearby, but there was no sign of him. By midnight she had exhausted her meagre knowledge of Ronnie's domain and they were forced back to Barnham Street. The other search parties had returned too. The high-sided court-yard reminded Hattie of the town of Hamelin, the adults sharing a look of stunned incomprehension. How had they let their children be spirited away? It had been a normal thing for the kids to roam free late into the night, finding their own entertainment or mischief among the ruins, and their parents, too exhausted by poverty and war, had let them go. Hattie saw guilt written large on every face, though on some, those whose children had been led home, she saw pure relief.

But there was nothing more they could do that night. As she and Joe walked back to the squatting colony together, she was so bone-tired her legs wobbled beneath her. Joe caught her and offered her an arm so they were walking in companionable silence, his stride matching hers perfectly, for they were of a similar height. When she and Alan walked arm in arm they always seemed to bump each other away, like two moored barges bouncing on the tide. The picture made her smile, but then her hand flew to her mouth.

'What's the matter?' Joe asked.

'Alan! Oh, bloody hell, I forgot all about it – he was taking me for a special night out and I forgot... poor Alan,' she groaned.

Joe laughed. 'He'll get over it. A missed meal's not the end of the world. He should count his lucky stars he's got someone like you.'

In spite of the warm night, she felt a chill raise goosebumps along her arms. Her chest tightened as she met Joe's gaze. For some reason, what she saw in his eyes was not a surprise. *Poor Alan*, she thought, as Joe took her in his arms and kissed her.

*This shouldn't be happening*, she told herself, yet his lips on hers felt so surprisingly tender and strong she was unable to pull away. What was the point of leaving Crosbie, only to fall into the arms of Joe, of all people? What was she doing? She put her hands on his chest, but before she could push him away, he jumped back.

'Sorry, oh, sorry. That shouldn't have happened.'

'Exactly what I was thinking,' she said, breathless.

'It won't happen again. Alan's my best mate.'

'I know that! And he's my chap!'

She realized she was holding Joe's hand. Joe, who'd hated her very presence in the camp, Joe who blocked her at every turn. Why was she holding his hand? And then he kissed her again and she knew why.

★ ★ ★

Alan had come to Clara at the hut asking after Hattie, his face flushed and clouded with confusion.

'I can't believe she's stood me up. She knew I had this date all planned...'

'Hattie wouldn't do that, Alan, not without a good reason,' she said, coming to the defence of her friend.

'Well, she never let me know, not a word!' he said. 'She was meant to meet me at the pub first, and then we were going to a nice Italian place over Soho, none of your British Restaurant rubbish! I waited an hour and then came here. Have you got any idea where she is?'

'No, Al, I haven't, sorry.' She felt so sorry for him that she asked him in, feeling she was safe to do that. After all, Hattie had said she was sticking with Alan, and he'd shown no signs of leaving her. She'd preferred to put down his declaration as a passing fancy, brought on by their closeness in watching over Martha. He was naturally thoughtful – he'd simply confused concern for her child with love for her. His face brightened suddenly.

'I won't come in, Clara, but why don't you come out? Come out with me! It's a shame to waste the reservations…'

He had seemed so deflated, she couldn't disappoint him. She asked Maisie to babysit and, feeling it was the most daring thing she'd done since stowing away on the ship home, she went with him. The meal wasn't as wonderful as Alan had promised – how could it be when the weekly meat ration was an inch square and sugar was a distant memory? But for Clara it was the company that dazzled her, and for a brief instant she allowed herself to imagine what would have happened if she'd not rejected him, when he said, 'Clara, I still feel the same.'

His words exploded into her fantasy, and the silence rushed around her. His eyes fixed on hers, and when she didn't reply, he went on. 'When you turned me down, I tried to forget… and Hattie seemed to be getting more attached. But, the truth is, all I think about is you…'

Now, as she lay awake in bed, Clara's heart quailed at the thought of all that had happened that evening. She heard Hattie come in and carefully remove her shoes by the door before creeping into the hut. They had partitioned the bedrooms; the walls were only plywood and every sound echoed around the wooden structure. Hattie had shed her clothes and had just slipped into bed when Clara emerged from her bedroom.

'Hattie, I've been awake, waiting… I've got something to tell you.'

'Oh, Clara, I've had a terrible day. I just need to sleep,' her friend replied in a voice hoarse with weariness. 'Can it wait?'

'No, it can't.'

Hattie sat up, wincing as she did so. She spoke into the darkness. 'What is it?'.

Clara leaned over and switched on the bedside lamp.

'Clara, you've been crying! What's the matter?' Hattie took

her hand and pulled her down to sit on the bed, but now Clara couldn't meet Hattie's eye.

'I spent tonight with Alan. He was meant to be with you...'

'I know, I know, don't go off at me again about him,' Hattie said with a guilty look. 'I stood him up, but there's a good reason. There was an accident – a building collapsed, and we think Lou's Ronnie might be under there.'

Shock forced Clara to meet her gaze, and Hattie seemed to use up the last reserves of her energy to explain what had happened.

'Oh, poor Lou, she'll never get over losing another kid.' Clara's heart went out to the woman who had saved Martha's life.

'I know. That's why I had to stick around and help, not that I could do much but search.' Hattie laid her head back against the pillow. 'Was Alan really upset?'

'Actually, Hattie, that's what I wanted to talk to you about. He wasn't upset, not at all.'

Now Hattie sat bolt upright. 'He wasn't?'

Clara shook her head. 'In fact, we had a really lovely evening together. Maisie babysat and Alan took me over to that Soho restaurant.'

Hattie laughed. 'That's the best news I've heard all day. Well, I hope you had a bloody good time on my date!'

Clara felt a blush rising and swallowed. 'The best time I've had for ages.'

Perhaps it was the breathless quality of her voice, or the flush on her cheeks that betrayed her. But in the glow of the lamp she saw a look of suspicion cross Hattie's face.

'Clara! Don't tell me you like Alan yourself?'

Clara's blush deepened. 'Oh, Hattie, I'm so sorry. I didn't mean it to happen...' She took a deep breath. 'The thing is – Alan's told me he loves me.'

Hattie let out a low whistle. 'Well, sod me. How long's it been going on?'

Clara dropped her head and began to cry. 'I'm so sorry. We got close when Martha was ill – you know what a soft-hearted feller he is. I thought he was just feeling sorry for me. 'Course I told him I wouldn't go behind your back, and then you said you were sticking with him. Oh, if only you'd kept that date, this would never have happened...' And she was silenced by her sobs.

'You love him too?'

'Yes, I do,' Clara said, wiping her eyes. 'But he doesn't know it.'

'Well, I think it's about time he did.'

* * *

Next morning Hattie woke early, her mind in turmoil and her heart torn in too many ways to count. Her first thought had been for Ronnie, crushed beneath Wardick's house, and Lou's agonizing wait for news. She realized she needed to push all her feelings about Joe and Alan into a small hidden place, an imaginary cell, a bit like the eyeless dungeon Joe had been shut up in. She incarcerated her confusion, her guilt and her surprising desire, slamming the door and turning the key. Love would have to wait, she told herself.

She propped herself up on her elbow and looked out of the hut window. The billowing canopy of trees, just beginning to turn red, filled her eyeline. Joe had suggested bringing Ronnie here once; now she knew it had been an attempt to protect him. She scrubbed a hand through her hair, and pulled down a golden strand to find it full of brick dust from last night. She'd have to wash it before she went anywhere today. Groaning, she eased herself out of bed and threw her coat on. She padded quietly along the duckboards to the NAAFI, praying she wouldn't bump into Alan. But as she emerged with the heavy bucket of water, she found Joe waiting for her.

'I didn't sleep a wink,' he said, dark-eyed and grey-faced.

'Cissie would say you look like a death-worn duck!'

'She'd be right then! Listen, Hattie, I think we'd better just forget about last night. Alan—'

She was unprepared for the disappointment and the imaginary

cell she'd constructed burst open. 'But I don't want Alan,' she said. 'I want you.'

The early morning sun peeked through the tree canopy, adding its gold to the burnished leaves, and Joe's face was gilded with light as he broke into a wide smile. 'I'm happy! But I shouldn't be.'

'There is no should or shouldn't, Joe. You can't argue with what you're feeling, nor what I'm feeling. And maybe Alan's been ignoring his feelings for a while too.'

They made their way out of sight, behind the NAAFI building, Hattie wearing only her pyjamas and jacket, with her feet stuffed into some old shoes. She felt that if Joe looked at her properly this morning he must surely realize the mistake he'd made. They walked to the tree line, and stood beneath the old fairy tree, its branches alive with the song of a solitary blackbird.

'What do you mean about Alan?' he said, reaching to push a wayward strand of hair from her cheek. She thought of the brick dust and didn't care.

'Clara told me he's been in love with her for a while and he felt too guilty to tell me—'

'In love with Clara! But why?'

'Oh, Joe, you can be thick sometimes. Why anyone? Why you? Why me?'

'A million reasons and I'd like to spend a million days telling you every one of them.' He drew her close and – to the music of the singing bird – she realized that however many tragedies might be going on around her, love just couldn't wait.

Afterwards, when she'd said goodbye to Joe and promised to meet him later that day, she made her way back to the hut, allowing herself a small smile at her failure to keep her feelings locked in that imaginary cell for more than an hour. But for the moment, there was Clara to face. She imagined there would be an awkwardness between them, but as she let herself in, Clara rushed over and dumped Martha into her arms.

'Where've you been all this time? We'll be docked half-hour

now. You give her some breakfast, she takes it better from you.' Martha had become a picky eater since her teeth had started to come through, and Hattie was secretly proud that she could coax more spoonfuls of mashed food into her tiny mouth than her mother could. She used sleight of hand and misdirection. Martha was clever, but not so clever that she couldn't mistake a spoonful of food for a choo-choo train. Hattie was relieved. Perhaps it would be different when their confidences had sunk in, but for now it seemed she and Clara had shared too much to let their love lives come between them. So, while Clara got ready for work, Hattie tricked Martha into eating rusks and milk, and then washed the baby's face and hands.

'I'm not going in today!' she called through the thin plywood wall. 'Will you let Harper know for me?' Chris Harper had been understanding about her coming back to the Alaska – too understanding. It wasn't like any of the Harpers to make her life easy and Hattie suspected an underlying motive. She just wasn't sure what it was yet. Lenny had been lying low since his first attempt to muscle in on the squat. Perhaps he had something more lucrative and less trouble to occupy him, but she knew she hadn't seen the last of him.

'So, what shall I say – you're sick?' Clara asked, coming to lift Martha from her arms.

'Tell him the truth. Ronnie's my ward – it's a court order. I can't just go back to grooving and leave Buster to deal with it all. If Harper wants to make a fuss he can go and argue with the judge.'

'All right. Well, I should go, and, Hattie…' Here a faint blush rose in Clara's cheeks. 'We'll say no more about Alan. He's yours and that's that. I can't trust me own judgement where fellers are concerned anyway. Probably all end in tears…'

'It's not just up to you, though, is it, love? There's four of us now.'

'Four?'

But Clara was late and Hattie ushered her out of the hut door, promising to explain everything that night.

She'd arranged to meet Buster at Barnham Street Buildings. The whole place had an unusual quiet hanging over it. Normally the courtyard was full of shouts and children's cries, foul-mouthed exchanges and raucous laughter, mothers calling down from balconies to their screaming kids, throwing money for errands or generally scolding. There was more often than not an explosive row of some kind going on, with f's and b's reverberating round the courtyard. But today, even the trains thundering along the viaduct behind the tenements seemed to be muted.

Buster opened the door.

'Any news?' she asked.

He shook his head. 'All the other missing kids come home last night, all accounted for except our Ronnie and Norman.' He looked over his shoulder at Lou. 'I've spent all night trying to keep her from going out looking for him. She thinks he's with Sue. Poor cow, he might be.'

'What can we do with her? We can't take her to the site again.'

'Norman's mum's promised to keep an eye on her. I'll let her know we're going to the site.'

They left Lou in the woman's care and were just crossing the hushed courtyard when a policeman ran towards them, out of breath and sweating in his blue serge uniform and helmet. Normally the tenants would run in the opposite direction to any policeman, or at least close their doors, but today heads poked out, and before long the constable was surrounded. 'Looking for the families of Norman Gates and Ronnie Payne?' the policeman gasped.

Buster nodded.

'They've found another body.'

The clearance gang had been working since dawn, Wardick's house had been almost entirely excavated before they had made their discovery. As Hattie watched with the others, the last bricks and tiles were lifted out of the crater that had once been the cellar. Two crewmen jumped in and manoeuvred a stretcher into the tight space. It all seemed so ham-fisted and graceless. The small body was mishandled and limbs fell awkwardly from the stretcher; the young round head lolled to one side. There was an almost audible intake of breath as the stretcher lurched and the body began to slip off. The men struggled for a moment, then recovered the stretcher and carried it to a waiting ambulance.

'Is it Ronnie?' Buster hissed. 'Can you see?'

'No, but I can hear something,' Hattie said, craning her head. As the stretcher drew nearer, the sound continued, a thin but strident wailing, almost like a song. Then a cry burst from Norman's dad standing beside her, and she heard clearly. It *was* a song!

*APPles red and yellow... won't you come and buy...*

'It's my Norman!' Norman's dad ran forward, followed by Hattie and Buster. The boy's eyes were open but glazed. 'Is that you, Dad?' He broke off singing. 'Knew if I sung loud enough you'd hear me... *APPles fo' your apple tart...f'o ap pie...*'

'It's all right, son,' Norman's dad said, tears streaming down his face. 'You can stop singing now.'

Hattie stood back to let the doctor do his work, but as she did so the boy's hand shot out and grabbed her. 'Did Ron get out? Tell 'im sorry we didn't get Wardick... sorry I ruined it.'

'Ronnie? Was he with you?'

But the boy's eyes closed and the ambulance doors shut. As they stood watching it recede, the clanging bells echoing off Bermondsey Wall, she allowed herself a small hope.

'Sounds like Wardick escaped, and that means Ronnie could have too!'

Buster looked unconvinced. 'If he did, I don't think we'll be the only ones looking for him.'

# 18

# The Children's Flats

## September 1947–January 1948

Hattie and Buster had spent all day searching farther afield. Down river steps and along the foreshore beneath Tower Bridge, they clambered on to linked barges that bobbed with the tide, dug beneath tarpaulins and rummaged under sacks full of peanuts. They scoured the wharf sides wherever there was access, asking dockers and stevadores to keep an eye out for Ronnie. They traipsed up to the Borough market, asking the traders if they'd spotted a boy, scavenging for food. Many of them knew of Ronnie, but none had seen him.

If Ronnie had escaped the collapsed building, it was likely he knew Wardick had too. She suspected Ronnie would want to go to ground, hide like a hunted animal, and she had asked herself over and over again, where would he feel safest? She wasn't sure why she hadn't thought of this place before. But it had occurred to her as she'd been walking home and thinking of Joe, how he'd come out of captivity only to choose a life of isolation at the squatters' camp – until she'd come along. They'd both preferred their familiar wartime life of huts and camps, and she'd been pondering what it must have been like for him, all those dark days and nights locked in an underground hole, when it had dawned on her – all Ronnie's hidey-holes were like little dungeons in themselves.

Now she found herself outside the old air-raid shelters in the park. Pressing her hand against cold metal, she pushed. The creak of the iron door jagged on Hattie's already raw nerves. Evening sunlight spilling down the stairs from the doorway cast a long shadow, her own, which moved before her as she descended the stairs into the black depths of the concrete bunker. Outside, the autumn evening had been golden, but down here it was freezing and she shivered in the darkness.

There was no air down here. She gulped quick breaths trying to fill lungs that felt as if they'd been crammed with the pulverized stone and ash from Wardick's ruined house. She got out her torch. The beam illuminated the row of wooden bunks and as she walked along them, her footsteps echoed in the dank cavern. She walked the length of the shelter, listening to faint whisperings. They might have been echoes of hushed voices long gone, the murmured prayers of all those terrified souls who had once sheltered here, but though the place was cavernous as a cathedral, there was nothing holy about it.

Air from a side tunnel fanned her cheek, and then there came a rattling that made her start. She froze, feeling sweat trickle down her back, and a chill crept up her arms. What if Wardick had come to hide here? It was a ridiculous thought, but all the same she swung the torch in a wild arc, bouncing its light over wartime graffiti and redundant official signs advising those sheltering to avoid exertion and refrain from smoking. The torchbeam caught a movement beneath one of the bunks. 'Who's there?' she called, her voice trembling and her hand shaking, causing the torchbeam to waver.

A rat? No, bigger. She plucked up courage to move closer and saw a shadowed form, squirming, a small animal gone to ground, squashed deep under one of the bunks. Curled up in a writhing ball, the rattling she'd heard was caused by its violent trembling against the bunk frame.

And now she heard the whispering more clearly: 'Gawd's good, let someone save me, gawd's good... don't let him find me... gawd's good...'

Ronnie's grey shorts were covered in white rubble dust, but

a dark ruby-red area glistened at the top of one thigh. His back was covered by a ripped shirt, caked in blood. His eyes were shut tight and his blue lips moved as he muttered a hoarse imitation of his mother's rosary: 'Gawd's good'. When she reached down a hand to touch him, he screamed.

'It's me, Hattie! You're safe.'

But he seemed not to have heard her. Instead, he scrunched into an even tighter ball, alternately groaning and praying. She had seen such violent trembling after a wound, when the body went into shock and the jaw locked and the muscles spasmed. She needed to get Ronnie a doctor, and quickly. She was about to leave him to run for help when his eyes shot open and he put up weak arms. "Miss! It's you! I thought you was the smiling man.'

She reached under the bunk and he draped his bony arms around her neck. As she eased him out from under the bunk he cried out once, but she saw him bite his lip and carried on hauling. When he was finally out she sat with him on the cold shelter floor. He fell into her lap and his arms encircled her so tightly she could barely breathe. She wasn't sure how badly he was hurt, or if he could walk at all.

'Ronnie, I think I've got to leave you for a bit, go and get help.'

'No!' he protested weakly. 'Don't leave me, miss.'

The thought of leaving him down here while she went to fetch someone was too dreadful. She let him lay his head on her shoulder, and listened as his harsh rapid breathing gradually slowed and his violent shaking subsided a little.

'Is that what you call Wardick, the smiling man?'

He looked up at her and nodded, while his sharp chin trembled. 'I thought I see him get out of the rubble. He ain't dead, is he?' He was barely able to speak, he was shivering so much.

'No, Ronnie.'

'Oh gawd, that's bad, that's really bad…'

'It's good – you silly boy! You could have been up for murder if he'd died… what on earth did you think you were doing?'

His face screwed up and he clenched his fist. Batting away angry tears, he shouted at her, 'I was looking after meself, like I always do, 'cause no one else will!'

He pushed at her with two flat hands, but there was little force in them and she let him shove her again and again, never moving until he finally fell back into her arms, crying like the little boy he still was.

'I didn't know what else to do. You all said I had to go to Wardick's, but once he started on me, I knew I'd have it for months... I couldn't put up with it any more. I'm sorry, miss, I mean, Hattie.'

Soon her frock was wet with his tears and blood, and she found herself kissing his matted straw hair. 'Oh, Ronnie, love, it's not you who should be saying sorry, it's us. Why didn't you say anything?'

'You wouldn't have believed me.'

And Hattie supposed he was right. 'Well, you're OK now. He won't hurt you any more.'

'But he's not brown bread, so you can't say that for sure.'

'Maybe not, but my friend Joe got all the evidence we need for the police, and when they find him they'll lock him away for a long time.'

'Joe! You don't want to trust him – he's one of them!' In his excitement, he had forgotten his injuries and now uttered a yell of pain, grabbing the top of his thigh. She saw blood seeping through his fingers. She needed to move him, but was wary of doing more damage.

'No, no, Ronnie, he's a good bloke. He just likes photography, that's all. He wants to help you.'

Ronnie looked uncertain.

'He's been trying to get evidence on Wardick for months.'

'Well, he should've got a m-move on,' Ronnie stammered.

Hattie smiled, glad to see a spark of the old Ronnie. 'Yes, you're right. Joe can be a bit slow sometimes. But listen, we need to go now. Do you think you can walk?'

He nodded and leaned heavily on her as she helped him to his feet.

They came up from the shelter into the light of day. Once out from under the earth, they were greeted by the lingering warmth of the setting sun. Its last rays glinted through the trees so that black and gold bars striped the green grass. She walked with her arm round his waist, fearful that he would bolt at any moment. But he seemed content, stopping and smiling every time they walked into a patch of sunlight.

'Where you taking me?' Ronnie asked, as Hattie supported him. He hobbled along with his arm over her shoulder, grimacing with every step.

'To the squat, we can clean you up, see what the damage is, eh?'

Ronnie looked suspicious, still wary of a trap. 'Will I have to go to Borstal?'

'No!' she said, though she couldn't be certain. 'But you'll have to promise to live at home and stop running off. Your mum's been worried sick...'

'Surprised she missed me.'

'She missed you.'

'I been so cold, down there on me own, Hattie.'

'We'll get you warm soon enough, Ronnie.'

They were greeted by Clara, standing at the hut door, holding Martha in her arms. At the sight of Hattie and the injured boy she ran to them. As she jogged along in her mother's arms, Martha thought it was a game and laughed at Ronnie, holding out her arms to him.

'Hello, how's me baby?' He reached for her hands, but staggered against Hattie. 'Later, we can play later, eh?' he mumbled, his eyes losing their focus.

Martha leaned forward in her mother's arms and, with a look of intense focus, reached out to pat his cheek with her chubby hand.

'See, she knows... she knows me...' Ronnie said, before slumping, insensible, to the floor.

They called for help, and soon Joe and Alan came running. Lifting Ronnie between them, they carried him to Hattie's hut.

'I'll ring for the doctor,' Alan said, hurrying off to the phone box outside the park while Joe examined Ronnie's wounds.

'Looks like he's got some crush wounds, and he's in shock. God knows how he got himself out of there. Are you all right?' Joe looked up at Hattie with anxious eyes, and for the first time she noticed Ronnie's blood staining her frock.

'Yes, don't worry about me. Do you think he'll be all right?'

But Ronnie was already coming round and he drew back in fear when he saw Joe. 'It's OK, Ronnie. I told you, Joe's a friend.'

But she tugged Joe away. 'Still not sure he trusts any photographers yet!' she whispered.

While Joe retreated, Clara fetched scissors to cut away Ronnie's blood-caked clothing, and water to bathe his cuts and grazes. Remembering her army first aid, Hattie questioned him about what day he thought it was and how many fingers she was holding up.

'I might have had half a ton of rubble on me head,' he said, eventually growing impatient, 'but I ain't a bleedin' idiot.'

It was early evening before the doctor had pronounced Ronnie a very lucky young man and assured Hattie it was safe for him to be taken home. The tin bath from behind the hut was filled with hot water from the stove, and Ronnie allowed Alan to help him with a bath. They redressed his wounds and found some clothes of Maisie's brothers to fit him. And while he played with Martha, Vera cooked him a meal from their common supplies in the NAAFI. He looked almost like a normal schoolboy by the time they bundled him carefully into Alan's car.

Cars were not such a common sight in Barnham Street, and when they drew up outside the buildings they were immediately surrounded by a swarm of children. The shout of 'Ronnie's home!' reverberated round the courtyard, people lined the balconies, and a cheer went up as she and Alan helped Ronnie to the stairwell. He gave a little wave to the assembled neighbours, almost like returning royalty, though the surroundings were far from palatial.

It was agonizingly slow for him to get up the stone stairs, with a bandaged leg and bruises blooming on most of his limbs. But eventually they arrived at Lou's front door. Before they went in, Ronnie stood for a moment, with difficulty, and tried to smooth his hair.

'You look fine, very handsome,' Hattie whispered. 'Just be nice to your mum.'

But her warning was unnecessary.

'Oh, Ronnie! Gawd's good, boy, I prayed God not to take you!' Lou put out her arms and ran to him.

'Sorry you was worried, Mum, but I was so scared...'

'How did you find him, after all the places we searched?' asked Buster, who had returned to Lou's side.

'I suddenly remembered it was the one place we hadn't looked,' Hattie explained. 'Only me, Joe and Johnny Harper knew Ronnie had ever been there. It was the safest place for him to go – wasn't it, Ron?'

'You're the cleverest of the lot, miss – Hattie,' he said, giving her the elfin grin that no longer had a hint of wariness to it.

She left Buster to tell him about Norman and poor Frankie. She doubted she was the cleverest, but she realized she certainly wasn't the bravest or strongest, not when it came to children. Perhaps they were her weak spot after all – and perhaps that's why she'd never wanted one of her own.

Back at the car, Alan shooed away the kids clambering all over it. She got in and felt oddly shy, realizing this was the first time she'd been alone with him since before the building collapse; since before Joe.

'Fancy going for a drink?' he asked.

She shook her head. 'I'm so tired, I just want to get home to bed.'

He drove silently, concentrating on negotiating the heavy

early evening traffic around London Bridge. It wasn't until they neared the park that she plucked up courage.

'Alan, I'm sorry I missed our date the other night.'

'What date?' He seemed genuinely confused.

'The one you spent with Clara instead.'

'Oh! Yes, *that* date!' He smiled and his prominent Adam's apple rose and fell as he turned into Southwark Park Road.

'You had a nice night, I hear.'

'Yes,' he said, gripping the steering wheel. Never before had he seemed so enigmatic.

It felt like a game of chicken. Who would be the one brave enough to admit that they were both with the wrong person?

'Al, I've changed my mind about that drink. But why don't we get something at the off licence and have it back at the hut – we could ask Joe in, make it a foursome?'

They bought beers and Hattie insisted on buying them a bottle of whiskey. The price was extortionate, but she had a feeling she'd need the Dutch courage before the night was out.

'You get Joe, I'll warn Clara – she might be in her dinky curlers!' Hattie said, hoping she'd get a few minutes to explain to her friend.

Clara was standing at the metal kitchenette cupboard, slicing bread. 'I've just this minute got Martha off to sleep.' Her friend looked up with a frazzled smile. 'Want a sandwich?'

'Have we got enough bread for four? I've invited guests,' Hattie asked, shedding her coat.

Clara was about to reply when the knock came, and the two men walked through the door. The knife Clara was holding clattered to the floor. She fumbled to pick it up, glaring at Hattie. 'Oh, you should have let me know,' she said sweetly. 'I would have cooked something.'

'Impromptu!' Hattie raised her eyes in apology. 'We like to be impromptu, don't we, Al?'

Joe followed close behind, and the look he gave her mirrored Clara's. The two men set about pouring drinks, and when they were all seated round the stove Clara offered them meat-paste sandwiches. The men had identical sheepish looks on their faces, and both were avoiding eye contact with the women they loved.

Hattie took a gulp of her whiskey. 'I've got something to say.'

'No!' Clara and Joe said in unison, and Alan said, 'What?'

She took in a deep breath, hoping she wouldn't regret taking charge of the situation. 'Alan, I love Joe,' she blurted out, and heard Joe groan. 'And he loves me. So, you won't break my heart if you ask Clara out, and she won't break your heart either, because she loves you too. Anyone for another drink?'

★ ★ ★

It hadn't been an ideal way to announce their love for their new partners, but Hattie's nature was to take the lead and she couldn't have done anything else. She'd expected to be told off by Joe and Clara, but once Clara had realized she didn't have to let one betrayal freeze her heart forever, and Alan had been reassured that Hattie's heart was not secretly breaking, the four friends settled into their new relationships without a rift. In the weeks that followed, it became obvious that Clara and Alan were perfectly suited. It helped that Alan loved Martha, and his light-hearted nature was able to lift Clara's more cautious approach to life. But it was less straightforward for Hattie and Joe. The truth was that Hattie still found Joe the person who challenged her most, the one who made her think twice about everything she said or thought or did.

Through the rest of that autumn, Ronnie's wounds slowly healed. The damage to his leg was the worst and he developed a slight limp, which he seemed to enjoy exaggerating to impress his mates. Hattie took to visiting him and Lou as often as she could, taking them bags of potatoes when they were put on the ration, and anything else that could be spared from the squatters' allotment. She was conscious she'd let Ronnie down. Surely she should have seen something in Wardick? Why had she been so completely taken in? The police still hadn't managed to track

Wardick down and their enquiries into the building collapse and its consequences dragged on, so that it wasn't until Christmas that Ronnie's case reached the courts. The magistrate was far more lenient, she suspected, than if Wardick hadn't been a court-appointed predator. Ronnie and Norman were passed into the care of their guardians, with a proviso they attend a youth club regularly. Though how they would manage to enforce that in Ronnie's case she didn't know. He declared that all youth clubs were for Mary Anns and he wouldn't be seen dead in one.

But with Ronnie's escape, at least Lou had made one of her periodic emergences from that confusion of past and present where she lived most of her life. She went back to the Alaska and was greeted with more sympathy this time. For weeks, the talk there had been all about the building collapse and the boy who'd died. Lou's Ronnie had been elevated almost to sainthood, the women's condemnation of the probation officer who'd preyed upon him was so strong. There were many women who came up to Hattie and wanted to tell her their own stories of truant sons and daughters, already caught up in gangs like the Barnham Street boys, some on the edge of crime, others deeply ensnared in the Harpers' net. Frankie's plight was held up to their children as a warning by more than one of the Alaska mothers.

At the canteen table one day, after Lou had returned to work, Kate, a woman with four sons, broke down in tears. 'All my boys was on probation and they've ended up telling me the truth – that Wardick had a go at all of 'em! If they find him, I tell you there'll be so many mothers outside Tower Bridge nick there'll be murders!' The other women voiced their agreement and she went on. 'I can't give up me job here and my husband works all hours God sends. How we meant to keep our eye on our kids? The thought of what that bastard's been doing...'

'All they want to do is go on the bombsites and smash things up,' Daisy, a woman with a dozen children, said. 'Or nick stuff off of the docks.'

'It's not their fault,' Levin the nailer added. 'I've got five little

bleeders of me own, I give 'em a back hander now'n again, but
even I can't control 'em, so gawd knows how Lou manages.'

'Well, I don't, do I?' Lou said. 'It's better now my Ronnie listens
to Buster and Hattie.'

'Is your boy back on his feet, love?' Kate asked.

'Back to school an' all,' Lou said proudly.

Hattie smiled with the other women, but she was wondering
how long Ronnie's new leaf would stay turned.

*

Later that week she went to Barnham Street Buildings, largely to
make sure Ronnie had been at school that day. As she was turning
out of the stairwell after her visit, she sniffed the air. There were
plenty of smells to be experienced here, mostly unpleasant: rotting
food and rubbish from the chutes, coke and soot from the steam
trains, boiling cabbage, noxious smells drifting from the nearby
tannery and Sarson's vinegar factory. But this was something she
had never before experienced in Barnham Street Buildings – it
was the smell of fresh paint.

It was so uncommon she had to follow her nose. She discovered
the smell was coming from a ground-floor flat. In spite of a
December chill, the front door was wide open and she could hear
the sound of a woman singing. It was a sentimental tune from the
war, 'Tomorrow is a Lovely Day', all about how wonderful life
would be for them once the war was over. Hattie hadn't heard
it since VE day. The reality had been so different, it had seemed
to knock every ounce of gratitude out of her, but today she felt
the truth of it and she was grateful. Ronnie was safe and Lou
had found her own sort of peace, Joe loved her and Clara was
discovering happiness again. Tomorrow, it seemed, was indeed
a lovely day.

She poked her head into the tiny front room. It was bright.
Most of the flats' interiors boasted shades of dark brown and
green distemper, usually bubbled with damp.

'Oh, it's yellow!' she couldn't help exclaiming and the woman, holding a dripping paintbrush, turned round. She was wearing a scarf tied turban-style and a green boiler suit spattered with paint.

'Sunshine Yellow! I thought it would brighten things up!' the woman said, with a wide smile.

'It does. Are you moving in?' Hattie asked.

'In a way, I suppose I am, but I won't be living here.' The woman put down the brush and wiped her hands on the boiler suit. 'My name's Anne Lethbridge. I'll be running the children's flats.'

Seeing Hattie's confusion, she indicated one of two chairs. 'Come in and sit down. I could do with a break, I've been at this all day.'

Hattie could track Anne's yellow progress round the once dingy brown walls. She sat and nodded her appreciation. 'You're doing a great job.'

Anne sat in the chair opposite and wiped a sheen of sweat from her forehead. Rich brown curls were escaping from her turban, which hadn't protected them from the yellow paint. 'I've already got our little kitchen set up in the corner. Do you fancy a cup of tea?'

Hattie nodded, intrigued to know what this well-spoken young lady was doing in Barnham Street. Anne made tea at a kitchenette cupboard with a flap-down counter and offered her some home-made cake. Over tea she explained that two ground-floor flats were being rented by the Bermondsey Children's Council for the specific purpose of giving them over to the kids who lived in the buildings.

'So, they'll live here on their own?' Hattie said. 'I can think of one kid who'd just love that!'

The young woman had a pleasant, rich laugh. 'I dare say they all would! But no, my idea is that every day after school, they can come here and it'll be *their* place. To decorate, and furnish as they wish, to cook their own tea in the kitchen and make things for the flat – just as they please – obviously with a bit of supervision from me and my trusty helpers, when I get a few. You're friends with some of the kids here, you say?'

Hattie sighed. 'I suppose I am, one in particular. But it's been a sad time...'

'I heard about the little boy who died in the building collapse.'

'My friend's son, Ronnie, he was one of the boys involved. He was lucky to come home safe and sound, but we didn't know if he was alive or dead for days. At first we thought half the kids in the buildings were under the rubble – couldn't track them down!'

Anne nodded. 'Oh, I know, these kids are like a wandering tribe. They go out and roam the bombsites, mum and dad at work all day – and school? Forget it.'

'Well, most of them didn't get into the habit of school. It's the war, I suppose. It's not fair their lives got ruined as well as everything else.' Hattie felt heat rising to her face, as she voiced emotions she didn't know she felt.

'That's exactly why I'm doing this!' Anne exclaimed. 'These kids are roaming far and wide every night, just because there's *nowhere* for them to go. The flats are tiny – two rooms for families of ten? Of course the kids prefer to stay out. But if they'd been here, in one of these flats where the parents could pop down and check on them, that tragedy might not have happened.'

'But what about youth clubs?' She was thinking of Ronnie, and the approaching battle to make sure he went to one.

'Once or twice a week's not enough. They need something to occupy them every day, otherwise it's the gangs who win them. Besides, I've worked with these kids before. They don't fit into normal youth clubs. Can you imagine your little friend Ronnie – was that his name? – going off happily to play ping-pong and then hang around for prayers at the end of the evening?'

Hattie laughed. 'He's already told me he won't! It's hard enough to get him to sleep in his own bed every night. Mind you, it is a camp bed in the kitchen. But with Ronnie,' Hattie hesitated, 'there was someone else involved, someone who was meant to be protecting him but was doing the opposite.'

'I heard about that too. We've failed them all, haven't we?

They're the ones we wanted a better tomorrow for...' The young woman's sad expression brightened. 'Would you happen to have a few hours free each week to make sure they get it?'

*

Over Christmas and into the New Year, Hattie found herself giving every spare minute to helping Anne get the children's flats ready. She did everything from painting walls, to collecting art materials, to going round local businesses begging for donations. The council funding was small, just enough to cover a warden's salary and the rent on the flats. Everything else had to be fundraised. The squat had given Hattie plenty of practice in sprucing up the least promising of dwellings. She'd co-opted Buster to source some material so the kids could make their own curtains. Anne's one stipulation had been that they should do as much for themselves as they possibly could. The children's own homes were cramped and unsanitary; there was usually little enough money or hours in the day for their parents to lavish on them. Anne didn't judge. She just provided an alternative to the bombsites, one Hattie found she increasingly approved of.

Ronnie, however, did not. She'd persuaded him that going to the children's flats for the evening would be nothing like attending the youth club, and what's more, he'd still be complying with the court's sentence. But the opening night at the children's flats didn't go according to plan. Ronnie and a rowdy gang of kids tumbled in after school and made a beeline for all the neatly arranged craft materials. Ronnie was the first to see their potential as missiles, and before long pencils and crayons, milk-bottle tops and cardboard boxes were being propelled across the tiny room. A battle began with boys pitted against girls, the boys creating a barricade of whatever furniture they'd been able to amass and the girls deciding sound was their best weapon, screaming at increasingly high pitches. Halfway through the evening Hattie's sergeant-self took over. Overriding Anne's softer approach, she barked at the kids that there would be no tea and buns for anyone who didn't help clear up. The effect was instantaneous, and before chucking-out time order had been restored.

Afterwards she and Anne sat with feet up and cups of tea, pondering the mayhem of their first session.

'I think it was a great success,' Anne said. 'Don't you?'

Hattie didn't, but she wanted to match the woman's optimism. 'Hmm. At least I could keep track of Ronnie all night.'

'Exactly,' Anne said. 'Did I tell you Norman's dad offered to do weights with the boys? But I think we're going to need more help.'

Hattie nodded. 'A *lot* more help! Just as well I'm good at drumming up volunteers.'

# 19

## The Ashes

That winter was as mild as the last had been harsh. For Hattie and Joe, their own corner of Southwark Park became a secret, almost rural, mid-winter haven amidst Bermondsey's thirteen hundred acres of crowded streets and factories. They found secluded benches in the rose garden, which, deep in its bare-stemmed sleep, was largely unvisited. There, on those mild winter evenings and afternoons, she began to discover the man she'd so unexpectedly fallen in love with. There were things she already knew: his experiences during the war; his solitary nature. But one day, after they'd begun talking about the future, he made a surprising revelation. He'd been engaged during the war. His fiancée had stayed faithful to him through all the long years of his incarceration, but after he came home it became obvious to them both that whatever spark had held them before the war was no longer there. He said he wasn't bitter, that the thought of her had kept him going through the worst times at the camp, so in a way she'd saved his life and he'd always be grateful. In the end, he said, the failure of their love had been just like any other war wound. But from the tremor in his normally controlled, even, voice, she sensed it had been more like a bereavement. She was glad he'd told her, and she was about to commiserate when he followed up with something that made her heart lurch.

'While we're getting things out in the open, there's something else I need to tell you. The thing is, Hattie, the war made me see that you can't rely on another person to make you happy. Sometimes you have to do what's best for you.'

She felt her heart racing. Was he about to dump her?

'I don't want to work in the Alaska forever. In fact, for a long time I've been thinking of emigrating.'

'Emigrating? Where?' She pushed herself up from the bench and out of his arms. He wasn't looking at her. Instead, he leaned back against the bench and, with his legs stretched out and his hands behind his head, he stared up into clear blue skies above the rose garden.

'Australia. Me and Alan made a plan, not long after we met, that we'd go together.'

She sat back, keeping her eyes on the bare roses, trying to control her racing heart. So, he was trying to tell her their relationship would be a short-term one. The revelation had come like a swift, sharp blow that had knocked all the air out of her lungs. Once, she would have been relieved to find someone as unattached as herself. But her feelings for Joe were different than for any other man she'd ever known: neither the insanely irrational passion she'd felt for Lenny, nor the casual affection she'd felt for Alan and all the others before him, but something as slow and sure as Joe himself, which had been growing since he'd first told her she really wasn't his ideal neighbour. She looked down at his handsome face, the dark brown eyes turned to look at her. He blinked against the glinting sun and she reached up a hand to trace the perfectly arched eyebrows.

'You've gone quiet,' he said.

'Seems I have. Has Alan told Clara?'

He took hold of her hand. 'I haven't asked him.'

'Well, she'd never go back to Australia!' she declared. It felt like both she and her friend had been somehow hoodwinked.

'But would you?' he asked simply. 'Would you go to Australia? With me?'

Wind rustled the hedges that enclosed them and she didn't answer immediately. Why wasn't it easy to give him the 'yes' he was waiting for? She mentally pounded her forehead. If the question had come when she'd arrived in Bermondsey, without a home or work, wishing she were anywhere else in the world, she would have been hustling him on board the next ship out. Instead she swept her hand in a wide arc at the rose garden and the park, with their little cluster of huts in the distance, and she played for time. 'Go to Australia and leave all this?' She laughed. Then she saw a look of acute disappointment cross his face. Whatever stupid reasons she had for doubt were swept away in an instant. 'I'm joking! Of course I'll go to Australia with you!'

He leaped up to catch her in his arms, but before he could kiss her she put two fingers on his lips. 'On one condition. I go to Australia with you, so you have to come somewhere with me.'

'Yes, yes, anywhere,' he said, claiming his kisses.

But when she explained what she wanted of him, she discovered that the contrary side of his nature hadn't retreated entirely.

Joe was adamant. 'No! I'd be no good in a youth club. You saw what Ronnie thought of me!'

'It's not really a club. It's just a safe place for them to be. No rules to speak of, just a home from home really...' She hadn't told him about the wrecking spree of that first night. 'But keeping the kids interested, that's the key, Anne says. And what better than photography? You've got at least three old box Brownies you never use, and you could set up a little darkroom in the office!' The second room of one of the children's flats had been turned into a working space for Anne and a quiet room for the kids. 'It would mean we'd see more of each other...'

Joe's face lit up. 'Now you're talking,' he said, pulling her into his arms. 'All right, I'll give it a go – but if they kick up a fuss about me being there I'm not pushing it.'

'They'll love you.'

'Just like you do?'

'A bit less than I do...' And she laughed into his kisses. She was learning that awkward Joe could be the most amenable of men under the right circumstances, which were usually when he had her in his arms.

*

When Joe saw Barnham Street Buildings he was as shocked as anyone who hadn't been born there. As they passed through the railings into the black-walled, high-sided courtyard, they were met by the usual concoction of aromas that collected there: the sickening malty smell from Sarson's vinegar factory, effluent from blocked toilets and rotting rubbish from the chutes. He raised his voice against the screech and thunder of commuter trains coming in and out of London Bridge Station. 'Why don't they just pull the bloody things down?'

'They were going to, before the war – the first war that is!'

He raised his eyes and gripped her hand. She found it endearing that he was actually nervous. He carried an army rucksack on his back with the necessary chemicals and cameras. Anne had already provided everything else he needed to set up a makeshift darkroom in a corner of her office, but Hattie had warned him the chemicals might well be put to nefarious use if he left them in the flat overnight. There hadn't yet been thefts or break-ins by their own kids, but a raid from another gang was still a possibility.

Ronnie was already there and looked from Hattie to Joe, then seemed to make a decision. He left the fort of cardboard boxes he was constructing and strolled over to them. He shook Joe's hand and said, 'Thanks, mate, for dobbing the geezer in,' then returned to his fort. That evening Joe showed the kids how to use the cameras, and they went outside to take photos of each other before the light failed. Nutty Norman's preferred pose was to balance a football on his head while standing beneath the sign that read *No hawking, bill posting, cycling, fireworks or ball games*. Ronnie surprised her by wanting to join in the photography class. He ran upstairs with a box Brownie, dragged Lou on to the balcony and took a photo of her in slippers and pinafore. Hattie looked up and saw her patting down her thin pale

282

hair and covering her smile behind her hand; Lou's teeth hadn't survived the war well and she was always conscious of them. The kids were noisily disappointed when they couldn't see the results of their efforts instantaneously. But at least that meant they'd have good reason to return and help Joe develop the pictures.

Hattie knew she was good at persuading people to do what she wanted, but she surprised even herself when she'd soon added another handful of helpers to their ranks. Buster agreed to come and give dancing lessons to the girls – along with any boys brave enough to join them. Levin the nailer volunteered to give carpentry lessons, on condition that they relax the rule that only children from the buildings could join the flats. 'I'll only come if I can bring three of my little bleeders with me,' he declared. Her own contribution, apart from being the general sergeant major keeping order, was to give the girls ju-jitsu lessons, a skill she'd learned in the army. The classes were to take place in the largest room of the second flat, for which Anne had found some well-worn gym mats from a local school. She tried to hide her shock when Ribbons the twins turned up. Considering they'd helped see her off so fiercely on her first night home, she thought they might end up teaching her a few throws.

\* \* \*

As spring approached, the numbers of kids using the flats rose steadily from twelve to thirty and sometimes more. Eventually they were having two sessions a night, one in the early afternoon for younger kids and a later one for the older. Word got round the Alaska that the Barnham Street gang had stopped their 'raids' on other gangs' territories and that fewer of them were turning up at the magistrates' court for vandalism or petty theft. Several mothers at the Alaska asked if they could have a children's flat where they lived.

But when she put the idea to Anne, the woman's face fell. 'I'd like to have children's flats in every Bermondsey estate, but we can barely raise funding for ours. The council grant could be pulled at any time. I can't see them forking out for more. They don't see it as a priority.'

Hattie could understand why not. Every bit of money and energy was being poured into building new homes to replace those destroyed in the war – it seemed their children were again paying the price.

Hattie had at first just been glad to keep Ronnie out of trouble, in school and in favour with the courts, but she found herself looking forward to her stints at the children's flats. Part of the attraction was that Joe was often there, but she found the kids responded to her no-nonsense manner. They seemed to like it when she barked at them or had them quick-marching round the tiny rooms for misdemeanours, such as smashing cups or trashing the art cupboard. But when they started asking, 'Can we have drill, miss?', she knew she'd have to think up another punishment as they obviously enjoyed that one so much.

Though rationing was more severe than ever and goods were short, at least they hadn't frozen in an Arctic winter or been cut off by floods, as they had last spring. And though their clothes had seen them well beyond the war, they could just about be patched again. Hattie began to relax into the peace that had so far seemed to elude her. She'd said nothing to Clara about going to Australia, respecting Joe's judgement that it was best left to Alan. But she suspected when her friend found out it would end Clara's budding romance. This was the only cloud on her horizon. Today, as she and Joe walked home together from the flats, she broached the subject.

'Can't you persuade Alan to tell Clara about Australia?'

'It's none of my business. I can't tell him what to do with his life.'

'But Clara's my friend and I've always felt sort of responsible for her.'

'The only person you can be responsible for is yourself, Hattie. If she loves Alan, she'll go with him.'

'Aargh! For a clever man you are so dense sometimes, Joe! It's not whether she loves Alan or not that's the problem, it's what the last man she loved did to her, and that happened in *Australia*... see?'

He frowned. 'It's not the country's fault.'

'I give up! If Alan doesn't tell her soon, I will. Besides, I can't say anything to her about us going till she knows, can I?'

In fact, it had become increasingly difficult not to share her own future plans with Clara. She'd become the younger sister Hattie never had and, whatever Joe said about responsibility, she would protect her. If that meant spilling the beans about Alan's plans, she would.

*

When the cricket season started, Joe and Alan marshalled the Alaska cricket team and organized a match against the Camberwell Bus Garage's team, who'd offered the use of a London double-decker bus to get the two teams, wives, girlfriends and children to a ground in the heart of the Kent countryside. Lou and Ronnie came too, and Hattie had asked to take a dozen of the Barnham Street kids with them. It would be a rare treat, for many of them had never seen the countryside. The April day was bright and clear, and they sang on the bus all the way to the ground. When they arrived, they staked out their spots, and began spreading blankets round the edge of the cricket pitch, getting out picnics and drinks for the children. Ronnie, Norman, Ribbons and Jack – the small terrier of a boy who'd once snapped round her ankles – ran up and down the field, drunk with the open skies and pure air. Ronnie trotted like a horse with Martha on his shoulders as Lou looked on proudly. Alan and Joe distinguished themselves on the field, with Joe hitting several powerful balls for six and Alan's long strides clocking up the runs. She acknowledged the possibility that she was biased, but she thought Joe was certainly the most handsome of the team, in his white flannels, with his dark complexion and hair and his strong physique, but she saw

Clara's eyes fixed on Alan, and knew her friend was suffering from a similar bias. She couldn't see her looking on so adoringly, when all the while she was being kept in the dark.

'Clara? I've been meaning to tell you something – it's about me and Joe.'

Clara turned bright eyes on her. 'What? You're getting married!'

'Well, not yet. I'm sorry I haven't said anything before, but…' She found herself tripping up over the words.

'What?' Clara repeated. 'It's not bad, is it?'

'Me and Joe, well, we're going to Australia.'

Clara gave a hesitant smile. 'You're joking.'

When Hattie shook her head, she was alarmed to see tears brimming in Clara's eyes.

'Don't go!' her friend blurted out and threw her arms round Hattie, clinging to her as if she were a spar on a sinking ship. How could she not tell her the rest?

'Don't get so upset, love. It won't be for a while. We haven't got the money for the passage yet.'

Clara wiped her eyes. 'But what will I do without you?'

Hattie wanted to say, *you'll have Alan*, but she really didn't know if that would be the case. 'I've got to tell you something else, love. Joe says I should wait for Alan to say something, but him and Joe, well, they'd been planning on going together…'

'Going where?'

'To Australia. Hasn't Alan said anything about it?'

Clara shook her head. 'Not a word.'

Hattie squeezed Clara's hand, reliving her own emotions when Joe first told her he'd be going to Australia. 'Perhaps he's changed his mind,' she said softly.

When they broke for tea the shadows were growing longer, and the white wooden score board showed in favour of the Alaska. As the two men strode off the field, shedding gloves and caps, they expected praise for winning the match. Instead, they were greeted by Hattie and Clara's frosty glares.

'What have we done?' they asked.

And both women answered. 'Australia!'

The men clearly didn't know whether this was a good thing or a bad thing until Hattie grabbed Joe's arm and glared at Alan. 'I can't believe you never told her! Come on, Joe. Let's take Martha – these two need to talk.'

She picked up the child, who was tired and tottery after her day in the fresh air, and Martha nestled into her arms as she and Joe walked to the pavilion. Hattie looked back once. The field of bright green was dimmed now by approaching twilight, and Alan and Clara stood like two unmoving dark statues, he with his arms encircling her and she with her head on his chest.

'You shouldn't have said anything!' Joe said, keeping his voice calm because of the baby.

'Don't blame me. She needed to know!'

'It wasn't your place, Hattie.'

'Maybe not. But he couldn't do it, so I did it for him.'

They didn't see Clara and Alan again until they were seated in the pavilion with cucumber sandwiches and fatless cake before them. Clara's eyes were puffy with tears and Alan's face was drawn when they joined the table, and there was an awkward silence as Hattie poured them tea. But eventually Alan broke the silence. 'I was *planning* to tell her!' And Clara reached over for Hattie's hand. 'We're going too,' she said, breaking into a smile.

'Bloody hell, you are?' Hattie jumped up and clasped Clara tightly. 'Thank God, now we won't have to say goodbye!' Letting her friend go, she shot an accusing look at Alan. 'How did you persuade her? And I'm not complaining, Clara, love, but why have you forgiven him?'

'He said if I didn't want to go, he wouldn't either...'

'Oh, I'm in the dog house, don't worry, but she's not doing it for me!' Alan said with a shame-faced expression. 'I had to appeal to her maternal instinct, didn't I, Clara?'

He puffed out his cheeks, then blew a raspberry for Martha's entertainment, followed by several more till she was satiated. Clara put a hand on her daughter's dark curls. 'It just seems right somehow. I've always known she was a sun child. She's fine now it's getting warmer, but what with the diphtheria and then all the cold's she's had, I don't think she'll ever thrive here, Hattie. She deserves the sun...'

'And blue skies,' Alan said.

'Hattie didn't need any persuading,' Joe said, reaching for her hand. 'Even if she didn't love me, she hates Bermondsey so much, she'd have said yes!'

'But she does love you.' Clara said it for her. 'Don't you, Hattie?'

And for answer, Hattie gave Joe a loud kiss, which drew a long groan from Ronnie, who mimed being sick. He had been unusually quiet as they sat round the table, listening intently to their conversation.

'You and Clara won't be saying goodbye, but you'll have to say goodbye to me, won't you, Hattie?' Ronnie asked, his face suddenly serious and his eyes unblinking.

'Oh, you'll be glad to get rid of me! You always tell me I'm a worse nagger than your mum.'

'He's a cheeky little git,' Lou said, but her look was indulgent. Whenever she remembered she had a son, she started to spoil him. 'Here,' she said, fishing a threepenny bit from her purse, 'go and get yourself a packet of crisps.'

When he'd gone, she said in a low voice, 'He thinks the world of you, Hattie. He'll be heartbroken when you go.'

'Oh, it won't be for a while.' Hattie smiled. 'He'll have to come out and visit us!' But she knew it was a ridiculous thing to say, for Ronnie would be a grown man before she and Joe could ever afford to send him the fare.

After drinks and dancing to Perry Como and Frank Sinatra seventy-eights on the wind-up gramophone, the teams bundled back on to the red double-decker bus. One by one, the children dropped off to sleep as they left the countryside behind and reached the Old Kent Road. During the journey, Hattie stole looks at the sleeping Ronnie. Joe had warned her she should be responsible only for herself, but it seemed she always found herself in charge of someone. It wasn't always a position she used to her credit; she could manipulate to get where she wanted, but the flip side was that she'd never turn away from someone who needed her. As a child, she'd looked after Cissie, and later her ATS girls, then Clara and the others in the squat, and now she had Ronnie. It was hard to imagine him staying on the straight and narrow with only Lou's frail hand to steer him.

The bus dropped off the Alaska team in stages, and Hattie and her friends got off in Southwark Park Road. As they walked to the park, they saw an unusually bright red glow lighting up the sky over the park.

'Reminds me of the war,' Clara said with a visible shudder.

And then they heard the clanging of bells. The friends exchanged looks of alarm as a red fire engine sped past them.

Hattie felt a cold wind, raising the hairs on her arms. On the wind came soft white flakes, settling on her cheeks like the insistent snows of last winter. Instinctively she knew. 'It's the huts!' she said, and Joe sprang forward, sprinting across the park, closely followed by Hattie. Alan was hampered by having Martha in his arms, but Clara grabbed the baby. 'I'll catch up – you go!' she ordered, and the fear in her voice woke Martha, who began to wail.

As Hattie ran across the grass of the Oval she could see flames shooting into the sky from the area of the camp where the NAAFI was situated.

She was keeping pace with Joe now and as they ran she shouted breathlessly, 'Which hut is it? Is it the NAAFI?' She was scanning the camp, praying that none of the inhabited huts had caught fire.'

'Think so, can't tell for sure!' Joe called back, pulling ahead.

As they sped into the colony, she saw many squatters had already formed a chain. They were passing buckets of water from the ablutions block, then throwing the contents on to the roaring pyre which had once been Vera and Brian's hut. She could see it was hopeless, like spitting on a flat iron to cool it down. But she, Joe and Alan joined the chain anyway, swinging bucket after bucket till Hattie felt her arms must drop off. The firemen ran a hose from the fire engine parked in Hawkstone Road and took over from their ineffectual efforts, until all that was left of the hut was a steaming mass of charred timber and sodden ashes.

Only now did she look around for Vera and Brian. She pushed through the crowd of exhausted, ashen-faced squatters, looking for them at the forefront of the crowd where she would have expected them to be. A dread overtook her, and she grabbed Maisie, who stood with her arms round her youngest brother. 'Vera and Brian? Maise, where are they? Did they get out?'

But the girl shook her head. 'I don't know, Hattie. Please God they have, but I don't know. I've just been running for buckets!'

'Vera!' she called, and the crowd parted. Vera stood at the back of the crowd, dressed in her nightdress and slippers, arms tightly wrapped around herself in an effort to stop the trembling that wracked her entire body. Brian, in striped pyjamas, stood next to her, his bullish frame stooped and exhausted.

Hattie ran to her. 'Oh, thank God you're safe! I'm so sorry, love,' Hattie said, taking Vera into her arms. 'But you're not on your own. Whatever it takes, we'll fix you up another hut.'

'It's all the home I had, Hattie. All what come through the war. I ain't got the energy to start again.'

Vera collapsed on to the grass, sobbing, and Hattie kneeled beside her, taking the woman's ash- and tear-stained face in her hands. 'You listen to me, Vera. We all came here with nothing and we built it up together. The rest of us have got enough energy to do it for you. So don't you worry.'

'Suppose we've got to be grateful.' Vera sniffed, lifting her head. 'We're alive, and at least it wasn't one of the other huts with kids in. They could have been dead in their beds. The bastard that done this needs to swing for it...'

When it was certain there was nothing more anyone could do, the squatters drifted back to their huts. For Hattie, the heady mood of the day was all but forgotten as she convened a meeting of the squatters' committee in the NAAFI. An exhausted Vera and Brian insisted on being there.

'First off, Vera's certain it was arson,' Hattie said. 'So, what makes you think it wasn't just an accident? Did you have the stove on?'

'No, no, no – me and Vera's been very careful!' Brian said defensively. 'That lid goes on the stove and the door's closed. We didn't have no candles and the paraffin lamps wasn't lit.'

'I don't like to say it, as I'm the sparks, but what about the electrics?' Alan asked. 'I should have a dekko at the wiring to the hut, see if anything's blown.'

'It wasn't no accident,' Vera said wearily. ''Cause I see who done it, didn't I?'

Every eye was upon her. Hattie found she was clenching her jaw so tightly it hurt.

'It was that Dickie Harper, and he didn't mind me seeing him neither.'

Hattie had been dreading the day when the Harpers would make their move. Now, when she heard the name, it came as an odd relief, the sort of relief she'd once felt when the bombers finally appeared in the sky above a gun emplacement. For her, it was always better to engage in a battle than to anticipate it. She let out a long breath. 'What did you see?' she asked.

'Me and Brian was just going to bed when I thought I heard a noise outside the hut. I looked out the window, in case it was kids. I know we've had less trouble with them Barnham Street boys, Hattie, but there's others around that's just as much nuisance. I see someone moving about and I was just telling my Brian to get his arse out of bed when I see the feller strike a match.' She sobbed, and put a hand to her mouth. They waited till she was able to speak again. 'He looks me right in the eye and grins, like it's a bloody game, and then he sets light to a rag in a bottle and chucks it straight at me.'

'Molotov cocktail,' Joe said. 'We used them against the Japs when we ran low on ammo.'

'If my Vera hadn't looked out of the window, we'd have been crispy bacon by now,' Brian said.

'What do you want to do?' Hattie asked everyone, and several jumped in with suggestions. 'One at a time! You first, Brian and Vera.'

'Go to the coppers. Vera's a witness!' Brian said.

Everyone agreed, but Hattie knew it wouldn't be enough. 'We can report it, no harm in that. But the Harpers have been getting away with worse than this for years. They're not scared of the police. We need to be responsible for ourselves, for our own safety and our own lives. We can't rely on anyone else to help us.' She glanced at Joe, who nodded encouragingly and gave a discreet thumbs-up sign.

That night, Alan gave up his hut for Vera and Brian, saying he would bunk with Joe, but before the four friends parted they sat in Hattie's hut together, voicing their shock.

'What were the night patrol doing off?' Hattie asked Joe.

'I don't know. I haven't asked them yet, but I will – first thing tomorrow,' he said wearily.

'Well, you *should* know, you're their captain! They got sloppy, that's what – probably in the NAAFI drinking bloody tea all night!' Hattie wanted someone to blame, but in her heart she blamed only herself. It was her fault that the squat had attracted Lenny's interest in the first place.

'It's not the war any more, Hattie,' Joe said mildly. 'We can't court martial them for dereliction – it's voluntary!'

'Well, they should have been more vigilant. Someone could have died!' she said, hearing the tremble in her own voice.

'It's not your fault either. Harper would have targeted us whether you lived here or not.'

'Who said I thought it was my fault?' she snapped, blushing to think she'd been so transparent.

Alan shifted awkwardly in his seat. 'Come on, Joe, mate, let's leave these lovely girls to get some sleep. We can go over it all night, but none of us knows what Harper plans to do next.'

Hattie was now regretting her sharpness with Joe, but it wasn't in her nature to apologize in public. 'I know what he'll do,' she said, and instantly wished she hadn't claimed any special knowledge where Lenny Harper was concerned.

She and Joe exchanged only the briefest of goodnights, and when Hattie was in bed she could still smell woodsmoke in her hair. She let herself run through the litany of things Lenny would do. It was like a rosary – she knew it so well. His modus was to begin patiently. He would wait for the right time, but she suspected these past months when they'd all been anxious about another attack had been the waiting time, and now it was the slow escalation of pressure. Lenny knew how to terrorize people and it wasn't by using a sledgehammer. He'd no doubt given his brother Dickie strict instructions to be seen and had targeted an inhabited hut purposefully. Now it was the squatters who were backfooted and waiting for his next move. The only time she'd bested Lenny was when she pre-empted him. Many times, when she'd left it too late, she'd paid the price, as with her broken collarbone. She decided she must go to him first, just as she had when Ronnie took Martha. She hadn't been intimidated then, and she wouldn't be now.

The camp was alive with activity early the following morning. Although it was a work day, Brian and Vera went to report the attack at Paradise Street Police Station, while Hattie and Joe did the rounds of the camp, knocking on doors to see if someone could add anything to what they already knew about the arson attack. Their numbers had risen to over twenty families, each one carefully vetted by the committee, but there were at least another fifteen empty huts.

After knocking on all the doors and finding out very little more, she asked Joe, 'Shall we see which hut would be best for Vera and Brian to move into while we're at it?'

'All right.' Joe had been a little tight-lipped with her. 'But I need to get a move on. I'm meant to have come up with a new silver dye formula by this week, but I've been a bit distracted...' He wasn't looking at her, but she took his remark as a criticism.

'Oh, so sorry to have taken you away from your work!'

'Hattie! I didn't mean that!' he said, taking her hand and turning her to face him. 'If there's something the matter, you can't just feel it then snap at me and expect me to know what's going on! You need to tell me.'

'You seemed to know it all last night when you accused me of being to blame for this. I'll never live bloody Lenny Harper down...' she said miserably.

'I didn't say that at all. It's only you carrying him around like a piece of useless luggage. No one else thinks you're the reason he's coming after us.'

'But do you?'

'No,' he said firmly. 'But just promise me you'll keep out of his way and leave this for me and the other blokes to deal with?'

Just then they came to the unoccupied huts, which ran parallel to the occupied ones. They had their own duckboards connecting to the NAAFI and ablutions.

'What about this one?' she asked, as they came to the first hut in the row. They'd taken the precaution of padlocking them all after Lenny's first foray, and now Joe gave her the master key. She struggled with the padlock.

'Typical, someone's forgotten to lock it!' she said, and gave the door a push. The door had warped in the frame and required a further shove, but as it swung open Hattie gave a cry of alarm and stepped back. It seemed the hut already had a new resident.

# 20

## *Hobo*

### *April–May 1948*

The bundle of ragged blankets came alive, squirming like a soggy, smelly dog, caught in some mischief. At Hattie's scream, Joe leaped in front of her, and now she wished she'd shown more composure.

'Come out of there!' Joe called, and at his command a man's head emerged from the grey, army-issue blanket. His hair was an unruly mat of black, tightly coiled ringlets, and the walnut-coloured face was almost entirely hidden in a springy black beard of a few weeks' growth. He sat up, blinking.

'Not disturbing you, are we?' Hattie stood in front of him. The smell was not so ripe as Pissy Pants', but it did suggest a man who'd worn the same clothing for weeks.

'Sorry, mate,' Joe said, 'but you can't kip here. These huts are for squatting families – you have to be approved by our committee.'

The man stood up slowly. He was shorter than Hattie, but well-built, and he held his palms face out, spreading his arms wide. 'I'm not a vagrant. I only got in late last night, and saw you'd had a bit of trouble, so I thought I'd leave my business till today.'

'What business is that?' Hattie asked, noticing the man's accent.

'I'm looking for my wife.'

Back at their hut Hattie was glad to see that Clara was holding Martha in her arms. She knew Clara wouldn't allow herself to faint or scream or do anything to alarm her child. And when

Hattie told her who they'd found in the empty hut, Clara simply held her baby tighter and widened her eyes.

'No! I don't want to see him,' she said in a quiet, urgent tone. But the baby buried her face into Clara's chest, sensing the fear in her mother's voice in spite of Clara's attempt to control it.

'You don't have to, Clara. Barry just asked if we'd pass on the message. So, I've told you and now we'll forget about it,' Hattie said.

'He's already messed up my life once and he's not doing it again!' Clara put Martha into Hattie's arms. 'Hold her while I make a bottle.' She opened the tin of formula and began spooning it into the bottle, spilling half the contents on to the table.

'Damn it, now I've lost count.' She slammed down the bottle and began again. 'Why now? That man! I'm sure he's got a bloody radar that points to when Clara's happy, just so he knows when to step in and ruin it. Well, not this time...' She began spooning and again lost count. 'Come and do this, Hattie, for gawd's sake.'

'I said, you don't have to see him.'

Hattie sat Martha on the rag rug and gave her a wooden pull-along horse to play with, while she went to finish the bottle.

Clara let out a long groan and slumped on to a kitchen chair. 'What am I going to tell Alan?'

'It's not as if you've kept any secrets from Al, and if Barry takes it into his head to come halfway round the world to see you, it's not your fault.'

'What did he say again?'

'He said, "I've come to see my wife." Well, there's not many women here who've been married to Aborigine servicemen, so we knew who he was. But I'd have known even if he hadn't opened his mouth.' Hattie looked down at Martha.

'She's got his eyes, hasn't she?'

'And his smile.'

'Oh, that bloody smile! Smile of a charmer.'

Clara was twisting and twisting a coil of her dark brown hair, and Hattie reached over, gently forcing her to release it.

'Don't get yourself into a two and eight. See him or not, no one's judging, and I'll tell you the advice Joe's always giving me – you're not responsible for him, Clara. You do what's best for you and for Martha, and if you decide you want to see him, I'll come with you when you meet him.'

'Would you?'

Hattie put down the bottle and sat next to Clara, putting an arm round her shoulders. 'Of course I will. Joe's told him he can stay another night – just to give you time to think. But after that he's got to move on. Unless of course you decided something else...' For Hattie had seen the look on her friend's face when she'd told her that Barry was here, and for a brief moment it was as if the sun was reflected in her eyes. True, the light died a second later, but it had definitely been there.

Clara gave her a puzzled look. 'What? You think I'd ever take him back? Never!'

'Well, love, just think it over, decide what you want to do today, and then we can tell Barry tonight. Joe felt a bit sorry for him actually – took him a bowl and shaving gear, so he could have a wash and brush-up. If he's come all this way, he'll wait another day, won't he?'

'Did he look rough then, Barry?'

'He's not come here on a luxury cruise liner, let's put it that way. He was carrying his old army kitbag and his clothes could do with a wash...'

'Really? He was always so neat and tidy,' Clara said, and then shook her head as if to rid herself of the memory of what Barry was, or used to be. 'But he didn't look ill?'

'Not ill, no. Just... like he'd had a long journey.'

'Oh yes?' Clara said, with a hint of bitterness in her voice. 'Well, I had a long journey too.'

Clara always left early in the morning, in order to get Martha to the nursery before work. So Hattie took the chance to pop in to see Joe before she set off for the Alaska herself. She'd not wanted to put undue pressure on Clara to meet her bigamist husband, so had given her only the minimum information about his appearance. But in fact, Barry had a hacking cough and it turned out was half-starved. He had wolfed down a whole loaf of toast and dripping while they'd decided how to break the news to Clara.

When she went into Joe's hut, Barry was drinking a mug of tea and eating a sausage sandwich. *Poor Joe's weekly bread ration must be all gone by now*, she thought,

'Well, you look better.' Hattie addressed Barry, whose handsome face was revealed now the bushy beard had disappeared, along with the layer of dirt. He'd managed to clip some of the shaggy hair and she could see how, with his strong jaw, wide smile and sparkling eyes, he would have bowled Clara over. His walnut-coloured skin was a shade darker than Martha's golden brown, and she supposed her friend could have taken it for suntan, but Clara must have been such an inexperienced innocent for it never to have occurred to her he was a coloured man. Still, Hattie knew of people who'd never ventured out of Bermondsey all their lives. It was as insular as a country village in some respects.

'He was still hungry,' Joe said.

'I couldn't get served in many cafés, coming up from Southampton. Told me to eff off back to India!' Barry explained, with a good-natured smile. 'It was a different story back when I was in uniform. Anyway, I went into a Salvation Army hostel and got a meal there, but other than that I've been on short rations. What did Clara say?' he asked, with a look in his eyes which spoke of a different kind of hunger.

'She's not made up her mind if she wants to see you, Barry. She'll let you know tonight.'

He pushed aside his plate and wiped his mouth with the back of his hand. 'I only want five minutes, just five minutes. There's not a day gone by when I've not regretted—'

But Hattie cut him short; she wasn't interested in his excuses.

'I daresay, but perhaps you should save that for Clara. I need to get to work.'

Joe came outside with her. 'Bit harsh?' he said.

'Harsh? The man's a bigamist. He bloody ought to regret what he did! And what about Alan, how did he take it?'

'Poor bloke, how do you think? His life's just fallen apart. He thinks the world of Clara and now he's scared he might lose her.'

'Is that what he said?'

'Didn't say a word. I just know.'

'Well, I'm just going to make sure Barry doesn't hurt her again,' she said, and felt Joe's hand cover hers, which had somehow balled into a fist.

'Hold on, Hattie, she's a grown woman. It's her choice...'

'I know, I know, but she's an innocent.'

'We're all innocents, it's only life teaches us any different,' said Joe, taking her in his arms.

'I was never innocent,' she said.

'No?'

She thought of the girl she'd been when Lenny had first charmed her, and lied. 'No!'

'All right, I believe you. So, about the Harpers... you stay out of their way.'

Joe, with his infuriating intuition, had made the connection whether she'd voiced her thoughts or not.

'OK,' she agreed quietly, though she had little faith in her ability to keep her promise.

Even though she had no real intention of staying out of Lenny Harper's way, she wasn't proved a liar. For that lunchtime, he was waiting for her outside the Alaska factory gates. He wore a draped, boxy-shouldered silver-grey jacket with a black shirt and a vivid tie. His blond hair was Brylcreemed into a shining quiff and his sculpted lips smirked when he spotted her. Clara had gone to see Martha in the nursery and Hattie had planned to have dinner with Buster in the canteen building. Now she turned abruptly into Grange Road and Lenny followed.

'We can't go to The Horns or the Red Cow. I don't want anyone from the Alaska seeing me with you,' she said, not looking at him. 'Let's go to The Grange.'

He stuffed his hands into his pockets and struggled to match her stride. She could feel his breath on her cheek and knew he was looking at her as they walked. He reached out a hand to touch her cheek and she slapped it away.

'Speck of soot!' he said, holding up his index finger with a look of mock innocence. 'Don't suppose you can get a good wash in that shithole, can you?'

She shoved open the doors of the pub and let them swing back in his face, so that he had to struggle to get through.

'No need to be nasty, Hattie. You know me, it's not personal, none of this.' He smiled, and she thought he might even believe it.

'All right, what do you want?'

'Hang on, let's be civilized. Whiskey mac, right?'

She nodded, and while he was at the bar she allowed herself a second to wonder what on earth she was going to say if he offered her a deal. Cissie had always taught her to approach relationships with men as if they were union negotiations. *Never go in without a plan, never let them know what you really want up front and always have a non-negotiable in your head.* The non-negotiable was the part that was worrying her. When she wanted something, she would go very far in order to get it. But now she had more to lose than she'd ever had: Joe, the squat, Ronnie and her work at the children's flats. What would be her sticking point? She didn't know.

'So, you was saying, Hattie?' He settled his draped jacket around him, so that it didn't crease. 'What do I want? I think you know!' He wagged a slender finger at her. 'I want in on the squat. Not all of it! I'm not a greedy bugger. I've held off 'cause I've had stuff going on that's kept me ticking over nicely. But times are hard and you got empty huts there, bringing down the tone of the neighbourhood.' He laughed and then, abruptly serious, he leaned forward. 'Give me the empty huts. I'll find your tenants for you and collect the rents, you get a cut and your lot carry on happy as Larry, no interference from me. I don't see the problem, Hattie, for the life of me, I don't.' He grinned.

'Maybe we don't want a vicious bastard who'd murder innocent people in their beds hanging around our kids, that's the problem!'

'*Your* kids? You ain't got no kids and last I heard you never wanted none, neither. What's got you all maternal? Is it your age, darlin'?'

He lifted his beer and sipped at it, and then patted his mouth with a spotted handkerchief, in the delicate way of his that she remembered.

'They're my responsibility.'

He leaned back and looked at her with narrowed eyes. 'Didn't do a very good job with that little git who posed for the photos, did you?'

She went cold. 'How do you know about that?'

'That was a good little earner, while it lasted. Little cowson cost me a ton a week when he scared off Wardick. So, you've got young Ron to thank that I'm looking for another business proposition now. Got to keep me profits up somehow!'

'You were in it with Wardick?'

'There's a demand! And that nonce Wardick was happy as Larry with the arrangement. He used to be my PO! That's how I knew about him in the first place, told him I'd slice off his John Thomas if he started on me. It was me come up with the idea of selling the photos. Bloody goldmine,' he said proudly.

'And you let him carry on, doing it to other boys just so you could make a few bob? You're sick, Lenny,' she said quietly, the whiskey turning sour in her mouth as she realized his racket with Wardick must have been going on while they were together.

Lenny had always been a 'bad boy', that's what she and her friends used to call him, with a hint of admiration, when they were growing up together. She'd discovered he was vicious too, yet this revelation was a new low that shocked even her.

'He never hurt the kids! And the photographs – well, it's no different from beach snaps, is it?'

'Never *hurt* them? Why do you think Ronnie thought he'd bury Wardick under a ton of rubble rather than face another session with him?'

'Mary Ann, same as his Uncle Buster.'

'Do you know where Wardick is?' she asked, ignoring the comment.

Lenny shook his head. 'If I find out I'll finish what that little git of yours started. I've still only got half the photos due to me. Wardick run off owing me photos I paid for.'

She felt a small rush of relief. At least Wardick seemed to have gone for good. But Lenny's revelation had just clarified her 'non-negotiabattle' – it was the kids. She wanted nothing to do with any deal or compromise if it meant having Lenny anywhere near them. She shoved the half-drunk whiskey away and got up.

'The answer's no. You're not having the empty huts and we don't want your filthy money either. I feel dirty just looking at you, Lenny, so stay out of my way in future.'

His face, which had worn a perpetual arrogant smirk, hardened and he lunged forward, grabbing her wrist.

'Don't make the mistake of thinking I've got any feeling left for you, you tart.' She pulled away, but he squeezed harder, crunching the bones in her hand. 'You'd better get those useless effers in your night patrol off their arses 'cause Dickie will be paying you another visit if I don't get what I want.'

Hattie found herself back outside the Alaska gates with no idea how she'd got there. She'd walked in a daze from the pub, feeling near to tears as she remembered her own carefree, thoughtless years when Lenny had seemed the most exciting thing in life. She'd been sleepwalking into her future, while all the time Lenny was sowing the seeds of Ronnie's nightmare. At first she'd blamed only Wardick, then today she'd blamed Lenny, and now she thought if only Cissie hadn't given her such a useless upbringing, she could have been different... But every accusation felt like an excuse: she was as much to blame as any of them. She'd turned a blind eye to Lenny's 'bad heart' back then, but she wouldn't now.

'Penny for 'em?' Buster said, as he and Lou joined her at the factory gates. 'Where were you, thought you was coming to the canteen?'

They turned into the yard, along with a stream of returning workers. The clatter of shoes on iron staircases and gantries drowned out her reply, and she had to shout. 'Lenny Harper wanted a chat. We went for a drink.'

'No wonder you look a bit tom and dick.'

'I'm all right. Just had a rough night of it. The Harpers burned down Vera's hut and now they want the rest of the empty huts.'

'We heard about the fire from Levin the nailer. So, Lenny's threatening to burn you all out now?'

Hattie nodded.

They punched their cards and she turned to Lou. 'Can you tell Anne that me and Joe can't make it to the children's flats tonight?'

Lou nodded, but grabbed her elbow. 'You be careful of that Lenny. Just let him have what he wants.'

'No!' she and Buster replied in unison, and Hattie wondered if poor Lou would be so eager to give in if she found out Lenny's part in her son's misery. Hattie lagged behind with Buster, watching Lou make her way up the iron staircase to the bambeating floor.

'So what you going to do about Lenny – have you got a plan?' Buster asked.

'Not really. But if the park still had ack-ack guns in it, then my plan would be to point them all at the Harpers' house.'

*

Hattie sat with Clara and Martha having their tea. She'd seen nothing of Clara all day and was pleased that her friend seemed calmer this evening. They ate tinned tomatoes and sardines with the last of their bread ration. The allotment had provided some apples, which Hattie stewed and served with a dollop of condensed milk. But it seemed a meagre enough tea. At least she'd found a supply of Picadillys in Lush the greengrocer's, opposite the factory. The shop had no fruit, but they had cigarettes under the counter, and so the queue was out of the door. She shared the cigarettes with Clara after the meal.

'So, what should we do with Barry, love? Send him packing? Joe says he's been making himself useful today, clearing up after the fire. He's waiting in Joe's hut now for his answer.'

'Is Alan there? Oh Jesus, whose bright idea was that?' Clara said, her calm veneer cracking.

'Haven't you spoken to Al about it at all?'

Clara shook her head. 'I never got the chance. We were so busy up on the bambeaters...'

'Rubbish, you bottled out,' Hattie said, knowing that Clara always found time to nip down to the electrician's shop to see Alan during the day.

'Well, I couldn't tell him anything because I hadn't made up my mind!' she said, blushing.

'And you have now?'

'He's come all this way. I'll hear him out.'

'Do you want me in there with you?'

Clara shook her head. 'No, I won't be in there long. Five minutes, that's all he wanted, wasn't it?'

Hattie took a long drag on her cigarette and said a silent prayer that the quick conversation would turn into nothing more, for Clara's sake – and for Alan's.

* * *

On the boat coming home, Clara had once regularly been rocked to sleep while imagining such a meeting with Barry, but sleep always claimed her before he had a chance to speak – perhaps because she wasn't capable of imagining anything he might have to say that could ever make it better. In her fantasy, she said plenty, pouring out all the words that hadn't come to her before she'd left, all the questions that should have been asked when she had the chance. But what she hadn't ever foreseen was that the meeting would actually take place. That he would come after her.

Alan was waiting for her outside Joe's hut. She was so ashamed of her cowardice in avoiding him that she could barely meet his eye.

'I know this changes everything,' he said. 'But Clara, the one thing that won't change is how I feel about you. I promise you that. You go in and see your husband and decide if you want to take him back. If you don't, I'll be here.'

'He was never my husband.' She put a hand to Alan's cheek. 'You're a good man, Al,' she said, and left him before she lost her courage.

Barry was sitting by the stove and stood up hesitantly when she came in. His physical presence was a shock. He looked so different from the man she'd fallen in love with. His eyes immediately filled with tears. 'Clara,' he said, but his greeting was cut off by a hacking cough, which gave her time to take in his changed appearance. He'd always kept his hair clipped short at the sides, even after demob, but it was now a matted mass of tight curls, while his skin had lost its glow and deep worry lines furrowed his forehead. The cough she recognized, knowing the English climate had never agreed with him. He and Martha had that in common.

'Sit down, Barry,' she said, and waited before sitting opposite him. The early evening sun slanted into the hut, glinting like liquid gold in his tear-filled eyes. He clasped and unclasped his hands, then dropped his head.

'You came a long way to talk to me, Barry. I'm giving you your five minutes. Ain't you got nothing to say?'

He nodded and sniffed back his tears, then looked up at her. 'I have. I came to say I'm sorry, Clara. Sorry I lied, sorry I hurt you, sorry I betrayed you. I'm so sorry.' Here the threatened tears began to spill down his face, and he covered his eyes with his hands. He took a deep breath and went on. 'I came to say that I always loved you and when you found out about me being married already... well, I was trying to figure a way to tell you, I promise I would have told you. I just waited too long. I made a big mistake and it cost me you and my daughter, and I'll pay for the rest of my life.'

Barry got on to his knees in front of her. The sun had moved in the sky now, and it blinded her. 'But the main thing is that I've divorced her and I've come here to ask you to marry me, again – properly this time. Will you give me another chance, Clara? Will you come back to Australia with me, as my wife?'

His hands reached for hers and Clara felt the powerful pull of his touch. It lit her skin like a fuse.

# 21

## *Burning of Leaves*

### *May–June 1948*

Police promises of a couple of bobbies patrolling the squat at night and an interview with Dickie Harper – who'd wriggled out of any involvement by paying half a dozen witnesses to prove he was elsewhere at Molotov cocktail hour – gave Hattie no confidence in the law's ability to protect the squat. When she reported back to the committee that she'd talked to Lenny, Joe's face flushed with anger.

'He approached me!' she countered, and when she explained what his demands were, it was no surprise that the committee backed her decision to turn him down.

'So, that leaves us with the problem of how to defend *ourselves*. He doesn't make empty threats. He could come tonight or tomorrow, but sooner or later he'll send Dickie back and we've got to be ready. Joe, any ideas?'

Joe took the floor. 'I think we turn the squat back into what it used to be – an army camp. Double the night patrol: everyone needs to be on the rota. Then we reinforce all the old army fencing round the camp, make an entrance – one way in, one way out – and put a guard on it. If anyone's going to be late home, you let someone know.'

There were protests. 'It'll be like living in a prison camp!' Maisie's dad said.

'No. Nothing like. I spent years as a Jap POW, so you can believe me – this is a holiday camp in comparison!' Joe said.

'Besides, it's only temporary, till we can find a more permanent solution. Hattie and I are working on that.' He nodded towards her and she wondered what on earth he was talking about. If he had a plan he hadn't yet shared it with her. Hattie could understand people's grumbles, she and Joe had somehow both become tethered to the war, albeit for different reasons, and neither had ever really lost their wartime mentality. But most people wanted to shed the war like a worn-out old coat. They wanted a normal life, bringing up kids in the better world they'd been promised. Living on a decommissioned army base was quite enough of a reminder as it was.

Afterwards, as Joe walked with her back to her hut, he said, 'Are you telling me the truth, or did you go and find Lenny?'

'He was waiting for me outside the Alaska.'

'But you didn't *have* to go off with him, did you?'

'It was a chance to find out what his plans are, and besides, I don't need you mollycoddling me!'

'Sorry, but I can't be blamed for wanting to keep you out of harm's way.'

She put an arm through his, forgiving him. She found it touching that he wanted to protect her, but it chafed too. 'Lenny chased me off once, Joe. I left Bermondsey like a frightened little girl. That's not me any more. Anyway, what was all that about us working on a plan?'

'I had to wing it a bit in there. I sensed a mutiny.'

'Well, I hope it wasn't all bluff. You have got another idea, haven't you?'

He put his arm round her waist and drew her close. 'I have got an idea, but it requires some privacy and it's got nothing to do with the Harpers!' he said, nuzzling into her neck. They drew away from the huts and strolled across the open expanse of grass, heading for the tree line and the ruined boating lake. The inky sky sat like a dome above the open expanse of the Oval. It was awash with hundreds of stars and a quiet settled over Hattie's heart as they walked. She began to imagine what it might mean, to have a future far away from here, to look up at a night sky and see an alien pattern of stars. Perhaps there she would be able to feel herself part of the peace.

'Sometimes I wish we could go now – to Australia. Just pack up and leave all this behind.'

He didn't answer her immediately. 'That sounds a bit like Harper chasing you off again.'

'No! I just want to be rid of it – the war, fighting, hurting, destroying everything that's any good in life… Look at how hard we've worked to make something here. And it could all be wiped out in one night by a bully boy like Lenny. It always comes down to that, who's the strongest, doesn't it?'

'Or who's the cleverest,' Joe said.

She thought for a moment and then said, 'Listen, I just might have an idea… Lenny told me something else. Wardick was working for him, supplying photos of kids.'

'What?' Joe stopped dead.

She nodded slowly. 'Seems Lenny's been running the porn racket for years. What's more, he'd just taken a delivery of photos from Wardick before he disappeared. What if Lenny's got some of those photos at home, and what if the police found out about them?'

\* \* \*

Clara was already in bed when she heard Hattie come back to the hut that night. Her friend called softly at her bedroom door. She knew Hattie would be desperate to hear how it had gone with Barry and she was tempted to get up, but what could she tell her? Her feelings weren't clear-cut at all. To speak about a spark, the memory of a passion, seemed too airy-fairy. Even to herself it was pathetic, and she'd been lying awake trying to fathom that forgotten part of her own heart which had flickered into life to betray her tonight. How could she even think about going back to him? How could she ever want to be loved and cherished by this man who'd betrayed her? She couldn't.

The answer came to her, like a soft whisper, rustling on the wind as it picked up around the huts and whistled along the duckboards. She couldn't. Once, the fuse of Barry's touch would have caught to unquenchable fire, robbing her of any other desire but to be with him, but tonight she had felt the flames fade almost as soon as she'd run for the door, leaving Barry in the hut still on his knees. They'd been replaced by the balled-up hurt of betrayal that she'd carried with her on her long journey home from Australia. That was the fire that burned in her now.

She awoke to the crackling of leaves. It must be that autumn had come early, usurping the summer. Her sleep-fogged mind tried to make sense of the noise. The crackling was persistent, not the sound of children crunching dry leaves underfoot, nor the rustle of their gold and brown in the branches, nor their eddying around the wooden huts. But she smelled woodsmoke in the air too. Someone was burning leaves. She took in a deep breath – she had always loved that smell. But as she breathed in, she choked, coughing and gasping for air as her lungs burned.

'Clara! Clara!' Hattie was screaming her name. 'Wake up!'

Clara sat bolt upright, at once fully awake. It wasn't leaves that were burning. It was the hut.

'Martha!' She shrieked her daughter's name, but now the flames took hold more fiercely, their crackle and roar drowning out her cry.

Hattie stood holding a wet sheet. Ripping some off as easily as tissue paper she shoved it at her and ordered, 'Cover your face! Follow me!'

How could she sound so calm? 'No! Get Martha,' Clara sobbed.

Hattie lifted a corner of the sheet. 'I've got her, under here!'

Now the flames had caught Buster's curtains and they licked like red voile at the windows. It seemed every pane had turned to molten gold. Hattie grabbed her hand.

'Crouch down, like me!' she yelled and dragged Clara through their kitchen, round the stove towards the door. Flames were already creeping along the wooden floorboards when suddenly

Hattie stopped dead. A sheet of fire sprang from wall to wall, blocking their way. Clara screamed at Hattie. 'Give her to me, Hattie. I'll take her through!' She wouldn't let her daughter's life end this way.

'No, wait. Other door! Stay close to me!'

There were doors at each end of the hut. The second one had been made redundant when they'd partitioned the rooms, and it was now in what had become Hattie's bedroom. Clara felt Hattie's strong grip and was dragged back through the kitchen, her vision obscured by thick black smoke billowing from all sides. There were loud pops and bangs as glass exploded and timbers turned to crackling charcoal.

Hattie banged the door of her bedroom shut behind them. Curls of bright flame were licking through the wooden slatted walls, but the fire was tamer here. Grabbing the door handle, she yelped in pain and pulled her hand away. Clara fumbled with her sheet, ripping off a corner for Hattie to bind her hand. The door was locked. Not only was it locked, but it had been nailed shut by Levin the nailer as a security precaution. Hattie lifted Martha out of her arms and shoved her under Clara's sheet.

'Stand back!' Her voice was gravelly as an old man's, and her eyes shone white with terror out of a blackened face. 'Cover Martha.'

Hattie picked up a chair and swung it with all her might at one of the bedroom windows. It bounced out of her hands and the army construction wooden frame held. But, undeterred, she picked up the chair and battered the window again and again. Clara sank to the floor, covering Martha with her own body. She heard Hattie's screams for help being obliterated by the roar of the flames, and then darkness blotted out all the searing light.

*

Above her was a pearly sky, opalescent with a gentle light that bruised her eyes. Clara was lying on her back, aware only that the blistering heat was mercifully gone and so was the pain. She must be dead. 'Thank God.' The voice that came out of her mouth wasn't hers; it was a dry, gruff whisper as if her vocal chords had atrophied. Perhaps there was no need of a voice in heaven. But she tried to speak again. 'Martha?' She remembered cradling her baby under the blanket, crouching over her to protect her from the flames. She remembered thinking she would die, that the fire would burn her to a crisp, but that she didn't mind. It was no sacrifice to die, not if she could be a shield for her child, keep the flames from harming her. Where was Martha? Perhaps she'd left her back on the earth, safe and sound. She rolled over and pulled herself up on to her elbows, and as she moved pain shot through her. This wasn't death! But it might be hell. There was a figure lying beside her, the face burned red on one side and the hands blackened, veined with oozing red cracks. A sickening smell of charred flesh met her.

She kneeled and looked for a part of the body she could hold without causing pain, for the eyes were wide with agony and a single, uninterrupted groan escaped the lips.

'Barry, oh, Barry,' she rasped, ineffectually patting the air around him.

'I got her out...' he whispered through swollen lips. 'Our baby, I got her out. Find her, Clara. Tell me she's alive.'

'I will, I will! Hold on, Barry.'

Jolted into action, she sprang up, running in wild circles, calling her daughter's name until strong hands grabbed her.

'Shhh, shhh, Clara. It's all right, you're safe.' Alan held her tightly to his chest.

'Martha? Is she alive?' She felt his ribs heaving beneath her cheek and it seemed an agony of slow seconds before he answered.

'Alive? Yes! Thanks to Barry. He got you all out.'

'I want to see her.' She collapsed into his arms and felt tears streaming down her cheeks, and she tasted salt and soot as he picked her up and carried her to the hut. Hattie was there, holding Martha.

With Clara still in his arms, Alan kneeled beside Hattie. 'Here, my darling. Here she is.' He made no attempt to hold back his own tears.

Hattie said nothing. She simply raised the sleeping child for Clara to see. Martha's face was untroubled, her eyelids resting on her plump cheeks and her mouth half open, as the lips puffed out gently with each breath. Clara leaned in close, to feel the breath on her own cheek, and to see for herself the rise and fall of the baby's chest.

'She's all right?'

'Fine,' Hattie croaked. 'We'll get her lungs checked, but she's been sleeping like this ever since Barry pulled us out. We've sent for the ambulance. He saved all our lives, Clara.'

'Barry! He asked me to find Martha, to let him know. He's out there – why's he out there? Can someone tell him?'

'I'll go. We didn't want to move you two till the ambulance came.'

When Alan was gone, she had the chance to look at Hattie. Someone had bound her hands with strips of the sheet she'd been holding. Her pyjamas were in shreds and her legs were striped with vicious-looking cuts.

'From the exploding windows...' Hattie followed her gaze. 'But nothing seems to hurt. What about you?'

Clara shook her head. 'Everything hurts.' She touched her throat. 'I can't speak very well. Here, let me take her,' she mouthed.

Hattie transferred the baby into Clara's arms, careful not to wake her.

'Was it the Harpers?' Clara asked.

'Who else? But there was no warning this time. He told me there wouldn't be. Why didn't I just let him have the sodding huts... what's the point in fighting any more? I've put Martha in danger, for what? A load of poxy sheds, barely fit to keep animals in!' There was an uncharacteristic bitterness in Hattie's voice.

'We're fighting because they're our homes,' Clara said. 'They're all we've got.'

'Well, we deserve better.'

Hattie sat back and closed her eyes, and Clara stroked the baby's cheek, letting her child's peacefulness permeate her. If her baby was unharmed then nothing was wrong in her world.

'We *will* have better, when we go to Australia,' Clara said, but Hattie didn't respond.

Alan returned with Joe and both women looked up. 'Take us now,' Hattie said, her voice dull with defeat. 'Take us away from this arsehole of a place. For chrissake, take us somewhere better.'

In two swift strides Joe was at her side. He put his arms round her. 'I'm sorry I let this happen, Hattie. I should have got rid of Harper the first time.' He kissed the top of Hattie's head.

'I don't give a toss about Lenny. Let him have everything. Let's just go.'

Clara had never seen Hattie so beaten down. Nothing had ever seemed to deflect her from getting what she wanted. Clara looked at Joe mutely, but the worry on his ashen face matched hers.

'If you really want to go, all right,' he said finally. 'But you told me you'd never let him chase you off again...'

Hattie didn't look up. 'I was wrong.'

* * *

Hattie's wounds had been dressed, her lungs tested, she'd endured her bed rest, and after two weeks she'd been pronounced fit to leave the hospital. But she wasn't fit. Something was broken, though she didn't know what. She felt physically sick at the idea of returning to the squat. She simply couldn't face the stench, nor the blackened fragments of her attempt to build a new life here in Bermondsey. Joe wanted her to stay in his hut, but she made the excuse that there was barely enough room to put up Alan and Clara and Martha. She would be fine camping out in one of the empty huts, she told him. The hospital released Clara and Martha soon after her, the doctor saying they'd undoubtedly been saved by Hattie's quick thinking with the wet sheets. Barry's case was more serious. His burns were severe, his lungs damaged irreparably.

She had got the story of their rescue from Joe and Alan, served in tiny pieces like milk sops to a sick baby, as she lay in the cool white of the burns ward. It had been in the early hours when the two men were woken by the glare of flames and the choking smoke. But Barry was already at the blazing hut by the time they'd rushed there. Apparently, he'd been awake in the empty hut and had seen the glow. Hattie's screams for help had led him to the back door and somehow, though how they couldn't imagine, he'd found the strength to tear the door open. He'd made light of the four-inch nails and all Levin's years of nailing experience.

'Barry should never have been able to do it,' Alan said, with a shake of his head. 'What Levin nails stays nailed.'

*

When she went back to work Hattie was surprised at the reception she got from the other Alaska girls. As she walked on to the grooving floor, those women already at their benches called out greetings. 'Y'all right, love?' Lal Martin, the supervisor came up to her. 'How's that poor little Clara getting on – is her baby all right?'

'She's back at work today and the baby's doing well,' she answered.

'Vera told us about the fire.' The woman dropped her voice. 'And she said it was them Harpers again. I can't believe anyone could be so wicked. Vera said you'd have all been dead if it weren't for Clara's hubby.' The woman gave a decisive nod. 'That's what I say, there's good and bad in all sorts.'

'The police are looking into it.'

'Coppers are bleedin' useless!' Lal scoffed. 'Probably all getting a bung from Lenny Harper anyway.'

Hattie had never been popular at the Alaska, even less so since the Crosbie affair, which had tainted her in most of the women's eyes. But it was clear that both she and Clara had been forgiven their indiscretions, for as each woman came on to the floor, one by one they offered her their sympathies. Some brought parcels of hard-to-come-by soap or household items, while others brought odd bits of clothing, precious nylons or a blouse. She tried to refuse. They were all still re-patching and darning their pre-war clothes, and no one had any to spare. One woman had made up a parcel of baby clothes. 'Give that to Clara, will you, love. Vera said you've lost it all.'

Hattie nodded, feeling tears prick her eyes for the first time since the fire. 'Yes, we did, we lost everything. Thanks,' she said. 'Thanks, girls, it means a lot...'

Her burned hand was swathed in a thick white bandage, and it was impossible for her to hold the grooving brush, so Lal put her to tidying the benches and fetching and carrying. But halfway through the morning Chris Harper came in. Ostensibly it was to check on an order for an important West End outlet, but she could feel his eyes on her all the time he was speaking to Lal. When he'd finished he strolled over to her. She was sweeping up one-handed.

'You ain't much good in here with that hand. You'll have to go home.'

Lal's head shot up. 'She's making herself useful, Chris!'

'We're on three-day weeks and I've been putting other people on short hours! I can't justify no dead weight, Lal.' His excuse was plausible enough, but she knew it had nothing to do with the austerity hours. 'Go home – oh, I'm sorry, you ain't got one, have you?'

She heard Lal suck in a breath, but she didn't expect to be championed by the supervisor, nor expect her to risk her own job.

'I'll go back up on bambeating,' Hattie said. She couldn't afford unpaid sick leave now, of all times. 'I can do that one-handed.'

'They're full. I don't need no more girls up there.'

'Sorry, love,' Lal said, as Hattie relinquished her broom. 'Wish you better...'

And as Chris Harper escorted her out of the grooving room, several girls echoed her good wishes.

She said nothing to Chris as she followed him across the iron gantry linking the two factory buildings, but halfway along he stopped, barring her way.

'You're finished in the Alaska.' His Neanderthal Harper features were set in hard lines. 'And you're finished in that shithole of a squat. You did a wrong'un crossing our Lenny. He won't stop now till you're out of Bermondsey. You should've known better.'

He turned abruptly and thudded on heavy feet down the iron staircase. She felt it bounce with his every step, and waited till he'd gone before continuing herself. She expected rage to surface, and had a defiant retort on the tip of her tongue. Yet whatever force would normally catapult it from her lips was absent, and she walked slowly to the canteen, marvelling at how little she cared that Lenny had won, again.

She stopped off at the canteen. She wanted to give Clara the girls' gifts but she also wanted to talk to her about Barry. Hattie had been to his bedside, to thank him for saving their lives, and at that stage his burns had been hidden in thick bandages. All she'd been able to see of him were his eyes, Martha's eyes.

'What's going to happen with Barry?' she asked. Clara had made her stop for a cup of tea after hearing of her treatment at the hands of Chris Harper.

'He'll have to stay in Guy's for the time being. But he's not on the panel, so the lady almoner told him he'll have to pay – until the new National Health comes in, that is.'

'So he's got nothing at all?'

'No.'

'Same as us then,' Hattie said, feeling the irony of it.

'But listen, something really strange happened. I went in to see him yesterday and it turns out someone's offered to pay his doctor's bills.'

'Really? Who?'

Clara shook her head. 'Don't know. Anonymous donor. That's all the lady almoner would say. Of course, he's grateful, but it's odd. He doesn't know anyone in this country, only me.'

Even this piece of intriguing news couldn't lift Hattie's heart.

She felt as if cotton wool had been stuffed around every feeling or reaction, especially anything to do with the fire or the squat. She made an effort. 'So, the night of the fire. I never did manage to ask you, what did Barry say?'

'He asked me to marry him – again.'

This succeeded in jolting Hattie out of her apathy. 'What a bloody cheek! I hope you said no!' But then she checked herself. 'Still, he's not all bad. He did save our lives, after all – and Martha's.'

Clara shook her head. 'I didn't say no, I didn't say yes. To be honest, love, I was so confused I just ran out, and I've not had a chance to talk to him since. I don't know what I'm going to do now. How can I say no to him, after what he's done for us?'

Hattie was stunned. Before the fire, she knew she would have fought for Clara to follow her advice, to never forget his betrayal.

'You do what you think's best for you and Martha.' She sat back and ran her finger round the thick rim of the canteen cup.

'No advice to give?' Clara asked, a puzzled look on her pretty, pale face. 'That's not like you, sergeant major!' She laughed nervously.

'I'm learning that it's better if I stay out of other people's business. If it hadn't been for me you'd have stayed in Cissie's basement, safe and sound, but no, I knew better. Like Joe says, we should only be responsible for ourselves.'

'I don't think he means it like that, Hattie. He just says that sort of thing to you 'cause he knows you're always feeling guilty if you don't help people.'

Hattie didn't recognize that view of herself.

'No! Don't laugh. It's true. You're not interfering – you just care! I'd have been lost without you, and so would Lou and Ronnie and all the others at the squat. But you're right about Barry, I suppose. I'm the only one who can decide about him...'

Hattie stopped off at Cissie's. Her mother's house in the Square had undergone a transformation over the past months.

Mario hadn't taken much persuading to return to Cissie, but he'd insisted their relationship continue on a more equal and permanent footing. He'd set about making their home more comfortable, repairing the roof and the top-floor rooms himself. Back in his home village, he said, people were used to building their own houses. No one would wait all these months for a landlord to make repairs when they could use a hammer and saw themselves. Now they had spread out over two floors, and as soon as she arrived Cissie offered Hattie the front bay room all to herself.

'Come back and live here! You've not got a pot to piss in now, so you might as well come home. We've got all the mod cons. Mario's put a bath in the kitchen and he's even doing up the basement. Perhaps you and Clara can come back when it's finished?'

Cissie's offer only confirmed how right it was for Hattie to leave. Her return to Bermondsey had resulted in nothing. She'd be going with far less than she'd come with. She would be glad to see the back of it.

'Thanks, Ciss, but I won't be staying in Bermondsey for long.'

'What d'you mean? Where else can you go?'

'Australia.'

Her mother's face registered shock and then anger. 'Don't tell me you're letting that little bastard Lenny run you off? I thought you had a bit more gumption than that.'

'Joe's asked me to go with him. Alan and Clara are coming too. It's got nothing to do with Lenny.'

'My arse it's not.'

'Well, I haven't got a job either. Chris Harper's put me off on indefinite sick, so there's nothing left for me here.'

She was surprised to see Cissie's lip tremble. Her maternal feelings had never flowed freely and Hattie for a moment didn't know how to respond.

'Ciss, you won't miss me. You've got your own life... you always have done.'

'It ain't that I'll miss you! It's just I don't recognize you, love. You won't get on in Australia, you won't get on nowhere – not now you've you let him rattle you like this.'

Cissie offered her more tea and as the conversation turned to finding other work for Hattie, Cissie brightened with an idea. 'Do you want me to organize a protest strike – unfair discrimination on the part of management, if you can call Chris Harper that! Your firm's a disgrace anyway, saying you've got no right to a union in this day and age!'

'If you want,' Hattie said. Her mother's activist days were long over and the protest would never materialize, but Hattie was glad of anything to divert Cissie from the disturbing accusation that she'd turned into a coward.

That evening when she got back to the squat, it looked almost beautiful. A low mist veiled the Oval, and a halo of stately trees, with leaves of lush green, softened the stark outline of silver-grey huts. It looked more like a village tonight. Some squatters had made front gardens outside their huts, with low picket fences round them. Their NAAFI had been painted a leaf green and now there were children playing a game of rounders on the Oval. But the two ugly scars of the burned-out huts spoiled the idyllic scene, reminding her that all they had built up was being destroyed by someone who wanted to take away her home. Perhaps she'd brought it upon herself. The secret part of her that hadn't wanted the war to end had finally got its way.

Joe had found her some blankets and a camp bed to put in the bare hut she'd chosen, and he'd cleaned out the stove so she could boil a kettle. And later that night he pleaded with her one more time. 'What's the difference between a camp bed in here and one in our hut? I don't like the idea of you staying here on your own. I'll sleep in here with you,' he offered.

She raised an eyebrow. 'What, and scandalize the squat!' She still liked to tease him about his ideas of propriety, but she found it a refreshing change that he had wanted to court her, rather than jump into bed with her straight away.

'No one's going to be scandalized by my wanting to protect you,' Joe said, pretending to ignore her jibe. He pulled her close and stole a kiss, which she eventually broke free from.

'You've changed your tune. Anyway, there's no need, we'll all be safe in our beds for now. Lenny's made his point. He wanted me to see what happens when I cross him. He'll wait for me to make the next move.'

'For *us* to make a move. It's not just you fighting this battle, you know.'

She pulled him down on to the camp bed. It was narrow and they held each other so as not to fall off. She spoke into his chest and was glad that he couldn't see her face.

'Actually, you're right, Joe,' she said quietly. 'It's not just me fighting the battle. But to be honest, I don't think I want to fight it at all any more.'

# 22

## *Dancing to Paradise*

Dance night at the children's flats usually ended with a fight. Dancing had proved almost as popular as fighting with the Barnham Street kids, so popular that they'd split the class into two groups, to avoid the continual bumping into each other or treading on one another's toes, which was the usual cause of the fight. Anne always took the fracas in her stride – every club needed a rounding-off ritual, she said. For most it was prayers, but for the children's flats it was a fight.

This evening, as well as old favourites, the hokey-cokey and waltz, she and Buster planned to teach the palais glide and the jive. For weeks after being laid off work, Hattie had been hanging around the squat doing nothing much but washing Martha's nappies, digging over the allotment or rattling around in her own depressingly empty hut. Dance nights were always a welcome distraction. In fact, her work at the children's flats was the only thing that didn't feel hopeless in her life at the moment.

She arrived early to set up the little room in the second flat where they held the dance class. As she crossed the courtyard she heard Ronnie's foghorn voice call down from the third-floor landing.

''Ang on, Hattie, I'm coming down! Got something to tell ya!'

She heard his helter-skelter descent as he swung on stair railings and leaped four of the stone steps at a time, till he came bounding to a halt in front of her. It was good to see him running and jumping again, though she noticed he still favoured one leg. The dancing would help with that. He grabbed her and spun her round as he'd seen Buster do. 'Dance night, tonight!' he said with a grin.

She unlocked the second flat. 'Come and help me get the gramophone and records,' she said, letting them both in. She retrieved the gramophone from Anne's office, where it was kept under lock and key. It had been a gift from a musician friend of Anne's, who came along to teach piano once a week to any kid who showed an interest. The piano was on permanent loan from Old Bermondsey Church, which already had two. She kneeled in front of the storage cupboard, and as she was sifting through the small collection of heavy shellac records in their brown sleeves she asked him what he'd been in such a rush to tell her.

'I know a secret!' he said, with an exaggerated wink.

'Oh yes.' She carried on sorting. '"Paradise", Guy Lombardo for the waltz? Geraldo for the palais glide and Lou Preager for jive? What do you think, Ron?'

'Suits me. Don't you want to know what it is?'

'What are you meant to do with secrets?' She was enjoying teasing him – his prickly exterior had for so long forbidden it. If she went away from Bermondsey with nothing else, at least she'd helped to soften the edges of Ronnie into something resembling a normal boy.

''Course I effin' well know, but you're me friend and you can tell friends secrets!'

Sobered, she looked up from the records. 'Go on then.'

'I know who paid for Martha's dad's hospital bill.'

She wasn't expecting this. 'How the bloody hell could you know that?'

'He told me!'

'Who?'

'The geezer who paid the money – cash! I see him count it out before he took it up Guy's.'

'Are you pulling my leg, Ron? I haven't got time for this. The others'll be here in a minute and there'll be a riot if I'm not ready.' She attempted to leave the office but he stopped her.

'Shhh, no one else can know... well, Joe can and Clara, but no one else, in case it gets him in trouble.'

'No one's getting into trouble for doing a good deed!'

'Well, *he* bloody will!'

'Go on then, tell me – who was it?'

'Pissy Pants!'

Now the heavy records slipped through her hands and she juggled to catch them before they hit the floor. 'What! Are you sure?'

'Don't you believe me?' he asked, seeming disappointed by her reaction.

'Actually, I do believe you. He was fond of Clara and Martha, and if someone told him about Barry rescuing them...'

'I told him! I told him!' Ronnie said eagerly.

'But where did he get the money from?' she asked, thinking of the scavenger's derelict camps all over Bermondsey. Then something occurred to her, and she found herself wondering if she really wanted to know where Johnny Harper had got the money.

'He's got piles of wedge. Stacks of it, all in ten bob notes and whites, he hides them all over the place! He's made good money on the old newspapers and stuff he's lifted from sites.'

'But surely not *that* much?'

Ronnie dropped his voice. 'I think a lot of it's Lenny's. He stashes it with Johnny till he needs it. Nobody's gonna go digging around Pissy Pants' blankets looking for it, are they? But, Hattie, that bunce didn't half pen and ink! I bet that lady almoner stank for days!' He gave a throaty laugh.

'Listen, Ronnie, I don't want you to tell anyone else... not even Norman. Promise?'

'Already told him, but he won't say nothing.'

She sighed. 'It can't get back to Lenny. He won't like Johnny helping out anyone from the squat.'

Ronnie nodded. 'Come on. I'm dying to learn how to chuck you over me shoulder, miss!'

'I'll chuck *you* over my shoulder, you cheeky little sod!'

The kids were already gathered in the next room, and as she wound up the gramophone Buster arrived. She wasn't quite sure what Ronnie's revelation meant, but she would have to tell Joe. She may have retired from the fight, but Joe was determined to stop Lenny and he still thought the best bet was to use Wardick's photos against him. If Johnny had used his money to help the squatters, that might just be another chink in Lenny's armour. But for now, she wanted to drift away to another more sophisticated, civilized time, and she put on 'Paradise'. It was always easier to start them off with something they knew and the waltz had been the first dance she'd taught the kids. The rich tones of Guy Lombardo and the lyrics about the paradise of innocent young love always seemed to calm them down, for even the most belligerent sometimes showed a deep sentimental streak. After the waltz's stately rhythm, she lined up the kids to learn the light-hearted steps of the palais glide. The boys with their grazed knees and grey shorts and the girls with their faded ribbons and darned cardigans were a million miles away from the elegance and glamour of the pre-war Hammersmith Palais. But they had fun pointing toes and back-stepping, tripping over their partners and bouncing off the walls of the tiny room without the usual deterioration into a 'bundle'. When it came to the jive, she and Buster demonstrated. There were whoops of laughter and cheers as he swung her high to either side, then whirled her in the air, tipping her upside down, with her head brushing the floor and her feet pointing skyward.

'Me first, me first!' Ribbons the twins, insisted. Hattie paired Ronnie and Norman with the two girls. They were impatient to get to the throw-aways, but she made them learn the basics and was delighted with Norman's light-footed precision and Ronnie's unembarrassed abandon. After an hour, they were all exhausted and went into the other flat, where tea and buns were served by the little girls who'd been doing cookery with Anne.

She pulled Buster to one side and whispered the details of

Johnny Harper's charitable act of defiance. 'Do you think there's a way Joe could use it against Lenny?' she asked.

'Joe? I thought you'd both thrown in the towel, now you're upping sticks for Australia.'

'It's me taking a back seat, Buster. Joe wants to do what he can for the squat before we go.'

'You might be able to use a split in the Harpers if it was Dickie or one of the others branching out, but Johnny? He's no threat to Lenny.'

'Maybe not, but I know he's about the only person Lenny gives a tuppence for.'

'Well then. There's your leverage – might be enough to rattle him.' Buster took a bite of the currant bun and pulled a face. 'What's this, find the bleedin' currant!'

'Shhh! You'll hurt their feelings.' Hattie glanced at the young girls who'd baked them. 'We have to apply for all the ingredients on extra rations. You should count yourself lucky you've got any currants at all!'

'Sorry. Has Joe dug up anything on Lenny paying for Wardick's filth yet?'

She shook her head and leaned in closer. 'That's why I was asking about using Johnny. I don't like Joe's plan.'

'What's that?' Buster said, who in spite of his complaints was tucking into another bun.

'He's going to break into the Harpers and make sure Lenny's still got the photos!'

'Is he nuts?' Buster said, half choking on the bun.

'I think he is. He says he'll only need ten minutes in the Harpers' place. He's just waiting for the right time, when he can be sure they're not in!'

'Well, I can pump Chris Harper, find out when the boys are likely to be out. Old Ma Harper's an invalid now, deaf as a post and bedridden, shouldn't think she'll give Joe any trouble.'

'Thanks, Buster. See what you can find out. I don't like it, but Joe's not easy to talk out of anything he's set his mind on.'

'Same as you.' Buster paused. 'Or same as you *used* to be.' He took a gulp of tea and stared at her.

'Oh, leave off, Buster. There's no shame in walking away,' she said, but her words were like a stuck record, repeated on a loop whenever she needed to justify her inaction.

'I'm not saying you should tackle Lenny yourself, like you did before. That was bloody stupid. I'm just saying it's not like you to give up on something. We're all worried about you.'

'I'll be fine. I'm leaving! It's the poor sods staying that deserve your sympathy.'

Just then a chair came flying across the room and she ducked her head, pulling Buster down with her. A little girl was wailing and three of the younger boys were lobbing broken buns at each other. 'Chucking-out time!' Hattie said, glad for an excuse to escape Buster's questioning.

\* \* \*

Ronnie missed the bombsites. He liked having his mum back and he liked going to the children's flats, he liked the dancing and the carpentry lessons from Levin the nailer, and most of all he was glad Wardick was gone, but sometimes he felt the draw of a patch of land that was all his to discover and claim. Making useless cardboard forts in the children's flats wasn't a patch on using timber beams from bombed-out houses to build a proper camp, with sash windows and corrugated-iron roofs. He missed their potato-baking on the fire, he missed the fighting when another gang tried to muscle in, and he missed staying out all night. But when Frankie had died, him and Nutty Norman had promised each other to stay off the sites, although they still reminisced, like old soldiers talking about the war, debating the merits of this site over that. This morning they were walking towards Southwark Bridge, where, on a day like this when the pavements were slick with a pale frost, there was fun to be had. The bomb-damaged bridge was still shorn up with wooden struts, and half of it was paved with temporary wooden blocks. The repairs had given the bridge a steep incline down to the north side of the river, and the game was to run up the south side and launch themselves over the crown, then skid down the other side. It wore out their shoes, but it was the best fun to be had outside of a bombsite.

'D'you remember when we went down that one?' Nutty Norman asked, as they passed a ruined riverside brewery. Ronnie peered over a low wall and into a deep pit that descended at least thirty feet. They had once climbed down to the bottom on a precarious lattice of collapsed beams. At the base of the pit was a stone slide, used to roll barrels of beer to the quayside, ready for loading. They had tobogganed down the stone slide all the way to the river.

'Yeah, it was a good lark, weren'it?' Ronnie said.

'Fancy going down?' Norman asked.

'No! We said we wouldn't no more. We don't want to end up like Frankie.'

Norman shook his head. 'Poor old Fishie… he was a good'un. I miss him, d'you?'

Ronnie gave a brief nod. He hated thinking about Frankie. Sometimes he wished it had been him, dead under the rubble. It might be better than feeling guilty all the time for drawing Frankie into his scheme. As they walked on to the bridge, a bus slowed its progress as it neared the central span, but its brakes locked and the bus slewed snake-like for the rest of the way, sending the foot passengers on the bridge scurrying in case it should mount the pavement.

The boys were not deterred and Norman roared with laughter at the horrified faces of the bus's passengers, fearing they'd be tipped into the Thames at any minute. The boys were about to start their own skidding when Ronnie felt a hand grip his shoulder and he was spun round.

'What you pair doin' off?' Lenny Harper grinned at him. 'Up to mischief again, Ronnie boy?' He tutted. 'I reckon I should I report you to the PO!'

Ronnie's mouth went dry and he shook his head. 'We ain't doing nothing!'

Lenny ignored him and stared at Nutty Norman. 'Piss off home, you.' And when he didn't move, he shot a hand out to grab one of Norman's red ears. 'Go on, jug ears, sod off,' he said, twisting hard till Norman yelped and ran.

Lenny put an arm round Ronnie's shoulders and steered him to the parapet and back towards the bombed brewery. When they came to the low wall above the pit, Lenny stopped. He placed a hand between Ronnie's shoulder blades and pushed him forward, till Ronnie was slung like a sack of coal over the wall. Ronnie was sure he would be sick and swallowed back bile.

'Now, listen here. You owe me something. Just cos that nonce Wardick's run off, don't mean I can't find another photographer for you. You're a very popular little boy, know that? Handsome bastard, with all that blond barnet of yours. Mummy's little soldier boy, eh? So, you're getting your arse down to my place for a little photography session just as soon as I can set it up. I'm getting the rest of what I paid for.'

'No! I ain't doin' that no more!'

'Don't you piss me about!' Lenny shoved Ronnie's head down and he was forced to shut his eyes tight so as not to see the dizzying drop to the pit below.

'All right, all right!' His voice sounded like a girl's, and he wanted to smash Lenny's grinning face as he was hoisted back on to his feet.

'And no blabbing to your girlfriend Hattie or it'll be the worse for her. You do me a few favours, I might even lay off the squat.' Lenny ran his hand through Ronnie's hair and twisted it round a be-ringed finger. 'So you just be ready, hear me? I'll let you know when I want ya. And make sure you wash your barnet before you come. I don't want you looking like a street raker and turning off the punters.'

Lenny hunched up the velvet collar of his wide-shouldered overcoat and patted Ronnie's face, before nimbly trotting back down Southwark Bridge Road to a waiting car.

Ronnie shoved his hands into his pockets to stop them from

shaking, bunching them into fists as he walked, sniffing against the cold. 'I've had me chips now, oh God, well and truly had me chips,' he muttered as he walked, not knowing where to go or what to do. All he knew was that if he didn't turn up at Lenny's when he was called, Hattie would pay for it; but if he did, then he would pay.

He turned into a side alley which hugged the riverside, and passing under the railway arch he found himself in Clink Street, a black cobbled place, where warehouse walls closed in on him like dark wings. A gap between the buildings gave him a glimpse of a parapet with the river beyond. He ran to it, gasping for air. *I might as well chuck meself in*, he thought, imagining the slap of the water and the icy grip of the tide bearing him off downriver to the sea. Tears, hot and salty, trickled into his mouth and he suddenly remembered Sue, how she'd always hated going over the bridges; even when he carried her on his back, she'd squeal. She didn't like the water. Perhaps she wouldn't be where he was going. He sobbed and tore his eyes from the eddying green tide surging towards London Bridge. Looking up, he saw the square, pennanted tower of Southwark Cathedral blocking out the sky above him. He pushed off from the river wall and began walking towards the cathedral. He only went in because he didn't know where else to go. But once he'd slipped inside the dark interior he felt safe. He crept along a side aisle and found a small, pointed arched entrance into a side chapel. It was quiet. Coloured light from a stained-glass window spilled across the short pews. He picked up an embroidered kneeler and laid it on a pew, then, with his head on the kneeler and his legs curled up on the pew, he fell asleep.

When he woke up, the sun had moved round and the coloured light was dimmed. He uncurled his legs and shivered. It was cold in the side chapel, but he wished he could stay there forever. His neck muscles protested as he lifted his head. He sat up and his eye fell on a small wooden altar on which was painted a scene of Jesus on the cross, with the two thieves on either side. Ronnie thought it was horrible. Nails in your hands and your feet were the sort of thing Lenny Harper might do to you if you upset him. He leaned forward to read the gold lettering beneath the painting. *This day shalt thou be with me in Paradise*, it said. And then Ronnie knew what he had to do.

* * *

When Barry was finally discharged from Guy's Hospital, the committee had told him he was welcome to stay at the squat. He could keep the hut he'd appropriated for as long as he liked, they'd said. Clara couldn't argue with their decision. After all, she owed him her life, and Martha's too. But she worried for Alan, who, so far, had done everything to assure her she should take all the time she needed to decide which of them she wanted. He'd been almost too accommodating. It would have made it easier for her if he'd raged or insisted, or claimed her as his own. But that wasn't Alan, and perhaps she wouldn't have loved him if it was.

Alan wasn't exactly avoiding her; they were living in the same hut after all. But she had felt him withdrawing and it made her panic. She didn't want Alan to make the decision for her and simply drift away, but neither was Barry in any condition to talk about the future. He was still in pain from his burns, and she and Hattie went daily to his hut to change his dressings and take him food, making sure he had fuel for the stove and a bucket of water. But as the weeks passed and he grew stronger, Clara knew the time had come.

Tonight, after tea, she went to fetch Barry's covered plate, which was keeping warm on the stove. She noticed Alan glance up from the table, where he and Joe still sat. Their eyes met and he smiled. Hattie usually ate with them, returning to her empty hut to sleep. Until now, Clara had made sure she was never alone with Barry, and seeing her readying his tea things, Hattie joined her. But tonight, once they'd left the hut, Clara said, 'Hattie, I think I'll take Barry's dinner in on me own tonight.' Her hand, holding the plate, trembled. Only now did she realize how nervous she was to be stepping out on to the precipice of her future.

'Oh!' Hattie said, understanding immediately what this might mean. 'You've made up your mind then?'

'I think so.'

'You *think*!' Hattie said in a hushed voice, for they were still in earshot of the hut. 'Don't you know by now?' She was unable to hide her exasperation.

'It's not easy! He's Martha's dad and he's saved our lives. I do think he's changed. I always told you he really loved me, didn't I?'

Hattie shook her head. 'I never bought it, Clara. Actions speak louder and all that…'

'Actions? He would have died to save us! But I've started think-ing about Martha more than myself. Will she blame me later on, when she finds out I sent her dad away?'

Hattie groaned. 'You've got that all arse up'ard. He's the one broke up your family when he decided to be greedy and have *two*! Remember? Besides, Alan would be a great dad for Martha.'

'I know you want me to choose Al…' As Clara said the words, she felt a wave of sadness almost knock her off her feet. It was the realization of what it would be like to give him up, send him away.

'It's not that,' Hattie said, gripping her by the shoulders. 'I just want you to decide what it is *you* really want and then fight for it!'

It was good to see the fire back in Hattie's eyes, even if it was directed at her. 'I could say the same to you, Hattie.'

Hattie's face reddened. 'That's different.'

'Is it?' Clara replied, shocking herself with her own directness. 'Anyway, I'm going now, Hattie. Before I lose me bottle.'

As she steadied her hands around the dinner plate and walked towards Barry's hut, she heard Hattie call after her, 'Just follow your heart!' And Clara reflected how unusual the phrase sounded on the lips of her unsentimental friend.

'Hello!' she called, pushing open Barry's door. 'Your tea's ready.'

He was dressed, washed and shaved, and sitting on the bed waiting for her. He gave his broad, sunny smile.

'No chaperone tonight?' he said, clearly pleased. 'Stay for a cuppa while I have my dinner?' he asked, as Clara pulled up a camp table and produced a knife and fork for him.

'OK, I'll stay,' she agreed, going to boil a billycan of water on the stove. The hut was bare of any comforts and she was grateful that Barry hadn't made it a home yet. She watched him eat and remembered the days in Sydney, when he'd come home after being away for a few days, supposedly doing labouring jobs.

'When you used to come home – from being with her – and I'd make you your tea, I suppose you must have already eaten with her... I never thought of it before; couldn't have been pleasant, trying to eat that second meal,' she said, speaking her thoughts, and remembering how she'd always tried so hard to make something nice for him to come home to after his days eating in greasy cafés.

He paused with his fork midway to his mouth. 'I always preferred your cooking,' he said with a grin.

'I don't care about *that*, Barry!' she said, enraged at his reaction. How could he believe her remembrance had anything at all to do with whose dinners he preferred. 'I put my heart into *everything* I did for you! Dinners, or making our home, or looking after our baby... I did it all because I loved you, and I thought I had the same from you! It's nothing to do with a bloody cookery contest!'

He tried to get up and grimaced, holding the thigh that had been burned raw. 'Oh, Clara, I'm a stupid feller sometimes. I put my foot in it all the time, but I did love you like that, same as you did me. It was just the bind I was in with... her.'

She wished he would use her name. 'It was only *you* who got yourself into that bind, Barry,' she said, fixing him with a look that made him flinch.

'I know. There's no excuse. But I need to tell you, Clara, soon I'll have to be moving on... unless. Well, look, I might not get you on your own again, so I need to ask again.' He tried to drop to one knee and his face contorted with pain. She leaped up to stop him.

'No. Don't do that, Barry. Stay where you are – it's hurting you.'

'I don't care. I just need an answer. Will you give me another chance?' His warm brown eyes pleaded for her to remember the man he was when they first met. But the gap between then and now was a vast gulf, a chasm of disappointed hopes and dreams.

'Barry, I'm so grateful for what you did, for saving me and Martha and Hattie. But you took me away from everything I'd ever known. I gave up my family and I went to a strange country just to be with you. You said you loved me then, but what sort of love is it that ripped out my heart and threw it away? Why would I ever give you a chance to do that all over again?'

His eyes filled with tears. 'But I've given up everything for you now – to show you what a mistake I made! I've worked my passage here and I'll work for you and our daughter till I drop. I promise. I'm so sorry.'

'I know you're sorry. But, Barry, it's too late. My family still won't talk to me. I've had to bring Martha up on me own. You don't know how hard that was. But I've found some good friends here, and I've met a man I love with all my heart. He beat you to it, Barry. He's already asked me to marry him, and he ain't got another wife on the side. He loves Martha – she'll be just fine. We'll both be just fine.'

She felt exhilarated, free. She opened the door of the hut and breathed in a deep draught of cold air, feeling that all the corners of her heart were being swept clean of past hurts. But then she heard the strangulated sound of a man attempting to suppress his sobs. There was no doubt in her mind that Barry's remorse and regret were genuine, but did that mean she should ever trust him again? She had almost reached their own hut when she heard heavy footsteps on the duckboards. He was behind her and she felt his hand on her shoulder and flinched away.

'I'm sorry. Don't look at me like I'm a monster. Just try to believe I love little Martha. If you don't want me back I understand, but please, do it for our daughter. She deserves to have her dad!'

She brushed away his hand. 'Don't. You might be her father, but Alan's been more of a dad to her than you've ever been!' She could see how much it hurt him, yet there was an arrogant streak in Barry that she'd chosen to ignore, and it had fuelled his return. He couldn't believe anyone would deny him what he wanted. She went on in the face of his shock. 'When did you last change her nappy, or laugh at her babbling, or be proud of her first words and her first steps? Never! You just weren't here, Barry. If you want forgiveness, you've got it. But you'll never have me.'

In a few strides she was at her hut door; she didn't look back. But once inside she felt her limbs turn to water and she leaned against the wooden door, holding on to the handle for support. Alan was sitting by the stove. He looked up, a question in his eyes if not on his lips.

Joe got up. 'Just popping out,' he said. 'Something I forgot to tell Hattie.' And he gave Clara an encouraging smile as she moved aside to let him out.

Alan stood up and all Clara's world narrowed to the space separating them. His distance and her vacillation seemed to have made those few feet into an uncrossable chasm.

'Alan, I've made up my mind. I'm going to Australia,' she said finally.

His sparkling eyes dimmed with sadness, but he attempted a smile. 'If that's what will make you happy, Clara, love, I'd never stand in your way. 'Course, I'll move back in with Mum and Dad till you've gone.'

For a moment she wondered if her indecision had broken them, but then she understood.

'Not with Barry, you idiot! I'm going with you!' she said, flinging herself across the room into his arms, and suddenly the space between them was no space at all.

# 23

## *Traps*

### October–December 1948

Hattie and Joe had been arguing for over an hour. They were in the narrow camp bed, which was still virtually all the furniture her hut contained, apart from the stove. A comforting red glow filtered through the edges of its closed door and the only other light was provided by a couple of candles that guttered in the draught from the rotting sash windows. She hadn't chosen the best of huts, but it would only be for a short while, and she could put up with it till they left. They lay fully clothed beneath the grey army blanket, her head on his chest. He never raised his voice in an argument, but she could register from his heartbeat when he objected to anything she offered.

'I'm just saying there has got to be a safer way – and I know that's usually your line, but this time I'm just being cautious for you,' Hattie said, in as even a tone as she could manage.

'Buster's told me the Harper brothers will be out all next Saturday till gone eleven. They're going to the races and then on the piss. I'm not worried about their old mum. I don't think she'll be chasing me off with a poker!'

'You *think* they'll all be out, but that family's massive. Any one of the cousins or uncles could decide to pop in for a visit and you'll be caught like a rat in a trap.'

'So, what other "safer" way do you suggest I can make sure he's still got Wardick's photos? I've been waiting for this chance for ages and it's our best bet! It's no good waiting any longer. If the photos are sold the police won't be able to do a thing!'

She sighed. 'I don't want to fight.'

'No, I've noticed that,' he said, and there was an edge to his voice which she didn't like.

'Oh, I wish you lot would stop going on at me. I'm sick of it. I get it from you, from Buster and even Clara, of all people! But none of you know Lenny like I do.'

'He's not going to burn every hut down. He'd have nothing left to rent out!' Joe said, with maddening logic.

'Maybe not, but if the scare tactics don't work, he could just decide to walk in mob-handed and turn us all out of our beds.'

'Which is why we decided to stop him first.'

'Yes, but it was meant to be a "clever" move, and this ain't clever. Why can't we just tip off the police and let them deal with it?'

'Because they've got to collar him when the photos are on the property. If they raid the place and he hasn't got the photos, we've lost the advantage. Once I know for certain, I'll go to the police. Don't worry. I'll be in and out in no time.'

'Joe, I just don't want Lenny to get his hands on you. He'll hurt you.'

'Nastier people than him have tried that in the past and failed.'

She still wasn't convinced the risk was necessary, and wondered if his motivation was simply male pride not to be bested by her ex. Her retort was silenced by his lips on her mouth.

'You always shut me up like that when you can't win,' she said eventually.

'Complaining?' He smiled, and for answer she put her lips to his.

*

Hattie had promised Anne she'd go to the children's flats to help ring around for donations. They'd lost half the council funding, and if things didn't improve the flats would have to close for the want of £100. She'd completed a morning of dispiriting phone calls to businesses and charities before deciding to walk off her disappointment. She was locking up the flat when she saw Lou on her landing, peering down into the courtyard. Hattie waved. 'No work today, Lou?'

But Lou didn't seem to have registered who Hattie was. She stared at her and gave a vague smile. She had forgotten to cover her mouth and was pulling at her flyaway, unwashed hair. Knowing instantly that something was wrong, Hattie ran for the stairs, and when she saw Lou dressed only in nightdress and slippers, her heart lurched.

'Lou, it's Hattie.' She put an arm round the woman and led her into her flat. 'Has something happened? Is Ronnie all right?'

'Oh, Hattie!' Lou said. 'It's you, gel, I didn't recognize you! Gawd's good, I know, but I think he's taken my Ronnie. The boy's gone out of here this morning in a terrible state. He never got up for school and when I told him off, he says to me, *Mum, I'm the man of the house now, I ain't got time for school, I'm gonna sort out them Harpers once and for all*. Did I tell you, he was ever so upset about Lenny burning your place down?'

'Yes, you told me, Lou. Did he say where he was going?'

Lou tried to speak, then sobbed into her hand. 'I didn't hear him properly, but he says, *Don't worry about me, Mum*, something about *I'm going to paradise*… He had such a funny look on his face. Oh, I don't know… I gets so confused.'

Hattie licked dry lips. It seemed as if all the men she cared about were determined to go up against the Harpers. It was much easier when she was indifferent. 'Don't you worry, Lou. Buster and I, we always find him, don't we?'

Lou nodded. 'So, I'll just stay here and wait?'

'Don't go anywhere. I'll tell Buster.'

She sprinted all the way to the Alaska, arriving out of breath and windblown. The yard was quiet, empty of the delivery vans that usually filled it, but peering into the electrician's shop, she found Alan drinking tea.

'Hello, Hattie.' He beamed. 'What's up?'

'I need to find Buster.'

'He's up with the nailers, last I saw. Fancy a cuppa?'

'Sorry, can't stop. Urgent.' And she dashed off, leaping the stairs to the nailing room.

But when Levin the nailer finally heard her and removed the nails from between his teeth, he told her that Buster had already left for the shearing shop. When she got there, he'd moved on to bambeating. She cut across the iron gantry linking the old and new buildings, but halfway across it, her way was blocked by a grinning Chris Harper. She tried to push past him without speaking, but he grabbed her arm.

She decided to be civil. 'Sorry, I'm just a bit busy now, Chris.'

'Oh, *busy*? Too busy to talk about a job I've got for you?' he said, a disarmingly pleasant expression on his face.

'For me?'

'You do still need a job, don't you?'

'Yes, I do.' She nodded. 'Perhaps I'll come in and see you about it later.'

'Now or never. It might be gone tomorrow. Come to the office and I can give you your cards now...'

She hesitated. But wherever Buster had gone she'd find him soon enough, and the job offer might not come again. She followed Chris to his office, but as soon as the door closed behind her, she knew it had been a mistake.

'Hattie, darling! Where've you been hiding your pretty little self?'

Crosbie was dressed in a sleek, light-grey suit with blue silk lining, and his bronzed face showed that somehow he'd found money to travel abroad. He uncurled himself elegantly from the chair and walked over to her, holding out his arms to give her an unwanted embrace. The mere smell of that expensive cologne caused her to blush with shame that she could have ever been taken in by his sharp veneer. He stood back, pretending to admire her, and she resisted the urge to smooth down her windblown hair. Crosbie looked at Chris Harper. 'As I was saying, she's a stunner, absolutely wasted on that factory floor.'

She looked from one to the other, and had the uncomfortable feeling that the two of them were jaws in an elaborate trap. Soon she would hear the snap and feel the pain.

'What's going on, Chris?' she asked, ignoring Crosbie. 'I don't know what Mr Crosbie has told you, but I'm not interested in working in sales again.'

'I know! That message came over loud and clear last time we met.' Crosbie held up his hands and gave a hearty laugh, as if they'd parted the best of friends. 'No, this is just a temporary stop-gap sort of thing.' He glanced at Chris. 'Perhaps you should explain.'

Crosbie went to the grimy window and, turning his back on them, lit a cigarette. She recognized the strong, exotic smell of Gauloises, and saw that his silver cigarette case was packed with the impossible-to-get French brand that she'd become addicted to when she was stationed in Europe. Chris saw her staring at Crosbie.

'I can see you've noticed Mr Crosbie's doing very well, Hattie, and the other thing you should know, it ain't all on that sales-man's salary of his. Sit down, make yourself comfy.'

She sat on the edge of the chair, ready for flight.

'See, Mr Crosbie's told me how you come home with a fur one night. Did anyone ask you for it back?'

'You're not doing me for that! I did send it back – clean!'

Chris waved his hand and she heard a chuckle from Crosbie at the window.

'Yeah, yeah, but did anyone come after you for it?'

'Of course not.'

''Course not,' Chris repeated. 'Because Mr Crosbie *loaned* it to you. Turns out you're not the first girl Mr Crosbie's sent home with a coat on that weren't hers. It's just you sodded it all up, getting it filthy and then taking ages getting your boyfriend to clean it.' Chris paused, enjoying surprising her with his knowl-edge of her secret. 'Anyhow, what normally happens is that the coat never goes back to the sales showroom, 'cause he never logs it in as stock in the first place! No, that coat goes straight to my cousin Lenny, who sells it on for Mr Crosbie at a fair price. Fair price?'

He shot a look at Crosbie, who inhaled deeply and nodded. 'But your cousin certainly takes a good cut for himself.'

Chris grinned. 'That don't surprise you, does it, Hattie?'

No, it didn't surprise her at all. She should have realized that Crosbie's lifestyle would take a lot to fund, far more than the salary of a fur salesman. And she wasn't surprised to hear Lenny had a finger in the pie.

'There's bloody good money in furs, Hattie,' Chris went on.

'So long as you're not at the dirty bambeating end, you mean?'

'You can be at the clean end.' Crosbie quickly turned round, and his slightly mocking tone was replaced with something sharper, perhaps fear. 'It's a couple of jobs, that's all. My girl's got cold feet and we need to get a few sables and minks into Lenny's hands. He doesn't like the supply drying up.'

'Why me?' she asked, already knowing the answer.

'Because Lenny asked for you. And if you do well, he says he'll lay off your squatting camp.'

'Oh, bollocks. He'll never lay off the squat, not till he's run us all out! Well you can tell your employer *Mr* Harper that I'm not interested. I won't do it!'

'Hattie! Please. You don't want to upset Lenny, and nor do I. To be honest, I'm in a bit of a jam here. Help out an old friend?' Crosbie pleaded.

'You were never my friend. You used me; I used you. It was barter,' she said bitterly. 'And I think I came off worse. It won't happen again.'

Crosbie's face showed even more shock than when she'd told him she wouldn't be sharing his bed more than the once. She flung the chair back so that it clattered to the floor, and slammed out of the office. She flew down the iron staircase and, forgetting all about seeking out Buster, ran to the drug room. Joe stood at a bench in the far corner of the room, carefully pouring some sapphire brew into a balloon-shaped glass vessel suspended over a Bunsen burner. Her entrance hadn't gone unnoticed; other men in white coats turned curious eyes upon her. Joe finished decanting the blue liquid and turned round to find her standing behind him.

'Hattie! What are you doing here? I thought you'd be at Barnham Street!'

She didn't want to embarrass him in front of the other chemists, so she smiled brightly. 'Sorry to interrupt. No joy with the fundraising. All those rich people pleading poverty, broke my heart!' She gave a false giggle and Joe's eyes widened.

'What's up?' he mouthed.

'Thought we could go for a drink at lunchtime, cheer me up? Meet you in The Horns?'

He looked up at the wall clock. 'Ten minutes?' She nodded briefly and made her escape, before her boiling anger rose up and shamed him. Joe was a private man. She would spare him a scene in front of his workmates.

She waited for him on the corner outside the pub and saw him leave the factory. When he spotted her, his face grew serious, and he ran across the road to where she stood. 'What's going on?' Joe asked, taking her elbow. 'You got me worried in the drug room.'

The pub was only half full; no one was splashing out on beer these days. They easily found a seat at a window table. 'Get me a whiskey mac, Joe. I need it.'

He raised his eyes, but kept back his questions until she'd taken a gulp of her whiskey. 'So?' he asked, tipping up the bitter glass, and draining it in a few gulps.

'Thirsty?'

'I know trouble when I see it, and I know you, Hattie. This has got nothing to do with the children's flats.'

'No, it bloody well hasn't. You've got my blessing. Do it, Joe. Raid the Harper house and get something on that bastard. I've had enough of him interfering in my life. I didn't fight

Germans all those years to come home and be bullied by Lenny Harper.'

She slammed her glass down, drawing stares from the few drinkers at the bar. And then she told Joe about Crosbie and Chris Harper's offer.

He surprised her with a chuckle.

'It's not sodding funny! I'm bloody angry.'

'So, he can try burning you to a crisp and that makes you give up. But if he asks you to thieve for him, you bounce right back to your old Bolshie self. You make me laugh sometimes.'

'Well, I don't like you laughing at me, so you can wipe that grin off your face.'

'God, I've missed that old fire of yours.' He reached across for her hand. 'Tell me off all you like.' And she smiled at the mischievous expression that danced in his dark eyes.

But when she told him about Ronnie, he grew serious. 'Any idea what he's planning?'

'Can't think, but the last thing we need is Ronnie getting caught up with the Harpers again. I'll see if I can track him down today. Someone at the buildings usually knows if there's trouble.'

It was a dull, damp day and already the light was failing. She popped into Lush the greengrocer's to see if by any small chance there were some tangerines that she could take to Cissie's. They had come off ration and she knew they were her mother's favourites.

'Sorry, love. This is all I could get.' Lush looked with disdain upon the one crate of shrivelled specimens. 'I'm ashamed to be selling 'em at that price, but we can't get 'em for love nor money.' He was so apologetic that she bought two, but at five and six a pound she was equally apologetic that she could afford no more.

Outside, a fine rain now fell from the leaden skies. Hugging the two tangerines as if they were a pair of sunshine capsules, Hattie walked back to Barnham Street, imagining bright blue skies and sunset-streaked beaches. It was her regular fantasy of Australia. From Clara, she knew the reality was different, and that the new world had its share of slums. But only the thought of a perfect life in the sun would get her through another winter in Bermondsey. The gas lamps dotted around Barnham Street Buildings only highlighted the unremitting drabness and squalor of their peeling paint and crumbling brick. She crossed the court-yard to speak with the inevitable gang of roll-up smoking truants hanging around the dust chutes, but they had seen nothing of Ronnie that day, and Norman was still dutifully at school. So, if Ronnie was up to mischief today, he was on his own. She hoped this wasn't the first sign that Ronnie's new resolutions were already failing. She'd thought Frankie's death had helped him turn a corner. Perhaps she was wrong. She'd been wrong about so many things in her life. But Australia! She looked up at the heavy, rain-filled clouds and smiled secretly to herself. About that she was right.

Before going home, she stopped at the Square. Mario answered the door.

'How's the invalid?' she asked.

He raised his eyes. 'She see too bloody well, now! The place is filthy, she says. She got me cleaning this, tidying up that...'

Mario led her to their newly decorated front room on the top floor, where Cissie sat, wrapped in a silk kimono dressing gown. She had just been operated on to remove her cataracts, courtesy of the new National Health, and her restored eyesight was proving a mixed blessing.

'Come in, darlin', let's have a good look at yer,' she said, beck-oning Hattie to her side. 'Good gawd, you're looking your age, love. What's that I can see?'

Hattie yelped as her mother pulled out a strand of hair.

'That's a grey one! Talking of which, why did you let me go round looking like a fluffy red pillar box? When I first see me hair properly, I sent him out for a new shade. What do you think?'

She fluffed up her new soberly coloured hair.

'I thought you liked it red!'

'Well, to me it always looked more chestnut. And I changed me lipstick too.' She puckered her lips.

'Yes, it's better,' Hattie said. But as she handed her mother the tangerines, she couldn't help a twinge of sadness that Cissie the Red was no more.

*

On Saturday night she needed a distraction from going mad with worry as Joe put his plan into action. She was going to spend the evening at Buster's. She'd seen Joe off, wearing the old woollen hat that always reminded her of the night she'd first met him. Tonight he'd pulled it even lower over his forehead, but still the stray lock of dark hair found its way out. He wore an old army pullover and dark trousers.

'All you need now are the mud smears across your cheeks!' she'd said, trying to keep the mood light. But she'd felt anything but light-hearted and was regretting her impulsive decision to let him go through with the scheme. 'Be careful, promise?' she asked, giving him a lingering kiss.

'Walk in the park!' he said, spreading his arms wide as he walked backwards from her across the Oval. She knew it was ridiculous, but tears pricked her eyes as she shooed him off, feeling almost as if he was going off to war. Through all those years of fighting she had managed to avoid this frightening, stomach-clenching anxiety, but here she was now, gripped by fear over the man she loved going off to another kind of battle.

'Come and wake me up, doesn't matter what time!' she called and he stuck a thumb in the air, before turning round and trudging off in the direction of Southwark Park Road.

She found Buster in good form. He wound up the gramophone as soon as she arrived and put on some Perry Como. The little room was draped in so many paper chains the ceiling was invisible, and the table looked set for a special occasion, with a white cloth and the best cutlery. Aiden again performed a culinary miracle. He'd queued for hours down the Blue for a piece of cod, and had eked it out with potatoes and a cube of cheese to make a surprisingly good fish pie. He produced desert with a flourish – banana fritters, made with the single banana he could find – and some tinned cream.

Hattie was suitably impressed. 'Blimey, what are we celebrating? Or has Christmas just come early?'

Buster and Aiden looked at each other and both spoke at once. But Aiden let Buster continue. 'Christmas come early, darlin',' he said, lifting the glass of bitter that Aiden had poured him. 'Looks like we might not be able to spend Christmas with you, so we thought we'd do it now, didn't we, Aide?'

Aiden nodded and to her horror Hattie saw Buster's eyes begin to well with tears. Aiden swallowed hard and got up to clear away the plates.

'Don't get upset, Buster. I'm not going to Australia right this minute!'

'You tell her,' Aiden said. 'I'll just go and wash up.'

'Thing is, love, it's not you leaving. It's me. I might not be here by Christmas.'

'Oh God, no. Are you ill?' she said, her mouth dry and her heart beating faster.

He shook his head. 'No, love. Might be better if I was, though.' He pulled a resigned face.

'Tell me, quick. You're scaring me,' she said, her nails biting into the palms of her clenched fist.

'I did a silly thing, Hattie. I was walking back from a club up the Old Kent Road one night and I had to stop for a jimmy riddle. So, I went in the conveniences up Tower Bridge Road...'

She groaned. 'Oh, Buster, you didn't! Poor Aiden.'

'No, love! He was *with* me. And you know me when I'm pissed, I get sentimental, don't I? I just give him a little kiss – just a peck, no tongues! Well, some bastard keen-as-mustard copper collared us. Looks like we're both going away, darlin'.'

'Oh no! When?'

'Haven't got a court date yet, but it'll be before Christmas.'

Buster's lower lip trembled. She stood up and went to put her arms round Buster. 'Oh, love. Maybe you'll get a decent judge, eh? They don't all send you down, not for a first offence.'

'Well, it ain't exactly me first offence. There was that time I said I was reading the electric signs outside the lavs and the beak let me off.'

The irony wasn't lost on her. 'Guiltier then than now?'

He nodded sadly. 'I'm more worried about him...' Buster inclined his head towards the scullery. 'He's such a softie, they'll make mincemeat of him inside.'

'Don't talk like that. Joe says you've always got to think of the best thing that could possibly happen and not the worst...'

A tear trickled down Buster's face. 'I'll try, love, I'll try. But if it's the worst, you'll look after my Lou and Ronnie, won't you?'

Of course, she promised. But how she'd accomplish it from the other side of the world, she had no idea.

The rest of the evening was a noble attempt by the two men to be cheerful, and she tried her hardest to match their bravery. But she found herself wondering at the so-called justice in the better world she'd fought so hard for, when the likes of Wardick and Lenny were walking free, while two men who only wanted to be left in peace to love each other were facing ten years' hard labour. She remembered how her GI boyfriend in Belgium had described liberating the camps and discovering for the first time what the pink triangle meant. She couldn't see how this was any different and, though she smiled and, to please him, danced the jive in Buster's tiny front room, her heart was all the while silently breaking for her sweet-natured dancing partner.

She left earlier than she normally would have. She'd wanted a distraction, but this had been too much of one. And once back in her bare hut, with the doors locked against the world, she got into bed, fully clothed, and allowed herself to cry for Buster. She dozed fitfully and woke when the moon was high. By its light, she checked her watch. Midnight. Joe should have been back long ago! Where was he? She got up and peered out of the window. The moon was smeared with a mist that hung heavy on the bare branches of trees surrounding the Oval. The fog and the darkness made it impossible to see more than a few yards beyond the hut. But, as she watched, she spotted movement in the mist and then an elliptical beam of light, spreading out across the grass.

'Joe!' She put her face to the cold, wet window, tapping on the glass till the figure halted and held up the torch to dazzle her.

She dashed to the door and let him in. 'You gave me a fright – where've you been? Why did you leave it so late?'

He pulled off the woolly hat and she saw his hair was soaked in sweat. 'Got into a bit of trouble,' he panted. His face was wet and streaked with black, which she found odd, as he'd said he wouldn't be mudding his face.

She helped him off with the pullover, which was damp with mist. His shirt was soaked in sweat and he slumped on to the edge of the bed, arms resting on his knees, head dropped forward. 'Blimey, that was a close shave. I've had to run all the way from the Harpers.'

'But it's only ten minutes away. How d'you work up such a sweat?'

'I went the long way round. I've had half the clan chasing me down like a pack of wolves. I didn't want to lead them straight here.' He was still breathing heavily and she sat next to him. She took his hand and, resisting the urge to say 'I told you so', waited for him to explain.

'You were right.' He took a heaving breath. 'The racing was called off and they got home early. I'd just come downstairs from the bedrooms when the door opened, and I had to jump into the coal cupboard!'

'Oh no! How did you get out?' She took out her handkerchief and wiped away the coal streaks.

'Well, there I was, stuck between old Ma Harper's downstairs bedroom and the sodding kitchen. She had her door open and they were pissing it up with a crate of beer in the kitchen. I just had to wait until they all went to bed. I stayed there another half-hour after they'd gone up, and when I heard the boys all snoring I went to slip out through the back garden. Just my luck Dickie's got a weak bladder. He was going out to the lav at the same time.'

'Did he recognize you?'

'No, I don't think so. Too dark, and I had the hat pulled down. So, then it was pandemonium. There's old Ma Harper going off alarming, shouting at the boys to cut my balls off, and then Lenny, Denny and Dickie – all half naked – chasing me down Southwark Park Road.'

'How did you lose them?'

'Just pretended they were a Jap patrol and used my bush craft. Climbed a tree!'

She giggled at the picture he painted, and soon they were both rolling on the bed, laughing hysterically. When they'd calmed down, she asked, 'So, did you find the photos?'

His face was drawn with tiredness as he shook his head. 'Nothing! After all that, it was a total waste of time! Not a sign of the photos and I looked everywhere apart from under Ma Harper's mattress!' He was angry, at himself, Hattie knew, but also a little at her. He insisted it was his fault for delaying, but the unspoken accusation was that she'd been the one who'd persuaded him to wait till it was safe.

'God knows what we're going to do,' he said, and thumped the wooden wall of the hut. 'If I had the money, I'd go out tomorrow morning and buy us all our tickets to Australia!'

# 24

## *Caught*

### December 1948

Martha was tugging at the turn-up of Alan's trouser leg. Her smile and pleading dark eyes won him over in minutes. He scooped her up, launching her skyward, letting her go, then catching her over and over so that she laughed until she got hiccups.

'Mind her head, she'll go through the roof!' Clara scolded.

He dutifully placed Martha on her feet and she tottered off to her next target. Hattie hoisted the toddler up on to her knees, where Martha stood surveying the room. She liked to be eye-to-eye with the adults, and Hattie was sure sometimes that she followed every word they were saying. Now she noticed the child's eyes grow serious as she stared at Joe. His face was wretched with worry as he spoke to Alan about ways they might raise the money for their passage to Australia. Since his failure to find the photos at Lenny's he'd spoken of little else. Martha's solemn eyes followed Joe's pacing, and Hattie saw the child's mouth turn down in the beginning of a cry. She stood up swiftly, whirling Martha round to distract her from the puzzling adult concerns which were clearly upsetting her.

'Perhaps Clara will get an anonymous donation from a secret admirer – you'll share it with us, won't you, love?' Hattie said, trying to lighten the mood. 'Mind you, we'll have to fumigate it first!' she said, grinning.

Clara raised her eyes. 'I wouldn't take his money! Poor Johnny needs it more than I do.'

Hattie handed Martha to Clara. 'It's probably all Lenny's anyway, in which case I wouldn't want it either.'

She shrugged on her beaver lamb as she looked out of the window. A sharp sleet was falling and she was reluctant to leave Joe's warm hut, which Clara had made more cosy since she'd been living there. Hattie had resisted all their urgings to move in as well. She liked her own sparse hut, the fact it felt so temporary.

'I'm off to the court. If it turns out bad, I want to at least be there to say goodbye to Buster.'

'And I'm going to say goodbye to Barry,' Clara said, glancing at Alan, who gave her an encouraging nod.

She waited while her friend put a woollen coat and bonnet on Martha and wrapped her in a blanket. Outside, the sleet was soaking the duckboards and the grass. Hattie grasped Clara's hand. 'Good luck, love. Don't let him make you feel guilty…'

Clara looked down briefly. Her pale face had become leaner over the past year, and the dark eyes, that had forever flitted about like a nervous bird's, now looked up at her fearlessly.

'I'll stick to me guns,' she said. 'There's nothing he can say to change my mind. Good luck to Buster. If you get a chance tell him we're all thinking of him.'

Hattie watched as Clara hurried down the duckboard to Barry's hut. She believed her. Clara had gone through too much to be swayed now.

*

Tower Bridge Magistrates' Court was a forbidding place for the innocent. The guilty seemed to take it in their stride. She saw some spivs and their girlfriends outside one courtroom, laughing and joking, dressed up as if for a day trip to Ramsgate, ignoring the shushing of a passing clerk. She slipped into the courtroom and searched for Buster and Aiden. They were sitting in the dock, looking nervous and solemn. Both were dressed in sober suits. She guessed Buster's, black and far too tight, had last been worn at his parents' and little Sue's funerals. She shuffled along a bench towards the back and was surprised to see Ronnie already sitting there, with Lou beside him. On the bench behind them was Levin the nailer, who nodded a hello, along with a group of the Alaska girls who'd come to offer Buster support.

It was the first time she'd seen Ronnie since he'd gone missing, promising to 'sort out the Harpers'. Now she frowned at him. Settling herself on to the bench, she reached round to squeeze Lou's hand. She'd obviously washed and waved her thin hair, and she wore an old-fashioned pre-war suit that had been patched at the elbows. She gave a brave smile. 'Gawd's good, he'll look after my Buster.'

Hattie heard a grunt from Ronnie and nudged him in the side. 'Leave off!' he said as she shushed him.

'What were you thinking of, going missing again!' she hissed. 'You frightened your mother and you had me running around like a blue-arsed fly looking for you!'

'Don't jaw him, Hattie. He come home, didn't he?' Lou kissed the top of Ronnie's fair head and he wriggled away.

'Gawd's not good,' he muttered stubbornly. 'If he was, it'd be Wardick up there, not my uncle!'

By the end of the very short trial Hattie found herself forced to agree with Ronnie. The judge took into account that it was Aiden's first offence and he was, he said, inclined to be lenient as the younger man had obviously been led astray by the other defendant. Aiden was given six months. When it came to Buster, the judge's voice grew stern. 'I cannot ignore the fact that the defendant, Mr Golding, has been before the court on a similar charge and was shown leniency. Furthermore, as a legally appointed guardian for his young nephew, he has shown a woeful disregard for that young man's moral welfare and a contempt for this court! The defendant will serve a term of no less than three years with hard labour.'

As the gavel hit the bench Hattie heard a cry from Lou, and Ronnie shot out of his seat. 'You bastard, you can't do that, my uncle's a good man!'

Levin the nailer uttered a series of loud expletives, mostly aimed at describing the judge's parentage, and the Alaska girls began weeping, saying it wasn't right. But within minutes the clerk had begun clearing the court. Hattie remained silent. She stood up and made sure she caught Buster's eye before he was led away. As he spotted her, his gentle eyes, drained of all their usual bright humour, were cold with terror. But he called out to her. 'Look after them, Hattie!'

And she nodded. 'I will, Buster!'

She tried to put on a brave face in front of Lou and Ronnie, but before she left the court buildings, she went to the toilets and was sick. She couldn't imagine how Buster would survive the hard labour. His hands were softer than hers, and so was his heart. It was a sombre walk back to Barnham Street, with Ronnie stomping ahead, hands thrust deep into his pockets, and Lou hanging on to her arm as if her legs would give way at any minute. When they got to the tenements, Ronnie peeled off to talk to the gang, who'd been waiting eagerly for news. Cries of disbelief rose up from the little group, and lanky Micky Driscoll smashed a fist into a wall. She waited anxiously for Ronnie, knowing from the kids' expressions that they would use this as an excuse for a raid on another gang, a useless protest against their own powerlessness. She walked over to them.

'I've got the key. I'll open up the flats early. Come in.' She saw Micky Driscoll hesitate until Ronnie nodded. 'Giss the key. You bring Mum. Best not leave her on her own, eh?'

She and Ribbons the twins made tea in the little kitchen and she found a bag of Peek Frean's broken biscuits, which she handed round. Lou was treated like an honoured guest, the girls proud to show off their housewifery skills, putting a pretty cloth on the table, laying out cups and a tin of condensed milk. The boys, leaning back in their chairs, eating biscuits, were discussing the court case as if they really were the men of the house. One of them tried to roll a cigarette, but Hattie took it from him. 'Just

'cause Anne's not here, don't think you can come the old acid!'
she said, silencing his protest.

'Has Anne got any solicitor friends could help my Buster?'
Lou asked suddenly.

Lou always surprised her. Sometimes the things that should
most send her spiralling into confusion actually seemed to sharpen
her thinking. It was no secret that Anne had connections to a
very different strata of society than the tenants of Barnham Street
Buildings. She'd persuaded many of her friends to volunteer at the
children's flats. There was the famous artist who gave drawing
lessons, the concert pianist who taught piano on the old upright,
the Shakespearean actor who helped them put on little plays and,
amongst the others, there was indeed a solicitor. But she doubted
anyone could help Buster now that the sentence had been passed.

'I'll ask her,' she promised Lou, reasoning that any hope would
be better than none at the moment, even if it came to nothing.

It was while Lou was distracted by Bonny, one half of the twins,
who needed the yellow ribbon in her hair retied, that Hattie took
Ronnie aside.

'Are you going to tell me where you went missing to? And
what was all that about going to Paradise? You must have known
it would frighten her!'

She was surprised that he was eager to confess.

'Lenny collared me a while back, up Southwark Bridge.'

'What did he want? Why didn't you tell me?'

'Shhh!' Ronnie said, casting a quick look at his mother. 'I'm
telling you now, ain't I?'

And when she'd heard his explanation, she smiled for the first
time that day.

As soon as Anne arrived and the mess was cleared up, Hattie
hurried to the Alaska, eager to relay Ronnie's news to Joe the
minute he left work. She waited, leaning against the red telephone
box outside the factory, for the hooter to signal the end of the day
shift. But her timing hadn't been the best, for just as the hooter

sounded she saw Crosbie get out of a black cab. He leaned in through the cabbie's window to pay, as someone else got out of the taxi. Doris Axmouth spotted her and smirked. She made a show of gathering a luxurious mink coat around her and raising its collar to flash the gold silk lining. Crosbie took her elbow and Doris swayed forward, self-conscious on new, overly high heels. Hattie didn't move or acknowledge them, but as they passed Doris muttered, 'You had your chance.'

She followed them with steely eyes, but just as they were about to mount the iron stairs to Chris's office, Crosbie turned back and strode towards her. 'Best you don't mention this to anyone, Hattie. Lenny's such a vicious thug – wouldn't want you putting yourself in harm's way. Very poor taste in men you've got, my darling.'

'And didn't I hit bottom with you.'

He grinned and flicked away his cigarette. 'Doris isn't complaining.' He gave a white-toothed smile and went to join Doris, who made sure Hattie heard her giggling as Crosbie slipped his arm round her.

Workers began streaming through the gates, and she searched the crowd for Joe. He was one of the last to emerge and, as he offered her his arm, she was glad that he'd not been there to witness her encounter with Crosbie.

'What's the news?' he asked.

'Buster got three years, Aiden six months.'

'Oh, I'm sorry, Hattie.'

'Anne's going to ask her solicitor friend if they could appeal…'

He put his arm round her and they walked to the bus stop. 'But listen, Joe, I did get some good news,' she said, smiling secretly.

'It must be very good, if it's brought a smile to your face today of all days. What is it?'

'Walk me to Cissie's. I promised to pop in, and I'll tell you on the way.'

They turned down Spa Road and she pointed across at the

bombsite. 'That's where I got my first introduction to Ronnie and the gang. Can't believe the council's still not cleared it.'

There were a few bombsites that had been cleared, with blocks of flats replacing the bombed terraces, but every street in Bermondsey had a similar tract of wasteland. She drew Joe closer as the fine stinging sleet started again. The tall, smoke-belching chimney of Young's glue factory split the steel-grey sky like a gargantuan tree trunk, and soon the bombsite was shining with inky wetness, highlighting jagged shards of broken windowpanes and twisted sharp-edged corrugated iron, which stood up like unnatural shrubs in a ruined garden. 'Wouldn't it be lovely if we could turn them all into gardens, maybe even playgrounds?' she mused.

Joe sighed. 'It'll be a long time coming. The council's got its hands full trying to build new homes for people as it is. Anyway, tell me this good news.'

'Well, you know Ronnie went missing and Lou thought he'd died and gone to heaven?'

Joe nodded. 'Because he was talking about Paradise? I take it he's not dead.'

'He was talking about going to Paradise Street nick!'

'Is he in trouble again?'

She shook her head. 'He had a revelation... in Southwark Cathedral of all places!'

Joe's eye's widened with shock. 'So, he went to confess to all his crimes?'

'Don't be stupid. This is Ronnie we're talking about. What happened was Lenny got hold of him, up near the Borough, told him that once he'd found another photographer he was going to make Ronnie pose for more photos. Lenny's after the rest of what he paid for.'

'What a lowlife! But the boy's not going?' Joe's face reddened with unusual rage.

'He is – on Saturday morning. And before you explode, he's already been to Paradise Street nick and told them all about it.

The police are going to wait till he's inside the Harpers' with the cameras set up – then they'll raid the place, catch Lenny red-handed!'

Joe stopped dead, threw back his head, and a slow smile spread across his face. 'Hattie, you know what this means? That little street raker's only going to save the squat! Ronnie'll save us all!'

They burst into laughter and hurried on, but Hattie looked back at the deserted bombsite, seeing once again Ronnie, with his fierce, wide-legged stance and his feral eyes, staring down at her as she lay wounded on the ground that first night. Back then, she could never have foreseen that one day she would grow fond of him, let alone be proud of him. He was the most unlikely saviour she could ever have imagined.

*

When Saturday came, the weather turned mild for December and Hattie woke to a day of scudding clouds that sometimes admitted a patch of rare bright sky. She hoped it would be a good omen for the day. She couldn't help feeling worried about Ronnie walking into the Harpers' den. The police had said they would have men in place early that day, some in plain clothes. An air of anticipation hung over the squat. The children were in that state of irrepressible excitement that seemed to possess them once Christmas was in sight, and the adults were trying not to hope too much that this might be the day they'd be free of Lenny. She attempted to keep herself occupied and distracted.

Her hut was packed with cardboard boxes full of plastic swans. Between each bird's crudely moulded wings, an oval cavity was designed to take a bar of Imperial Leather soap. It had been Cissie's idea for Hattie to take in home work. She'd had no income for weeks and Joe had been keeping her afloat, buying her food and fuel. But Christmas was a good time for home work, and she set about assembling the swans, inserting the soap, wrapping them in Cellophane, which had to be tied with a ribbon in a neat bow. Clara had come to help, bringing

Martha, who was snoring softly in her pram. After an hour of rhythmic, companionable work, Hattie's heart finally stopped beating loudly in her chest. She and Clara spoke in whispers.

'What time do you think the boys will be back?' Clara asked, for Alan and Joe had insisted on joining the police, reasoning that two more pairs of hands would be useful in catching all those Harpers as they slithered from the nest.

Hattie shrugged and tied the red bow deftly. The whole hut was full of the cloying scent of the soap – a luxury Christmas gift this year, with soap scarcer than sugar and spice for the Christmas puddings.

'I just hope it's soon. I wish I could be there to see Lenny's smile wiped off that vile mug of his.'

'I used to think that about Barry, but when I met him again it was all different, and I just felt sorry for him really.'

'I never felt sorry for Lenny. Do you think you'll ever see Barry again, when we get to Australia?'

'Suppose it depends if we decide to stay in Sydney.'

'Do you really think you'll want to stay in touch with him?'

Clara looked over to where Martha lay sleeping. 'It's hard to say no. He's asked to see Martha... Who knows, perhaps one day we'll even be able to sit in a room together and not remember how painful it all was.'

'When did you turn into a wise old bird? I can't say I ever want to sit down in a room with Lenny again. The nearest I want to be is when I go to see him in the dock!'

They were laughing when the door of the hut opened, and Hattie spun round with a smile on her face, expecting to see Joe and Alan. But it wasn't them. It was Ronnie.

'Hide me, Hattie, hide me! It's all gone wrong. Lenny's comin' after me!' He hurled himself across the room, scattering swans and skidding on Imperial Leather soap until he was in her arms.

'Where's Joe and Alan?'

'Don't know. Something tipped Lenny off, he scurfed me down the garden. Dragged me under a fence panel and we was away before the police could even get in the house. But they set the dogs after him. I made a run for it and Lenny's shot the bleedin' dogs! Oh, Hattie, I'm sorry, he's followed me here…'

He was breathless with fear and trembling, and now the noise had woken Martha. She let out a loud wail. Clara was halfway to the pram when the door burst open. Lenny kicked it shut behind him. Hattie froze, pulling Ronnie closer into her arms, as if that could hide him. Clara sprang towards Martha.

'Shut her up!' Lenny ordered, pointing to the pram.

A white-faced Clara lifted Martha in her blanket and swaddled her close to her chest. Lenny lunged forward to grab Ronnie from Hattie, shoving him on to the floor in the centre of the room.

'Let Clara and the baby go, Len,' Hattie said.

'What, so she can go and blab? What d'ya take me for, my dozy brother!'

'She won't say anything! If you keep them here, the baby will be screaming the place down in a few minutes.'

Lenny reached into his jacket pocket. The gun shook in his hand, which she noticed was covered in blood. The arm of his pale blue suit was ripped and blood was oozing through it. Lenny saw her gaze resting on the blood.

'Police dog bit a chunk out of me,' he said, and sounded almost like a whining child.

'Don't expect any sympathy from me!' She laughed at him and he took a step forward, slashing her across the cheek with the gun barrel. Clara screamed and set Martha off crying again. Now Ronnie picked himself up and frowned at her furiously. 'Shut up, Hattie,' he said.

Lenny smirked. 'Listen to your little soldier boy, Hattie. Get up!'

As she stood, he grabbed her arm, flinging her towards the door. 'We're going for a little walk.' He prodded her chest with the gun. 'I warned you it was a bad idea coming back, didn't I, Hattie?' He prodded again, harder, so that she flinched. 'I told you to piss off, didn't I?' This time as the gun slammed into her ribs, Ronnie charged like a little bull, toppling Lenny amongst the swan soap dishes and red ribbons. 'Run!' he roared, and all three of them plunged out of the hut. Hattie pushed Clara out first, and she ran towards the NAAFI, clutching Martha, whose screams ripped the air. As they tumbled out after Clara, Lenny recovered just in time to catch Ronnie by the ankle, toppling him to the floor.

'Go on, leave me, Hattie! Leg it!' he cried.

She couldn't. She grabbed his hand, but Lenny was on him and the gun was touching his temple. 'This is all your fault. You Bolshie bitch, you can never do as you're told, can you?'

He thrust the gun in her face and, holding firmly to Ronnie with the other hand, he herded them out of the hut and on to the Oval. He kept Hattie ahead of them, urging her on with a tap of the gun in her back. Several of the squatters, who'd been going about their normal business, attempted to follow, but Hattie screamed, 'He's got a gun, keep away!'

Lenny kept up a steady trot, but she could hear his laboured breath and could only hope that blood loss from his wound would slow him long enough to allow the police to track him here. She knew that once they'd left the park, Lenny could take them to any number of safe houses dotted around the borough. The police would never find them, not till their bodies washed up on Tower Bridge beach, for she hadn't a doubt that Lenny's violent side had grown to eclipse anything good in him. He pushed her forward once more and she tripped, sprawling headlong on to the grass. It was as Lenny stooped to pick her up that Ronnie pounced, leaping on to his back, trying to wrestle him to the ground. She heard the bang as the gun went off, smelled the bitter sulphur, and waited to feel the bullet rip through her.

A scream escaped her lips. But as she looked up, it wasn't Lenny's face she saw but Ronnie's. 'He's down, shot himself in the leg!' Ronnie tugged at her arm.

Lenny lay on the grass beside her. Blood was seeping through a burn hole in his pale blue trousers, the gun still in his hand. But then she heard him groan and he began to stir.

She sprang up and grabbed Ronnie's hand. 'Quick, we've got to get away from him!'

Together they sprinted towards the Jamaica Road gates, and as the familiar wedge-shaped structures of the shelters came into view. Ronnie veered to one side. 'Follow me, Hattie! I know where we'll be safe.'

In unthinking terror she followed him to the nearest shelter entrance. He was already scrabbling for the hidden padlock key and they both stumbled inside and down the steps into the concrete cavern beneath the park. All she could see was blackness and she felt around like a blind woman till she'd found Ronnie's hand.

He grabbed the candle from its hiding place and now struck a match. 'He won't find us down here. It's only us kids who know you can even get in!'

She sniffed the air. The lingering smell of Pissy Pants reminded her there was someone else who knew of this place. 'What if Johnny's told Lenny about it?' She saw Ronnie blanch in the guttering candlelight.

'He don't speak to Lenny much.' He hesitated. 'Better go further in, though.'

And she followed him down the long line of double bunks, their shadows rippling on the vaulted ceiling like the ghosts of those who'd once sheltered here. It was as they neared the far end that she heard the sound of scuffling coming from the entrance.

'Put it out,' she whispered, and heard the hiss as Ronnie pinched out the candle flame. They hunkered down. Hattie's limbs trembled so much, she feared they must be making some sort of noise, and Ronnie gripped her hand so tightly that her fingers throbbed. For an instant, Hattie hoped it might be Johnny Harper – the stink down here was enough to let her know he still used it as a haven. But then the footsteps got louder, with the click of a leather sole on stone, followed by the scrape of a foot being dragged along the floor. She heard the snap of a lighter and smelled petrol. The little dancing flame held beneath Lenny's face seemed to distort his puckish features, the neat ears elongated to points, the small nose bent to a hook, the delicate chin splayed. 'Rats in a trap? Come out, come out, wherever you are…' His voice sounded tight with pain and she heard a gasp at every footstep. 'Cat's coming… I can hear your snotty breathing, Ronald, you dirty little tyke. Use your hanky.' Lenny cackled like a schoolboy and Hattie was wondering if now was the time to rush at him, when another flame joined that of the cigarette lighter. Someone had silently lit the paraffin lamp.

'Johnny boy!' Lenny's voice sounded pleased. 'Give me the lamp.'

'Sod me, it's Pissy Pants!' Ronnie hissed.

Johnny Harper held the lamp aloft in his massive hand, his squat-headed, broad features contorted by fury. Suddenly he rushed at Lenny like a troglodyte defending his cave. 'Ge'rout, ge'rout!' he shouted at his brother. 'Leav'em lone!'

She saw the shock on Lenny's face as his brother charged with all his force. Lenny screamed as the weight of his thicker-boned brother pinned him to the floor. And she heard him pleading. 'Johnny boy, it's Lenny, your brother, mate. What you doing, you dozy sod?'

But Johnny straddled Lenny and banged on his chest like a drum, and the words she heard were: 'No bruvver! You burned my girl, you burned my baby! No bruvver!'

'Let's get out of here,' Ronnie said and, still holding hands, they crawled together towards the side tunnel leading off from the main shelter. 'Down here,' he said, 'before Lenny shoots the poor bugger.'

'But we'll only be trapped! Let's go towards the entrance!'

Ronnie ignored her, crawling ahead.

'Where does it lead?'

'You'll see!'

And then she heard the gunshot.

## 25

## *Requiem*

### *December 1948–January 1949*

Hattie heard the crack, then a high-pitched pinging sound, like the whine of a wasp. The sting was like burning liquid fire piercing her back, and then the darkness of the tunnel misted over with red as her eyes closed. She became aware of hands shaking her and resisting them; she only wanted to stay asleep. A slap across her cheek finally roused her.

'Help me, Hattie. I can't carry you!' It was Ronnie's voice.

She felt herself dragged like a sack of coal into the side tunnel, and in an excruciating instant realized what had happened. The bullet hadn't hit Johnny. It had bounced off the cavernous ceiling, finding her. And she knew that if she wanted to live, she had to move. But the pain was worse than a hot poker being driven into her flesh, and she stifled a scream as she began to drag herself along the narrow tunnel. There was no light at the end of it. She didn't know where it would take her. She had to trust Ronnie – that he knew where he was going, that he knew better than she how to save them. Inch by agonizing inch, they followed the tunnel. At one point Ronnie stopped, hesitating between two forks. She heard him muttering to himself. 'That way? No, that's the bone yard. We go this way,' he said decisively, and tugged her again, jolting her back into the world of pain. Soon they came to another junction where two tunnels joined, but this time Ronnie paused for only a second before following the fork which bent round to the right. As they followed the bend, she thought she saw a distant play of light on encrusted walls. But every sense was alert to what was behind her as she repeatedly looked back and strained to hear.

'Is he coming?' she whispered hoarsely.

Ronnie didn't answer immediately. He was intent on half-pulling her along, his feet scrabbling for purchase on the slimy algae-covered floor of the tunnel. She knew she must be hallucinating when he finally answered. 'I hope so.'

Finally, he stopped and let her go, so that she slumped against the tunnel wall, closing her eyes. Ronnie was grunting and swearing, and she heard the scrape of metal on stone, then from behind closed lids she was aware of a glow. She opened her eyes to what felt like an explosion of light. The light was made of pain and she put up a hand to block out what appeared to be the late evening sun, glancing down through a manhole cover. Ronnie's body disappeared and then his legs, as he clambered out of the manhole. Then he was reaching down for her. 'Come on, Hattie, nearly there. Hold on tight!'

She gripped his hand and with an effort that made her legs tremble she got to her feet, allowing the agony to spur her upwards to the light. He grasped her forearms and then pulled her free of the tunnel. Out in the open air, feeling cobbles beneath her back, she found herself staring up at the grim, drunken walls of an ancient building with bars at every window.

'Where am I, Ron?' she asked.

He looked down at her and his smile had a seraphic sweetness about it. 'You're in Paradise, miss.'

And as she gave herself up to the darkness, there was comfort in knowing that she had been right all along. She'd always known that coming back to Bermondsey would be the death of her.

*

The two coppers who'd been returning from their beat found Hattie's bloodied body spread-eagled on the cobbled courtyard of Paradise Street Police Station. Ronnie kneeled beside her, sobbing and useless, begging Hattie to wake up. When he saw the two bobbies he leaped to his feet. He'd never been so happy to see the coppers turn up.

'I think he's killed her!' he said, and one of the policemen pushed him to one side, kneeling to take Hattie's pulse, while the other ran into the station for help. Ronnie watched as she was stretchered into the station, but he wasn't allowed to follow. They held him, demanding to know how he'd got into the locked courtyard. But neither of the coppers seemed to understand what he was telling them.

'It's a tunnel, it goes all the way to Southwark Park bomb shelter!' he said, pointing down the manhole. 'Don't you know about it?'

They were looking at him as if he was an imbecile. 'It's *your* nick. You should know there's a tunnel under it, you clots!'

One of the constables gave him a sharp slap on the back of his head. 'Less of your lip. Did you climb over them?' one of the bobbies asked, pointing to the heavy double gates which opened from the courtyard into Cathay Street.

Ronnie shook his head and shouted, 'Oh yeah, and I lugged Hattie over 'em as well. I'm telling you we came up from that hole, and you've got to get down there before he gets away!' He was shouting at them now.

'Calm down, son,' the other older constable said. 'You're not in no trouble – yet. Just tell us the truth.'

'I am!' he yelled. 'Don't you know about the stake-out at the Harpers? Come down there with me yourself if you want to catch Lenny Harper!'

The two policemen exchanged looks, and the younger one said, 'Lenny Harper? Sod me, I'll get the inspector.'

Soon the courtyard was filled with a half a dozen policemen. Ronnie recognized the inspector immediately. He was the genius who had let Lenny escape.

'Thank God you're all right, son,' he said, patting Ronnie's back as if they were old pals, which they weren't. 'We've had men looking all over Bermondsey for you and Lenny! Where did he take you?'

Ronnie, jumping up and down with frustration, shrugged off the inspector's hand. He felt he might need to punch someone if they didn't listen to him soon. He tried to slow down and speak clearly. 'He's down *there* – at the end of the *tunnel*. It goes into the bomb shelter in Southwark Park. Lenny chased me and Hattie into it, but Pissy Pants belted him, and Hattie got shot…' Then, to his great shame, he started to blub like a baby. 'And I think she's dead, but no one'll tell me nothing…'

The inspector put an arm round him. 'Steady on, son. Your friend's being given the once over by the station doctor. Last I saw, she wasn't dead.'

'Not dead?'

'No.'

Ronnie drew his cuff across his eyes, but he couldn't stem the flow. The inspector gave him a hanky. 'You've been brave enough for one day, young man. You go back in the nick with my constable and leave Lenny Harper to us, OK.'

Reluctantly he agreed. It was all useless anyway. Lenny would be long gone by the time these cloth heads found their way to the shelter. He watched the inspector prepare to lower himself into the manhole. He'd be down there for hours, silly sod, trying to find the right tunnel. One would take them to the old workhouse graveyard at St Olave's, another was a circuitous dead end, another led back down to the riverbank, and the one that he'd exited in the courtyard led to the bomb shelter.

'Hold on!' he called, running back. 'Let me show you the way. You'll be running after your own arses all day down there.' The inspector was about to refuse, then held up his hands. 'Get yourself down here. You can lead the way, but when I say get behind me, do as you're told.'

Ronnie nodded. He only hoped this lot had a gun between them – if Lenny was still there, they'd be needing it.

He crouched low and, creeping forward, came to the first fork, where he sniffed the air. A breeze brushed his face: it was full of the dank river smell, sewage, algae and mud. He followed the left-hand bend and didn't stop till he reached the next junction. It was like having an army of hobnail-booted ants following him, but it was easy for him. He was much smaller than the universally tall coppers and it was an uncomfortable squeeze for them. He could only think that in the olden times, when the grave robbers used these tunnels, men must have been much shorter. He paused again to get his bearings. 'Don't tell me you're lost?' the inspector hissed. 'Is it this way? That's the direction of the park.'

'No, no. Not that way. It leads to the old workhouse grave-yard. Follow me.' And he was off. Certain now he was on the right track, certain there were no other diversions, he soon left the police behind. He felt a tug, as the inspector grabbed his ankle. 'That's far enough!' he whispered.

There was a light ahead.

'Johnny's got a paraffin lamp in the shelter,' Ronnie whispered, as the inspector shoved in front of him.

'You stay back now, son. Keep out of our way.'

He squashed himself against the tunnel wall, letting the bobbies overtake him. It wasn't until they had all disappeared into the huge bomb shelter that he followed, sticking close to the rows of wooden bunks lining the walls.

A low wailing noise came from the direction of the light. It sent shivers up Ronnie's spine. What if it was the ghost of one of them robbed bodies come down the tunnel? He crept forward so that he was hiding directly behind the broad, blue-clothed back of the biggest copper, and then he stuck his head out. The sound was coming from Pissy Pants, who was sitting on the floor surrounded by wads of fivers and tenners.

'Woohoo, woohoo!' Johnny Harper wept as he tore up the notes and flung them into the air. 'Woohooo, nobruvver's dead'n gone. Woohoo, dead'n'gone!'

Ronnie stepped forward and crouched beside him, fighting off the inspector's attempts to stop him. 'He's me friend!' he said, and put his arm round Johnny's shoulders. It was then that he saw Lenny, lying beside Johnny, eyes wide open and almost half buried in ripped-up white fivers, brown oners and mauve tenners. Johnny continued to tear them up and – like flower petals – scattered his offerings to the dead brother who had always protected him. He half sang his requiem. 'Nobruvver, dead'n'gone, he burned my girl, he burned my baby. Woohoo.'

Ronnie gently prised the wad of money from Johnny's hands. 'What happened to Lenny?' he asked.

'Johnny,' Pissy Pants replied.

★ ★ ★

Hattie was struggling with her blouse buttons. 'I need to find out what's happening. I'm not staying here!'

The police doctor fixed her with a look that was meant to intimidate. 'Young woman, I don't advise it. I have just removed a bullet from a muscle in your back. You risk tearing it open, infection—'

'It's a flesh wound, Doctor! Believe me, I've had worse than this with shrapnel from our own ack-ack guns! Look at me, I'm covered in scars.' And she showed him her forearms, where there were indeed several jagged scars from poorly sewn-up shrapnel wounds. 'Field dressings did fine then. I'm sure you've bandaged me up nice and tight.' She took a deep breath and regretted it, for the stitches he'd put in pulled and stung as if the needle was still stuck in there.

The doctor sighed and then gave a resigned smile. 'Ex-gunner, eh? Where are the delicate flowers of my youth? You ATS girls are a different breed, I'm afraid. Hard as nails!'

She smiled, knowing she'd got her own way. 'I'll take that as a compliment, Doctor.'

'I was a medic in the artillery. Take it from me, it's true! All right, young lady, just don't go anywhere until I've given you some painkillers.'

Soon he was back with a bottle of pills and an outsize woman's jacket. 'Unclaimed lost property,' he said, draping it over her shoulders. It swamped her. 'I can see why it's unclaimed!' she said. 'But thanks anyway. Do you know what happened to the young boy?'

'All I can tell you is that I saw him take our inspector back down the manhole.' He pointed out to the courtyard, where there was now no sign of activity. 'Just don't tell anyone I told you!' he said, and she gave him a smart salute and slipped out of the police station without challenge.

The station was an ancient building on the corner of Paradise Street and Cathay Street. It was out of character with the mean buildings that surrounded it, which were largely warehouses interspersed with crumbling terraced houses, along with a pub and an old mission hall. Once the house of a surgeon who'd employed body snatchers to bring him the corpses of paupers buried at St Olave's Workhouse, it was now a dilapidated ghost of its former imposing self. The rusted wrought-iron arch above the door held a cracked lantern and all the sash windows were rotting. She descended the front stone steps, which had been hollowed out by the footsteps of thousands of hopeful or despairing souls who had entered there in search of healing or justice. She looked both ways along Cathay Street, on the off chance Lenny might be hanging about. Its cobbles were running with water from a blocked drain, and only a little boy was visible, playing with a paper boat in the gutter outside one of the narrow, shuttered houses. Beyond was the Angel pub and the river, riding high. She could just see the red sail of a Thames barge as it made its way swiftly downstream. She doubted Lenny would be anywhere in the vicinity now, but the inspector had thought it worth going back to the park shelter and that was where she decided to go. She lifted the large jacket up around her ears and headed away from the river. The pills had dulled her pain, but even the short walk to the park entrance left her breathing heavily and flinching at every step.

She approached the shelter cautiously. The heavy iron door

was wide open and she descended, shivering as she relived their flight of just a few hours earlier. Light spilled up the stairs and she heard an inarticulate wailing. She could make out no words, but the tone was one of unmistakable grief. No one saw her approach, but what she saw by the light of the paraffin lamp made her recoil. Lenny lay on the floor, surrounded by piles of money, his quick, light frame stilled and stiff with death. It took her by surprise that she felt a surge of grief, but perhaps it was only the keening sound coming from Johnny Harper that had infected her. It was crazy to be sorry, and yet there had been something that once made her care about him, and she hadn't wanted him dead. A constable tried to prevent her from approaching, but Ronnie had spotted her.

'She's with me. Let her in. Hattie! You all right?' He left Johnny's side and ran to her.

'What happened?'

The inspector stood, hands in his pockets, surveying Lenny's body. He looked up at the sound of her voice. 'What are you doing here?' he asked sharply. 'I'll have to ask you to leave.'

Ronnie clung to her. 'No, she's me guardian,' he said fiercely, which seemed to satisfy the inspector.

'It looks like Lenny's had a heart attack. Not sure of the cause, but Johnny seems to think it's his fault.'

'No, it's not his fault. Lenny had a bad heart,' Hattie said, a dullness around her own.

'Oh!' the inspector said, suspicious of anyone with intimate knowledge of the Harpers. 'Friend of yours, was he?'

She shook her head. 'Not a friend. I knew him once, a long, long time ago.'

The police allowed them to go and, with Ronnie supporting her, they walked back to the camp. It seemed a long way to Hattie, up the avenue of battered trees, round the bombed bandstand, past the rose garden and the ruined boating lake, each step an increasingly painful effort. When the huddled group of huts came into view it seemed such a poor patch of land to have been fighting over, and yet it was all they had to call home, so she supposed it must have been worth it. She was waiting to feel relief, but there was only a sense of heaviness. It seemed that no matter how many wars you fought and won, there was always another one waiting in the wings.

They were halfway across the Oval when she saw Joe running towards her, his normal reserve thrown to the winds. He called her name when he was still yards off, and then caught her up in his arms so that she cried out in pain.

'Sorry, sorry! What have I done?' he asked, hastily putting her down.

'Don't fuss. It's just a little bit of a bullet wound. How did you know I was coming – did you hear the bells from the police cars?'

Joe paled and looked as if he might be sick. 'No! I've been pulling my hair out looking for you. A bullet wound? My God, Hattie, what's happened, have the police got Lenny?'

She hesitated. 'Yes, in a way. They're at the bomb shelter with him now.'

Joe ran his hands through his hair. 'Ronnie!' He clasped the boy to him. 'We were meant to be protecting you! I'm sorry, son.'

Ronnie gave him an awkward pat on the back. 'What a cock-up, eh, Joe? But it weren't your fault,' Ronnie said, disentangling himself.

'I don't understand – why was Lenny in the bomb shelter?' Joe asked Hattie.

'I'll tell you all about it on the way, but now I just need to see Clara and then get Ronnie home.'

'I can get home on me own. I ain't a kid!' Ronnie said with a scowl.

And looking at his weather-worn, lean-cheeked face, Hattie had to admit it was hard to believe he was just twelve.

'You're right, Ron,' Joe said. 'You've done better than all us men today. Thanks for saving my Hattie.'

Ronnie smiled. 'She's mine too. You'll have to share her with me!'

They were laughing as they arrived at Joe's hut, where Alan and Clara had been waiting anxiously for news.

'I'm glad you're laughing – we haven't been! We've been going mad here, haven't we, Al? Thank gawd you're safe!' said Clara, throwing her arms round Hattie.

'We can thank Ronnie for that,' Hattie said, explaining what had happened.

Martha trotted over to her, but halfway across the room decided Ronnie was the more interesting prospect and veered towards him. He lifted her up and said, 'It's not me you've got to thank. It's this little girl. Poor old Pissy Pants only turned on Lenny 'cause he loves you, don't he?' he said to Martha, as he hoisted her up and planted a kiss on her cheek. 'Oh, and you too, Clara,' he added, causing her to blush. 'Worst thing Lenny ever done was set fire to you two.'

'So, do you think Pissy Pants killed Lenny?' Alan asked.

'Hattie says he had a bad heart, and the police think it was an accident,' Ronnie said doubtfully. 'But I saw Pissy Pants chargin' Lenny…'

'It was the shock,' Hattie said, knowing it was true without any proof. 'The shock of Johnny turning on him. He was the only one Lenny ever loved.'

Joe gave her a questioning look, from under the stray lock of hair.

'And I think Johnny was the only one ever really loved him,' she said, answering his unspoken question. 'Everyone else was just scared of him, even his mother.'

Joe put an arm round her. 'Well, he won't be troubling her, or us, ever again. Shall we go and tell the others?'

They gathered the squatters in the NAAFI and told the events of the day. There were cheers when people realized that their homes were safe from Lenny and his arson attacks, and there was universal praise for Ronnie's bravery. Hattie stood to one side, reflecting on how Ronnie had gone from a reviled truant and petty thief to an unlikely hero. But the knife-edge between the two was precarious. He'd chosen not to be lured back into the dark by Lenny. How much that was due to the children's flats and the time she'd spent with him, she wasn't certain, but she found herself hoping it had made the difference. And if the children's flats were forced to close? What then? She'd be in Australia, Buster banged up, and Lou couldn't steer her own way down an unlit street, let alone guide Ronnie away from the dark.

After the meeting, Joc borrowed Alan's car and drove them back to Barnham Street. Lou was pleased to see Ronnie with Hattie and Joe as she opened the flat door, even though it was obvious she hadn't noticed that Ronnie had been gone all day.

'Come in! I've made me fairy cakes and I've got real milk, so I'm ready to entertain guests!' She seemed almost perky.

'Go and wash your hands, boy,' she said, giving Ronnie a rare instruction and a kiss on the head. The house looked neat. True, there was little enough of furnishings or belongings to be tidied away, but the kitchen didn't smell of mouldy food, the water bucket was filled and the few bits of crockery Lou owned were stacked neatly on a kitchen shelf. The newspaper that usually covered the table had been replaced by a cloth. It lightened Hattie's heart that Lou was acting like a proper mother, or what she imagined that might be, for Cissie could never be described as a proper mother.

'You three had a nice time today? Has he been making himself a nuisance round your squat?' Lou asked, pouring tea and handing out the minute fairy cakes which must have taken up four weeks' fat ration. She'd also cut several chunky slices of the grey national loaf, spreading them with jam.

'Ronnie's been... a real help today,' Hattie answered truthfully, for they'd already agreed it might be better to spare Lou the details of Ronnie's dangerous day.

They stayed for the rest of the evening. Lou was lucid, and even hopeful that they would get Buster out of prison. 'Anne promised she'd come to see me this afternoon. She's a good 'un, don't break her promises,' Lou said, proud of a visit from the well-spoken lady with important contacts. 'That's why I'm all tidy, tell you the truth. Anyway, she's spoke to her solicitor friend and he's said it's a disgrace – Buster's sentence. He's taking on Buster's case, and if he can't get him off he'll get him less time. And the man's not charging a penny for it!' Lou put down the cracked cup and drew a tattered handkerchief from her pinafore pocket. 'Gawd's good, Hattie,' she said, dabbing the corners of her eyes. 'Gawd's good.'

* * *

It wasn't until the end of January that Hattie could go back to helping at the children's flats. Although she'd made light of her bullet wound, she'd had to admit that she wasn't up to the rigours of controlling the Barnham Street kids, and nor had she any appetite for dancing. It reminded her too much of Buster, who, in spite of the efforts of Anne's solicitor friend, remained locked up. But she knew that Anne needed her, and Joe, so one evening after they'd been visiting Ronnie and Lou, they paid a visit to the children's flats, which were just winding up for the night.

Anne was herding the kids towards the door. Sometimes it was hard to persuade them to return to the confines of their over-crowded bedrooms. Although they encouraged parents to collect their children rather than risk them slipping off into the night for a couple more hours of probably illegal entertainment, this had never taken off. Joe and Hattie stood back as a stream of kids jostled out into the courtyard. It always amazed her how many the small flats could hold.

'G'night, miss!' they called out to Anne, and then, seeing Hattie, 'Hello, miss! Where ya bin?', before charging out into the courtyard, tonight an evil-smelling paddling pool, the result of a burst downpipe. The kids whooped and splashed, till someone shouted for them to cork it and threw a bucket of water on their heads, which not surprisingly had the opposite effect.

'Quickly, come in!' Anne dragged them into the flat and shut the door with an audible sigh. She slumped down on to the nearest chair, looking exhausted.

'I can't do anything about them when they leave here,' she said apologetically and then paused. 'Nor when *I* leave here, I'm afraid.' Her face, which was invariably brightened by a broad smile, crumpled and she hid her face in her hands.

'Oh, Anne, you're not leaving, are you?' Hattie said, drawing up a chair beside her. 'You can't!'

'I don't want to, but we really have run out of money. We can't pay the rent or my wages come to that. The LCC simply won't renew our funding and the borough's spending all its money on building flats, never mind that the kids living in them have nowhere to play!' she said, preaching to the converted.

'But we've drummed up money before.'

Anne shook her head. 'I'm worn out with it. You two have been such a boon, but none of the charities think this idea is worth the money…'

She choked back tears and Hattie thought of Ronnie, just one among many, who would lose an anchor if the flats closed.

Joe had been listening thoughtfully, but now he spoke up. 'We won a big victory before Christmas, Anne,' he told her. 'We beat a bully boy who wanted to take over the squat, and we succeeded because Ronnie, one of your boys, decided to help us rather than the villains. It's the kids that'll get us out of the mess we've made. You can't give up.'

Hattie had never heard him speak so passionately about the project. She thought he had only ever come along to be with her for a few hours; she'd never realized he'd been converted.

Anne drew in a deep breath. 'This morning I was on the telephone for half an hour, trying to persuade a banker friend in the City to give us a few hundred pounds. He wouldn't. One of the richest people I know, sits in an office not a mile from here, and won't give two hundred pounds to help some of the poorest. I haven't given up, Joe, but the world has.'

# 26

# Flower of Life

The children's flats were closing down. Anne had not been able to face giving the children the bad news and, always hopeful that some wealthy friend or council official with a conscience would step in, she'd delayed and delayed. But one night, in early spring, the doors of the children's flats remained closed. Ronnie told Hattie there had been a near riot when the kids turned up for an evening session and nobody was there. A crowd of them banged and kicked the doors of the two flats, till eventually they dispersed in search of other entertainment: they'd decided a fight with the Vine Street gang would be a good choice. The second time the flats remained closed, bewilderment turned to fury. Windows were smashed. Disappointed children reverted to an earlier, fiercer version of themselves and broke in, redecorating the flat with the meagre ration of flour and fat and sugar meant for baking class, with a smattering of powder paints for icing on the cake.

'Well, I hope you didn't join in?' Hattie asked Ronnie sternly.

''Course not, what's the point? It's only us'll suffer. But what's going on, Hattie, and why ain't miss opening up any more?'

'If I tell you, promise me you won't say anything?'

Ronnie agreed and Hattie went on. 'Well, Anne thought it'd be easier on everyone if she stopped opening one or two nights a week, so you'd get used to it.'

'Get used to what?'

'The flats not being there any more.'

'Why?' he asked innocently. 'Have we got to move somewhere bigger?'

His expression was one of hope – which she would have to dash. It had been fruitless to try easing the kids into their loss.

'The flats have got to close. There's no money left to keep them running.'

'But I thought the council paid for 'em!'

Hattie shook her head. 'We get a small grant, but not enough to pay rent, Anne's wages and to buy all the craft materials and other stuff.'

'OK, how much do we need?'

'Five hundred to keep us going another year.'

'That's a lot of bunce!' he said thoughtfully, and then brightened. 'Bombsites are free!'

'Maybe, but there's nothing to do on bombsites but smash things up. The point is, at the flats you can learn to build things, do crafts and dancing and chess. You decorate the places and you make the rules. *And* you don't have other gangs muscling in, taking your place away.'

'True. But, Hattie, I think we should tell the other kids. It's not fair letting them think they've got something when they ain't.'

\*

Ronnie had been right, and she resolved to persuade Anne of his wisdom as soon as she got the chance. A few days after her conversation with Ronnie, she got up early and left the squat before Joe and the others were stirring. Hattie arrived at Anne's home along with the milkman, who swung his crate as he walked, clinking bottles to wake those still snoozing. Bermondsey Street where Anne lived had an early morning quietness about it. Tulls, the printing works, had not even started up its clattering Victorian presses, and the trains steaming towards London Bridge Station hadn't yet reached their rush-hour volume. The ancient narrow house, which Anne loaned from the church, was usually full of students or volunteers, and sometimes the Barnham Street kids, who came knocking at all hours, hoping for cakes or baked potatoes. But this morning it had a deserted feel about it, and even the blue window boxes were empty of their usual flowers. After getting no answer to her knock, Hattie began to wonder if Anne had simply decided to leave without saying goodbye. She'd been so heartbroken about the flats closing that it wouldn't have come as a surprise. Hattie was reminded of a gunner sergeant she'd once dumped, who'd been so devastated he'd asked for a transfer to the Far East. Sometimes disappointment was best starved of all reminders.

It was after the third knock, when Hattie was about to leave, that the door was opened.

'How did you *know*?' Anne asked, throwing the door wide open and beckoning her inside.

'Know what – that you're planning to do a runner?'

Hattie followed her up to the first-floor sitting room. She had been there a couple of times for planning sessions and once for Sunday dinner. It had obviously been done up on a budget, with orange-crate shelves and second-hand furniture, though there were some expensive-looking paintings on the wall, which had been loaned by Anne's artist friend. Once in the sitting room, Anne turned to her with the familiar beaming smile. Her fresh face was clear of all the anxiety that had clouded it lately, and Hattie felt a ripple of anger that she wasn't suffering more – that she could just walk away and leave the kids with a smile. But a small voice accused Hattie too. Wasn't she planning to do the same? When Anne threw her arms round her, Hattie extricated herself quickly.

'Were you planning to leave without saying goodbye to the kids?' she asked, her voice betraying her irritation.

'But, Hattie, I'm *not* going at all! I thought somehow you'd already found out.'

Seeing her confusion, Anne pushed Hattie down on to the ragged sofa.

'Sit! You'll need to be sitting down for this. We've had a donation, and it's all the money we need, and more, to keep us running for another year. The flats won't have to close!'

She was aware of staring with her mouth open. It was rude, but the news was too good, and to say anything might prompt Anne to explain that she'd misunderstood. Anne looked back, triumphant, and eventually Hattie ventured, 'Not close?'

Anne laughed, shaking her head.

Now Hattie allowed all her forbidden delight to surface and she laughed back. 'But who is it from?'

'Anonymous benefactor,' Anne said, her eyes wide with wonderment at their good fortune. 'It just *appeared* – all in cash, piles of it, stuffed through the letterbox! The thing is, I had to take it straight to the bank. I couldn't possibly keep it in the house. As it was, the cashier gave me a very funny look when I handed it over.'

'Why?'

'Those bank notes absolutely reeked!'

Hattie got a sinking feeling. 'What of?'

Anne thought for a moment. 'We had a dog once, would slink off to odd corners to pee on the carpet. The money smelled exactly like that!'

'Really? Perhaps the donor had a dog too?' Hattie said, a hollow feeling replacing her short-lived happiness.

They spent the next hour discussing the best way to use the windfall, and one of Anne's suggestions came as a surprise.

'I want to put you in charge of a new venture I've had in mind for quite a while. Ever since you told me how your kids at the squat thrive in the open spaces of the park, I've thought we should do something outdoors, but I don't know what. Have a think about it?'

'You want me in charge? But you know I'll be going to Australia?'

Anne shrugged. 'We're only ever going to have funding for a year at a time, so we'll do what we can while the money lasts. Besides, if it works, you can hand it over.'

Hattie agreed, allowing herself a surge of excitement for what might be possible. She walked along Bermondsey Street and took a shortcut across the bomb-flattened Larnaca and Stanworth Streets, picking her way carefully over mounds of bricks and stones, towards Abbey Street. She thought of the buried nave of the old medieval abbey beneath her feet. So little changed in Bermondsey. It was ruin upon ruin, and somehow, life went onatop of it all, each generation shoring the ruins of the past with fragments of new dreams. This was the exact route she'd taken on her first night back in Bermondsey, and in that time nothing had been rebuilt. In fact, more destruction had been visited upon the place by bored kids. She stood stock-still, in the middle of the razed streets, and in an instant, the plan came to her.

* * *

She looked up at the sad-eyed seal carved into the entrance arch while she waited for the Alaska gates to open. As they were swung wide, the entire width of the yard was jammed with workers hurrying to clock on for the early morning shift. Hattie had returned to the Alaska after her wound had healed. Production was up, they were now on a four-day week and in need of skilled workers, so that even Chris Harper hadn't been able to give the factory manager a good reason not to re-employ her. She jostled shoulder to shoulder with the others, as they tried to get to the clocking-on machine, but the line came to an abrupt halt.

'Come on! You're moving slower than my old mum, and she never gets out the effin bed!' She looked over her shoulder to see Levin the nailer grinning at her.

'It's Lal's fault!' Maisie shouted back at him, and Hattie saw Lal struggling with the machine handle, which appeared to be stuck.

'Hold your horses, Levin. I can't get the bloody thing up!' Lal said.

'That's just what my old woman says about me!' Levin said, causing a ripple of laughter along the queue.

'Don't be filthy, Levin!' Lal said, struggling. Hattie was leaning forward to help her with the brass handle on the clock when someone shoved her forcefully in the back.

'Out the way, let me see it. Trust it to be you sodding things up, you stupid bitch.' Chris Harper elbowed her out of the queue, and she staggered on the cobbles. She saw Levin reach his long arm over the head of another nailer and grab Chris by the collar of his foreman's blue overall. 'Oi, oi. Watch your language... And you can keep yer bleedin' hands to yourself, Harper.' Levin's fingers curled like gnarled old tree branches into the tendons of Chris's neck, and Hattie saw the foreman cringe.

Lal managed to pull the clock handle and the queue began moving again, quickly syphoning through into the yard and up the iron staircases that zigzagged up the various factory buildings. Chris rubbed his neck.

'You watch yourself, Levin,' he said. But his tone held little conviction, for there wasn't a faster or surer nailer in the factory than Levin, and they couldn't afford to lose him. So instead, Chris aimed his venom at her and, as she tried to scoot round him, he muttered, 'Our Lenny's dead and Johnny's gone back in the nuthouse. I've told 'em it's all down to you. I'd watch your back if I was you.'

But without Lenny, the Harpers were like a snake without a head – they might wriggle and thrash about, but none of them had his brains or will. They'd lumber about, but there'd be no one to orchestrate any vendetta against her.

'Lay off, Chris,' she muttered. 'Apparently, the directors have been looking into stock discrepancies over at the sales offices. Wonder what they'd say if they knew why you and Crosbie are so pally?'

Chris's face paled.

'Not so brave without Lenny to fight your battles? Excuse me,' she said politely. 'Some of us want to earn an honest bob or two.'

She walked away, waiting for his retort, but there was only the chatter of the women and the rhythmic cranking of the time clock. His silence told her that she'd have no more trouble from Chris Harper.

Lenny was dead and everything was different. She finally felt free of the past she'd been running from. Yet she was aware that the change had begun before his death, even as she'd followed Ronnie along that tortuous, dark tunnel to Paradise Street nick and up into the light of day. She owed Ronnie her life. And now she found herself in need of his advice, if her budding plan to extend the children's flats was to bloom. For the moment, she settled down to a morning of focusing on painting straight lines on to dyed and sheared sheepskins. One after the other, she striped the mahogany-coloured furs, never losing concentration or breaking her rhythm, apart from the inevitable coughs caused by the fumes from the resin paint. And, as she lost herself in the repeating lines, she imagined her plan in all its details coming to fruition.

At the dinner-time hooter she hurried up to the bambeaters to find Lou.

'Hello, darlin'.' Lou greeted Hattie with a smile. 'Clara's already gone to the canteen.'

'Are you going home?' Hattie asked.

Lou was folding her green overall neatly and putting it away in her bag. 'Yes, love, got to give Ronnie his dinner – he's out-growing his strength! My Vic was tall,' she said, without the usual timbre of regret.

'Can I come with you?'

''Course, love! But I'm using the last of me rations on the boy. I ain't got nothing to give you, only bread and dripping.'

'No, don't be silly, Lou. I wasn't inviting myself! I just want a word with Ronnie.'

A shadow darkened Lou's bright expression. 'What's he done?'

But Hattie linked arms with the woman and laughed as they left the bambeaters and clattered across the high gantry. 'Nothing this time! It's about the children's flats.'

'Oh? He told me they was closing? It's such a shame for the kids.'

She allowed herself a moment's irritation that Ronnie had ignored her warning to tell no one.

'Actually, Lou, the flats have been saved. Anonymous donor.' And as she said it, she realized her earlier suspicions about the donor must be wrong. For, according to Chris, poor Johnny Harper was once more locked up in Stonefield Asylum, the very place that had ruined his mind as a young boy.

Lou was long into one of her clear-minded phases and Hattie had almost forgotten to look out for signs she might be drifting away. She hoped that this time her clarity would be permanent. On the way, Lou talked about Ronnie and how proud of him she was, that he was sticking with school and even talking about what he wanted to do when he left. 'He told me he wants to be a surveyor! Where'd he get that idea? I prayed gawd he wouldn't turn out a villain, and he ain't, has he, Hattie?'

'No, he's turned out all right, Lou,' Hattie said with a smile, for it was she who'd given Ronnie the idea. His constructions on the bombsites went beyond the normal bodged camps of other kids, and she'd been astonished when he'd shown her how he planned them out meticulously on paper first.

Ronnie opened the flat door and grinned. 'Hello, Hattie! What you doin' here?'

'I've come to see you,' she said, and to her surprise he blushed. She forced herself not to echo Lou's earlier question about what he might have been up to.

'Why's that?

Lou busied herself with frying up some bread slices for him, along with a precious egg, while Hattie took off her coat.

'Make Hattie a cuppa, Ronnie,' Lou ordered and Ronnie obeyed.

'I went to see Anne before work this morning, and guess what? She's only had an anonymous donation – the flats can stay open! She's asked me to use some of the money to set up an outdoors club!'

Hattie was so excited to share some of the ideas that had been bubbling under the surface all morning that at first she didn't notice Ronnie's blush returning. When she did, she supposed he was of the age when unwanted blushes would arise with embarrassing frequency.

'Staying open, eh?' Ronnie said, with a little nervous laugh.

'My God!' She fixed him with a wide-eyed stare. 'It was you!'

'What's he done?' came Lou's refrain.

'Nothing!' Both she and Ronnie answered as one. Hattie wasn't about to spoil Lou's newfound good opinion of Ronnie, so for the moment she carried on the conversation as if she hadn't realized that Ronnie was the mysterious 'donor'. She took in a deep breath, fixed him with an unblinking stare, and tried to ignore the dilemma he'd put her in.

'I wanted to ask what you think of my idea. You said to me once, bombsites are free, remember? Well, what if we turned a bombsite into a playground?'

'What, clear a site and put swings and slides on it?'

'No. What is it you like doing on the bombsites – apart from smashing stuff up?' she added hastily.

'I like making camps,' he said.

'Right, and they're bloody good camps. Walls and windows – and that one you made in Spa Road's even got an upstairs. Wouldn't it be good if you could build your own playground? The sites are full of timber just rotting away. But with the help of that kind *donation*,' she paused just long enough to let him know the subject wasn't closed, 'you could have proper nails and screws and tools. You could do technical plans and build anything you liked – a proper cabin for a club house, or even an assault course, like the one we had in army training. What do you think?'

Ronnie's face lit up. 'Levin says I'm a good chippie. Nutty Norman would love it, and so would the others. It's a brilliant idea, Hattie!' he said, excited and then wistful. 'I miss the bombsites. Can we still bake our potatoes in the fire?' And he rubbed his hands together as if warming them at the flames.

'Yes, but there'd be an adult supervising, just so you didn't set

Bermondsey alight... So, if Anne goes for my idea, you reckon the other kids will want to join in?'

He nodded. 'Which site shall we use? Spa Road?'

She screwed up her face. 'Too small.' Which was true, but Hattie had other reasons for not wanting to use it. The memories of Lou's losses and her own miserable return to Bermondsey hung too gloomily over the Spa Road site. She wanted a fresh start. 'Got to think big, Ronnie. The bombsite around Larnaca Street is massive, at least a couple of football pitches.'

'Would we be allowed?'

'If the council didn't worry when you were pulling everything down, I don't think they'll object to you building it up! So long as they don't have to pay a penny.'

After Ronnie had finished his dinner, he accompanied them to the Alaska, which was on the way to his school in Grange Road. But as they parted at the Alaska gates, Hattie held on to his blazer sleeve. 'Lou, you go and clock in. I've just remembered another question for Ronnie,' she said.

When Lou disappeared into the shelter by the timekeeper's lodge, Hattie turned, grim-faced, to Ronnie.

'What you looking at me like that for?' Ronnie asked.

'I know it was you!'

'What?'

'You bloody idiot, you've given Anne a pile of dodgy money and now she's put it in the bank! All her good work, all my "brilliant" ideas that you like so much will go up in smoke if those notes are traced!'

'I don't know what you're talking about, Hattie,' Ronnie said, his face a study in innocence.

'The donation stank of piss.'

'So? Must have been Pissy Pants done it.'

'He's locked up in Stonefield.'

'No! Poor old Johnny, he don't deserve that. Perhaps he posted it to her...'

'Don't come the old acid, Ron. I'm not stupid, but you are.

You've put Anne in a terrible position. How can she take dirty money?'

'Oh, keep your hair on. She don't have to know where it come from,' he said, finally giving in.

'So it was you?'

'I only grabbed a *few* bundles, stuffed 'em under one of the bunks – while the coppers was busy sorting out Lenny's body. Johnny was tearing up all the money. It would have only gone to waste!'

Hattie blew out a deep sigh of frustration.

'Better for it to go to a good cause... eh?' Ronnie gave her a wink.

She gave up and decided to say nothing to Anne; at least if anything came to light, the woman could claim ignorance. And though she'd never tell Ronnie, a part of her took a secret delight in knowing that from Lenny's ending would come a new beginning for Bermondsey's kids.

*

Shortly after Lenny's death Clara moved back in with Hattie, and now that the threat to the squat had passed they were inspired by the spring weather to start refurnishing their replacement hut. Living at the army camp was only ever meant to be temporary, but after they'd first moved in, the glacial rate of the council's reconstruction programme had persuaded them they might be there for years, and so they'd added all the extra touches that made a mere shelter into a home. But this time they had far less enthusiasm. One Saturday afternoon, as they were arranging the few bits of furniture they'd put together, Clara asked, 'Is it worth us buying proper curtains? We'll never get anything as good as poor old Buster made us.'

'Actually, last time I visited him, Buster told me he's got spare curtains in his flat we can have. But to be honest, I just don't fancy going there. It's too sad.'

'Has he heard anything about the appeal?'

'Nothing. Anne's got faith in this lawyer friend, so he's keeping his hopes up. I hope to God something happens soon. That place is crushing him.'

'So he'll still be in prison, when we leave…'

'Probably,' Hattie said, with a dullness in her heart. She didn't know how it had happened but now, when she thought of Australia, the joy was always entangled with sadness.

Anne loved her idea of a junk playground, but Joe took more convincing. When towards the end of spring they began to clear the bombsite at Larnaca Street, she took him along to help her work out what waste materials were already there and what they'd need to provide.

'A pickaxe, definitely,' she said, adding it to her list.

'You're going to give kids of ten and eleven pickaxes?' he asked disbelievingly.

'And shovels, and saws and nails and screws… and a bit of supervision, but not too much. The idea is to give them the tools and let them get on with it.'

'But get on with what? You've seen their antics on the bombsites. They'll just go on a smashing spree, Hattie. It'll be anarchy.'

'You're wrong, Joe. I've seen the camps they build and I've seen how they decorated the children's flats. They want to build homes!'

'Just like Bermondsey Borough Council!' He chuckled. 'Let's hope they're a bit quicker at it!'

'You can laugh, but it's true. Given half a chance, they'd rather build something than destroy it. It's just they've never known anything but this bloody wasteland.' She turned round in a circle, surveying the raw material to hand. Sword-like shards of glass and razor-sharp scraps of corrugated iron were still to be cleared, but she could see plenty of timber, bricks, iron girders, oil drums and old tyres for them to make use of. She struggled for the words to describe what she'd seen in her first flash of inspiration as she'd walked over these very ruins.

'The kids are just like those…' She pointed to places amongst the detritus where self-seeded patches of hardy wildflowers and grasses had grown up, pink and purple lungwort, bright blue speedwell and yellow cress gems dotting the otherwise uniform grey-and-dun palette of the ruins. 'They've already started to make the best of the bad mess we've left them. Just imagine what they could do if we give them a little bit of help…'

'All right, I'm sold. Besides, you're very pretty when you get worked up about stuff like this.' Joe put an arm round her and looked steadfastly into her eyes. 'They're sparkling – your eyes. Little glints of gold in the green. Tell me more about your plans.'

She thought for a moment. His support meant everything, but perhaps he might be more sceptical about the other plan she'd been mulling over.

'You might think I'm crazy, but Anne reckons I'm a natural with the kids. She even said I should go on the same course she did, get a proper youth-work training. I'd go to evening classes at the LSE, where she went… I think I could do it, Joe.'

In fact, ever since Anne had mentioned it to her, she'd thought of nothing else. It had been a moment when the world seemed to shift and all the pieces of a long running puzzle had fallen effortlessly into place. She'd believed an office job would be her way out of the Alaska, out of Bermondsey, but that had only been because she couldn't imagine another way. Now she could and she held her breath, waiting for his response.

'This means a lot to you, doesn't it?'

'It just feels important, as if this is why I made it through the war. There must be a reason,' her eyes welled with tears, 'when I think of all the ones who didn't come through. Lou's mum and dad, her little Sue… there must be a reason.'

In the middle of the open wasteland, he kissed her. 'There is. It was so I could meet you and you could make me happier than I've ever been.'

They sat on an upended water tank and she leaned her head on his shoulder.

'How long would the training take?' he asked.

'I've got time… we haven't even got our passage money together yet.'

She made a pattern with her foot in the fine sandy debris around where they sat, and Joe said, 'One day, that could be Bondi Beach.'

'Yes,' she said, absently staring at the pattern. She scraped her shoe across it, smoothing out the sand. 'This would be the perfect spot for our playground cabin, don't you think?'

Joe was quiet for a moment, then took her by the shoulders. He turned her to face him. 'Hattie, you don't want to leave, do you?'

A deep stillness settled into her heart. After her next words, nothing would ever be the same. 'No, Joe, I don't want to leave.'

She placed her head on his shoulder and they were both silent, watching the sun burnish the crushed yellow bricks at their feet to a lowly gold dust.

★ ★ ★

What do you mean, you're not going to Australia? But you've got to!' Clara protested. 'All right, me and Alan, we'll stay here – I can't lose you. I've never had a friend like you, Hattie…' She choked back tears and couldn't finish. Hattie gathered the young woman in her arms and let her own tears fall.

'Don't be silly. It's what you want, for yourself and for Alan, and for Martha! She'll thrive there. You know, I'll miss you and Martha so much, and if I could split myself in two, I would! It's just I've found something I want to do with my life, Clara, and I've been looking for so long…'

They were both crying and Hattie shared her handkerchief. She'd waited to tell her when they were alone. Martha was having a nap outside in the sunshine, and now she and Clara sat in the hut together with the door open. The fresh green smells of spring wafted in from the park, and the young leaves on the surrounding trees trembled in the air, almost vibrating with eagerness to unfurl.

'Hattie, if it hadn't been for you, I wouldn't have got through. What am I going to do without you?'

'You'll be fine. You've got Alan, and he's a good 'un!'

'Alan! I only found him because of you!' Clara sniffed and swallowed a sob. 'But what about Joe?'

Hattie hadn't known what his response would be. Telling him she wouldn't be going was like a leap in the dark. Either she would be caught in his arms or he would let her fall. Either way, she knew that she had to follow her own path. It would break her heart to lose him, but to give up her newfound dream would break her soul.

'He said he'd rather be in hell with me than paradise without me…' She paused. 'Don't say much for Bermondsey, does it?'

And they laughed and cried and laughed again, until they didn't know which was which.

'Come on, it's such a lovely day. Let's take Martha for a walk. I'll show you the other project we've been working on with that anonymous donation!'

They walked the length of Southwark Park Road, enjoying the pink-blossomed cherry trees planted by Ada Salter's beautification committee, or at least those that had survived the bombs. Under the shorn-up John Bull Arch and along the Blue they walked, passing so many bombsites on the way that sometimes it felt as if they were walking through meadows of grasses and wildflowers, for the greenery of April had overtaken them. Eventually they turned down Rouel Road, and rounding the corner at Pearce Duff's, reached Spa Road. They soon arrived at the bombsite where she'd suffered her humiliating defeat at the hands of Ronnie and his gang. She could never pass it without remembering the lowest point of her life. Now it was full of a small army of children wielding, not bricks and iron bars, but hoes and spades, garden forks and trowels. A couple of women were there to oversee the work and one looked up to wave at them. Her hands were dirty with earth, her hair flying, and a sheen of sweat covered her brow, but she was smiling broadly

– a gap-toothed smile, but one which Hattie found beautiful none the less.

'Hattie!' Lou called, beckoning them over. 'Come and see what we just planted.' They pushed the pram round the strewn rocks to the garden that Lou and the children were making. They had cleared all the large boulders and piled them up to make a rock garden. Nutty Norman was working hard with a rake and sieve to sift the soil clean of stones, glass and shrapnel fragments. Ribbons the twins held packets of seed and Anne was showing them how to sow in rows. But Lou and Ronnie had some flowering spring plants in pots that they'd been planting out in a bed. A dozen of the purple, violet and yellow violas were already in the ground, splashing bright colour across the once bare ruin.

'Heartsease!' Lou said. 'Ain't they lovely? They remind me of my Sue. She loved these. Flowers always brought a smile to her little face.'

'They are so pretty, Lou,' Hattie said, the words of the poem learned at school so long ago returning to her all at once, so that she spoke them softly to herself.

> *Heartsease I found, where love-lies-bleeding,*
> *Empurpled all the ground:*
> *Whatever flowers I missed unheeding,*
> *Heartsease I found.*

When she looked up, tears filled Lou's eyes. 'Never a truer word, darlin'.'

Martha woke up and Clara lifted her from the pram, handing her to Ronnie, who rubbed dirty hands down his shorts before taking her. Clara and Hattie walked with Lou to read a small painted sign that had been erected on the edge of the cleared area. It read *Sue's Garden*, and underneath were the dates of her birth and death.

They looked on in silence until Lou said, 'Gawd's good. My Sue's getting her garden, after all, ain't she?'

And Hattie reflected that in a way the garden was for them too, herself and Clara and Lou. In the dead ground of Bermondsey the seeds of their futures had somehow pushed up small green shoots of hope, up through the stony ruins and up through tangled roots of destruction, shoots of hope which were even now reaching for the sunshine and blue skies of a new world.

# *Acknowledgements*

I would like to thank my agent, Anne Williams, and my editor, Rosie de Courcy. Without their invaluable help and insight, this book would have been the poorer. Thanks also to the team at Head of Zeus for their enthusiasm and professionalism in bringing the book to publication.

Grateful thanks are also due to the following people:

Mrs Veronica Kelland, who wrote to me after recognizing her sister on the front cover of *Gunner Girls and Fighter Boys*. Aged ninety-five, she generously shared her still vivid memories of what it was like to be a war bride and set sail for an unknown country on 'The Bride Ship' *Athlone Castle* in 1946. She joined her husband in New Zealand, where she was welcomed into his loving family and spent many happily married years.

Local historians Debra Gosling and Patrick Kingwell for the valuable background information on Southwark Park during World War Two and also the occupation of ex-army huts in the park by twenty-nine homeless families after the war.

The many people who have shared their memories of the bomb sites and factories of post-war Bermondsey, especially Michael Gibson, Bill Gibson, Violet Henderson, Dave Riseborough, Maureen Riseborough, Roger Metson and Anne Chivers, whose mother worked in the Alaska fur factory as a teenager during the war.

I would like to acknowledge the work of Anne Lethbridge Shells, who worked tirelessly for the children of Bermondsey from 1941 to 1953. The children's flats were her brainchild and you can read more about her work in her autobiography, *The Stout Lady in the Brown Coat*.

Many thanks to my writing pals at Bexley Scribblers for their continued encouragement and to my lovely family. Finally, special thanks to Josie Bartholomew who makes it all possible.